CHOPPED

A Novel

CHOPPED

A Novel

DALE M. POLLOCK

SHADOWBROOK PUBLISHING   WINSTON-SALEM, N.C.

Design and production by Julie Allred, BW&A Books

Library of Congress Control Number: 2022922495
ISBN: 979-8-218-11701-6 (paperback)
ISBN: 979-8-218-11702-3 (hardcover)

To Pamela O'Keeffe and her daughter Susie,
who never gave up.

*There is no such source of error as the
pursuit of absolute truth.*
—Samuel Butler

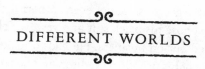

DIFFERENT WORLDS

November 23, 1849
Garden Street, Cambridge, Massachusetts

Professor John White Webster had a firestorm raging in his head. He was naked. He was trapped alone deep in a primeval forest. A growing blaze approached him rapidly from all directions.

A murmur that began softly in his dream now wailed, the dissonant melody of a thousand crows. It was what hell would sound like.

All around him embers and chunks of wood were falling. He knew from his chemistry experiments that wood bursts into flame at 572 degrees Fahrenheit. It was much hotter than that—a nearby tree went with a whoosh, vaporized.

For all his scientific training, he could see no way out. He crouched low under a tall oak, its trunk still standing defiant before the flames, and assumed the fetal position. Just as a burning branch hurled itself downward to set him alight, he reared up, awake.

He was not in a forest. There was no fire. He lay on his featherbed mattress, in his second-floor bedroom at 22 Garden Street in Cambridge, just blocks from the campus of his employer, Harvard University. He grabbed his spectacles off the night table and peered at the timepiece across the room. It indicated a few minutes after seven. He had not moved from his bed, but he was still breathing heavily from his dream.

The fiery vision was not unprecedented. Webster dreamt iterations of it at least once every week; the setting sometimes changed, as did the threat. Once there was a nor'easter that propelled him through the air and threatened to blow him out to sea. Usually, he awoke in fire, cowering and gasping, his lungs still trying to suck air from a suffocating, blazing forest.

The dream's fatal conclusion had not yet arrived. His dreams always stopped short of disaster's final visitation. Webster knew the source of his nightmares. The greater the financial pressures on him, the more vivid the natural dilemmas in which he was placed by his sinful imagination. And George Parkman always held the match.

Webster hurried to get dressed, not even bothering to wash his face and hands. By habit, he chose his black suit and vest, which he wore when he lectured or ventured out on business. He had to make an early-morning stop at the residence of his principal creditor, and he could not afford to be late. Dr. Parkman never waited patiently, least of all for a timid chemistry professor who was doubly in his debt, and after today's meeting, possibly triply so.

In point of fact, Parkman waited on no one. He had the easy condescension of the very rich, thought Webster, his brooding resentment of the morning's business growing every moment. Why must a man have to prostrate himself continually before his financial benefactor, as if he were chattel?

Webster went downstairs to the calming odors of the same breakfast his wife offered every morning: hot, lumpy porridge; steaming, bitter coffee; and a hunk of salted bread with a smear of glistening butter on it. John Webster loved his butter, and so it was always there, expensive as it might be. Harriet was not creative, but she was reliable, and in the scattershot world of her husband's personal affairs, that was an essential quality.

"When do you see Doctor Parkman today, John? Before or after midday?"

"I will arrange a time when I call on him this morning at his home," Webster replied, ruffled by Harriet's question. He preferred she not examine him in the way she did; her voice implied that he had forgotten or neglected something important. The fact that he often did forget and neglect only augmented his irritation.

Harriet pulled out a chair for her husband, but he demurred by passing a hand distractedly in front of his face, its complexion already florid with his aggravation and haste.

"I have no time to eat, all of Boston knows of Doctor Parkman's punctiliousness, he delays for no visitor," Webster said as he grabbed his black greatcoat from a hook in the back hallway and shuffled his way into it.

"He departs his mansion for his daily duties at half past eight," he continued, "so I must be at his door at least one hour prior. And how will I find a cab, cross Craigie Bridge, and make it up to Beacon Hill, all by half past seven?"

He looked at his wife pleadingly, as if somehow she could magically right things in his upside-down world, but she could not, did not, and never would. John Webster, as he had known since his earliest childhood memories, had no one to rely on but himself, and the finality of that conclusion had given him little stead in his life.

Soon he was half-running, half-walking down the wooden sidewalk on Garden Street, his breath freezing in the cold air. He hailed every passing carriage frantically until one proved to be a hansom cab. Webster clambered in, and in his usual breathless and high-pitched delivery, instructed his driver to ferry him to Beacon Hill, the most elite neighborhood in Boston, as soon as his horses could get there. The cab went clattering off, and Webster tried to gather his thoughts.

He was at a crossroads with Dr. Parkman, and he knew what that meant. Parkman would demand full payment of all of his outstanding loans; Webster wouldn't be able to accommodate him; and then what would happen? The underpaid Harvard Medical College professor could find no more unsolicited lenders, and even if he did, for how much longer could he borrow from Peter to pay Paul? Debt was debt, no matter who was owed, and John White Webster was swimming in it.

His last brilliant idea had been to leverage his valuable mineral cabinet, the essence of his chemistry teaching, as collateral for a loan from Robert Gould Shaw, Dr. Parkman's brother-in-law. Except the same collection had already been mortgaged by Parkman himself, a fact that only John Webster was aware of—but not for long. The two men, relatives as well as business partners, now each thought he owned the mineral cabinet, which was of no practical use to either of them.

Of course, Webster should have foretold they would speak about the matter. There was little doubt that both of them were outraged by the duplicate transaction, which benefited only Webster, and neither of the richest and most powerful men in Boston.

John did possess a new plan. He had saved $200 by canceling the party he had originally planned for the day after the Thanksgiving holiday and would offer it to Dr. Parkman as a significant down payment on his debt, which now amounted to $2,400. He had drawn up a new agreement that called for him to pay the loans down monthly, with interest. It would take almost seven years, by Webster's calculations, to finally emerge debt-free, but with self-discipline, and fear of the consequences of his failure, he believed he could do so.

The hansom driver pulled up in front of 8 Walnut Street, and as

Webster descended and reached up to pay him, the Irish driver whistled through his teeth. The handsome Georgian brick house stood haughtily on its perch atop Beacon Hill.

"Mighty fine digs, sir," he said, looking down at the rotund figure below him, his short arms and small hands trying to reach the driver in his seat. "Be the man who lives 'ere a friend of your'n?"

Webster looked at him, not understanding a word the man was saying. He just wanted to pay the driver and be done with him.

"Yer friend, yer pal, the rich man what must live 'ere? Ye know who he be? Just me own bein' curious, ye know," he said, trying to reassure Webster. The driver shook his head, abandoned the conversation, and took the coins Webster, using his fingertips, extended upward. The coachman tipped his hat, and his horse trotted off.

Webster was sweating, despite the freezing temperature; he could see rapid breaths appearing and disappearing before him. He had constructed a sound proposal; he must now adhere to it, and show neither fear nor panic, nor supplication. This was a meeting between two businessmen who had an economic matter to resolve; no more, no less.

Webster's legs trembled as he approached the three-story dark brick house, smoke already trailing out of its two chimneys. He tried to calm his breathing, a trick his mentor, Dr. Harold Vaughn, had taught Webster during his medical internship in London, decades ago. Webster practiced the technique often, and it had aided him in maintaining his composure when his students' classroom behavior tested it.

He would need more than composure to triumph over Dr. Parkman. He would need bravery. He would need persuasiveness. He would need steel.

Walnut Street, Beacon Hill; Cambridge Street; Endicott Street, the North End; North Grove Street; Boston, Massachusetts

Once again, the breakfast service was slow. George Parkman fumed as he waited for the serving girl, Glynnis, to bring out his eggs and fried cod, and the frighteningly hot coffee he needed to send him on his collection route with a full head of steaming anger.

It was approaching half past seven when Glynnis—round-faced, round-bottomed, and possessing nary a sharp angle in her body or her personality—stumbled backward out of the kitchen and into the richly appointed Parkman dining room. She reached for a wall to steady herself, and the grilled cod slid dangerously close to the edge of its plate, inches from becoming a flying fish.

"For God's sake, straighten up, Glynnis, before you dash my breakfast to the floor," Parkman said in a voice that was like a blade slicing meat. It was one of his special tools, that quality of speaking that could cut someone to pieces.

The Irish housemaid looked as if she might faint. If one hand had been not occupied with the tray, she would have clutched the doorway with both.

"I be sorry, Docter Parkman, sir, but tha boy be late comin' with tha eggs, and I needs keep the cod warm, so ye see . . ."

Parkman cut her off, as he always did when she prattled on. It was the one thing the Irish did well, he thought, then reflected. No, there was no way to judge this gibberish good or bad. He couldn't parse their terrible tongue, and he had long since given up trying.

"Set the plates and be done with it, Glynnis. Leave me be. I'm sure the mistress has duties for you. She's in the solarium."

The girl carefully set his plate and a mug of coffee on the enormous dining table, built to seat twelve large New Englanders. The lanky Parkman was not intimidated by its size and comfortably held sway over his half of the mahogany expanse. Glynnis had nothing more to add to their encounter. Her goal was to get out of the dining room as soon as possible, which she did.

Parkman set to his meal. The eggs had congealed into a yellowish, puckered mass; the fish was burned to a crisp. Thanks to this worthless Irish trash, that for some reason his wife insisted upon employing, he was going to be ill fed in beginning his collections. He could send back the breakfast and choose to be late in inaugurating rent day, but that was not an option.

George Parkman was an unusual man. Everyone in Boston knew it.

Some—never in his presence—called him "The Chin": his conspicuous, protruding jawbone was characteristic of the Boston Parkmans. Adamses had prominent foreheads, Saltonstalls had significant noses, Parkmans possessed notable chins.

George was tall, at five feet eleven inches, but attenuated; at fifty-nine, almost bald, with a colorless face and ill-fitting (if expensive) false teeth— one of his few vanities. He was a person of strict and stern principles, and unflagging energy. He was simple and frugal. He abstained while others indulged. He worked while others slept. He walked while others rode.

He wore a long, black wool coat whatever the weather. He strode across Boston with hands clasped behind, head thrown back, chin thrust forward, eyes darting in every direction from their perch. George Parkman was alert to the world around him, which for the most part feared him.

He was mindful of his community. Parkmans always gave donations anonymously, to avoid the embarassment of gratitude. The land George had personally donated for the relocated Harvard Medical College was a notable exception to the maxim that the proper Bostonian did not seek credit for his good works. There had been a recent public ceremony celebrating Parkman's generosity to his alma mater.

Family was important; Parkman considered it his greatest asset. Although they breakfasted separately, he and his wife Eliza had dined together at two o'clock every day of their thirty-three-year marriage. They were not close.

The sole affection George Parkman reserved was for his ailing daughter, Harriet, who lay in the large house's largest bedroom. Now twenty-eight, she had been a sick child, then an equally unwell young woman, confined to her bed and her room for the past fifteen years.

George strode up the stairs, checking the watch in his pocket—the one with the gold face that he liked his tenants to see, a visible representation of his power. At seven-day intervals, he controlled time itself for those unlucky enough to occupy one of the many habitations he possessed.

Parkman knocked softly on Harriet's bedroom door, and then paused, something he rarely did, until he heard a soft, "Come in, Papa."

It sounded like a deep sigh, not an articulated command. The sigh was understandable. Harriet's illness had defied diagnosis. Parkman had engaged no shortage of medical men, including himself, although he specialized in diseases of the mind, not the body. Physicians paraded through this room with regularity, yet none had solved the puzzle of what beset poor Harriet.

Despite being in her early adulthood, she occupied the emaciated body of a starved fifteen-year-old, one who had not yet reached pubescence. She kept down little food and subsisted primarily on weak tea and hard biscuits, which she chewed relentlessly. She slept for much of the day but little of the night. This caused ominous dark circles to appear under her coal-black eyes, giving her the appearance of a sickly raccoon.

George moved to his daughter's bedside after entering and grasped her hands, which were folded above the coverlet that hid her frail frame.

"How are you this morning, my darling?" Parkman inquired, in a radically different manner than he had employed with Glynnis. There was actual affection in his voice.

"Much better, thank you, Papa," Harriet lied, trying to flutter her sparse eyelashes in an unsuccessful imitation of flirtatious health. "I experienced a restful sleep. God heard my prayers last night, and He granted them."

"We must be grateful," agreed Parkinson, who would have scorned the sentiment in any other room but this one. He was grateful for anything that dulled the pain he saw in his daughter's gaunt features.

"I'm about to go out. What may I bring back that will brighten your day?" he continued, letting go of her feeble hand and looking around the room. "Some flowers? Possibly some fresh herbs, something to make your room smell like your beloved garden, even if it is almost Thanksgiving? Tell me, Harriet. Anything you wish."

His daughter shook her head as she sighed, from both physical discomfort and the sameness of this routine, in which her father attempted to buy her some sweet or another as if he could purchase good health for her. Still, she tried to brighten her voice.

"Perhaps some lettuce if you go to Mister Holland's shop? And any other greens he has that would make a salad for our supper today. Mama so loves her greens."

His daughter, thought Parkman, unlike him, put her mother before herself, and chose Eliza's special extravagance instead of any of her own favorites.

"Your soul will receive a great welcome in heaven, my dear," Parkman murmured, kissing his daughter on her forehead, unable to avoid her odor, the stench of sickness on her. If he were an actuary—and God knew Parkman employed enough of them and their endless calculations for the annuities he sold—he would not estimate her time left on this earth to be more than a few months.

To contradict her father's dark thoughts, Harriet gave his hand a firm squeeze and sat up straighter in bed. "It's not heaven I think about, Papa, but you, and how hard you work yourself. There is no end of business for you, not when you are out, nor at home."

Parkman, already on his way to the door, turned around and faced her with his usual self-deprecating gesture, a distracted wave across his face. "Oh, Harriet, you know 'tis the work which keeps me youthful and useful. Regard my trim figure!"

Parkman, the last man ever to draw attention to himself in public, patted his firm stomach, puffed up his chest, and assumed the classic boxing stance: legs bent, arms raised, fists closed.

"Time to go to battle with the Irish!" he yelled, startling Glynnis, who had just entered bearing a tray with Harriet's breakfast of bone broth and brown bread. Another Irish serving girl followed directly behind her, carrying a teakettle and two cups.

Parkman quickly abandoned his comic pose, and the smile he had bestowed on his daughter disappeared as though someone had switched it off.

"Because of that goose Glynnis, I will be late and can't stay to tea with you this morn, Harriet. But I promise to return with your lettuce and greens, and I look forward to supping with two contented women today."

With less of a clipped bow than he bestowed on the rest of the world, George took his leave from the only person he really cared for. As he neared the staircase, the house servant, George McGowan, reached its top after a brisk climb. He was slightly out of breath as he bowed to Parkman.

"Beg your pardon, Doctor, but you have an unscheduled guest who has appeared at our door. He would not give his name, but he said you had anticipated his visit and wouldn't be troubled by its early hour."

"Wouldn't give you his name, you said? How dare a man call on me and refuse to identify himself. I will have to educate him on the proper manner of presenting oneself."

Parkman hurried down the stairs, and McGowan followed at a respectful distance. He did not witness the ensuing encounter between host and visitor, other than to hear his employer exclaim as he entered the room, "By God, sir! What are *you* doing here?"

The door to Dr. Parkman's study slammed shut just as McGowan reached the main floor. It remained that way for the next twelve minutes; the clock was loudly ticking nearby, impossible to ignore. Then the short, squat visitor opened the door to exit the study, looking down in consternation. For a moment McGowan wondered if he were weeping.

"We shall meet at half past one at the Medical College, sir," Parkman called out from his study as the visitor departed. "You do not wish to disappoint me."

Disappointing him about what was impossible to tell, because in a sudden draft of cold air from the front door, the short man was gone, or at least there was no trace of him that McGowan could see. Before the servant could gather his thoughts, Parkman strode out of the dark-paneled study as quickly as his guest had exited.

A prodigious scowl covered his face, and McGowan looked down when that gaze turned his way. Parkman was rarely this riled so early in the morning. It made the servant grateful that his master would soon depart, allowing McGowan the luxury of remaining behind. George Parkman was a fearsome man in any circumstances; when under the black cloud of choleric anger, he was to be avoided at all costs. McGowan gathered up the stiff, black wool overcoat and silently assisted Parkman in getting his arms into its heavy sleeves. He handed Pafkman his cane and hurried to open the door. Parkman set off in cold, hostile silence.

Dr. Parkman's reputation was not one of benevolence or generosity. He was the "Tiger Creditor," always in ferocious pursuit of those who failed repayment. If a debtor would not see Parkman at his office, Parkman went to his home. If he were not at home, Parkman would badger his wife. If the debtor occupied a stool in the King's Head Tavern or Hancock House, Parkman would pursue him there, brooking no demurral, no matter the time of year, the weather that day, or the cruel circumstances life had provided.

Parkman's curt manner, the glare he bestowed on everyone who addressed him (save his wife and beloved daughter), his loud and cutting voice: these attributes alienated everyone he interacted with, save his loyal brother-in-law, Robert Gould Shaw. They would meet briefly, as they did every day, to coordinate their mutual interests. For anyone else, when doing business with George Parkman, it was best to do it quickly; there was no joy in lingering.

On this Friday morning following his conversation with Shaw, his famous chin led Parkman down from atop Beacon Hill, through the Common, and across the odiferous streets of Boston. The further west he strode, the more rooting pigs and mounds of horse dung there were to maneuver around.

His mission was one he spread over three days of each week: to collect daily, weekly and monthly rents from the tenements, boarding houses and dilapidated homes he owned in nearly every section of the city. Parkman never employed carriage or horse, though he possessed both, choosing instead to walk, no matter the distance, the weather, or the time involved. As a result, he was exceedingly fit, a state unusual in his social class.

He strode down Vine and Blossom Streets through the West End, the neighborhood in which he had been raised, toward the Irish slums of Fort Hill. He was only a few blocks from the small two-story brick building that housed the Medical College, where he had agreed to meet his early-morning visitor that afternoon.

Shortly after ten o'clock, Dr. Parkman entered the grocery store of Paul

Holland on Cambridge Street. The warm air inside felt comfortable, coming from a small blaze in the iron stove. There were few customers when he approached the wooden counter, carrying a small bag of lettuce. He asked Holland to add it to some greens, along with sugar, butter and fresh milk for his daughter. It was a familiar order; the grocer knew of Harriet's infirmity, and her father was a regular customer, purchasing fresh ingredients for her meals almost every day. Parkman promised Holland he would return later that afternoon, after he collected his rents; he stated he was off to the Medical College for a brief meeting.

Parkman's first two stops loomed ahead, tenements located on Merchant Street just blocks from Holland's grocery. Both buildings were two stories high, and neither looked steady on its footing. Despite the smoke pouring out of the buildings' numerous chimneys, Parkman knew it was even colder inside than out, given that the walls were paper-thin.

The properties Parkman trafficked in were never the darlings of their neighborhoods. They reflected the fortunes of their tenants: crude and crowded living spaces filled with the shabby children of the working and nonworking poor who owed their shelter to George Parkman.

And he loathed them for it. These particular real estate investments were highly profitable, especially on the scale of Parkman's holdings. But he detested these weekly encounters with people whom he considered, to a person, his inferiors in every respect.

There was a certain grim pleasure he took in the badgering, the cruel verbal jousts he wielded, even if their recipients often received them with incomprehension. Mean is mean, no matter how well dressed the words are, and Parkman was a mean man.

Ten minutes later, with eighteen more American dollars in his coat pocket, Parkman was on his way to the North End, where his most severely distressed, and therefore most crowded, houses were located.

Not far from the famous Old North Church, Parkman turned down Endicott Street and approached number 82. The bland appearance of the black-painted door hid the crowded conditions that lay beyond it; Parkman had fourteen tenants in this small, narrow building.

On the ground floor, a sodden anchor to the rotting wood-frame building, sat O'Malley's grog shop, which also served as a local tavern of sorts, and whose rent made the structure the most profitable one Parkman owned in the North End. He could see why; it was not even eleven o'clock in the morning, and the establishment was already crowded with men drinking, and men already drunk.

Parkman approached the barman, one Seamus Rooney, whose name he confirmed as he checked the leather-bound accounting ledger that never left his side on his collection route. Rooney took one look at his new customer and busied himself at the other end of the pine planks that sat on two oak barrels. His hiding bought him little time.

"Mister Rooney, you are aware of the day?" Parkman called in his ringing voice, which silenced the noisy establishment.

With no response offered, he continued. "In the absence of a denial, I will assume the affirmative. I will also assume you have the rent you owe me, and the percentage of your sales to your," Parkman turned and surveyed the drunkards surrounding him, "customers."

Still not verbally acknowledging his landlord, Rooney turned around and reached low behind a group of barrels containing the rye and whiskey he watered down, and then watered down again, before it reached the parched lips of his ever-thirsty patrons. He removed a metal strongbox, and from it a wad of bills tied with a bit of string and a worn leather pouch filled with coins.

Rooney silently handed the money to Parkman and returned to his end of the bar. Parkman stood, counting first the bills, and then the coins, large and small.

Even if he were not their landlord, every renter in the North End—there being almost no one in the North End who was not a renter—knew of Dr. Parkman. After all, he visited every tenant every week to collect their paltry coins and grubby, twisted bills. He never missed a visit, and they had best never miss a payment.

If they did, they were soon dispatched from their premises by two large and extremely hairy men, and deposited, with all their belongings, on the street. Standing by was usually a new group of Irish immigrants hoping for the opportunity to suffer Parkman's predations. He was, indeed, a tiger, and they were the terrified villagers living at his behest.

Perhaps not all of them. One man leaned back on the plank bar and broke the silence that usually prevailed until Parkman's exit. He appeared to be in his early forties; his brown hair, mixed with strands of gray, rose in the exaggerated frontal wave his people favored. His collar, stained and loose, topped a dark vest that had been washed several times too often; whatever shape it once possessed had departed, leaving a garment that hung loosely on its wearer.

"G'day ta ye, Docter Parkman, sir," said the middle-aged man. "I hope ye be 'avin' a productive mornin'."

Parkman, already thinking about the next stop on his route, a twenty-room tenement across the street that looked ready to topple over, halted.

"Do I know you, sir?" he said, boring his eyes into the man at the bar. "Do I have business with you?"

"I be William Haggerty, at yer service, Docter, sir," the man said. "And ye 'ave bizness wit' all o' us, if ye please, sir."

Parkman looked quizzically at the Irishman. Once again, he could make no sense of what these people said.

"There ain't a man standin' here what ain't owes 'is rent to ye, Docter Parkman," Haggerty said, as if proud of his fellow tenants for surviving Parkman as a landlord.

"And we pays, oh, we pays, 'cause we know what a man sech as yerself will do if we dinna," Haggerty continued. Parkman realized this complaint was nothing but some Irishman's drivel, and he turned toward the way out.

"Tha money go out, but nun ever come back, Docter. The roofs, they still leak. The wind, she still blows right inna where the babes sleep, Docter. Ye be killin' tha little babes!"

Parkman ignored the speaker even as Haggerty's voice grew ever more indignant. The landlord walked toward the door, presenting his back to his interlocutor, when an attractive young woman with vivid, bright red hair bustled into the saloon and made a beeline for the complaining Irishman.

Parkman gave the woman a glance. He was on to Charter Street, where $35 in rent awaited him. He wondered if this beauty could silence that squawker but would not stay to see. Business awaited.

In the wake of Parkman's departure, the redhead, Ellen O'Keeffe, admonished Haggerty as she approached. "What trouble be ye causin' us now? That'd be a great aid to the neighborhood, turnin' George Parkman agin' us fer nae good reason! Tell me, William, why must ye make yer troubles everyone else's?"

Haggerty looked outraged. "I only be sayin' what all be thinkin' and needin' someone wit' the balls to say ta that wolf! He be robbin' us, and we all be like little lambs wit' our throats cut!"

Ellen looked at Haggerty as if he had lost his mind. He possessed no wherewithal to stand up to a man like George Parkman. Unemployed, drunken, loud, and obnoxious Irishmen were numerous, but that made them no more attractive.

She approached Haggerty to lead him away, but he pushed her back and made as if to strike her if she came closer.

"I nae be needin' yer help, Ellen. I do me best ta treat ye like me own dottir, but nae dottir would do fer me as ye do." He tried to look affronted. "Here I done saved yer mum from a life o' sin, and all ye can do is terture me, fer nae good reason,'" he added, feebly twisting her words back on her.

"We have nae choice in who be our true mother and father," said Ellen. "But we do on the second go-round, and ye be no father to me, of that ye can be sure."

She turned and strode out of the rough tavern. Next to the door was a set of wooden steps, crudely finished with uneven borders. This was not turning into a good day, she thought, as she carried her bustle above her boots and ascended. Not good at all.

Endicott Street, the North End, Boston, Massachusetts

Ellen O'Keeffe entered a cramped apartment and stumbled into a battered wooden stool that was not where it should be. Someone had knocked it over when leaving and given it no further thought. Ellen knew exactly who that someone was.

"Damn this place," she muttered, knowing that she was not to curse or take the Lord's name in vain. She was relieved to see that the room's only inhabitant, her pregnant mother, was sleeping on the rush mattress set atop four wooden crates. There was no one else in the room to hear her; her two sisters were attending a school for Irish children at the Sisters of Mercy convent. The single room, while large, served as parlor, kitchen, dining area, and bedroom for five inhabitants.

The apartment was carved out a former mansion on the corner of Endicott and Lafayette Avenues, built by Henry Fowler, a livery magnate who owned several stables throughout Boston. When the Irish immigration to America began to swell in the 1830s, Fowler and most of his neighbors relocated to Beacon Hill, a safe distance away, and a promontory easily kept separate from the grubby world below it.

Soon after the mass emigration, George Parkman and Robert Gould Shaw came hunting for real estate bargains and were not disappointed. Each room of a grand home could be turned into a separate apartment with just a few additions or removals of existing doors. What matter if there was hardly a ray of light or a breath of a breeze ever felt in those dank, poorly ventilated spaces; the stream of immigrants arriving with little money, yet desperate for shelter, was never-ending.

Ellen and her family had been among that number, and here they were, in a typical Irish tenement slum from which there was no likely escape. Like so many young women from the southwest counties of Ireland, Ellen had traveled to the United States on her own in 1845, the first year of the great famine.

Back in County Cork, there had been potatoes aplenty; then suddenly none were to be had. Ellen had watched her youngest sister, just three weeks old, starve to death in the arms of her mother, who was too weak to make the milk the baby required. Six months later, her father was trampled by a horse; he never regained consciousness and soon died, not that he would have desired to see the tragedies that awaited his family.

Ellen's two older brothers worked what crops remained, but John, the oldest, had finally had enough of the blight on his life and his potatoes, and set his sights on London. He was not heard from again. Brendan, older than Ellen by just ten months, met a semistarved girl he fancied, and off they went to her relations, who had a fishing boat on the coast of Kinsale.

It was determined that the family's survival depended on Ellen freeing herself from the tortured grasp of Ireland. She was provisioned to set sail for the New World, where she would undoubtedly find success, and pay for her poverty-stricken family's passage to join her in Boston, while sending home whatever funds she could to aid her relations.

Like many Irish girls in their teenage years, Ellen boarded an ocean liner by herself: the Phaedra, in Liverpool. She had little trouble with the seasickness that beset all those around her, and within two days of landing in Boston had secured a position as a scullery maid. She served in the fine home of Albert Atkinson, a counselor of the law who saw every Irish girl in his employ as a temptation to succumb to his worst instincts, and succumb he did.

Ellen was not of a mind to suffer his depredations, so her employ at the Atkinson home ended quickly. The lack of proper references, essential for obtaining a place in domestic service, hampered her ability to find another position in a wealthy household. Ellen was saddened that her widowed mother—living in Skibbereen with the two surviving girls, aged four and six—was taking in needlework to make some money. Her mother remained dependent on the meager generosity of her two sisters, who had little to spare from their own beleaguered households, and of Ellen. The letters Ellen's aunts wrote to her complained about the burden her family put upon theirs. It was time, they said, for her to bring her mother and sisters to America.

This left Ellen but one viable way to make money. She began taking in laundry from the households where the single women in her building and those nearby labored, and she saved the pennies she made in the hopes of paying the $70 for passage for three from Liverpool to Boston.

Ellen was diligent and reliable, thus contradicting two of the stereotypes that native New Englanders held about the Irish. Six days a week, shortly after daybreak she would pull out the aged water tub (only a barrel cut in half), pump it full of water from the communal well down the street, and drag it back to the dirt area behind O'Malley's groggery, trying not to spill her load.

There she and her neighbors built a steady fire in a stone pit and hung a battered and blackened iron pot above it. An iron rod extended from each side of the pot's bottom. When the water was boiling, the pot was moved off the flame and the water tipped into various wooden tubs. Then the hard labor—scrubbing with lye, rinsing, and scrubbing some more—commenced, and by the time each day was done, Ellen's hands were redder than a Boston lobster: chapped, raw, even bleeding after a large load of bed linens needs be returned blinding white.

This was her duty as a caring and responsible daughter, and eventually she succeeded in saving the funds to purchase one adult and two child fares from Liverpool to Boston. To her shock, as she awaited her family at Central Wharf, she saw her mother emerge from the ship's hold accompanied by a bewhiskered man who held one of Ellen's sisters in his left arm and the other in his right. Ellen had never seen him before in her life.

This was William Haggerty, who apparently had known Sophie O'Keeffe through mutual relations in County Cork, where his brother had married Sophie's cousin, Mary. They had reunited on the boat, and poor Sophie, husbandless and grief-stricken, had proved an easy mark for a man who was a grifter and a hustler. Conveniently, Haggerty had made the acquaintance of a priest on the voyage, so barely moments after she accepted his proposal of marriage, Sophie found herself with a new surname and a putative father for her children, including the one waiting for her in Boston.

From the time Haggerty moved in with Ellen's mother and siblings in the single room she had secured for the family, he had acted the maggot. Never had she met such a fool. When he was not fluthered with drink, he was in the process of arriving in that state, or reluctantly departing it, usually by passing out wherever he stood or sat.

Ellen detested the man. To her dismay, this antagonism seemed to delight her stepfather, who teased her, made lewd comments and obscene gestures, and generally tormented her whenever possible, which, given their close quarters, was often.

Haggerty's irritating presence had had one positive effect. It made her more determined than ever to abandon 82 Endicott Street, O'Malley's groggery, and the dispiriting sight and sound of William Haggerty, and make her own way in the world.

She knew the obstacles that faced a young Irishwoman, even an attractive one. Domestic service or prostitution summed up her primary options. Neither was acceptable, so Ellen needed to find another path to independence and freedom. She knew other women did this; she had heard about them while serving dinner in the Atkinson dining room, when she overheard the banker's daughters gossiping about a friend who actually attended a men's college. And another female friend who was attending the Harvard Medical College.

Ellen had no aspirations to those heights; they were beyond her ken. But to obtain a position that allowed her to use her brain instead of her body was a dream she believed attainable, even for one as lowly an Irish immigrant with a sickly mother and an Irish langer she refused to address as stepfather.

William Haggerty, it turned out, proved to be her greatest motivation.

Bowdoin Square and Washington Street, Boston, Massachusetts

Despite the bitter wind and chill in the air, Dr. James Stone set out as usual on his morning constitutional at ten o'clock. He had made the decision when dressing that morning to be unconventional, a state of mind he greatly enjoyed, even if the effect on others would be lost when he put on the voluminous greatcoat required to keep warm in the Boston winter. He was delicate in this regard, susceptible to the cold and its drafty penetrations.

Beneath the dull black wool wrap, a peacock spread its variegated feathers. The twenty-five-year-old had donned a dark blue sack coat, the linen garment buttoned only at the top and hanging fashionably open to show a blue and green checked vest and a gold watch chain. The collar of James's tailored white cotton shirt was stiffly starched and turned up under a flowing black cravat. His pinch-legged trousers were perfectly pressed (his Irish maid, Sharon, had accomplished at least that task successfully) and fit low around his waist, accenting his slender, trim form. Atop his head sat a hard black felt bowler, sliding around slightly on his well-macassared hair.

James would have slowed his gait as he strolled toward the Mall, adjacent to the Tremont Street side of the Common, had the weather been more favorable. The trees weighed heavy with ice. The wind carried the frozen but still salty scents of the nearby harbor. James nodded slightly to the occasional passerby, but the pickings were slim on this Friday morning: mostly older spinsters drowned in black capes, bonnets, and mittens.

The threatening skies had kept at home all who had no pressing reason to be about. No sight of any of Boston's famously inveterate strollers: Senator Daniel Webster, the politician Edward Everett, and defense counsel Rufus Choate. At the right time of year, when the right sort of people were in town and not at the seashore of Nahant, the Mall, like the walk atop the Mill Dam, was an ideal location in which to see and be seen.

Given this was not one of those mornings, James drew his scarf across the lower half of his face and departed the Common. It was time to change his identity and adopt conventional business attire. He returned to his rooms to change. He had made an appointment for early that afternoon to have a calotype portrait made at the Litch, Whipple and Company studio at 96 Washington Street; this would provide a second opportunity that day to design his idealized self.

The formal portrait James envisioned required that he look like every other serious doctor of medicine in Boston: white linen shirt, black silk cravat wound round his neck to his chin, black waistcoat and frock coat, black trousers, and black silk hat. On second thought, he decided to abandon the hat. He intended this calotype to present a gentleman who could impress and interest a suitable marriage partner, as well as future wealthy medical patients. He would hang it in his dispensary.

The calotype was a new process of photography invented by Henry Fox Talbot in Boston eight years earlier, and Mr. Simon Whipple, whose studio James was now headed for, was a follower of Talbot's method. It provided a larger portrait than the shiny daguerreotypes, which had to be tilted to be viewed properly, and it cost less—only $6, versus $10 for the daguerreotype.

When James had visited Whipple's studio some weeks earlier, what he'd admired most was how the portraits mounted on the studio's walls lacked the sharp clarity of the daguerreotype. The subjects seemed softer in their appearance, gentler, less harsh. James thought a calotype would lessen the effect of his pointed nose and sharp chin, features that embarrassed him.

Leaving Bowdoin Square shortly before one o'clock, James passed the imposing Revere House hotel, a five-story building with four tall columns supporting the roof over the front entrance. It dominated the former bowling green where Dr. Thomas Bulfinch, grandfather of the famous architect, had first settled in Boston.

Boston was altering itself before his eyes, James thought. The city was already so different from the one he had been born in barely a quarter century earlier. Beacon Hill, whose residents constituted his trade as a physician, had not even existed at the time. Now it was the apogee of his aspirations. A proper three-story brick house on Walnut Street would do just fine.

The other great change was the omnipresence in Boston of the Irish immigrant. Irish workers unloaded ships, hauled coal, gathered trash, dug canals, laid bricks. James could not imagine how Boston had functioned prior to their arrival.

As he turned on to Washington Street, where Whipple's camera awaited him, James looked around and saw an Irish woman or man in every direction, doing some task or another that required physical labor. *Can they become American if they are never required to think?* James wondered. *Can they ever stop being Irish, and become another thing, an American thing, if they are Catholic?* James knew so little about the religion or its adherents that he didn't waste time thinking about the faith of the Irish and why it elicited such hissing despisement. Those like his brother Anson saw popery as the country's next great threat.

Arriving at number 96, a sturdy brick edifice displaying a Georgian front, James wiped his boots on the iron scraper provided and climbed the steps to Whipple's studio. It had only been at this location for a matter of months. James had heard, when the photograph maker was first recommended to him, that Whipple had journeyed to the wilds of Michigan and Wisconsin to capture the wonders of nature with his chemical magic.

James entered the large room that served as the picture maker's studio. Two giant calotype photographs of the White Mountains were mounted on the wall, breathtaking in their ethereal beauty, the soft tones leaving the landscapes looking befogged. A large black velvet backdrop had been erected with two-by-fours, the edges left rough and unfinished.

Whipple came forward bearing an obsequious smile, already bowing slightly and extending his hand. James was not enthusiastic about this growing practice of everyone grasping each other's bare hands and wriggling them about. It seemed unclean to him, and his hands had a tendency to sweat; he would rather keep them to himself.

DALE M. POLLOCK

Still, he shook Whipple's hand vigorously, and Whipple turned to a chair positioned in front of the velvet wall.

"Doctor Stone, I have awaited your arrival with great anticipation," he said. "As I explained in your previous visit, the calotype process we use in our operation was developed by our good friend Mister Talbot. Some even call this style of portraiture Talbot-types," he added, with a dismissive smile. "But not here. In this establishment, we present calotype portraits by two of the most experienced and artistic operators in Boston, nay, the entire East! When beholding your image, people will know it is one created by Whipple and Litch!"

Whipple is nothing if not enthusiastic about his product, James thought, also noting that the photographer had reversed the order of the firm's partners. Conveniently, Mr. Litch was nowhere to be seen.

James had never posed for any portrait, let alone a formal one using the latest mechanical marvel. Whipple explained the calotype process, which relied on a translucent paper negative, and told James, with great satisfaction, that the time needed to hold a pose was now greatly reduced to only a few minutes.

"Would you like to rest your arm on a table, Doctor Stone? Or perhaps stand in a position of rest? I also possess a device that aids you in maintaining a firm posture."

Whipple gestured to a wooden contraption that James had imagined to be a torture device. But applying its purpose to it, he saw how it would maintain his back, neck, and head in a rigid position that he thought would look serious and respectable. A man of purpose.

"I will offer myself as a sacrifice to that device you employ, Mister Whipple. I trust you will allow me to emerge generally unscathed?"

"Most certainly, most certainly," Whipple wheedled. "A most dignified choice."

James felt better hearing Whipple's approval. He allowed the photographer to sit and pose him in a three-quarter profile, his face and his white shirt the only pale variations in an otherwise black sea of felt, wool cloth, silk, and hair. Whipple turned up his subject's shirt collar and reknotted his tie.

James had given considerable thought to the best facial expression he should don for the occasion. Did he aim to convey that he was serious and respectable? Confident and aggressive? Humble and plain? He would not have preferred a pose that revealed what he considered his lack of courage, or his desire to impress those around him. He hoped this odd-looking device would not capture those inner fears.

As if sensing his confusion, Whipple moved closer to James and settled him against the metal stand. Invisibly, it supported each arm, his back, and his neck. Then Whipple adjusted James's profile at a stronger angle.

"You are a most impressive man to be a doctor at your young age, Doctor Stone," Whipple breathed, reminding James of the way prostitutes sometimes solicited him in the street. "Allow your nature to emanate, and the camera will capture its essence."

James allowed a half smile to emerge on his face; he thought it might humanize his sharp nose and weak chin. Then he remembered.

"Oh, Mister Whipple, I decided not to bring my hat with me. Do you believe me in need of *un chapeau*?" James said, trying to employ the limited French he had learned at Harvard.

"No, no, Doctor Stone," Whipple said. "Worry not, worry not. You have a fine head of hair; many men would envy you. You may as well display it."

The half smile returned. James was glad he had abandoned the hat.

Whipple stationed his subject as precisely as he could, then dashed back to his camera apparatus, which rested on a tripod of tall wooden legs. Underneath a large black curtain, mounted atop the tripod was a square wooden box, with a brass lens protruding from its front and a brass-framed peephole at its rear. A flimsy paper negative was framed in front of it.

From beneath the curtain, Whipple called out: "That position is very good, Doctor! Please do not alter it in any manner!"

James heard some loud clicks, then nothing. He tried to breathe as little as possible, but of course, his ear needed scratching, his nose began to itch, and he felt he was about to sneeze.

"Just another three minutes," called Whipple, still busy beneath his curtain. James felt rooted to the spot; had time ever passed this slowly?

Finally, Whipple emerged from his photographic cavern waving a paper negative, a wide smile on his broad face.

"Allow me to print a positive image from this negative, and I will have your portrait, mounted and framed, by this time tomorrow," Whipple said.

James was eager to get a look at his image. But when Whipple showed it to him, he was completely confused. His image was the darkest part of the photograph, and all around him was lighter. Everything that was light and dark was reversed.

Whipple was familiar with this reaction. "Don't be alarmed, Doctor

Stone, this is not the final image. This is its opposite, its negative, as we call it. From this, I'll print a positive image that will restore the natural balance of light."

James was not completely reassured, but he trusted that Whipple was familiar with his apparatus. James stared at the paper negative and could see the outline of all his features, including his tentative smile; even in this rough form, he felt reassured. The camera had not laid bare the timid, puerile, unmoored James Winchell Stone.

Now accustomed to the reversed image, James could imagine that, if he were to see this portrait prominent on the wall of an up-and-coming young doctor's dispensary, he would not be reluctant to enter and place himself in that doctor's care.

His negative was more positive than he had expected.

Walnut Street, Beacon Hill; Boston, Massachusetts

George Parkman had vanished. He had not done business after one o'clock, he had not collected his rents, and he had not been seen by any who knew him after that time.

If he were not such a punctual man, his absence might have gone unnoticed for longer. He was not present at supper that afternoon, an occurrence so unusual that it greatly disturbed his family. His brother-in-law, Robert Gould Shaw, was contacted by his sister, Mrs. Parkman, via messenger, and the results were immediate: first, advertisements were printed in every New England newspaper, large and small; then a flood of more than twenty-eight thousand broadsides appeared on every major Boston thoroughfare. They read:

SPECIAL NOTICE!

GEO. PARKMAN, M.D.,
*A **well known, and highly respected** citizen of Boston, left his House in WALNUT STREET, to meet an engagement of business, on **Friday last, November 23d**, between 12 and 1 o'clock P.M., and was seen in the Southerly part of the City.*

> ***Any person who can give information** relative to him that may lead to his discovery is earnestly requested to communicate the same immediately to the City Marshal, for which he shall be liberally rewarded.*

And the next day:

$3000 Reward!

DR. GEORGE PARKMAN,
A well-known citizen of Boston, left his residence
No. 8 Walnut Street, on Friday last, he is 60 years of age—about 5 feet
10 inches high—grey hair—thin face—with a scar under his chin—light
complexion—and usually walks very fast. He was dressed in a dark frock
coat, dark pantaloons, purple silk vest, with dark figured black stock and
black hat.

As he may have wandered from home in consequence of some sudden
aberration of mind, being perfectly well when he left his house; or, as he had
with a large sum of money, he may have been foully dealt with. The above
reward will be paid for information that will lead to his discovery if alive; or
for the detection and conviction of the perpetrators if any injury may have
been done to him. A suitable reward will be paid for the discovery of his body.

ROBERT G. SHAW.
Boston, Nov. 26th, 1849
Information may be given to the City Marshal.

And, finally, two days later:

$5000 REWARD!

Whereas no satisfactory information has been obtained respecting
DR. GEORGE PARKMAN,
Since the afternoon of Friday last, and fears are entertained that he has been
murdered, the above Reward will be paid for information that leads to the
recovery of his body, and those that might have perpetrated evil upon him.

ROBERT G. SHAW.
Boston, November 28th, 1849

There was no shortage of applicants for these bounties. Numerous Bostonians came forward with eyewitness testimony that Parkman had crossed Craigie's Bridge over the Charles River on foot on his way to Cambridgeport late Friday afternoon.

Yet someone else had witnessed him tromping into the woods in Woburn, gun in hand and intent on suicide. He was seen variously on the streets of Milton, Braintree, even New York City. It was reported that Dr. Parkman went into a barber's shop in Boston's West End in the company of an Irishman to whom he exhibited his wallet; he was promptly robbed of its contents, and left senseless in a nearby ditch, the story went.

Given the prominence of the Parkman family (and the fear instilled within Boston municipal officials by the fury of Robert Gould Shaw), the search undertaken by Marshal Tukey and the recently formed police force, whose total number was only thirty-five constables, was exhaustive.

Each building and tenement owned by Parkman, a substantial number throughout the city, was thoroughly examined. The Charles River and Boston Harbor were dredged by a flotilla of small boats. The flats surrounding East Cambridge were gleaned more thoroughly than a well-picked field. Every ticket master on the various railroads leading out of the city was questioned, and handbills with a reasonable likeness of Parkman were distributed liberally.

There was only one observation concerning the afternoon of Friday, November 23, 1849, upon which the majority of witnesses agreed: Dr. Parkman was seen entering Harvard Medical College at around half past one o'clock. Despite many unreliable accounts to the contrary, no one had presented any proof that he ever exited.

CHAPTER 1

December 1849
Bowdoin Square and North Grove Street, Boston, Massachusetts

The blows rained down on Dr. James Stone's door. He woke up feeling drugged, stunned, as if he had just been in a barrel rolling down a hill. It took a moment to overcome his disorientation and realize he was indeed in his bed at number 6 Bowdoin Square, above his medical dispensary, and that it was the evening of Saturday, December 1. He possessed a dim memory of taking to bed early with a bad headache.

What time was it? And who was keeping up that infernal banging? James searched for his dressing gown, eased into his slippers, and made his way, stumbling in the dark, to the bedroom doorway, where he lit a candle in the sconce on the nearby wall.

He looked at the mantelpiece clock in the sitting room—nearly one o'clock! What affliction had beset one of his patients now? None other than a very sick individual would roust Dr. Stone from his warm bed linens after midnight.

Opening the heavy oak door to his chambers, James encountered, instead of a worried parent or spouse, Dr. Wynford Lewis Jr., who was looking frantic and agitated, his arm poised to deliver another resounding blow to the door. Next to him stood James's Irish maid, Sharon, wild-haired and trembling from the excitement of it all.

Dr. Lewis had been James's anatomy professor at Tremont Medical School and was a Harvard Medical College lecturer whose diagnostic and surgical courses James also had attended. Lewis shouted at James, his relief at rousing him evident. "Thank God you're here, Stone! I feared you had gone out of town to tend to a patient."

Aside from the fact that he had no patients out of town, and precious few within it, James was bewildered by Lewis's dramatic appearance. He could not imagine what would bring this respected physician and teacher to his door at this hour.

The hair rose on the back of James's neck. Could this untimely visit concern the disappearance of Dr. Parkman, the subject of all speculation in Boston, who appeared to have disappeared from this earth one week previous?

"What is it, Doctor Lewis? Did they find Doctor Parkman, or some news of his whereabouts?" James asked.

"They've found parts of a human form, aye, thus my purpose in gathering you, Doctor Stone," Lewis said. "We suppose it will constitute a body; it may prove to be parts of several. The circumstances allow no easy identification to be made, which is why I'm requesting your assistance. You're the only anatomist I could locate."

The slight was unintentional, but James perceived it nevertheless. Still, it was thrilling to be involved in a notorious case. James wanted to understand exactly what Lewis expected of him. The last thing he would allow himself to do was disappoint.

James said, "Are these remains Doctor Parkman's? Are you saying he was vivisected, Doctor Lewis?"

Lewis reached out and seized James by the arm, pulling him toward the door.

"Stone, you must dress quickly. We are anxiously awaited. Together we may be able to bring some clarity to this confounded mystery, but we must make haste to the Medical College."

James was perplexed. *The Medical College? Surely Parkman had not been found there. He was the donor of the land on which the new building stood, for God's sakes! What a terrible irony that would be! Who at the Medical College would dare lift a hand to one of the most powerful and wealthiest men in the city, let alone sever him into pieces?*

James turned to his bedroom to throw on whatever was available. For once, he cared neither about his wardrobe nor its suitability for the occasion. Nothing was suitable for this occasion.

$\sim$

Dr. Lewis's phaeton pulled up to the Medical College on North Grove Street, which was adjacent to the property housing Massachusetts General Hospital. The hospital stood some distance away on Fruit Street. Through the carriage window, James immediately recognized the janitor Ephraim Littlefield, who was dressed in a workingman's smock, standing outside the college. James remembered him from anatomical demonstrations he had attended just three years earlier. Littlefield had supplied the cadavers.

DALE M. POLLOCK

The janitor stood next to a man James did not recognize: Francis Tukey, the chief of Boston's new police force. Tukey had his back to the new limestone and wood structure that housed the Medical College. A broad granite staircase led up the front of the building to a landing and a set of tall wooden doors.

As James and Lewis disembarked, out of the building's shadows emerged Dr. Jacob Bigelow and Dr. J. B. S. Jackson, both prominent members of the Medical College faculty. "James, I'm obliged you have come to assist us," said Bigelow. "I would have fetched you myself, but I'm too concerned about the impact of all this to leave for even an instant."

James felt out of place in the company of these esteemed physicians, but it was clear that Dr. Bigelow, long his patron and mentor, had chosen him to be there, along with Dr. Lewis.

Dr. Jackson hurriedly explained that he had been called upon at his residence by the janitor Littlefield earlier that day and told of the man's suspicions regarding the privy beneath the laboratory of Dr. John Webster, the college's professor of chemistry. The entire building, including Dr. Webster's rooms, had been thoroughly searched during the first week of Dr. Parkman's disappearance and had yielded no clues.

Dr. Jackson now motioned Littlefield over. To James's surprise, the man he remembered as a surly loner displayed remarkable equanimity in telling the gaggle of important men surrounding him that he had been suspicious of Professor Webster's comments and actions in recent days. Littlefield said he was struck particularly by an encounter the previous morning with Webster in which the professor repeated a rumor of a woman seen putting a bloody bundle into a hansom cab. Webster assured Littlefield that Dr. Parkman had fallen into mean hands and his body was unlikely to be discovered, the murderers no doubt having done away with it.

Littlefield told the doctors and Tukey that he had remained suspicious of the chemistry professor. On November 30 the janitor used a trap door in his apartment to descend to the crawl space beneath the college, where he advanced on hands and knees to the brick wall of the vault built for Webster's privy. It drained directly into the Charles River.

James looked at the small crowd and found everyone closely following Littlefield's account. James had expected a reaction to Littlefield's effrontery in invading a professor's privacy on his own presumption. Dr. Oliver Wendell Holmes, the dean of the Medical College, would have never authorized such an action. That was probably why he was not invited to this gathering, James realized.

Dr. Bigelow, the senior doctor present, asked the janitor why he had acted so abruptly of his own volition.

"It was to satisfy myself and the public," Littlefield said in a self-important tone. "Every other part of the building had been searched, and nothing could have passed this space but through the privy."

Once authorized by Dr. Jackson to proceed with his plan, Littlefield said he had used a hammer and chisel to break through the privy's thick brick wall. He'd set his wife to watch the door to their apartment and had given her instructions that in the unlikely event Professor Webster were to appear, she was to rap four times on the kitchen floor with her heel to alert the janitor of his presence.

Sure enough, as Littlefield labored to dislodge the first of five layers of brick masonry, he heard the telltale tapping. In a panic, he'd hurled away his tools and hurried upstairs. It was not Professor Webster who had arrived in his apartment, but Parkman's business manager, Charles Kingsley, and Police Constable William K. Jones. Covered in dirt, Littlefield disclosed his scheme to the police and Kingsley, and thus through him to the Parkman family, and the police for the first time, promising that in a short time he would have a hole punched through the privy wall that would reveal what he suspected was hidden in the vault.

Kingsley hurried off to tell Parkman's brother-in-law, Robert Gould Shaw, of Littlefield's suspicions. Constable Jones departed to inform his superiors, after promising to return to see the results of Littlefield's endeavors.

Littlefield continued his account of that night, telling the assembled doctors and Tukey that he had returned to the basement, this time armed with a crowbar. Minutes later, he'd succeeded in knocking a hole through the final layer of bricks, finally allowing him a view into the privy vault. He'd peered into the darkness, holding a candle close by his head, and was shaken to his core by what he saw dimly illuminated. Now, he said, tonight he would lead them to the horrible sight.

"Let me show you, gentlemen, what I saw, because you are knowledgeable in these matters and I am not," Littlefield told the group of four doctors and Tukey as he led them to the left side of the building. He now displayed more humility than James knew him for; still, he saw Littlefield as a man resentful of his low station in life.

The group, each man bearing a candle, followed the janitor into his apartment and through the trap door to the earthen floor below. One by one, each crawled through the dark cramped space, following Littlefield and his candle as he made his way to the brick privy wall. Eventually the men reached an area where they could all stand in the dim light in a hunched position. Before them was a hole in the brickwork, about eighteen inches wide by ten or twelve inches high, from which emitted a putrid smell more foul than even a privy would produce.

The four medical men and Tukey hung back, initially reluctant to view the vault's contents. James's curiosity overruled the bile he felt churning in his stomach; he stumbled forward, stretching out his hand to push his candle into the black hole of darkness as far as possible, and peered in.

He saw a bulky shape or two hanging from what looked like large fishhooks. James squinted to bring clarity to what he first perceived: the hanging form resembled a human pelvis, or at least most of one, with the genitalia still attached, and two additional pieces that appeared to be appendages, one possibly part of a leg. He felt faint and nauseated. His gut's instincts had been accurate.

Bigelow, Lewis, Tukey, and Jackson were right behind him and also peered in with their candles, but the darkness was hardly vanquished. Tukey demanded Littlefield bring a lantern to better illuminate the dank space. While waiting for the janitor to return, the men stood silently, unwilling to look at each other or back inside the vault.

When Littlefield returned, he handed Dr. Lewis the lantern, which he extended unsteadily as he and James searched the cavern more carefully this time. Yes, these were most definitely human remains; the pelvis was now quite clear, along with the genitals, one upper leg and thigh, and what appeared to be a section of a leg from the knee down to the foot. Now he understood why Lewis had fetched him at Dr. Bigelow's instruction. It would be their job to identify which parts of the human body these random pieces were, and to answer the most delicate question of all: from whose body or bodies had they come?

～

The evening's chill seemed more penetrating to James as the doctors gathered again outside Littlefield's cottage. Bigelow said it was confounding that the police had searched the college so many times, invading lecture rooms, laboratories, and private offices in a rough manner that had put the faculty into an uproar; yet here were these remains, right beneath where they all stood.

"I must go to Doctor Holmes and President Sparks immediately,"

Bigelow said as he looked around the shivering group. "This discovery will do no honor to Harvard and may cause grave consternation in the community. We'll all be blamed for this foul deed."

"This is only the beginning of our troubles," said Dr. Jackson, the most senior faculty present. "Remember whose laboratory is above that privy."

The assembled doctors looked uneasily at each other. They had heard Littlefield's story of his encounters with Professor John Webster. All were aware that Webster was frequently in debt and had borrowed money from George Parkman. They also knew that Webster, as a professor of chemistry, had no connection to the department of anatomy. There was no reason for anything to be in that vault other than waste, much less distinguishable portions of a human body.

"Can we be certain that what we just viewed are indeed the remains of Doctor Parkman?" James asked in a voice more confident than he'd intended. He was a bit cowed in the midst of these learned men who had been his teachers, but he felt he must pose the most logical questions. "Shouldn't we do a closer examination, and first determine to a certainty that these specimens are indeed human? And if so, were they recently deposited in the privy vault? And only then, try to determine from whose body they were detached?"

A fleeting smile crossed Bigelow's face. "This is why I sent for you, James," he said. "Not only your anatomical skills, but for your common sense." Jackson and Lewis looked at James with respect, not for his insight, but because Bigelow was rare in bestowing praise.

Bigelow called over Marshal Tukey, who had been standing nearby, overtly eavesdropping. He directed Tukey to have his men break fully into the vault, carefully remove the specimens from the hooks that had been used to suspend them, and lay them on a clean board so they could be examined in one of the dissection rooms. James could see that Tukey did not like taking direction from a Harvard College know-it-all; the marshal now was sure that someone just like these professors was in all probability the perpetrator of this terrible crime.

Lieutenant Derastus Clapp's police carriage pulled up, and he hurried out to join the group huddled in the cold. He told the doctors that Professor Webster had seemed nervous and flustered when he'd met the first search party in his laboratory, several days earlier. He had pointed hurriedly to various articles in the room and directed the constables to his private storeroom, where he kept his dangerous chemicals. These actions now could be interpreted as diversions to keep the police away from his privy.

After bestowing a withering look upon his top lieutenant for not mentioning this earlier, Tukey assigned three constables to aid in the removal of the body parts and sent another patrolman to fetch Suffolk County Coroner Jabez Pratt. He took his most trusted constables with him and went back into the Medical College, followed by the klatch of doctors.

It turned out that a thorough search of Webster's rooms had never been accomplished. The largest space was set up as a lecture room, with a table centered on a low platform in the middle and a set of stairs on either side of the platform, leading up to it. As the group moved toward the partitioned area of the upper laboratory and Webster's back rooms, the police and doctors saw dark brown stains on the floor. In a cabinet, behind another locked door that they forced open, they found a pair of bloodstained pants and slippers. There were also several blankets that presumably had come from Webster's home, since Littlefield said they were not part of the Medical College's supplies. These could have been used to cover laboratory windows from prying eyes. Bigelow, James, and the other physicians looked at each other, their hearts sinking. The worst possible conclusion seemed likely.

"Can you contemplate any other solution to this mystery?" Bigelow said to James under his breath, unwilling to have the others overhear them or to draw attention by leaving the group to speak privately. "Doctor Webster seems the guilty party to this abominable crime, as much as I hate to state it."

James's cautious nature once again held sway. "Let's not jump to conclusions that may prove premature," he whispered back to Bigelow, turning so that no one else could hear him. "We must find and speak to Professor Webster and observe his reactions to this discovery."

As Bigelow and James spoke, one of Tukey's men opened the grate of a small wood-burning furnace, located near the door to Webster's private rooms. Every instructor in the Medical College had one of these iron stoves in his rooms to ward off the cold northwest wind that swept down the Charles River unobstructed and blasted the college at all hours of the day and night, but none possessed what lay inside Webster's.

The doctors were called over to confirm what was plain to see: a jawbone, along with a partial set of false teeth, rested among the ashes. Bigelow's posture sagged; he knew the pride Dr. Parkman took in the teeth he'd had specially commissioned for his long jaw, even if they never fit properly. There was little doubt remaining for anyone who knew the late gentleman: what was left of George Parkman was before and below them.

Bigelow and the other physicians could not meet James's gaze but stared fixedly at the ground.

The police were not done. Constable George Fuller poked through a pile of battered wooden crates and rubbish in a partitioned area to the left of the laboratory, and there he discovered an old wooden tea chest, about two feet high and locked shut. Fuller tried to move it, but it was far too heavy for its size, and it barely budged. He pried off the cover and found the chest seemingly filled with minerals and geological specimens labeled by Webster for his lectures. Removing the top layer of contents, Fuller could not see what lay below, only some sort of dark mass. He forced his hand down into the bottom of the chest until it encountered something soft and damp. Before anyone could object, Fuller turned the chest over and emptied it on the floor. Everyone in the room fell silent.

What emerged was a jumble of body parts packed in a thick sludge of the tannic acid that Webster used in his demonstrations of organic chemistry, to preserve his human samples. James warned Fuller to be careful as the doctors rushed over to examine the chest's contents: a burned part of a torso, the abdomen cut open; a thigh forced into the chest cavity, the ribs let down over it; and a lone kidney. These were accompanied by a bloodstained Bowie knife, one of the few implements sharp enough to accomplish this apparent vivisection.

James's training in anatomy brought the gory picture into focus: the abdomen had been opened, and the intestines removed. The cartilage of the ribs had been separated, and the liver and the heart taken out, although one kidney remained. All these body parts had been forced into the old tea chest, with the tannic acid employed as an effective means of destroying the organs and bones. Now the contents were doing their putrefying best to assert themselves in the exposed air of the room.

James knew that if one were disposing of a body, the easiest way to begin would be with the appendages: head, arms, and legs. Lop off the limbs first, get them out of the way, sever the head, and begin to dismember the trunk of the body. He shuddered at the thought of Professor Webster performing this grisly business on Dr. Parkman, a man of wealth, high standing, and great beneficence. How was this possible? James's head swam with the import of what lay before them.

Another constable, poking about in a room adjoining the laboratory, found a small handsaw, clotted with what appeared to be blood. Tukey was furious that all of this evidence had been missed in the initial search. It was all he could do to contain his rage.

"This is enough, gentlemen," Tukey announced with a peremptory growl. "I need see no more." He turned to another constable, John Bryant. "Gather up all this evidence, and label where ye find each piece of it. Me, Officer Clapp, and Officer Fuller will proceed immediately to Professor Webster's house in Cambridge, and arrest him for the murder of Doctor George Parkman."

Tukey turned to Bigelow and James. "Would one or both of you please come with me? I have a plan in me mind, and it will be a great help to have a person familiar to Doctor Webster with us when we apprehend him."

Bigelow and James looked at each other. James was neither a friend nor even an acquaintance of Professor Webster; he had taken Webster's chemistry course three years earlier, as required, but enjoyed no personal contact with the professor. Bigelow shook his head; James could see that he did not have the wherewithal to witness Webster collapse, confess, beg for mercy, or any of the other depressing outcomes this journey promised.

"I'll stay with our colleagues to await Doctor Holmes and President Sparks," Bigelow demurred. "I believe it best if you accompany the police, James. Webster will think little is amiss if you're with them, but if it is I, he'll know the matter is grave, and he might act rashly."

Tukey wasted no further time: "So ye'll join us, Doctor Stone?" he demanded. The question required no answer, and the police hurried from the room, James following behind. The nightmare of this evening would not end. James wished it were a dream, not this reality that was more disturbing at every turn.

CHAPTER 2

December 1849
Garden Street, Cambridge, Massachusetts; Leverett Street and North
Grove Street, Boston, Massachusetts

By all accounts, Professor John White Webster was the meekest of men. During his four weekly lectures on chemistry at Harvard Medical College, it was not at all unusual for students to throw things about his lecture room, drop his minerals on the floor, and cause him to weep from their lack of respect. This was the Webster of James's acquaintance, which was why he could not fathom the timid professor committing this brutal crime. His students mocked and belittled him; none would have thought him capable of any such action.

As the dark brougham police carriage rattled over Craigie's Bridge, James could not refrain from contemplating Webster's fate. The chemistry professor was not an insubstantial man, professionally speaking. His accomplishments were many; he was the founder of the Linnaean Society, for God's sake.

James also knew of Webster's active participation in the Cambridge social scene. Many gatherings were hosted at his successive residences: first a large home on Harvard Street, and now a more modest Greek Revival house at 22 Garden Street. He, his wife, and his four daughters had lived there since 1837, close by the Harvard campus. James had heard it rumored that Webster, due to his untoward finances, had let go his household staff, with only one servant remaining.

The police carriage lurched left onto Garden Street, toppling James onto Tukey's shoulder. James's pulse was racing as he tried to right himself. He dreaded the imminent arrival at Webster's door. He could not imagine how a man he had only known as mild and ineffective would react to the unexpected appearance of the police to seize him for a crime that was unthinkable on every level.

James's palms were sweaty. Unable to breathe, he grabbed and loosened the black stock around his neck. He cursed himself for agreeing to Bigelow's request to make this agonizing journey. He had not realized to what extent his involvement in the investigation into George Parkman's untimely demise would grow. The horses drew up; they had arrived at Webster's residence.

~

Marshal Tukey knocked on the door at 22 Garden Street with a firmness that seemed to James to second his purpose. There was no response, and Tukey rapped again, this time more violently.

James could hear movement on the other side of the oak door, and it swung open. There stood a short, round man in his midfifties, wearing wire spectacles. He displayed a careworn expression on his round face emblazoned by large side whiskers, and a brow absent of worry or concern. Whomever John Webster expected on his doorstep late into this chilly December evening, the sight of the police marshal, two constables, and one of his former students did not seem to perturb him in the slightest.

"This is a surprise," Webster said calmly. Acknowledging James, he bowed and said, "Good evening, Doctor Stone." James silently returned the bow.

Turning to the marshal, Webster inquired as to how he might be of service. To James's surprise, Tukey downplayed the matter.

"As yer no doubt aware, Professor Webster," the police chief responded, "we've been much consumed with our search for Doctor Parkman. We're doing a careful inventory of the places he mighta visited; our efforts now are concentrated on the Medical College itself. Would you mind accompanying us to yer rooms and laboratory?"

Webster tried to demur.

"I've already accompanied your men on one such tour in which nothing of interest was discovered," he said. "Can't this wait until morning? I'll be happy to help in any way that I can, but I must regard your request at this late hour as an imposition."

James wanted to warn his former teacher how serious the matter really was, but Tukey cut him off before he could speak, and glared at him to hold his tongue. This was police business.

"We're imposing on many people, Professor, to offer some relief to the Parkman family. As you can reckon, there's great concern about the fate of Doctor Parkman. Several of yer professors will meet us at the college, including Doctor Holmes. Doctor Stone here was kind enough to come along to gather ye."

For the first time, Webster looked directly at James. He studied the ground, looked up at Tukey, his men, then back to James. His expression was clear-eyed and benign.

"Well, if Doctor Holmes will be there, it would be ungracious of me to refuse. Allow me to put on my boots, get my coat and hat, and I'll join you."

Webster shut the door, leaving Tukey with a murderous look on his face. James wondered if Webster might attempt some escape, dashing out the servant's door or hiding in his house or its outbuildings. Tukey looked as if he harbored similar concerns.

Abruptly the door opened again, and a smiling John Webster emerged, properly clothed for the chill weather. Tukey seemed surprised and a bit disappointed. James thought he might have enjoyed an actual pursuit, even with this little man as the sole prey.

James and the constables now surrounded Webster and repaired as a group to Tukey's carriage. Lieutenant Clapp entered first, helping Webster into the brougham to sit across from him. Constable Fuller followed, sitting next to Clapp; then James entered, ending up next to Webster. Tukey was the last to clamber in, jamming his chunky body beside Fuller's so he could surveil Webster's movements during the ride to the Medical College.

"Never before have I sat in a police conveyance," Webster said with some wonder as the two-horse brougham drove off, moving slowly under the weight of five men. "This is all quite exciting." James was stunned by the man's sangfroid. If Webster had committed this heinous crime, he was the most cool-headed killer imaginable.

As Tukey, Fuller, and Clapp stoically gazed at them, James and Webster exchanged idle talk on the ride back to North Grove Street. They spoke of Dr. Bigelow's botanical drawings, which he was assembling for a new volume, and Dr. Holmes's essay in the most recent issue of *The Atlantic*. It took all of James's self-control not to grab Webster by the shoulders and scream at him, *How could you? Why would you? What were you thinking?* Tukey's constant glower in his direction was designed to keep James from making any mention of the purpose of their journey.

James's head felt muddled. There were too many possibilities in this bizarre circumstance for the kind of clear thinking expected of him. *Harvard men do not commit murder*, James thought. He could not erase from his memory the images of that bloody torso with its half-detached leg hanging in the privy, and the horrible viscera in the tea chest. Someone had been brutally killed and hacked into the pieces that were found in the rooms of

Dr. John Webster at the Medical College. What other explanation could suffice, other than it was at the hand of the man who sat humming and smiling on the way to his killing ground?

As they chatted, James noticed Webster calmly reach into his coat pocket, then saw him cough. He coughed again, covering his mouth with his hand; the next thing James saw was the professor downing the contents of a small phial of liquid he had concealed in his hand. Webster immediately looked pained. James was horrified. Webster had poisoned himself.

Seeing James's reaction, the police finally noticed that something was amiss. Webster's hand at his mouth had blocked them from seeing anything.

"Professor Webster!" James exclaimed. "What have you done?" To the shocked constables, he shouted, "The man has poisoned himself, he has just swallowed poison!"

The carriage shuddered to a swaying halt. Tukey leapt upon Webster with a furious bellow, prying the phial from his hand and demanding the identity of the poison. Webster was sweating profusely; his eyes rolled back in their sockets as Tukey roughly searched his person for other contraband, emptying Webster's pockets and tearing his pants.

James sniffed the phial Tukey thrust at him, and his fears were confirmed. Webster had drunk strychnine, although it must have been a small amount, given the tiny size of the bottle. James knew what had to be done.

"Help me get him out of the carriage," James said to Tukey and Clapp, his voice steady and responsible. "Please, as quickly as possible!"

Clapp and Fuller manhandled Webster out of the conveyance, and Tukey rushed after them. James leapt to the ground and hurried to Webster's half-prostrate form. He had no medicines with him; he had not thought to bring his supplies on this trip. Always available, though, was the oldest remedy on earth to make a man bring up something he had just swallowed. James pried open Webster's waxen lips and shoved two fingers well down his throat.

Webster gagged, but nothing else happened. As disgusting as this task was, James redoubled the effort and shoved his fingers as far down as he could reach into Webster's gullet. The desired effect was achieved. Webster violently retched. James's fingers were covered in vomit, and he wiped them on the frozen ground near where the carriage had stopped.

Webster was on his knees, vomiting up not only the strychnine but also his entire supper and the red wine that had accompanied it. The man's eyes were glassy and his head swung back and forth as he tried to support himself. He slid down to his elbows, his mouth just inches from the vomit-strewn ground. James helped him sit up. Lieutenant Clapp stood by, regarding Webster with disgust, unwilling to help him to his feet.

"What is wrong with you, man?" James said to Webster as they sat on the ground, as softly as he could so the police might not hear. "Whatever your circumstance, suicide is no proper response!"

Webster said nothing but shook his head and moaned. He clutched his stomach, retched again, just missing James this time. He looked as if he might pass out.

Tukey said, "Should we ride him over to Massachusetts General, Doctor Stone?" He stood over James and Webster, frowning. *Little wonder,* James thought; *the marshal had apprehended the suspect with ease and then almost lost him to suicide on the way to the scene of the crime.*

James could see by the gross display before them that little was left in Webster's stomach. No one at the hospital could do more than James's fingers had already done. He knew Webster would likely not expire from the small dosage of strychnine he had consumed; he would have a terrible headache and upset stomach for hours to come, but he would live.

"We should allow him to lie down and regain his strength," James said. "I believe the worst of the danger has passed."

"I'm thankful ye were in this carriage, Doctor," said Tukey, helping James to his feet. He was a gruff man who rarely handed out compliments. "Without ye, we'd likelier not know what steps to take, medically speaking."

James turned to Webster, who remained slumped on the ground, covered in sweat. The poor man was now mumbling a plea to his captors: "My poor, poor daughters, do not let them know . . ."

James tried to calm him. "Don't be concerned, Professor, I'll share these events with no one, particularly not your wife and children. I give you my word."

After conferring with Clapp and Fuller some distance away, Tukey walked back over to the teacher and his former pupil. Webster lay half-recumbent on the ground surrounded by his filth; James hovered above him, a steadying hand on the professor's shoulder. James had the situation under control for now.

"We've decided to take Professor Webster directly to the gaol on Leverett Street," Tukey informed James. "It's where he'll end up in any event. If he's able, we'll transport him to the Medical College this evening. If not, it'll have to wait 'til morning."

Tukey looked closely at James before putting his plan into action.

"Now, Doctor Stone, you say you're confident he'll survive? I can't afford to lose this prisoner."

James tried to think matters through clearly. He realized that if Webster were to die or slip into a coma, he would be personally responsible. Yet the man had vomited up, if not all of the strychnine, the majority of it.

"He will not perish from this attempt," James said. "I cannot attest to his mental state, and he will be sick to his stomach, but his self-poisoning has failed."

Clapp and Fuller hauled Webster to his feet and led him back into the police carriage, this time with a man on either side of him, each clutching one arm and sleeve of Webster's coat. Once inside, the prisoner fell back against the rough horsehair seat, his eyes closed, his chest heaving. His moans were now quiet blubbering.

The ride to the jail was quick, less than ten minutes. When they arrived, several constables rushed from the building to half-drag, half-carry Webster inside. James, the last to leave the carriage, was shaking as if the ague had struck him. He saw dried vomit on his boots and sleeve but had nothing with which to wipe them off.

James followed the officers into the Leverett Street Gaol, where Webster was left on a cot in one of the cells. He was now a prisoner, whether guilty or not, James supposed. The wheels of justice turned exceedingly quick when oiled by money and public excitement. Along with Lieutenant Clapp and Marshal Tukey, James spent the next forty-five minutes waiting for Webster to recover.

James asked for water for the prisoner, but when it was brought, Webster trembled so that he could not drink. Sweat continued to pour from him, a reaction to the strychnine, James knew. He gently helped Webster lie back down, and the man's eyes fluttered closed. He checked Webster's pulse—it was beating strongly. Tukey walked over with a questioning look. James shook his head. It was still too soon, and what was the hurry at this point? Poor Dr. Parkman, if those were his remains, wasn't going anywhere. Webster might as well recover more fully before confronted with the grisly sight awaiting him.

When Webster finally dropped into a fitful doze, James left the cell and sat on a cane chair in the grimy anteroom. He closed his eyes, wishing he were somewhere else, not enmeshed in this bizarre situation. *Tukey or one of the other police officers should have entertained the possibility that a guilty man might take his life before undergoing the embarrassment and humiliation of a public trial.*

Webster had yet to be proven guilty of anything, James reminded himself. *The chemistry professor could have taken poison, a remedy he was well acquainted with, to avoid the shame of the accusation itself, although his success in killing himself would have spared his family none of the mortification he might have escaped.*

James must have dozed off because Tukey was shaking him, shouting that they must be going, the hour was late. Mayor Beacham, Governor Briggs, and Mr. Shaw were all gathered at the Medical College, where everyone awaited the police and Webster. It was well past three o'clock in the morning, and the patience of important people was wearing thin.

"Can we finally move him?" Tukey asked James, gesturing curtly to the still-prone Webster on his cot.

James examined his patient. Color had returned to Webster's face, although he still trembled, sobbed quietly, and mumbled his wife Harriett's name over and over. "Professor Webster," James said as calmly as he could. "We must go to the Medical College. Do you think you can stand?"

Webster looked up at James with pleading eyes. "Make them take me home, James," he begged. "Please tell them to just take me home to Harriet and my girls."

"That will not happen, Webster," Tukey broke in. "We need be going, and right now."

Two constables came over and yanked Webster to his feet. His body went limp, but they held him upright and propelled him first out of the cell and then the jail. A different police carriage waited on Leverett Street, a larger model with bars on the windows, and two constables already stationed inside. Webster was now officially their prisoner, no matter that he had yet to be charged with a crime.

"We'll have no more of the previous foolishness this evening," Tukey said to James, as if Webster's actions had been his doing. The appreciation he had expressed to James earlier was absent. "My men are instructed to take immediate action if Professor Webster makes any suspicious-seeming movement. We won't be waiting on ye to tell us this time around, Doctor."

"This man's in no condition to make a further attempt on his life, or anyone else's," James said, offended by Tukey's intimation that he was somehow in league with Webster or trying to protect him. *In the marshal's mind,* James supposed, *we're guilty of both being physicians and Harvard men. This is how our reputation will suffer in the public mind as the news of Dr. Webster's arrest spreads.*

The police carriage took off at a quick trot across the few blocks to the Medical College. When they arrived, James noticed a much larger knot of men gathered outside Littlefield's apartment than when he and Tukey had departed three hours earlier. Littlefield was at the group's center, obviously flattered by the attention of his betters. Upon seeing Dr. Webster helped out of the carriage, Littlefield went pale and turned toward his quarters, unwilling to look directly upon the man he had accused of murder, and worse.

Descending from the police carriage, Marshal Tukey's party was immediately engulfed by men in dark coats and silk top hats. James saw Tukey go over to Dr. Holmes, President Sparks, Mayor Beacham, and Governor Briggs, although it was so dark that he could not discern the expressions on any of their faces. Tukey was relaying the story of Webster's arrest and attempted suicide, James was sure.

He did notice one of the group surrounding the marshal; the hatchet-like silhouette of Robert Gould Shaw, the dead man's brother-in-law, his eyes like two glowing lumps of red-hot coal. They remained trained on Webster as he was pulled toward the Medical College by Clapp and his men. It was a look of vengeance James would rather have forgotten, but never could.

Dr. Bigelow strode over to James. "I understand Professor Webster attempted suicide on the journey here," he said in a low voice. "I'm sorry to have placed you in that situation, James. I was told you responded magnificently and saved the man's life."

James tried to say something, but Bigelow shushed him. "No explanation is needed. Now's the critical moment; let's see what unfolds. I must say, poor Webster is the worst sight I've ever beheld."

Tukey and Clapp dragged Webster up the steps to the college entrance, followed by a party of close to twenty men, including James. They ascended to the second floor and the chemistry lecture hall and laboratory. The group followed the trio into the lecture room, and everyone crossed to the back door that led to Webster's private rooms, which had been forced open in the recent search.

Tukey now demanded the key to the privy from where the remains had been lowered, since the police had been unable to examine the area upstairs. A confused-looking Webster said he had no knowledge of where the key might be; he never used it, but always kept the privy open. He could not explain why it was locked now.

Webster was next led over to where the pelvis and legs, hauled in through the privy vault, and the body parts found in the tea chest had been laid out in the vague approximation of a human form on a broad board of pine, a task supervised by Harvard anatomy professor Dr. Lewis. A convulsive shudder overtook Webster upon beholding the sight; he seemed deprived of self-control. A low moan escaped his lips. Sweat rolled in large drops down his forehead.

"Would this be yer handiwork?" Tukey said in a rough voice, looking directly into Webster's face. "Did ye murder George Parkman, and do this to his body?"

Tukey's extended arm invited Webster to behold the body parts on the board. Unable to articulate any response, he sagged to the ground in a shamble, a picture of the greatest woe. James thought, *He is the most pitiable creature I have ever witnessed.*

"An examination by these physicians ye see around ye will begin tomorrow to identify these remains." Tukey spoke loudly, as if Webster had turned hard of hearing. "If these indeed be the remains of Doctor Parkman, ye'll be charged with the willful murder of said person. Do ye have anything to say?"

Webster's response was to sob more effusively. James and Bigelow looked away in embarrassment. Not Robert Shaw, who walked over to Webster's prostrate form, regarding him as an insect he would just as soon crush with his boot.

"You'll pay for this crime, John Webster, hear me well," Shaw said in a low voice. "You'll pay for it with your life, for I will see you hanged in public for all to witness."

"Come, Mister Shaw, this is neither the time nor the place for these recriminations," Dr. Oliver Wendell Holmes said in a placating voice, his boyish face squeezed into a mask of sympathy as he approached Shaw. He attempted to extend a comforting hand to the tall man's shoulder, but Shaw, shrugging off the gesture, abruptly left the room. There was silence as everyone listened to the sound of his boots echoing throughout the room as he descended the stone stairs to the ground floor.

The mayor and the governor regarded each other bleakly, as did the assembled Harvard officials and medical men. Dr. Holmes looked frustrated; his overtures as peacemaker were usually successful, but this attempt had been an abject failure. The men began to file out of the room, not looking at each other, each preoccupied by what they might individually face in the next stage of the crisis.

"We have much work ahead of us," Dr. Lewis said, the first to speak when the doctors were again out in the cold and gathered together. "Let's obtain what sleep the good Lord will provide us. We'll meet here at nine

DALE M. POLLOCK

o'clock in the morning to try to make sense of what was discovered tonight."

Lewis carefully looked around the group. He had assumed an informal leadership of the autopsy, which reassured James, who felt considerably out of his depth, both in the assembled company and the gravity of the situation.

James was so tired that he feared he might fall asleep on the spot, standing upright. Bigelow took him by the arm, and they moved toward the carriages. *Would it have been better to allow Webster to take his own life?* James wondered. *It would have spared them all a terrible road that lay ahead.*

CHAPTER 3

Four months earlier: August 1849
Half Moon Place, Fort Hill; Summer Street, Beacon Hill;
Boston, Massachusetts

On the sweltering evening of Friday, August 7, 1849, Dr. James Stone gingerly made his way down the rotting stairs to the dark cellar of the house on Half Moon Place. This house call was not part of the training he had enjoyed at the Tremont Medical School and its successor, the Harvard Medical College. But these were not normal times.

The summer of 1849 had marked the beginning of a deadly cholera epidemic that had the potential to decimate the city of Boston, and as a recent medical school graduate, James had been directed to tend to its victims.

James was eight years old in 1832 when Boston's first cholera epidemic descended on the city like a pestilence from the Bible. He had but hazy memories of the commotion surrounding the plague. Seventeen years later, the city had accumulated new layers of dirt, refuse, offal, and dead animals. James knew it contained the worst wharfside slum conditions in America. Yet many in Boston believed the sole cause and sustainer of this feared outbreak were the Irish.

No wonder. The cholera's greatest impact fell on neighborhoods adjacent to Fort Hill, which were populated with three- to six-story buildings, each housing between forty and a hundred inhabitants. One hundred percent of them were Irish, James knew, because he had been visiting them for the past several weeks in a vain attempt to stanch the plague.

Now he was in probably the worst cholera locale in the city. The rotting, old wood houses were abutted by the perpendicular wall of Fort Hill on one side and the lofty buildings of Broad Street on the other. This meant little to no air circulation, a problem exacerbated by a central area of some fourteen privies, constantly overflowing and ill-constructed to begin with.

Even the cellars of the once-proud houses were occupied—dank, dark spaces whose only entrance for light or air came via the passage leading down from the sidewalk above. This was James's destination on this occasion, a cellar apartment on shabby, short Half Moon Place.

The building's landlord, who feared losing his tenants to the plague, had appealed to the Committee of Internal Health for medical assistance, and James had been directed to this residence. His new patient was an unemployed fish cutter who found only intermittent work on the wharves but brought the stink from his job search home with him nightly. The odor overpowered James as he arrived in the rear basement, where the fish cutter lived with his wife, child, and mother.

The room was at most twelve by twelve feet square and contained hardly a stick of furniture. There was no bed; only a pile of old clothes and bedding that served for one. Next to where the patient lay were two large oak barrels upon which a former pine door was laid as a rude table, a bench on either side of it.

The walls, or what could be seen of them through the darkness, looked slimy. The floor was littered with fish bones and emptied beer pails. The heat and humidity of an August Boston evening filled the small space, amplifying the smell of rotten fish. James took pains to disguise his desire to regurgitate his dinner of oysters and suckling pig, which he had consumed at the Spotted Owl before venturing onto Fort Hill. He did not wish to add to the mess on the floor.

James approached the man lying on the collection of rags; his family hovered nearby. James said, "My name is Doctor James Winchell Stone, and I've come to offer what relief I can as a physician." He spoke in as professional a voice as he could muster.

The man wheezed that his name was Albert Doyle; at least that was what James thought he heard. Doyle's face looked blue and pinched; his hands were darkened, their skin oddly drawn and puckered. He raised his head weakly and surveyed James as if he were the strangest human specimen he had ever beheld.

James had not intended to present such a sharp contrast between his clothes and those of his destitute patient. James wore a black frock coat, a purple vest, and a white cambric shirt, with a black velvet cravat wound around his neck. His trousers were slim and peg-legged, a sign that the doctor subscribed to the latest fashion—no straps beneath his shoes. James's chimneypot hat remained on his head, his leather medical case under his arm. Doyle wore a soiled fish cutter's smock.

The bedraggled woman tending to him burst into sobs at the doctor's introduction. The full pail at Doyle's feet testified to his inability to keep food down: it was filled not with beer, but vomit and diarrhea. James, who presumed the younger of the wailing women to be Doyle's wife, motioned to her to empty the waste bucket.

"You must remove that filth immediately. It is contributing to your husband's condition," James said. Then he worried that he had sounded dictatorial and peremptory, so he softened his tone. "It will help in his recovery if you remove all his waste as soon as you possibly can."

The woman did not bother to acknowledge anything James said. Her response was to kick the only child present, a boy of no more than seven years, and gesture for him to heed the doctor's order. As his mother shoved him toward the bucket, the boy's face lit up dimly with comprehension. The overflowing pail seemed to outweigh him as he struggled to lift it and carry it up the worn stairs.

A fierce cramp gripped Doyle. His eyes shut in pain and his wife's wails multiplied. James's experience with the plague had taught him that Doyle's death was imminent. Although it might be wasteful to give a dying man medicine, he had been instructed by his mentor, Dr. Bigelow, to bestow whatever relief was available.

James genuinely pitied this immigrant who had hoped for a better life in America and now was dying amid filth and squalor; cholera provided a horrid exit even from a miserable life. James hurriedly opened his case and removed three phials of calomel, a tasteless gray medicine made of mercury and chlorine that would act to settle his patient's stomach and possibly give him some relief.

"Now, take this, Doyle," James said, trying to sound professional and competent. "It will make you feel more comfortable."

James carefully poured the contents of one phial down his patient's throat, and handed his wife the other two, telling her to administer another dose every three hours. James knew the prophylactic was useless even as he administered it. It might provide the poor woman some hope, at least until the very end, which was near.

"Bleed me, would ye, Docter? I beg ye, get this poison out of me blood. Without me workin', none here'll eat."

James was startled to hear Doyle speak. But as instructed by the physician he most respected, Dr. Holmes, James knew that removing a patient's blood did nothing to alleviate the symptoms of cholera.

As gently as he could, he declined the request.

"I'm afraid that would do you no good, Doyle, and in fact, great harm. Losing blood will only weaken you."

His patient gave but a wheeze in response to James's refusal and turned his head away as if the doctor's presence now was of no interest to him. His wife's and mother's sobs swelled again as another painful cramp gripped the man, his body as rigid as iron.

And that was it. Albert Doyle's eyes, squeezed shut in his final death agony, now relaxed. His mouth hung open. No one in the room moved.

James had never actually had a patient die while in his care. It flummoxed him; he was unsure how long to give the family to grieve. What exactly should he do next?

After waiting for what he hoped was a reasonable period, James finally spoke.

"I must warn you not to have any contact with this man's body. This means you must not wash it. You must not touch it at all."

Three living Irish faces looked up at James, their initial incomprehension now turning to anger.

"And you must burn the bedclothes, all of his clothing and his personal effects immediately, all of them, everything!" James hurried through his final instructions, confident that he was doing everything wrong. The family looked ready to attack him.

"You have my deepest condolences," James threw out. He bowed his head and backed toward the stairs. It had just dawned on the Doyles that their loved one had expired right after James administered the calomel.

James felt sweat trickling down his back. He had to notify the authorities to pick up the body. If he didn't feel pity for this decimated family and others like them, he would have ordered the torching of the entire decrepit mansion, which doctors had the power to do in cholera-stricken neighborhoods. He also knew that Doyle's meager possessions no doubt would be divided up to infect another dozen friends and relatives. There was no more he could do.

James clambered out of the cellar on Half Moon Place, feeling saddened and frustrated. The wailing behind him continued, undiminished by his absence. He immediately made for the public pump and scrubbed his hands with a packet of soap powder he kept in his jacket pocket.

Making house calls to the Irish slums in Fort Hill was a new experience for James. It had been less than two years since Dr. Bigelow had presented him with his degree at the Harvard Medical College commencement ceremonies at Gore Hall in the Yard. His current practice, in his dispensary at 6 Bowdoin Square, was limited to fight-produced contusions on Colonnade Row boys, the occasional dyspepsia of a Mount Vernon Street matron, and the odd break or bone dislocation to a servant or groom from a mishap with the horse and carriage. Never before had he encountered disease on the scale of a cholera epidemic.

James's way was blocked by a distinctive presence who had materialized on Wendell Street. A prostitute dressed in vivid emerald green satin with a maroon shawl gazed searchingly into his eyes, a process aided by the omission of a bonnet that might have shielded her lightly powdered face and dyed blonde hair. James looked to the horizon as the young woman spoke aloud to him.

"Are ye looking fer pleasant company fer the evenin', sir?" the prostitute murmured, attempting to sidle up to James, whose progress had been halted. Pointedly ignoring her, James moved to the side and strode onward, now turning onto High Street in the direction of the temporary cholera hospital, the establishment of which had caused riots the previous month. No neighborhood or business wanted cholera patients anywhere near; even steamships and barges could not be procured to house the sick and dying, ship owners being as fearful as their counterparts on land.

As he had done in 1832, Dr. George Parkman had offered one of his many properties, a boarded-up tavern on Fort Hill, for use as a hospital of sorts. A mob had to be dispersed after threatening to burn down the old alehouse once its new purpose became known. As James entered the hospital, he saw men, women, and children scattered about what had been the drinking room. Some were somnolent on wooden gurneys; others sprawled on the straw-covered floor. Most were naked save for a soiled sheet or a disintegrating cotton blanket.

The commingled odors of human waste, unwashed bodies, and pervasive sickness made James feel nauseated again. *These people,* he supposed, *are going to die, and most of them quickly. Exactly as Albert Doyle had. It was all so sad.*

James looked up at the approach of an older woman in a rough gray robe surmounted by an intimidating black and white coif, followed by a striking-looking young redheaded woman who appeared to be in her late teens. Mother Bernadine, her cold white face framed above a heavy gold cross, was the abbess of the nearby Sisters of Charity. She usually brought James word of some new medical crisis; there always was another one in this jumble of twenty-hour days, snatched sleep, infrequent meals, and corpses, always more corpses.

Tonight's emergency had to do with orphans. The hospital housed twenty-three children who had lost one or both parents to cholera. The Committee of Christian Gentlemen was to come the following day bearing food, clothing, and money to aid the poor unfortunates. Mother Bernadine begged Dr. Stone to examine the children to make sure none were infectious. Members of the committee had expressed concern.

The abbess nodded curtly to the red-haired woman who stood next to her. "Miss O'Keeffe, please take Doctor Stone to the poor babes so that he may examine them," the nun said with the directness of one used to giving orders.

James took a moment to survey the young Irishwoman. She wore a dark green smock, cinched around her waist with a brown leather belt, a broad white collar sewn on her neckline. Miss O'Keeffe's vivid red hair was parted severely down the middle of her head and pulled back to just above her ears. James guessed that she might be eighteen or nineteen, in possession of strong features and sharp brown eyes.

He followed her up the broad wooden steps to the attic, reflecting on the reversal of social order that contagion encouraged. At no other time would an individual of James's background and aspirations have found himself alone in a darkened hallway with an attractive Irish girl. Their worlds would have rarely overlapped, let alone collided, except in the present peculiar circumstances.

James shared a few of the prejudices of his native Boston, but not the one that viewed the Irish as the greatest danger facing his beloved city. He had listened at the Presbyterian church to Rev. Lyman Beecher rail against the Catholic Church as a "ferocious beast" and the "mother of harlots," horrified by the rage and hatred that Beecher spewed forth. He had not returned.

James found that he carried no bitterness toward Catholics, nor the Irish. He did not go out of his way to court their company, and there was the depressing example of the Doyles to contend with in his acceptance of the "Irish problem." But he did not hate or despise them.

He agreed with the Catholic opinion on slavery: it was a human evil and an unnecessary practice in the New World of American freedom. Opinions on slavery had divided every aspect of American society, and James kept his antislavery views to himself, if only to avoid the infernal, never-ending arguments on the issue. The cholera epidemic, and the rumors and endless discussions of its impact on Boston, had at least changed the conversation.

Miss O'Keeffe pushed open a small wooden door, and the unlikely duo ducked their heads and entered the attic, the stench of unwashed sickness again filling James's nostrils. A dozen or so children lay on the floor like pieces of cordwood, each occupying a meager pallet of straw, some sharing a thin blanket, others trying to gain some warmth from each other or the scant clothes on their pallid frames.

The committee's aid was much needed, James observed. Most of the children were in fitful sleep, murmuring, tossing about. Others lay quietly, motionless. One dark-haired little girl stared wide-eyed about her but did not stir, as if any movement might catch the disease's notice.

James walked among the small bodies, trying not to step on them, peering intently for the telltale signs of incipient cholera: a bluish tint to the skin, darkened extremities, scabrous hands and feet. One boy sat up and vomited on himself.

"Remove this child at once," James ordered.

His imperious tone angered the young Irishwoman, who had no idea where to take the boy. "Where else might he go?" Miss O'Keeffe demanded of James, her Irish brogue hot and indignant. "This be the place of last resort."

As she hesitated, James tried a different approach. He tried to speak with the quiet urgency he had seen Dr. Bigelow employ with difficult patients.

"Miss O'Keeffe, we can't allow every child in this room the opportunity to catch cholera before daybreak. Please remove him now!"

Miss O'Keeffe said nothing in response, glaring at the floor instead. She hoisted the youngster to his feet, ignoring the mess that spread from his clothes to hers, and gently steered him out of the room. She looked back at James with a mixture of anger and helplessness, as though this hellish situation was somehow his doing.

Moments later, he joined the young woman and her charge on High Street, where she stood by a pump, washing the vomit from herself and the terrified boy.

As soon as he saw James approach, the boy shook and bleated softly, a lamb aware of its impending slaughter. He grabbed Miss O'Keeffe's skirts, trying to disappear into their rough twill fabric. James leaned over to wash his hands, too. He used the remainder of his soap powder after first offering it to Miss O'Keeffe, who declined. She pointedly washed her own hands in just the cold pump water, newly available from the Cochituate reservoir.

"He could have made them all sick," James reminded her, a defensive tone in his voice. He was still mindful of the furious glance she'd thrown at him as she exited the attic. "He is not like you or I, blessed with some natural defense against this scourge. Few children are, and I wish we understood why."

"I know, I know, but ye've scared the poor creature halfway to death," Miss O'Keeffe responded. "Truth be told, I don't have the slightest idea where to send him now. I must ask the abbess."

"Damn these pesthouses!" James said, the passion in his voice taking Miss O'Keeffe by surprise. "I often think we compound our problem by taking the sick in with the healthful. The miasma that causes this contagion thrives in this squalid wretchedness in which your people live."

"My people? Are ye of the belief that God be out to punish only the Irish, Doctor? Are not the tradesmen and the artisans also laid low by the cholera? Could even ye, Doctor, not be safe?"

James flushed, embarrassed by his ill-chosen comment. He wished he could take it back. Miss O'Keeffe gave him a cold, appraising look. *This young woman certainly has a mind of her own,* he thought.

"That's a risk I knowingly undertake. But you misunderstand me, Miss O'Keeffe. I don't blame the Irish for their conditions in this city. But vice, filth, and ignorance are handmaidens to contagion, and the Irish will continue to be this plague's chief victims until they display greater industriousness and temperance."

Ignoring James's lecture, Ellen bundled up the still-shaking boy and headed back toward the sagging tavern-cum-hospital without a word of parting. Feeling a bit frustrated, James made his way down the near-empty street toward the Common, the normal bustle of a Saturday evening eerily absent. There was a rope stretched across Chestnut Street above Spruce Street to indicate the quarantine area around Fort Hill.

A cholera cart creaked past; the morose driver sat in a slouch, his whip barely grazing the rump of his dispirited nag. He was headed across the bridge to South Boston, where dead Irish bodies lay for days before being stacked into shallow pits three or four feet deep, and then covered with a foot or two of loose earth. A family of pigs trotted confidently behind the slow-moving cart, certain that feasting opportunities would soon present themselves.

As he turned onto Summer Street, James passed the residence of Senator Daniel Webster. No candle burned in the window and there was no scent of camphor, so James knew the Senator must be in Washington. He

CHOPPED

51

caught a whiff of the acrid smoke that had followed him downtown, issuing from the houses of fearful families wisely burning the clothes and bedding of their friends and relatives who were cholera victims. It was the same ignored advice he had proffered the Irish fish cutter's family.

It will be days before I am rid of this smell, James thought, silently cursing his decision to wear fashionable clothes to Fort Hill. He debated going home to Bowdoin Square to change before calling upon Dr. Bigelow, but the hour was already late, past ten o'clock. Instead, he proceeded directly to Bigelow's house on Summer, near Tremont Street.

After pressing the new, modish iron bell affixed to Bigelow's front door, James fussed with his cravat, making sure the velvet bow was properly centered. Doctors such as James and Bigelow were society physicians, their clientele the Beacon Hill elite who lived on the other side of the Common. James knew that Bigelow would be smartly turned out no matter the hour and would expect the same of him.

The Black servant opened the door and bowed to James. "Doctor Stone, Doctor Bigelow is expecting you." James's eyes widened—he had made no appointment with Bigelow. The famed physician was much praised for his knowledge of everything going on in and around Boston, but did his divination include the meanderings of James Stone?

He followed the servant into Bigelow's study, which was filled with Egyptian objets d'art. A small model of the Great Pyramid of Khufu at Giza hung directly above Bigelow's massive desk. The new pewter whale-oil lamps on the walls shone brightly, illuminating the plain, substantial features of Jacob Bigelow, with deep-set dark eyes and long sideburns. To James's surprise, the light also displayed the gaunt, angular physiognomy of Robert Gould Shaw, sitting in stony silence in a wing chair across the large room.

Bigelow stood at his liqueur case, pouring glasses of Madeira for his guests.

"James, I am delighted you could join us," said Bigelow, moving forward to extend a glass and usher James into the room.

Visiting the distinguished Bigelow was a bit like being honored with a folksy royal audience. There could be genuine warmth, mitigated by an extreme brusqueness of manner.

"You are acquainted with Mister Shaw, no doubt?" Bigelow crossed the room to hand Shaw a glass of Madeira, which he silently declined with a dismissive wave of his hand.

James bowed, and Shaw rose to do the same, stiffly, performing a duty that he regarded as unpleasant but required. He was a lean, tall man, similar in bearing to his brother-in-law, the legendary George Parkman. Shaw's face was split by a long, aquiline nose over compressed lips that seemed to curl into themselves. He had a weak chin and large ears.

Dressed in an expensive smoking jacket with a black velvet collar and sleeves, Dr. Bigelow gestured to one of the fashionable plaid-upholstered wing chairs and motioned for James to sit.

"Your timing couldn't have been more fortuitous, James," Bigelow said. "Mister Shaw and I were just discussing the impact this foul pestilence has had on our city, as it has much of the country. You've just come from the cholera hospital, haven't you? I suppose we might hear of your experiences."

"Indeed, I was in Fort Hill, sir, and a rather disheartening visit it was," James said, sitting and removing his hat. Bigelow and Shaw remained standing. Bigelow did not look pleased; he was expecting a more positive assessment.

He said, "I have communicated to Mister Shaw our hopes that we are finally controlling the spread of this plague. Visits to the homes of its victims, such as the one you just made, are necessary to our efforts to stamp it out at the site of its inception."

James failed to pick up the signal Bigelow was attempting to communicate. He stuck obtusely to his story.

"The Irish fish cutter I hoped to aid instead died in my presence, and his family will now no doubt spread the cholera to all with whom they come into contact."

"That is an encouraging development, Doctor Stone," Shaw said. "I have no problem with the Irish choosing cholera as a most effective means of departing our country. It's quick and thorough, if not particularly clean."

James blanched at Shaw's bluntness. The man was without a conscience.

"But the disease has other, more costly repercussions," Shaw continued. "I was explaining to Doctor Bigelow the tribute this affliction has exacted."

James was puzzled. "How do you mean, sir?"

Shaw regarded James as if he were the village idiot. "Have you not eyes, Doctor Stone? Hotels are empty, railroads arrive without passengers, ships of all descriptions avoid our wharves. The mills are now silent; the banks have withdrawn capital. Cotton from the South sits rotting on our piers. Cholera could bring an end to all we have worked for in Boston, even if it does offer a partial solution to the Irish problem."

"Mister Shaw, we are containing the cholera, even more thoroughly than we did in 1832," Bigelow said in his most reassuring doctor's voice.

"Containment is no longer enough, Bigelow," said Shaw. He lifted a sepulchral finger and pointed at the two medical men. "You must find a way to limit cholera to those of least value to our society and protect those of greater value. The equation is quite simple."

James felt he must offer a disclaimer. "We still don't fully understand why the disease manifests when it does, even if we can guess where," he said. "How do we control something that we cannot fully comprehend?"

"We can contain cholera by prophylactic measures and restrict it primarily to the neighborhoods inhabited by the Irish and the colored," Bigelow said reassuringly. "But the disease must run its course."

Shaw rose and placed an expensive white beaver hat on his head, careful not to disturb his styled hair. He drew on a pair of black leather gloves.

"There are already five hundred dead, and only four hundred of those are Irish," he reminded Bigelow. "Best keep your promise of containment of this affliction to their slums, gentlemen," he said, with a particular emphasis on the words *your promise*.

Shaw paused for a moment to let the implication sink in, before he muttered, "Doctor Bigelow. Doctor Stone." He bowed again and promptly left the room, guided away by the quiet servant.

With Shaw gone, James was finally able to tell Bigelow of his two encounters on Fort Hill, one with a corpse, and the other with an insolent Irish girl he could not discard from his thoughts.

"What are the odds of an attending physician contracting cholera, Doctor Bigelow?" James asked abruptly, directly voicing for the first time the concern that had stewed in his mind since he had blithely assured the redheaded young Irishwoman that she and he were immune. "Do we put ourselves in true danger by treating these unfortunates?"

Bigelow leaned over to put a reassuring hand on James's arm. "We work and reside in a more healthful atmosphere, we're mindful of proper diet and the need for fresh water, and we recognize the symptoms, which we can certainly arrest within ourselves." He looked keenly at James. "Times of exigency are moments of opportunity for a clever young man, James. I seized just such an opportunity in New York, during the last cholera plague seventeen years ago."

"I know, sir. Your actions saved their community."

"My point, James, is that they also commenced my career. Now it's your opportunity to do the same."

"I wish I possessed your capacities, Doctor Bigelow, but I fall short and often embarrass myself," James admitted.

"Do not denigrate yourself to any but your closest friends, even in jest," Bigelow responded sharply, then smiled at James. "I'm proud to count myself among that number. You do yourself a disservice; you display a sound comprehension of the body's anatomy, and if you're invited into an established practice, you could make a great contribution to the furtherance of medical science."

Bigelow rose from his chair in typically abrupt fashion. "Given the great task that lies before us, I suggest we bring this evening to a close," he said. "Much hard work lies ahead."

The audience was over. Now Dr. Stone was the one hurried out by the wraithlike servant, who silently appeared at James's elbow and led him to the door.

CHAPTER 4

August–September 1849
The Mall and Bowdoin Square, Boston, Massachusetts

The darkness was pitch black, the moon absent as James made his way across the Mall under the leafy elms to Bowdoin Square. He walked toward the old mansion faced with dark stone at number 6 that housed his dispensary on its ground floor and his personal chambers on the second floor. James walked absentmindedly, his mind turning over the challenge posed by his mentor.

Bigelow had told him that success was there for the taking. For James, that meant associating with the people who danced at balls and attended horse races, the men who went hunting and the women who went riding, the people who attended the Congregational or Unitarian Church and entertained with lavish house parties and formal balls.

His oldest brother, Anson, had prospered, although not to the level to which James aspired. Anson had paid for James and his older brother Henry to attend Harvard, a fact the eldest sibling reminded James of frequently. He had also arranged an introduction for James to Dr. Bigelow, whose status at the Medical College approached that of the famous Dr. Holmes. James was thrilled when Bigelow took an interest in him: the prospects of an ambitious but lonely Harvard graduate had immediately improved.

James knew that he owed much to Anson's sense of family solidarity, so he maintained close contact with his brother Henry, older by two years, and his sister Lucinda, five years his senior. A strong proponent of slavery being vital to the economy of Massachusetts, Anson was too politically opinionated for James's taste, so he avoided dinner at his brother's house whenever possible.

As to his own character, James was aware that he could be an amusing and enjoyable companion. His skills as a raconteur were considerable; his long face and high forehead easily animated a story's telling, and his blue-gray eyes provided vivid accompaniment to his acute sense of timing.

Yet all too often he did his best to dominate any supper party or ballroom conversation, unable to control his delight in the sheer pleasure of hearing himself speak and exhibiting his supposed erudition. James was the type of person who knew many small things about great issues and lost no opportunity to expound upon them. In two words, he was self-consumed.

Reaching his residence, James climbed the once-grand wooden staircase between the first and second floors of the old mansion. James's dispensary took up most of the space on the ground floor; the two floors above were let as comfortable apartments for single gentlemen, one of which he occupied.

Still pondering the weaknesses of his character, James reached the top of the stairs and collided with Sharon, his Irish maid, who was bringing up hot water for his evening bath and was straining to open the door to James's apartment. He moved to help her. Sharon blushed, as she always did in her employer's presence.

"Excuse me, Sharon, I wasn't paying attention to where I was going," James apologized.

"It be nae a problem, Docter Stone," Sharon said, blushing again. She hurried inside to fill the bath, and then leave as quickly as possible. Sharon found James tremendously attractive and the perfect gentleman, so his presence made her exceedingly nervous, even after two years in his employ.

James waited until she departed, then hung his frock coat on the cherrywood rack in the corner of his bedroom. He was thinking, *a Beacon Hill doctor should be in possession of a cook, a housemaid, and a nurse, although the latter would necessitate a wife and child, too.*

James had only Sharon, a well-meaning and relatively competent Irish girl on whom he depended for cooking, cleaning, scrubbing, mending, and fetching. His sister Lucinda had searched for a suitable female Irish immigrant who was particularly unattractive, to deter rousing any untoward feelings on her brother's part, and she had achieved her goal with Sharon.

Since his mother's death when he was only three years old, at which time he came under Lucinda's stewardship, James had always relied on women to take care of him, and Sharon had become the latest iteration. He couldn't imagine doing by himself the many domestic tasks she undertook.

James hurried out of his clothes; the water was already beginning to lose its heat. He treasured his weekly bath, particularly the moment of immersion, the large iron tub steaming like a just-opened hot clam. James needed to be rid of the stench Half Moon Place and the cholera plague had left on him.

Most Bostonians confined their ablutions to washing their face, feet, hands, and neck only. James subscribed to the new movement that urged every individual to wash the whole person, on rising or going to bed, either in cold or warm water according to their constitution, at least one time a week.

James lay sweating against the cold back of the iron tub and regarded himself in the silvery glass of the mirror facing it. He was just under the median in height, an adolescent slenderness still apparent in his body. His dark, curly hair, parted to the right side, rose to a high and oiled but still unmanageable wave. His long, clean-shaven face abjured the fashion of muttonchop whiskers, a greasy moustache, or a bushy beard. He had a poorly defined chin and the full lips of a woman, characteristics that both satisfied and shamed him. He knew his mouth was sensual, yet it and his chin lent a feminine softness to his countenance that diminished his image as a gentleman. James often bemoaned to himself the sad state of his physical appearance. Why couldn't he have been born with the thin, pursed lips and aggressive chin of the New England ruling class?

James finally rose, the now-cold water streaming from him, and grabbed the rough homespun towel Sharon had thoughtfully left for him on the washstand. He vigorously toweled himself to stimulate his circulation, as modern thinking recommended.

He had ended up back at the identical place in his mind where he had started, following his meeting with Bigelow. What could distinguish James Winchell Stone? He thought back to the alarming redheaded Irish girl, Miss whatever her name was. No doubt she had aspirations, too. James had admired her passion, the animation in her limbs and face that reflected the profound emotions and vivid beliefs he found lacking within himself.

CHAPTER 5

September 1849
Bowdoin Square, Tremont Street, and Long Wharf, Boston, Massachusetts

It was a cool, overcast day in September when James set out on his morning constitutional. He strolled down the shady Mall, where the elm trees weighed heavy with turning foliage.

The breeze smartly carried the salty scent of the nearby harbor, and for once, the sandy walk was not muddy. The hum and buzz of Boston was ever present: the clinking of capstans, ringing of bells, barking of dogs, and clattering of iron wheels on cobblestones.

Leaving Bowdoin Square, James could have taken the omnibus, which stopped in front of Revere House, but he preferred to walk downtown. He entered the Merchants' Exchange on Tremont Street, passing between its grand Doric columns, and went down the steps to the lower level that housed the Boston office of the fledgling national postal service. James had a letter to post to his good friend and fellow Medical College graduate John C. Morgan, adventuring his way to California by sailing "'round the Horn," who had sent him several letters full of exotic descriptions of his nautical adventures south of the equator.

James wished he were as good a correspondent, but in this missive he had given Morgan an exciting description of the cholera epidemic and the manner in which it had been controlled, and finally extinguished, with minimal loss of life. The total number of victims was estimated at 611, and 500 of those were believed to be Irish.

James had made no mention to Morgan in this letter of the young Irish woman he was unable to banish from his thoughts; her likeness returned to him again and again, both day and night. The liberties he took with Miss O'Keeffe, even if only imagined, were unbecoming a gentleman.

Stepping up to the counter, James paid the clerk for the stamp, an exorbitant seventy-five cents (an outrage, since the letter would be carried westward from ship to ship and cost the postal service next to nothing). He folded and addressed the folio paper to John C. Morgan, Doctor of Medicine, San Francisco, California, and sealed it with the wafers supplied by the clerk. If fortune smiled on his post, it might reach Morgan by year's end.

The confluence of smells and sounds that James identified as the essence of Boston beckoned him as he exited the exchange and looked down State Street to Long Wharf. White seagulls soared above fresh and rotting fish, redolent oranges and lemons newly unloaded from Spanish and Portuguese traders, piles of cork and brimstone, and the earthy odor of domesticated animals. James had grown up on these wharves, and they evoked mixed emotions within him.

He was an infant when his father, Jeremiah Stone, normally responsible but on this night lost in a drunken stupor, careered out of the Hat and Helmet Tavern and toppled off India Wharf. There were no witnesses, and exactly how or when it occurred remained a mystery. He was not fished out of the bay for several days; when he did bob ashore near Rowe's Wharf, his body had provided hearty sustenance to the sea life that had feasted on him. He was unrecognizable to the distraught widow who brought her children with her to help identify him.

None of the Stone boys were old enough to take over their father's thriving wharfinger business. Jeremiah's shares were sold to his partners, and the purchase price of $10,000 became the basis of the family's estate, now greatly increased through shrewd investments in coal, railroads, and property by James's two elder brothers, Anson and Jerome. They remained convinced that their father's partners had cheated them due to their youth and inexperience, and they estimated the worth of their father's shares at closer to five times what they had been paid. They were unlikely to do anything about it. The Boston business community was a parochial one, and the Stones had best respect it.

James made his way to the News Room coffee house, where he purchased a copy of yesterday's *Boston Evening Transcript*. Today's edition had yet to come out. He had time to study the paper while waiting for the appointed hour to meet his brother Henry at the nearby Union Oyster House for their midday meal.

The news was more of the usual: uprisings throughout Europe, slavery both advancing and being repelled in the new southwestern territories won from Mexico three years ago, the cotton mills back to full output, and a great uncertainty in the financial markets over the slavery question. The news gave James a headache; he couldn't understand what impact, if any, all these reports had on his own life.

This was certainly true of the slavery issue, from which James felt particularly detached. He had known no slave owner in his life; nor any freed slave. Black men were considered free in Boston and the commonwealth of Massachusetts and had been so since his birth. Although James did not treat Black patients and had never socialized with any Black people, he held no animus against them, and he pitied them for the contemptible behavior exhibited against them by fully half the country, if not more. He knew prominent individuals in Boston who were just as racist as any Southern plantation owner, Robert Gould Shaw coming quickly to mind.

James's reverie was short-lived, as Henry finally arrived. They had roomed and graduated together at Harvard, despite their age difference, and they now possessed a comfortable ease in their relations. If James was socially ambitious, Henry was a devoted aesthete. At one point, under the severe influence of Henry David Thoreau, he went off to live in a hut in the woods beyond Lexington. He lasted just over two weeks. He now labored as a private music instructor, primarily teaching viola and violin. He barely made a living from the meager coins delivered by sweaty-palmed boys and girls, but he lived in a house owned by their brother Anson.

Henry and James repaired to the gambrel-roofed Union Oyster House. Seats were secured easily at its soapstone bar, given that James was a familiar and valued customer. Quickly set before them was a hearty meal: mock turtle soup, followed by a fish chowder, then a dozen Cape Cod Cotuit oysters, succeeded by twelve littleneck clams. Next came a lobster salad, oysters baked in their shells, and small lobsters broiled on a coal fire. The repast concluded with fruit and pastries.

The Portuguese Madeira wine loosened the brothers' tongues. They shared the latest doings of their siblings, mutual friends, and the minor celebrities of Beacon Hill. Henry mentioned that sister Lucinda would be writing to invite James to a ball in October. There would be an opportunity to dance not only the polka but also the redowa, a more voluptuous version of the waltz and the current rage in high society. Henry was very anxious to hear it played.

His sister always had a plan in mind for him, James thought. Henry said that Lucinda had met a young woman she considered the perfect mate for James, from a very good family in Trenton, New Jersey.

James disliked this turn in the conversation. He did not intend to serve as a piece of marketable merchandise, even for his beloved sister. He did enjoy the formal rituals and routines of the Boston high season, however. The balls could go on until two or three in the morning. James often had to be at the hospital by six to see patients with Dr. Holmes, but a successful ball made the physical exhaustion worthwhile.

He bid Henry an affectionate farewell, settled the bill—he was, after all, a Beacon Hill doctor and could afford to be generous with his artistic sibling—and, exiting the Oyster House, walked north toward Washington Street and Whipple's photography studio.

A ball probably was the most likely place for James to find a wife, but he had yet to accept marriage as a serious possibility in his life. His level of achievement needed to be greater. He had little hope of advancing into the higher echelons of Boston society without an appropriate and well-off spouse. The alternatives to the dress ball for meeting the opposite sex were the church or the lecture room, and James had little use for either of them.

He didn't like the women he met at church. They intimated that they knew a great secret that he was blind to: the Second Coming of Jesus Christ. A religious revival christened the "Great Awakening" was sweeping the nation from its old coast to its new boundaries. The prevalent sentiment among these eligible, if preoccupied, young women was that if Jesus hadn't saved you, there was no hope for you at all.

That left the lecture hall. James could feign interest only if the speaker held forth on a subject that appealed to him. The Boston Athenaeum hosted orations and public lectures at its three-story brownstone on Beacon Street, the best locale to observe the most attractive young ladies. He found the presentations often boring; they put him to sleep in a most embarrassing way, with violent shakes of his head as he fell asleep and woke up.

He also ventured to the Boston Lyceum at the Odeon, where he had enjoyed hearing Theodore Parker preach. He admired Parker's impassioned and dramatic speaking style more than his ideas regarding the sin of slavery. James did not consider slavery to be a religious question, but rather a legal and moral one. Human beings should not possess other human beings as chattel, was James's essential reasoning on the matter. That was a position both legal (concerning the nature of property and ownership) and moral (indefensible conduct that is impossible to justify). Did he need to hear speaker after speaker reiterate well-trodden opinions that had never changed his mind, and probably never would? He did not.

Only one recent presentation at the Boston Athenaeum had interested him: a speech given the past July, just before the outbreak of the cholera, on the language of sounds. The discipline of phonography, as its British founder Sir Isaac Pitman named it in 1843, used a system of phonetic markings to represent the sounds of human language.

James was transfixed by a phonographic report of the national Free Soil Convention in Buffalo accomplished by Oliver Dyer, which James read in the *Boston Evening Transcript*. It purported to relay the very remarks every one of the speakers made that night, down to their last syllable, pause, and throat clearing. James had never seen this level of transcription achieved previously, and he was intrigued by how it was accomplished.

Dyer, who established *The American Phonographic Journal*, had published numerous pamphlets on phonography, this new system of notation, using symbols based on sounds. James purchased all of the instructional pamphlets and spent hours reading and studying them.

He found Dyer's enthusiasm for phonography to be contagious. James realized that learning could increase exponentially if the words of great minds were recorded extemporaneously and accurately. Business would thrive when communication was simplified, and America would finally realize its manifest destiny. If the truth were in the telling, phonography would capture the truth. And his career would be the beneficiary.

James decided to embark upon an inaugural project, a phonographic report of Senator Daniel Webster's upcoming speech at the Festival of the Sons of New Hampshire dinner in Boston, to which James had been invited. He practiced phonographic dictation in his spare time, taking down every word Sharon uttered as she related all the neighborhood gossip while she busied herself cleaning his medical offices and his apartment.

Within a few weeks, he could write phonographic dictation six times faster than longhand. The most effective means of demonstrating phonography's power, he knew, was to record events of interest to the public. If readers were able to experience the true words spoken by an orator down to his last syllable, the public's learning would know no bonds of containment.

James wondered if he might make a mark, as Jacob Bigelow had so avidly encouraged him to do, in this new medium. At least there was little competition. He would never be a medical pathfinder, but he could be an avatar of the new science of phonography, a cause that could change the world, word by word.

CHAPTER 6

September 1849
North Allen Street, Howard Street, and Tontine Crescent,
Boston, Massachusetts

Ellen O'Keeffe made her way through the sunny streets of the West End toward the handsome Greek revival building on North Allen and Fruit streets that housed Massachusetts General Hospital. The structures near the water were a different kind of tenement than she was accustomed to in the North End, the buildings just as densely packed but more solidly built and better maintained.

Ellen felt trepidation whenever she ventured into Boston proper. It felt like an alien land—no one looked like her, spoke like her, dressed like her. If she wasn't invisible, as she was to most passersby, she was the object of leering by American men and frowns of disgust by American women.

Ellen's attitude was to ignore them all. How else would she ever escape the prison that was O'Malley's saloon, and her jailer, her horrible stepfather, Bill Haggerty? If she allowed the unexpressed emotions of others to halt her in her tracks, she might as well give in to one of those black-haired Brennan brothers who was always chasing her.

Miss O'Keeffe walked into the hospital's white Chelmsford granite building and across the ground floor of the Bulfinch Pavilion, to demand that a bewildered young porter please summon Dr. James Winchell Stone. The porter had no idea of whom she was speaking.

"Are you here to see a patient?" he asked. He assumed it was her father, husband, or brother, or maybe all three, who no doubt had been injured in one of the brawls that occurred nightly in the Irish neighborhoods. Many of the hospital's patients were the survivors of those battles, and the Boston morgue was filled with their victims.

By the manner of coincidences that often happen in life, just down the hall James Stone was exiting the Ether Dome, the surgery recently established to utilize the medical anesthesia process pioneered a few years earlier at Massachusetts General.

As he entered the hall, he was stunned to see Ellen approaching him. *An Irishwoman did not stroll into Massachusetts General Hospital unbidden,* James thought, and then felt guilty for the harshness of his sentiment.

As he recovered from his shock, he realized that he was inappropriately thrilled to see her. Ellen's mass of red hair was pinned up on either side of her wide forehead with large decorative wooden combs. Her simple blue cotton dress was clean and looked newly made. She was more vivid in person than in his memories of her. He was struck by her liveliness.

James moved quickly down the hallway and extended his hand.

"Miss O'Keeffe, I believe? I confess to surprise at your visit, but I'm pleased to see you again. At least we inhabit more pleasant circumstances than at our last meeting."

Ellen smiled. "Miss Ellen Margaret O'Keeffe, to make a proper introduction," she said as she firmly shook James' proffered hand with her gloved one. "I beg pardon for troubling ye so in this grand place, but I had nae idea where yer dispensary might be."

James's eyebrows arched as he tried to discern the true purpose of this visit. He assumed the worst: Miss O'Keeffe had come either to beg him to treat some dying relative for no fee, or to help her out of a bad situation in the event she was with child. He wanted no part of either business, but he was too stimulated by Ellen's physical presence to be dismissive of her.

A few doctors and male nurses were openly watching this strange encounter. No one could recall a female visitor previously calling upon Dr. Stone in the Bulfinch Pavilion. James looked around uncomfortably but did not want to appear so to Ellen; he suggested that they adjourn to one of the hospital's examination rooms, where they could speak privately.

Ellen smiled again as she looked around, the curious onlookers appearing suddenly otherwise engaged.

"To be sure, Doctor Stone," she said in a clear, bell-like voice. "I much appreciate ye receiving me with no warning." She added, "Though my seeking ye out is for a medical opinion, and nothing else, rest assured." She had noticed the glances between nearby doctors and staff. James felt the eyes of his colleagues upon them as he led Ellen down the hall.

He ushered her into one of the new examination rooms, another innovation by Dr. Holmes in his quest to make Massachusetts General the most advanced hospital in the United States.

"I am here on a matter that don't concern meself," Ellen explained, removing James's foremost fear. "Truth be told, Doctor Stone, if there was a real doctor in my part o' Boston, I shan't trouble ye at all. But there is none to be had, and yer the only doctor I know of that has a doctor's knowledge, so it's to ye I come."

James was crestfallen that Ellen was here only because she had nowhere else to turn. Still, she had come to him, and him alone.

"Go on," he encouraged her. He was impressed by how she had shed the exaggerated aspects of her Irish dialect.

She said, "My friend, a most valuable and loving companion to me, is herself a mother time and again, and now carrying another babe, the Lord help her. Her man could care for less, but I know she won't be up to living through another one. That last babe tore her up somethin' awful. Sure, the midwife in Cork said it was a miracle she survived at all."

James's heart sank. It was not Ellen O'Keeffe who was pregnant, but, as he had suspected, some slattern of her acquaintance. He knew of abortionists who preyed on single immigrant females, seduced on the boat to America or soon thereafter, pregnant and displaying their scandal, their reputation and prospects ruined. A familiar, sordid tale, and James's discomfort exhibited itself on his features. Ellen stiffened. She knew what he would say before the words came out of his mouth.

"I must offer my apologies, Miss O'Keeffe. This type of medicine is not my field. I fear that I can offer little assistance. Perhaps you should seek Madame Restell; I understand she aids women who find themselves in difficult straits."

Once he saw her surprised and hurt eyes, he immediately regretted his formal tone. Stupidly, he made the situation even worse by unnecessarily adding what he intended as a cautionary note: "I must remind you that a law was passed in our state just three years past prohibiting any interference with a pregnancy."

Ellen flushed but forced her face into a mask of rigid politeness. "I nae came to cause ye trouble with the law, Doctor Stone," she said sharply, her brogue now spirited. "I simply hoped for yer help, but I can see I'll nae find any here. Thank ye for yer time, Doctor Stone, and yer lecture on the law. It be most instructive. Now good day!"

Tight-lipped with the concentration necessary to contain her anger, Ellen curtsied and fled the examination room, flinging open its white pine door so hard that it banged against the wall. Again, all heads turned. The

DALE M. POLLOCK

sharp heels of her boots struck the granite floor as she hurried out the large doors that led to the Charles River, and down the walkway back to a world in which she understood the rules.

The nerve of that man, to call himself a doctor and then do nothing to aid a person in need! Ellen was furious with herself for assuming that one chance encounter with a presumed gentleman would somehow provide access to the help freely given to a proper Bostonian—a category, she knew, that would never include her.

A waste of her time, and she had precious little to spare, now that she had to complete her wasted trip and scrounge together tonight's dinner from street peddlers on her way home, or they'd have naught to eat.

In the hospital, heading for the changing room, James released a large exhalation of breath he had not been aware of keeping in. *What had that been all about? Was there really a friend whose fate was in jeopardy? Or was it Miss O'Keeffe herself with an unwanted life inside of her?* Why else would she have reacted so violently to his moral judgment?

In the dark-paneled room, he donned a dark gray frock coat, hanging up the plain dark blue one he wore during rounds. He left the hospital and walked toward Leverett Street, wondering why he remained so affected by Ellen's unexpected appearance and rapid departure. *Could have he reacted more thoughtlessly, more grossly, in a more unmanly way,* he wondered? No, James had failed his visitor on every count.

What was it about Ellen O'Keeffe that so distracted him? There was no proper way for a gentleman of his background to pursue an Irish Catholic girl with red hair who would be noticed wherever she went. Yet she was the first young woman with whom he could imagine spending more than a few idle hours. She was quick, sensitive, willful—or full of will, he wasn't sure which. Why was she not already married to some Irishman who dug trenches by day and drank himself to insensibility each night? Probably, James thought, *because she possessed a life spirit that such an arid existence would extinguish.*

James's agitation gave him a headache, in addition to his usual stomach distress. He needed to go home and lie down before enduring a concert that night at the Howard Athenaeum. It was to be followed by a late supper at his sister Lucinda's and her husband Jacob Dresser's home on Tontine Crescent. He could look forward to little enjoyment under his domineering sister's disapproving gaze this evening.

~

The Dresser carriage would come for him at thirty minutes past seven o'clock, so he began his preparations early. The Hutchinson Family, also known as the Tribe of Jesse, would begin their vocal performance at eight. His brother Henry had persuaded the entire Stone family to attend except eldest brother Anson, who often absented himself from these gatherings.

This was just as well, Anson being firmly proslavery and vocal in its defense. The Hutchinson Family was renowned for the antislavery content of their songs; they had set several abolitionist poems by Henry Wadsworth Longfellow to music. Anson knew he would be infuriated by the performance and so declined to attend.

James's evening dress was as close to a riding costume as someone who owned neither horse nor saddle could wear. A freshly pressed linen shirt went over linen underwear—one of the few areas in which Sharon excelled was laundry—and then James folded his indigo blue cravat into a triangle and tied it around the neck of his white cambric shirt. His dark gray pants were tight, if not as closely pegged as the ones he wore for his morning promenades. Next came an iridescent green waistcoat with traces of blue that drew out the color of his cravat, topped by a black riding coat, accented with velvet lapels, and a long velvet tail in back. His white gloves, which he used only for supper parties and balls, matched his white shirt. His black boots were newly shined, thanks again to the perspiration of Sharon.

Regarding himself in his new cut-glass mirror, James was not displeased. Perhaps he might be as eligible as Lucinda kept insisting he was.

The bell rang; the carriage had arrived. James looked down from his sitting-room window at the open landau with its low glazed half door and green upholstered benches on which sat Lucinda, Jacob, Henry, and Jerome, three quarters of all the family James Stone had in the world. He blew out the whale-oil lamp and carefully closed the oak door behind him.

The Howard Athenaeum was sold out for the Hutchinsons' engagement. Henry, a passionate antislavery advocate, was determined that his own family absorb the message of the Hutchinsons' worthwhile lyrics, as well as their stirring music.

James smiled as he listened to the musical family sing of abolition, of outlawing beer and liquor, and of voting rights for all Americans, including Blacks and women. *Which element of this concert,* he wondered, *would have enraged brother Anson to the greatest degree?*

The makeup of this liberal Boston audience, which James could see was filled with free Blacks and pairs, even trios, of women accompanied only by each other, would have been enough to dissuade Anson from ever setting foot in Howard Athenaeum again.

Seated next to James was Jerome, the quietest of the Stone siblings, guarded in judgment and speech, the business genius of the family. He had walked through Boston as a twelve-year-old, ascertaining vacancies and rents in various neighborhoods, fascinated by numbers and sums. It was Jerome who urged Anson to make speedy and low offers for residential and commercial property; often his wanderings led to profitable bargains.

Utilizing Jerome's commercial instincts and Anson's brute negotiating power, the Stone brothers had become powerful landlords in Boston. Nothing like Dr. Parkman, of course, who had so many rents to collect that they filled five ledger books.

The income allotted to James as part of his estate, beginning with his share of the proceeds from his father's business, supported him far more than the meager fees he collected as a doctor. That was but one reason Lucinda believed James to be in dire need of transformation. He had neither well-to-do patients, nor any young women eager for his solicitation of marriage. To his sister, he seemed to be doing nothing at all, occupying his days strolling on the Mall or the Common, buying the latest in male fashion, seeing an occasional patient in his dispensary, appearing infrequently at Massachusetts General Hospital, or volunteering his services for this outbreak of disease or that epidemic. Something must be done. For Lucinda, it was time to step into the breach. This evening's gathering would be an important first step.

Following the concert, the carriage pulled up to the Dresser home on the famous Charles Bulfinch–designed Tontine Crescent, still fashionable but trying a bit desperately to maintain its reputation as the most beautiful street in Boston. The horses were steadied, and the coachman leapt down to lower the stairs from the landau. Lucinda was the first to descend, her mission to put James's life on its proper course clear in her mind.

As if in condemnation of James's dandified appearance, all the other men wore dark clothing. The women displayed bright gowns that were neither too fashionable nor too ornate. Lucinda was joined by her sisters-in-law, Emily Willis Dresser and Cornelia Bouie Dresser, who arrived moments after the Stones.

The women gathered in the parlor to marvel at Lucinda's elaborate bird cage housing her new canary, a cunning little fellow who was feathered light yellow. With considerable passion, Lucinda unsuccessfully urged the bird to sing for her guests. She turned crimson when he would not comply, but she did her best to maintain a gracious smile.

A Black servant stepped forward and announced that the meal was served. The canary and Lucinda looked relieved. Jacob Dresser was proud of employing freed Blacks as domestic help; he thought it made a statement far stronger than pledging dollars to Reverend Garrison and his radical abolitionist cause. The practice embarrassed Lucinda. She always felt the need to explain that her staff was not slaves but hired servants.

Jacob took Lucinda by the arm, and they led the procession of couples into the dining room. Henry jokingly took James's arm, and solitary Jerome brought up the rear. A damask-clothed table resting on sturdy claw feet awaited them, attended by a white butler and two Black footmen. A fish course came first: turbot with lobster and Dutch sauces, carved on the sideboard by the butler, and a portion of red mullet with cardinal sauce. James was pleased to see his favorite dish, a bowl of hot stewed oysters, also on the sideboard.

Lucinda soon directed the table conversation toward her subject of choice: the upcoming ball to be given by Mr. and Mrs. John Stephens in honor of their niece, Jennie Ray Gillmer, who would be visiting from Trenton. There were general positive comments on the generosity of the Stephens in honoring their niece in such a public and expensive manner. She had been born in the Azores, the daughter of Mrs. Stephens's brother, a United States diplomatic officer on the island. He had succumbed to the yellow fever, and her mother had recently remarried.

The conversation shifted from the virtues of Miss Gillmer to the excitement about the event celebrating her, the first major ball of the season. In the time-honored tradition, it would be held the third week in October at the in-town chateau of the Stones' family friend, Ezra Deacon. Invitations for six hundred guests, including the entire Stone family, had just arrived, hand delivered.

The mention of dress balls did not please James. He reminded his family that he was not an accomplished dancer. These new polkas and other energetic dances required an agility he would never possess. He had only now just mastered the waltz, and it was already out of favor, he complained. If this Miss Gillmer were a dancing fanatic, there would be the end of it.

Lucinda didn't press the matter. There was time enough for her to plot the first meeting between James Winchell Stone and Jennie Ray Gillmer and aim it for a successful outcome.

The Stone and Dresser women withdrew to the drawing room for coffee and tea, while the gentlemen stayed at the dining table and indulged in Portuguese port and Cuban cigars.

The usual weighty subjects were touched upon: the pitiful performance of President Fillmore in place of the greatly respected President Taylor, the Conqueror of Buena Vista; the death of Edgar Allan Poe, a writer James admired for his tales of mystery; and the latest exploits of Lady Suffolk, an invincible racehorse who had just won a major heat and several thousand dollars at Saratoga Springs. Slavery was a topic best avoided in social situations such as supper parties, and James was relieved that it did not come up.

Eventually the men made their way to the drawing room, where everyone drank too much coffee that would keep them up for hours. By eleven o'clock carriages were summoned. One dropped James off at 6 Bowdoin Square, and the other took Henry and Jerome to Cambridge after crossing Craigie's Bridge, well-lit by new gas lamps.

It had been a long evening. James felt exhausted on the way home, unwilling to have engaged in anything but banal conversation with his relatives. He did not enjoy such late evenings. Not that there was anything pressing on his schedule to cause him to rise early the next morning. There never was.

CHAPTER 7

October 1849
Summer Street and Bowdoin Square, Beacon Hill, Boston, Massachusetts

The chateau of Ezra Deacon on Summer Street had never looked as splendid as it did for the grand ball hosted by the Stephenses, Jennie Gillmer's aunt and uncle on her father's side. Deacon was a business partner of Stephens in the manufacture of woolen stockings and had graciously lent his premises for the fête.

James had received his invitation four weeks earlier, delivered by a messenger boy. In elaborate calligraphy on linen board, the following was written:

> *Mr. and Mrs. John Stephens request the pleasure of Dr. James Winchell Stone's company at an Evening Ball in honor of the visiting Miss Jennie Ray Gillmer on* **Friday, October 18,** *at the Ezra Deacon residence at half past eight.*
>

An answer will oblige.
>
> *Dancing.*

James had replied with his own messenger well within the time-honored twenty-four-hour deadline. As the Dresser carriage pulled up to Bowdoin Square and number 6, James came down dressed in formal black trousers, a black jacket, and a black waistcoat with a white cravat atop a white shirt. White gloves covered his hands, as was required.

The ride was not a long one. Soon there came into view on Beacon Hill an enormous stone structure, constructed in the French style and lit in a brilliant manner. The wrought-iron front gates, the parade of carriages, an entrance hall that exuded baronial grandeur: all created a mood of splendor. Black servants in elaborate livery helped Lucinda, Jacob, and James disembark, escorted them inside, and announced them to the gathering.

The banqueting salon featured five enormous gilt-framed mirrors, reflecting gold and silver tableware, Sèvres china, Bohemian cut glass in various colors, dripping candelabras, and heavy wall hangings, all proof of Mr. Deacon's wealth.

The orchestra was situated at the top of the salon, the area farthest from the entrance. The musicians were discreetly hidden behind ornamental shrubbery: piano, violin, viola, cello, and cornet amid faux wax plants. They played music that sounded vaguely familiar to James; was it Handel? Mozart? Henry would have known instantly.

James often felt out of place in this world that he so ardently wished to join. He could not practice the pretensions and condescension he saw all around him at such gatherings. He felt inadequate to the social challenges that awaited him.

Still, his heart had thrilled a bit when a bawling footman announced their entrance: "Mr. and Mrs. Jacob Dresser, accompanied by Doctor James Winchell Stone."

Upstairs, the drinking had already begun in earnest. James was generally abstemious at such gatherings, unlike most of his male counterparts. Ladies also drank alcohol at the balls, although few became visibly intoxicated. It was a cause for disapproval if a man allowed himself to be seriously drunken in mixed company, at least before the dancing was concluded. For a woman, it was social ruin. James was pleased with this development in society. He abhorred a sloppy drunkard.

As he made his way through the crowd of young men and women near the bar, he heard the notes of a fast polka already shaking the largest ballroom next to them. James entered the dancing area where young couples whirled across the parquet floor. Each gentleman had a linen handkerchief carefully placed between his hand and his partner's back and concentrated on keeping it there as the couple traversed the dance floor.

James dreaded dancing at these balls; he was clumsy and awkward, possessing little skill in moving his body to musical rhythms. Dispiritedly, he turned to depart early and made his way out of the ballroom and into the adjoining courtyard. He ignored Lucinda and her alarmed expression as she frantically waved for him to join her. She was part of a large group of guests lined up to greet Mr. and Mrs. Stephens and Miss Gillmer. James had hoped to escape before Lucinda could corner him, and he estimated he just might make it.

As he approached the entrance, James noticed at the end of the receiving line a dark-haired young lady with a tiny mouth and close-set blue eyes. This must be the renowned Jennie Gillmer. She did look refined and intelligent, James thought, certainly in contrast to the jabbering women gathered around her. Still, he pressed on, determined to elude Lucinda.

On his way to the staircase that would take him down to the exit, James encountered Frederick Ainsworth, a classmate and old friend from his Harvard days. Ainsworth was now the demonstrator of anatomy at the Medical College, supervising the dissection classes and the preparations of the specimens for Dr. Holmes's lectures. This was an important faculty position, although it forced Ainsworth daily to deal with corpses. He also supervised the janitor Ephraim Littlefield in the preparation and disposal of the cadavers and body parts used by the faculty in their teaching, and the medical students in their dissections.

Ainsworth greeted James heartily. Encountering a familiar face made him feel better, so he reconsidered his decision to abandon the evening. Someone handed him a drink, a rum concoction that he sipped absent-mindedly as he chatted with Ainsworth, his smile quickly turning to a grimace. Damnation, these rum punches were powerful! How could any-one be expected to dance under the influence of such spirits? Perhaps that was the key to success: drink until all of one's inhibitions were loosened.

James gazed across the room and again saw Miss Gillmer, this time suf-fering a startled reaction identical to his, at the power of the rum punch. She looked up and caught his eye. They smiled at one another in mutual sympathy. James bowed, and Miss Gillmer curtsied, before she returned to her conversation with the young woman next to her, whom James recog-nized as her cousin, Mary Jane Buckingham Bailey Stephens. With only two names after his first, James had learned that the number of family affiliations in a name was a symbol of the social status of a family that had married generations of their offspring well.

Now the redowa began, a dance even more energetic than the polka. To James's relief, he could join Ainsworth and his friends in avoiding the exercise and repairing to the ground floor, where the supper room offered a bountiful feast. As they descended the drafty limestone staircase, the men passed a room where ladies sipped lemonade and cups of hot tea. For the third time, James caught the eye of Miss Gillmer, who had likewise relo-cated. James was unwilling to stare at the guest of honor; so embarrassed, he turned back to his friends.

Ainsworth was recounting a long and digressive tale concerning an er-rant corpse. Hearing enough, James left the bar, bearing a small glass of sherry. He was startled to discover at his side his sister Lucinda and the formerly shy Miss Gillmer, now staring directly into James's face. He had not heard them approach in the din of the music and voices.

"James, here you are, at last!" Lucinda said in her pronounced Yankee accent, squeezing James's arm unnecessarily hard. She knew he had tried to escape and was triumphant in having foiled him. "I would like you to finally make the acquaintance of Miss Gillmer."

And then, in the same long breath, she recited Miss Gillmer's pedigree, including the fact that her stepfather, the esteemed Captain Matthew C. Jenkins, built all the new docks and wharves in New Jersey.

"Welcome to our fair city," James said hospitably, bowing deeply and receiving a small curtsy in return from Miss Gillmer. "I understand you have traveled the high seas from the Azores, so I fear Boston may be too tame, given your apparent thirst for adventure."

"Terceira can hardly contend with the cultural capital of our country," Miss Gillmer said, a faint accent in her voice that suggested a more exotic background than James was accustomed to. "I have been told much about Boston, and that I needed to view it with my own eyes. Now that I am here, I agree with this position; there is so much to see."

"Such well-formed eyes should not be put under any unusual strain," James said, surprising himself with his declaration; he found gazing into blue eyes set so close together to be a surprisingly intoxicating experience. Lucinda looked astonished.

"That is purely a medical opinion," he added, an attempt to turn his compliment into a jest. Miss Gillmer smiled faintly, but James was unsure just what reaction he had elicited. Jennie's brown hair was pulled back in a tight bun; it restricted her moon-shaped face from revealing much emotion.

"I wasn't aware that my eyesight required a medical opinion, Doctor Stone," Jennie said. "Perhaps you assume that the source of the problem is the strain of looking at so many handsome Boston men."

"If my presence is causing you eye strain, I can cure that affliction easily," James responded, beginning to back away. He felt something faintly mocking in Jennie Gillmer's tone.

"James, where are you going?" Lucinda said sharply. She was familiar with her brother's technique of first fading into the background and then vanishing from social occasions. Miss Gillmer looked between brother and sister; she understood the game that was afoot. James liked that Miss Gillmer noticed this. To his surprise, he didn't really wish to depart.

"I have two dances remaining upon my card," Jennie said coquettishly to James. "I hope you will guide me in at least one of them."

There was no way to decline without being insufferably rude. Miss Gillmer had chosen him for a signal honor, the final dance of the evening, a selection that was simultaneously flattering and mortifying.

James felt his sister's eyes bore into him, urging the proper response. He bowed deeply and said, "I am honored, Miss Gillmer."

Jennie curtsied her consent and was led upstairs for the next dance by Taylor Wentworth, a tall young lawyer with an unusually pale complexion and a high-pitched voice. Lucinda quivered with pleasure as Wentworth and Miss Gillmer were swept away by the rollicking redowa. "James, I do believe she likes you," Lucinda breathed into his ear as she sidled up to him, her arm cradled in his. Her brother affixed the same glare upon her he had earlier.

"Oh, stop pouting," Lucinda snapped. "I arranged for your invitation tonight, you tell me you're thrilled to be in society, and then you act like a recluse. Can you not see that Miss Gillmer has taken a fancy to you?"

"It's not Miss Gillmer I object to, it's the cursed galop," he explained, causing Lucinda to burst into laughter at the name of an outdated dance.

"Let her lead and you follow, James. Remember that the patient must reveal the illness to you before you can treat it. If you can keep pace with Miss Gillmer on the dance floor as well as you did in conversation, there's a future in this relationship."

It was soon time for the evening's concluding dance. James made his way back up the stairs to the ballroom, fearful of publicly embarrassing himself.

James tried to take Lucinda's encouragement to heart. He did possess assets: he was a well-educated, moderately successful physician, a partisan of the noble science of phonography, a welcome friend to men as diverse as Dr. Jacob Bigelow and Senator Daniel Webster. Was not he, too, "a good catch," as Lucinda had described Miss Gillmer? James straightened his shoulders and lengthened his stride to enter the ballroom in a more manly and forthright manner.

James's burgeoning self-confidence grew as he approached Jennie. He didn't perceive her as airy or birdbrained, traits he saw in most of the single young women he had met in Boston. There was a depth of intelligence, a fully formed consciousness behind her blue eyes. He wanted to understand better what that meant in a young woman with her background.

As he reached the ballroom, he surveyed the sparkling decorations, the well-dressed guests, the dramatic lighting. He saw Jennie's long neck crane anxiously in search of him. When her amused aqua eyes alighted on his, they widened in pleasure, and she beckoned him forward. As they took their places on the dance floor, James's nervousness eased. He readied his handkerchief. He bowed; Miss Gillmer curtsied. He'd do the damned galop, and he'd lead, too.

CHAPTER 8

December 1849
Court Street, Summer Street, and North Grove Street, Boston,
Massachusetts

James was at the Old Cornhill Coffee House on Court Street when he purchased a copy of the *Boston Herald*. The headline on the December 3 edition marched in bold type across the front page:

Startling Intelligence! The Body of Dr. George Parkman Found,
Murdered and Cut Up, in the Medical College—
Arrest of Professor Webster, Charged with the Diabolical Deed—
Tremendous Excitement—A Riot Anticipated!

James was thrilled to be an intimate in matters that so consumed the city, even if any mention of the heroic physician who had stuck his fingers down Dr. Webster's gullet and saved his life was absent from the account. According to the newspaper, it was Marshal Tukey who had leapt upon Webster and dislodged the fatal dose from his hand before it ever entered his throat. Dr. James Winchell Stone was not even placed at the scene.

The *Herald* article, written by John French, the paper's editor and chief reporter, went on to describe the suspect after his incarceration: "Webster manifested the utmost trepidation. . . . His conduct at the gaol was that of a maniac. . . . An examination is now going on at the College to ferret out the whole affair. The greatest excitement pervades the public mind on the subject, and it is supposed that the building will be torn down."

These words disturbed James enough to plan a consultation with Dr. Bigelow. He was the sole nonpolice eyewitness to the previous evening's events. He had seen Webster play the pathetic fool, all blubbering innocence and exclamations about the shame he was bringing upon his family.

Yet the prisoner's attempt to kill himself was the reaction of a guilty man, or so it seemed to James. *Why else attempt to desert his beloved family for an unmarked plot in Mt. Auburn?*

If Professor Webster was responsible for murdering and dismembering George Parkman, he was unlikely to have acted alone, James reasoned; as he knew Webster, it was beyond the man's ken. James could not imagine this meek, rotund chemistry teacher overpowering and then killing the taller, angrier, and more physically fit Parkman. *Someone else must have been present to lend assistance, an accomplice strong enough to lift the dead weight of Parkman's body, move it, and help chop it up. But who?*

James's head was still fuzzy, even after two cups of the potent brew at Cornhill's. He had suffered several nights of fitful, troubled sleep, and the cold air that greeted him that morning when he stepped outside the coffee house offered little comfort. As he set off for Jacob Bigelow's home, a keen wind blew dead against him, and a hard frost prevailed on the ground. The low temperature was only slightly more tolerable.

He hurried his step as he rounded Tremont Street and turned onto Summer. He must persuade Bigelow to protect Webster's rooms and their contents at the Medical College. The evidence that could identify Webster's accomplice, should James's suspicions prove true, had to exist somewhere inside the building.

James knew that many of the initial rumors concerning Parkman's disappearance had him coming to a bad end at the hand of a murderous and greedy Irishman. The Medical College was not only the murder site; it was also the Harvard facility closest to the neighborhoods of the North End, from Broad Street to Fort Hill, now dominated by the Irish.

That very proximity gave rise to another concern James had. If an Irish-led, anti-Harvard riot started in the vicinity of the Medical College, he surmised, Marshal Tukey and his constables would be quickly outmanned, given the proximity of the Irish-dominated neighborhoods of Fort Hill and the North End. Reinforcements would be needed immediately, and they still might not be sufficient to protect the evidence contained within the college's walls if the riot got that far.

These morbid scenarios played out in James's imagination as he pressed the iron button that rang a bell in the Bigelow residence. The familiar Black servant greeted him and ushered him into the parlor. Bigelow soon came thumping down the stairs, each step thudding in James's overstimulated senses.

"You must be a mind reader, James," Bigelow said as he finally gained the ground floor and entered the parlor. "I was about to send a boy to inquire as to your whereabouts, and here you are, as if I'd ordered you up and had you delivered."

"I hope it is because you share my concerns, Doctor Bigelow," James said, unable to disguise the worry in his voice. "We must hurry to the Medical College and makes sure all within is preserved as it stands. I fear a mob may destroy it in a fit of rage."

"Rest yourself, James. Your concerns have been addressed. President Sparks has requested of Mayor Beacham and Marshal Tukey a special force of men to surround the Medical College, who will keep it free from any and all who might wish to harm it. They are in place as of this morning."

"What of Doctor Webster's residence? On my journey here I heard rumors of a mob on its way to Garden Street, determined to set the man's home ablaze, and damned be his wife and daughters."

Bigelow patiently explained that President Sparks had also requested a special patrol of twenty-five handpicked constables under the Cambridge city marshal's supervision to guard the Webster residence. So far, there had been no attempt to molest the innocent occupants of the home.

Like James, Bigelow was preparing to go to the Medical College, and he invited James to join him. As soon as their conveyance entered the roadway, the stream of humanity subsumed them. Bigelow's landau was surrounded by weavers and diggers, laborers and tanners, dockworkers and deliverymen, some accompanied by their wives and children. The festive air that seemed to animate the crowd moving east toward North Grove Street set James slightly more at ease.

Bigelow touched his coachman's arm to stop when the street became impassable due to the sea of humanity. Descending quickly, Bigelow and James hurried through the crowd, afraid of what awaited them at the college, which they could now see ahead.

As they approached the stone staircase that led to the Medical College entrance, Bigelow and James were recognized for who they were: Harvard doctors. Men in the crowd pointed and yelled at them, elbowing fellow protestors and pushing toward them. James felt the tension grow, and his stomach tightened.

Bigelow grasped him by one elbow and forcefully pulled him toward the bottom of the staircase. A burly constable was planted in front of the steps, cudgel in hand. James was jostled, and a hand struck the back of his head, propelling him directly into Bigelow's back. The constable, seeing this affront, lurched forward, his thick wooden stick aloft, and James's attacker scurried back into the crowd, which grudgingly moved back a few steps. It was enough for the two doctors to slip behind the policeman and quickly ascend the granite steps.

James was breathing heavily as he and Bigelow paused at the top of the landing; this doorway, too, was guarded. Marshal Tukey strode over to them and looked closely at James before speaking.

"Ye'll survive, Doctor Stone. Ye just received what they call the Irish love tap. I'm glad ye caught it on the back of yer head, and not the front. It might have spoiled those pretty features of yer's."

Tukey led James and Bigelow down the interior stairs to the building's basement. They passed through the furnace and fuel areas, turned left down the corridor, went through the front laboratory, and entered the dissecting room, where Dr. Lewis and Coroner Jabez Pratt awaited them. The sections of human flesh discovered the day before remained laid out on the same pine board.

"What we have assembled of the body remains intact," confirmed Lewis. James and Bigelow hurried to put on white aprons like the one Lewis wore. Pratt, who had a greenish tint to his complexion, remained in his dark suit and moved back a few paces. He was there only to observe. James wondered what qualified the man to be coroner. *It was not the possession of a strong stomach; Pratt looked likely to retch any moment.*

The medical men set to work. With great care, they transferred the body parts onto one of the stone dissecting tables. They determined that the lack of arsenic acid or chloride of zinc in the pelvis and legs meant they did not come from a body prepared for dissection. If Littlefield didn't add arsenic or zinc to the corpses he acquired, the bodies decomposed quickly and became useless for study. Whatever had befallen the unfortunate soul whose remains lay before the Harvard physicians, the indignity of being a display cadaver was not among them.

The busy doctors were absorbed in their task and therefore oblivious to the growing mob outside, but Coroner Pratt was not. He roamed from under the windows in one corner of the room to the other, listening for the commencement of a mob attack he considered imminent. He looked terrified.

James surveyed what was laid out before the Medical College faculty. It was obvious that someone had lowered these portions of a dismembered body into the privy, not as a final resting place, but as only a temporary holding measure.

Webster would have been unable to use the dissecting laboratory, in any case, since he did not possess a key to it. He had no need for the room as a chemistry professor, so he was not provided access to it. Lieutenant Clapp had discovered large fishhooks in Webster's laboratory. These could have been used to fashion a grapple that Webster apparently had used to lower the leg and torso into the privy vault. He then could have hauled them up bit by bit as he worked on their eventual obliteration.

During the police search two nights earlier, Bigelow and James had discovered potash next to the furnace in Webster's laboratory and had brought it to Detective Clapp's attention. They knew that potash, heated over a fire, would reduce flesh and bone to liquid, but it was a slow process that required a great deal of time to complete.

The one thing Webster (or, James corrected himself, whoever the actual killer was) lacked was a receptacle large enough to hold an entire human body. It seemed clear that the murderer had had no choice but to hack it apart, fit what he could into the furnace, and hide the remaining body parts in the privy vault and the tea chest until they could be destroyed, too.

James could not envision Webster performing these tasks alone, unaided in any way. He had read that murderous rage sometimes gives the afflicted superhuman strength. Perhaps Webster had been so animated in a life-and-death situation, but it seemed unlikely, given the professor's temperament.

Had time permitted, James was sure the killer would have done away with the body as completely as if it had never existed, disposing of everything identifiable except the false teeth. These, being mineral, would not burn in a small furnace, as Webster and the police had discovered. James could see that the murderous plan had not been well thought through. A forge would have been required to melt such sturdy choppers.

James's ruminations were interrupted by the arrival of Jared Sparks, president of Harvard College, and Robert Shaw, who looked as agitated as James had ever seen him. Sparks was pale. He had been heckled and jeered as the police led a tight cordon around the visitors. Some belligerent had narrowly missed Sparks when tossing a paving stone at the party of bigwigs, all in their expensive dark suits and top hats.

Sparks had been a Unitarian minister before assuming the leadership of Harvard, and he seemed shaken to his core by the Webster arrest. It had most inflamed Shaw, who appeared ready to burst with frustration and anger.

Shaw carried a sheaf of papers he was determined to show the other men. He grabbed Coroner Pratt roughly by the shoulder and shoved the documents at him.

"Why has not murder been determined, and the killer imprisoned?"

Shaw did not expect an actual response from the pale man, who shrank from his touch. It was for the benefit of all those assembled. For the first time, Shaw saw the torso and other body parts laid out on the dissecting table. He stopped short and put the hand with the papers to his forehead.

"My God!" he breathed, swaying slightly.

Shaw, alone of those present, had recognized a signal feature of Dr. Parkman's anatomy: the virile organ that remained unharmed and completely attached to the pelvis. Dr. Parkman's penis was distinguished by a condition known as phymosis, in which the glans becomes blocked. Circumcision was the usual remedy to relieve the resulting swelling and pain, but Parkman had refused any such treatment. Therefore, the prepuce on his penis was large and hard.

Shaw knew of this condition only because Parkman had shared with him the discomfort it caused and his regret that the issue hadn't been settled in his infancy. He had been unable to muster the courage as an adult to undergo the painful procedure to address his swollen condition, which now remained visibly apparent.

Recovering his composure, Shaw addressed those present.

"This can be none other than Doctor Parkman. That is what I expect to see in your report, Mister Pratt. The condition you see to be obvious in his private parts was known to me, and I know it still. There is no need for further examination."

Shaw walked around the remnants of Parkman's corpse as if they were pieces of a broken Greek sculpture he was assessing for purchase. He remarked on several patches of fine hair visible on the legs and the back of the torso, saying the hirsute Parkman had been embarrassed by the quantity of the body hair that covered his chest, back, arms, and legs.

"I also bring you, gentlemen, proof of the motive for this heinous butchery." Shaw held out more papers to Bigelow and asked him to read them aloud for the edification of all present.

Bigelow looked embarrassed to be the town crier, but Shaw left him no choice. He began in his stentorian lecture voice:

"Know all men that I, John W. Webster of Cambridge, professor of chemistry, in consideration of the twenty-four hundred and thirty two dollars paid by George Parkman of Boston, do hereby give, grant, bargain, sell and convey unto George Parkman all my personal property, including all of my household furniture, all my books, minerals and other objects of natural history, and all utensils and apparatus of chemistry, mineralogy, and geology. I, John Webster, assign that they are free from all encumbrances, that I have good right to sell and convey them to George Parkman. I, John Webster, shall pay unto George Parkman, said sum of twenty-four hundred and thirty-two dollars within four years from date with interest, yearly. Provided I do so, then this deed shall be void to all interests and purposes. In witness whereof, I, John Webster, have hereunto set my hand and seal this twenty-second day of January in the year of our Lord one thousand eight hundred and forty-seven."

Affixed at the bottom in a shaky, almost juvenile scrawl, was the signature J. W. Webster. Shaw pointed to the contract, grabbing the papers back from Bigelow and shaking them above his head.

"This scoundrel pledged the same collateral on two occasions," he said in a low voice. "He sold it to my brother-in-law two years ago, and again, most recently, to me. The identical collateral! My brother-in-law learned of this from me in all innocence as I told him of my attempt to help poor Webster. It enraged him in a way I had never seen before. He was determined to have Webster pay off the loan immediately, in full, and then have no more dealings with him."

President Sparks tried to intercede with mollifying words, but Shaw rudely interrupted him and continued his harangue.

"On Friday week past I am certain Doctor Parkman went to Professor Webster's rooms here and demanded his due. None of us know exactly what transpired, but the results are clear, gentlemen," Shaw said, his voice now down to its calm register. "Doctor Webster murdered my brother-in-law and did all in his power to conceal his horrible crime."

The tension that paralyzed the room was broken finally by the deep baritone voice of Sparks. "Our professors do not commit murder, Mister Shaw," he said, defensively. "There must be another explanation."

Shaw turned on him in a fury. "You dare to contradict me on these facts, Sparks? You would deny that John Webster is a liar, a deceiver, and a man willing to trade his honor so that he can host parties? A man who would murder rather than repay his debts?"

Sparks demurred. "I am only saying the Harvard faculty believes Professor Webster to be a colleague worthy of trust and respect until proven otherwise. His standing within the college, his conduct since Doctor Parkman's disappearance, his artlessness and unfamiliarity with crime of any kind, attests strongly to his innocence, Mister Shaw," Sparks said.

"As we speak," Sparks continued, hurrying before Shaw could interrupt him, "Professors Longfellow, Felton, and Horsford are on their way to visit

DALE M. POLLOCK

Professor Webster in the Leverett Street Gaol. It is remains possible that he has in his possession a plausible explanation for these tragic events."

"What, do your minions hope to further his escape?" said Shaw. "Are you as great a fool as your man Stone here, who allowed Webster to take poison and come close to ending his life before facing justice?"

James recoiled as if he had been slapped. Yesterday he had been praised for his quick reaction in preventing Webster's suicide. Less than twenty-four hours later, he was implicated in aiding the man's futile attempt to evade justice. James knew that he did not possess the standing or the bluster to counter Shaw's accusation. He bit his lip and suffered silently.

"Please take no offense, Mister Shaw," the Harvard president said. "I represent the feeling of many who mourn the death of Doctor Parkman and cannot accept that a fellow of their rank and learning could descend to this bestiality. Should we not wait to pass judgment until charges have been made, a trial scheduled, and a verdict rendered?"

"I have rendered the verdict, Sparks, and I tell you John White Webster is guilty. Guilty! I will see it no other way, no matter what tricks you may conjure. The victim here is not Webster, nor Harvard, and certainly not you and your faculty, Sparks. The victims are the Parkman family, each and every one of us. We will have no peace until Webster is sentenced to the death he deserves and the hell that will follow."

Shaw stepped away from the pine board and its grisly display.

"By all means, gentlemen, continue your work. I greatly anticipate its results. You will keep me apprised of them, I trust."

As if there were no need of further discussion, Shaw turned and left the dissecting room. Sparks and Pratt used his departure as an excuse to slip out, too. They wanted to get as far away as possible from the sordid reality of what lay atop that board.

~

Bigelow and James were washing their hands with rough bars of soap in the laboratory's large iron sink when the tumult outside rose dramatically in pitch and intensity. The Medical College sounded as if it was now under direct siege, and James feared the attackers would head straight for the dissection laboratory.

Lewis, who was near one of the room's two windows, located high on the wall to vent chemical fumes, climbed on a chair and peered out through the thick glass. He could see little in the growing darkness of the December day, only flickering torches moving back and forth across North

Grove Street, leading up to the college. That was enough. The mob was on the move.

"I fear we will soon be under attack, gentlemen," Lewis said, his voice hoarse, the color drained from his face. The sounds of disarray grew louder, and James grew apprehensive. This assignment, which he had performed out of a sense of duty and in obligation to Dr. Bigelow, with no personal gain to himself, now could lead to injury or even his demise. He didn't wish to join what was left of Parkman on the cold stone table.

"The mayor and the marshal both assured me this building would be kept under constant guard, given the importance of our task," Bigelow said. He didn't seem convinced by his own words. "I think we should wait here and stand our ground."

The building shuddered, a large boom echoing in the air. With a start, the men realized that the mob was employing a battering ram of some sort and would soon break down the heavy oak entrance doors, giving it access to the entire college. The three doctors stared at each other. Matters had degenerated quickly. James thought it paramount to preserve the sanctity of the remains they had worked so diligently to identify.

In the panic of the moment, James was the only one to hear glass breaking on the other side of the building. Soon everyone became aware, as a huge commotion followed. It sounded as if the demonstrators had simultaneously gained access to two different parts of the college, one group on each of the lower floors. They could be in the dissecting room in a matter of minutes.

Gunfire sounded sharply, and the noise of the mob receded. Bigelow, James, and Lewis exchanged looks of relief. The forces of law and order were still present.

Marshal Tukey himself flung open the door to the dissecting room, relieved to find all three doctors present and unharmed. He turned to Bigelow.

"There's a large tumult going on outside, Doctor, I cannot vouchsafe ye and yer men if we stay here one minute longer. Come with me, or perish as ye wish!"

Tukey and two uniformed constables led the physicians into the cellar proper. They moved to the storeroom. On the dirt floor, amidst shards of broken glass, lay a little girl, bleeding and wailing. James ran to her aid. Her forehead was bloodied and she was stunned, but she otherwise looked unharmed. James looked up at the empty frame of the window high up the wall. He could see feet massing before it, jostling for space.

Apparently, the child had peered in through one of the lower windows, thinking perhaps it would give a view to the supposed horrors within. James guessed she had slipped and crashed through the glass, falling to the storeroom floor. The sound of the window breaking, along with the child's terrified screams, had brought a crowd rushing to the north side of the building.

As Tukey's men prepared for a second assault from the mob surrounding the Medical College, James snatched up the bleeding child, her screams ratcheting in volume and pitch. Ignoring Tukey's cries of objection, he made his way to the far storeroom door and ran up the stairs to the college entrance. Flinging the doors open, he raced onto the landing, followed by two of the constables.

James held the little girl aloft to demonstrate to the mob that she was safe. A woman came running up the left flight of stairs, her screams of fear and then delight resounding through the crowd. The child's mother grasped James's hands in her own before putting the little girl over her shoulder and hurrying back down into the mob. Some cheered, but more hurled oaths at the police and the Harvard doctor who was foolhardy enough to present himself to the angry crowd.

James and the constables retreated into the college entryway, afraid of what might come next. Tukey, Lewis, and Bigelow joined them. Should they remain in the building until help came? Bigelow suggested they try to get out and blend in with the crowd until they could make good their escape. *James wondered if that was even possible in this charged and frenzied atmosphere.* Tukey quickly ended the discussion. The group would stay where they were for the moment.

Paralyzed by fear, Lewis was visibly shaking, sweat wet on his brow despite the chill in the evening. James knew that if they did not do something, circumstance would dictate its own sorry course. Pulling at Bigelow's sleeve and shouting at Lewis to startle him out of his trembles, Tukey and James moved the group toward the front door.

The tall oak doors opened to let the doctors go out, and closed quickly behind them. Lieutenant Clapp appeared in the dim light and motioned for Tukey and the doctors to follow him. They moved rapidly down two flights of stairs, through the furnace room, down the corridor and into Ephraim Littlefield's apartment, passing between his kitchen and his bedroom as they headed for the carriage shed and hoped-for safety.

Several constables were grouped together at the entrance to Littlefield's apartment, whose full-time occupants were nowhere to be seen. Tukey and his senior officers were inside, standing in the kitchen, and Tukey addressed the medical men when they rejoined him.

"My men will form a ring around ye. Once we're clear of the college and the hospital grounds, all should be easy. Only when yer group is safe will the City Light Guard clear this rabble. It will be nothing for officers swinging on horseback with their lances and swords."

"Fine, but let's go now," said Bigelow, his peremptory tone indicating that safety seemed probable. "I have no desire to remain in these premises while your men test their mettle."

As if by unconscious command, a group of five grimy and blood-spattered constables, nightsticks in hand, helmets firmly secured with chinstraps, gathered around the doctors.

Like an awkward centipede, the eight men moved as a group that broke up as soon as it formed. They still managed to reach the stable doors of the carriage shed undamaged. The policemen were reluctant to proceed further until Tukey roared at them, "Blast ye, get yer arses out there!"

Lieutenant Clapp and another constable opened the stable doors wide enough for two men at a time to exit. Clapp and Tukey led the way, followed by James and Bigelow, another constable and Lewis, and two more policemen bringing up the rear.

The roar of voices and the sight of men running in all directions quickly dispelled the quiet of the carriage shed. Children were screaming, whether in laughter or terror, James could not be sure. It took no time for bottles and paving stones to come flying toward the party of eight; the policemen raised their cudgels to give the physicians some measure of cover from the missiles.

James could see a bonfire nearby, men burning wood that had been stacked outside Littlefield's quarters. The air was biting cold and getting colder as the darkness deepened. Everything went by in a blur. The group quickened its collective pace, the constables pushing from behind, and the officers in the lead muscling their way forward.

James caught sight of a figure waving frantically at him. He strained to see who it was and recognized, with a shock, Ellen O'Keeffe, gesturing to him from a spot not ten yards away. He was taken aback at the sight of her.

Ellen was indeed imploring him to join her; only now did James notice a huddled shape near her feet. An elderly woman had been knocked down in the rush of the mob, and Ellen was signaling for help.

James took only a moment to decide his course. Without saying a word, he detached himself from the fast-moving phalanx and ran toward Ellen.

He heard Bigelow's and other voices call after him, but he ignored them. Reaching Ellen, he grasped her hands. His unanticipated action startled them both. James quickly abandoned the physical contact.

Ellen held him in her gaze as she gestured toward the bloodied woman at her feet. "Please, Doctor Stone, if ye could help this poor creature. Old Missus Flinn was flattened by the mob, gathered for nae good, I promise ye that."

"Ellen, what in God's name are you doing here?" James said.

He now heard angry shouts and oaths directed his way, but he chose to disregard them. He would not ignore Ellen O'Keeffe's plea for help twice. This was the first time he had encountered her since their brief and unpleasant meeting in Massachusetts General Hospital, and he was determined to redeem himself.

"Looking after my people, who just came out for a bit of excitement. Next thing ye know, they're layin' on the sod poor folks like this granny here, the blood pouring from her. Can ye not help her, Doctor?"

James was rendered momentarily speechless—whether due to the medical emergency he was presented with or Ellen's sudden physical presence, he was unsure.

"I have none of my medical supplies in my possession," he finally said, unwilling to explain that he had been working on the remains of a dead man and carried no medicines for the living.

James knelt down, and pulled off his silk cravat, the initials JWS carefully embroidered on it by his maid, Sharon. To Ellen's surprise, he used the expensive garment to stanch the flow of blood trickling from the elderly woman's forehead. He could tell immediately it was only a superficial wound. Since the handkerchief was already ruined, he used it to bind the woman's head tightly.

Ellen reached down and gently helped the old woman to her feet. "Now, Mrs. Flinn, it be time to get yerself home, and quickly now. Do ye think ye can manage yerself?"

The elderly Irishwoman looked between Ellen and James with understandable confusion but did manage to nod. James was surprised Ellen would allow the elderly victim to make her own way out of this riot, but he had no wish to interfere with her relationships with her own kind. Ellen looked grateful for James's help, and she smiled at him as she shouted over the din of the mob, which still milled around the Medical College, looking for an excuse to breach its doors.

"I need help findin' my neighbor's boy, afore his brains be dashed to the ground by one of those fine police clubs that were gathered 'round ye, Doctor Stone."

James looked around in a moment of panic, realizing the group that had promised safe passage had moved along and left him the sole Harvard man on the Medical College grounds. It remained a scene of burning fires and small pitched battles between Irish youths and the police.

Ellen let out a sudden "Whoop!" and ran to her left toward a raggedy clutch of boys, seized the tallest one by the collar, and dragged him back to James.

"Here he be, the horrible creature!" she said. "I try to keep him in me sights, Lord help me, but he don't make it easy. John O'Brien, greet Doctor Stone with some manners, will ye?"

The dark-haired youth, a good two or three inches taller than James, sullenly regarded the physician. James gave him his warmest smile and put out his hand to shake.

"Do your pa know about ye and this fella?" was the youngster's only response, ignoring James's gesture of friendship. The question brought him a quick cuff on the head from Ellen. James was uncomfortable with the implication.

"That'll be enough of that!" she said to the teen. She regarded James, blushing. "To tell the truth, I don't know what ye be." She turned back to her nephew. "Ye say a word of this and ye'll be dealin' with me, John O'Brien, and it won't be pleasant. Do we understand one another?"

Since this question was delivered with a simultaneous grab of John's rough linen shirt and another cuff to his ear, it elicited an immediate response, a grunt of assent that seemed to satisfy Ellen.

"My business here is done, Doctor, I thank ye mightily for yer aid," Ellen said. She kept a hand firmly grasped on her captive's shirt and bestowed upon James a look of sincere gratitude.

"I'm sorry I could not do more, ill-equipped as I found myself," he said, fumbling for what he really wanted to say to this attractive young woman. But the presence of the boy bade him hold his tongue about his feelings.

"Good evening to you both," James continued, at a loss for how to communicate his desire to renew Ellen's acquaintance. "I hope our paths may cross again in more benign circumstances."

Ellen laughed at his strained formality. "Nae more riots, I promise ye," she said with a smile. "We seem to meet only when all hell is breaking loose."

"I don't wish to wait until we meet in heaven," he responded with a smile and a low bow. "I hope our next encounter will be on terra firma. It is far more convenient."

Neither Ellen nor her nephew looked as if they understood James or his Latin reference. With another quick bow and an embarrassed smile, he took his leave, joining the exodus of demonstrators departing the area. Through his contact with Ellen O'Keeffe, he now imagined he had entered the Boston Irish universe, without the slightest idea of what that meant.

CHAPTER 9

December 1849
Bowdoin Square, Boston, Massachusetts

5 December, 1849

My Dear Miss Gillmer,

The sun is just setting though it is but 4 o'clock, as I write to you to relate the amazing events that have unfolded in the last few days in the City of Boston. You seemed quite favored by our fair shores during your recent visit. Yet I am sure even in Trenton you have read and heard of the horrendous murder of one of our great citizens and benefactors, Dr. George Parkman.

To compound a terrible situation, another Harvard man and Professor, Dr. John Webster, stands accused of this heinous crime. I knew both men, if slightly, and it was an honor to be called as a medical expert, among the first to examine what have proved to be Dr. Parkman's remains.

Shortly I will testify before the Grand Jury as to whether Professor Webster should be indicted for Dr. Parkman's murder. I am most unqualified to render such an opinion, and I will tell the Grand Jury so. My only expertise is as a doctor with a decent understanding of anatomy. I will explain how the various body parts discovered in Webster's chambers and privy constitute part of the whole of which we believe to be George Parkman. There were certain distinguishing characteristics that confirmed my opinions, but deference and sensitivity forbid me from mentioning these to you. Rest easy that I am confident in my assertion that the mutilated victim was indeed, sadly, George Parkman.

Being at the center of these events has made me the object of unwanted curiosity and interest from those around me, including my own family. It is a most distasteful and unpleasant way to become known to general society, and I pray that whatever the Grand Jury decides, we soon will be done with the matter. I prefer accentuating the more positive aspects of our existence here on Earth.

I envy the peaceful life you must inhabit in Trenton, my dear Miss Gill-mer. Your beauty and charm are doubtless apparent to all, thanks to the warm glow of your internal grace. It reflects your deep faith and abiding trust in a Greater Power.

I eagerly await the next opportunity to share our thoughts and desires in person, as we have in our recent correspondence. Letters on paper are but a faint reminder of your indelible presence in my existence.

I remain anxious to hear from you. I live with faith in the present and hope in the future.

> *Your Obedient Servant*
> *James W. Stone, M. D.*

~

James put down his pen and looked at the pages he had just composed. *Was this literary flirtation some kind of prematrimonial web in which he was now enmeshed? Was Jennie Gillmer really the woman he wished to spend his life with?*

The major obstacle to what had long been a plan of James's—to secure the most suitable partner with the greatest resources—seemed to be coming from, of all places, the person of Miss Ellen O'Keeffe.

James could not move his thoughts away from Ellen in any direction. She had captivated him as no one else to date had; yet here he was, making love with a pen to a distant person he barely knew.

Jennie represented something desirable, of course: recognition, connections, wealth, and standing. Lucinda's instincts were unerring in this regard, and James had no doubt Jennie's bona fides would be substantiated. She was exactly the spouse he and his sister had imagined for him, and there seemed to be nothing now in his way to realizing his ideal.

Except Ellen. James often fell asleep imagining a future encounter with Ellen, and how gallant and helpful he would be. These rival sympathies were not in keeping with the growing warmth in his correspondence with Jennie.

He could not continue this way, James knew. *He would need to redouble his efforts with Jennie and move toward a formal engagement. That would aid in disengaging Ellen from his imagination. She barely existed in his actual life.*

James was unsettled by his growing fascination with the redheaded Irishwoman. If he didn't soon secure a future relationship with Jennie, Ellen might end up derailing his plans. James guessed that she had no idea of her power over him, but he did. And he feared it.

~

17 December, 1849

My dear Dr. Stone,

I was very pleased to receive your letter of 5 December. I marvel that it arrived as quickly as it did, just ten days later, given the horrendous state of the post in New Jersey—it is quite a scandal in these parts.

Indeed, we have all been consumed with the details of the Webster-Parkman affair, which is reported upon by every newspaper in the area. We came across your name in the account in the Bergen County Record—it was so exciting to confirm to our friends that we are personally acquainted with the estimable Dr. James Stone, the Expert in Anatomy in the Webster case! You're not deserving of the scrutiny you must endure. How unfair it is to punish you for no reason other than your God-given talent in your profession! I know you will be honest and truthful in your duty to both the State and the Lord.

Life in Trenton is shallow and commonplace compared to your lively affairs in Boston—I'm sure you are consumed by your medical practice, along with exciting developments in the Science of Phonography. Now the added burden of the Grand Jury and even a possible trial for murder! Is there any peace remaining in your life?

Know that you are in my prayers and thoughts daily—in fact, many times a day and night does your visage cross my mind. I, too, yearn for the opportunity to look deeply into your eyes, the window to the soul the Good Lord hath put there, and find the harmony that I hope awaits both of us.

We must be patient until the storm clouds in your life begin to clear. With God's Blessing and Providence this shall happen soon, I pray, and we will see each other again. I await that day with great anticipation.

With my sincerest affections
Jennie Ray Gillmer

~

25 January, 1850

Dearest Jennie,

Your favors are to me as manna from Heaven was to the Israelites. I read your letters again and again, never failing to gain sustenance and nourishment from your words. Your faith in Our Savior gives them special meaning.

The Grand Jury has discharged its duty and delivered an indictment of murder by my former Professor, Dr. John Webster. I remain stunned by the news—I feel as if I have been dealt one heavy blow after another. To see first-hand the results of Dr. Parkman's dismemberment and now to witness Professor Webster accused of it—at times it is too much to bear. Your loving presence in our midst would do much to see me through this time of stress and peril!

I say peril because this trial threatens the very way of life I've worked so hard to achieve. In what regard does the populace hold physicians, when one is snatched off the streets and massacred by another? Both Parkman and Webster shared my alma mater. For the first time in my life I do not hold my head high at the mention of Harvard or its Medical College.

I'm the recipient of disdain and mistrust from my patients and those unfortunates I see at Massachusetts General Hospital, although I still extend the care I always have. The same has befallen physicians as esteemed as Dr. Jacob Bigelow, my mentor who has guided and expanded my career. He too has counseled me to wait out the storm—eventually, affairs will right themselves and the medical profession will reclaim its dignity and public confidence.

You know how greatly I anticipate your next missive, how delighted I will be to receive it, and will read it over and over again.

You fully occupy my thoughts as the holiday season recedes. The greatest gift in my life this past year was your acquaintance, and paying witness to our relationship deepening and flowering, if only by post.

Each time I see the stars in the expanse of the night, I think of my only wish in the New Year, to gaze upon you in your totality, physically present before me. Only then might I rest, your presence the balm and salve for all that is wrong with the world. Would that we could be together to share this beginning of a new and exciting decade. Given that impossibility, my thoughts, prayers and dreams reside with you.

Your Devoted Servant,
James

CHAPTER 10

February 1850
Bowdoin Square, Richmond Street, and Endicott Street, Boston,
Massachusetts

As the Webster trial neared its start, James realized it would afford him a unique opportunity: to employ phonography to record the trial itself, a full and complete record of every spoken word at the most momentous event to occur in recent Boston history. If he could achieve this project, he had no doubt that Jennie would accept his proposal of marriage. Who would not want to be the spouse of the celebrated legal chronicler, Dr. James Winchell Stone?

James had mostly withdrawn from his declining medical practice, focusing more on his new passion of phonography. The most effective means of demonstrating the medium's power, James knew, was to record events of vital interest to the public and then recreate them down to the last syllable uttered. If readers could experience the true words spoken at a trial weeks after its conclusion, and not have to wait a year or more for their approved publication, the citizenry would be better and more quickly informed.

James would need to find a qualified copyist to help with the dictation of his symbols. He could do it himself, of course, but it was tedious work, and made his left hand, his writing hand, cramp terribly.

In conversations with his patients, James had become aware that young women were now training to be "secretaries," gaining instruction in a simplified American version of phonography called stenography, which James considered inferior to Pittman's original system. Still, its popularity was growing.

James had a sudden idea. What if he enlisted Ellen O'Keeffe, whose diction, despite her thick Irish brogue, seemed more than acceptable? He knew Mother Bernadine's nuns at the Sisters of Mercy had successfully taught a generation of Irish girls how to read, write, and master their numbers, and Ellen seemed to be a favorite of the abbess.

James was reluctant to acknowledge his additional motive: the opportunity to become better acquainted with the red-haired Irishwoman. *He could imagine dictating to her while staring into her eyes as she reproduced perfect written versions of his notes. Phonography could serve as the bridge between their differing backgrounds.*

But what was he thinking? He knew he would humiliate himself and his family if he pursued any relationship with an Irish person beyond employment. James could imagine Ellen joining him on an intellectual journey to further the knowledge of mankind, but it would never get beyond the realm of fantasy. If Anson Stone found out he had engaged an Irish girl as anything but a maid, he might even disinherit James from the funds that provided his income.

The person whose reaction James feared the most would be his sister Lucinda. He could imagine her saying, "What eligible young lady would wed a man who had been rooting about in the Irish trough?"

James could only imagine Jennie Gillmer's response to such a circumstance. He had found himself becoming gradually more enamored with Jennie, at least by post. He was contemplating a proposal of marriage in his next letter. What had begun as a performance for Lucinda's benefit had surprisingly evolved into feelings that now seemed genuine.

Yet here he was, ready to hire the most tempting young woman he had ever met. Working with Ellen in the intimate act of personal dictation would be an unwise decision, James knew, *yet he was unwilling to surrender this possibility.* He needed a transcriber, Ellen O'Keeffe was no doubt well suited for the position, and the relationship would be strictly professional. *He reassured himself that he could handle this.*

James decided it was time to visit Mother Bernadine, the abbess who had enlisted both him and Ellen in the fight against cholera at her small abbey, part of St. Mary's Church. She was the logical choice to help him recruit his Irish redhead for a new cause, the flowering of truth from the seeds of tiny symbols.

～

A nun's visage can be forbidding. Mother Bernardine's was more so. The abbess looked ready to call Jesus to task for not working more diligently at his carpentry. Two round spectacles enhanced the oval of her tightly coiffed face. One heavy black eyebrow rose slowly when James, almost stuttering, inquired as to the whereabouts of Miss Ellen O'Keeffe, for whom, he added, he had gainful employment in mind. The question itself disturbed Mother Bernadine. Why was this dandy of a physician seeking a young Irish woman he had complained was impertinent? For that matter, why would James bother to venture into this disreputable section of Boston unless required to do so?

The abbess had good reason to question James's motives. She'd been informed of the rude reception he gave Ellen at Massachusetts General Hospital, as well as the true cause of Ellen's unfortunate decision to call upon Dr. Stone that day.

"If ye should require an interview with Miss O'Keeffe, for what purpose be it, Docter Stone? I'm surprised ye even remember her name, yer encounters with her were so brief . . . and unpleasant, if memory serves."

"I have need of an intelligent and quick-witted girl," James said, trying to alter the direction the interview was taking. He spoke in as businesslike a manner as he could muster. Conversations of this nature were not something he was accustomed to.

James did not share the distrust most Bostonians held for the black-clothed women who proclaimed they were the brides of Christ. He had always gotten on well with the nuns; at least he thought he had, before the abbess had scowled at him when he mentioned Ellen's name.

"Miss O'Keeffe impressed me as such," James continued, hurrying along. "Because my need is immediate, I took the liberty of seeking you out as an intermediary, a go-between of sorts."

James immediately regretted his choice of words. There was an undeniable sexual meaning of the term *go-between* when applied to an unattached man and a single woman. The frown that further cramped Mother Bernadine's face confirmed James's faux pas.

He stammered out an apology and hurriedly told the abbess of his recent work in phonography, a field familiar to Mother Bernadine. The nuns were more current with the advances of modern civilization than many Boston Protestants, James realized. Mother Bernadine knew that if the Irish were to survive—and yes, even thrive—in Boston, it would come from the rare opportunity such as this, offered by an intelligent and well-placed gentleman. The abbess knew she could not deny Ellen this small hope.

"Miss O'Keeffe may visit my medical dispensary at 6 Bowdoin Square, if that be her pleasure, on Monday next," James said, trying to adopt a more cheerful tone. "With your approval, of course," he hastily added.

"If her decision be otherwise, I'll tell ye," said the abbess. "Make sure a proper chaperone is there when ye meet, Docter Stone. This girl has a reputation ye may easily ruin, if ye have not already done so, given the way ye spoke to her at the hospital."

He flushed with embarrassment. "My intentions are nothing but honorable," James said, "and do not extend at all beyond the sphere of phonography. Of this I may assure you."

Mother Bernadine did not look a bit chastened. "I'm sorry if ye take offense at me frank tone, Docter. I did not mean to impugn yer reputation, only what I was told of yer manner in speaking to Miss O'Keeffe. It took great courage fer her to approach ye regarding her dear mother and—"

James was dumbstruck. "Her mother! She described the party in question as a friend, so naturally I assumed it was really herself she was concerned with."

The forbidding frown, whose lines were well established on Mother Bernadine's face, reappeared.

"Of course ye did, Docter," she said through thin, pale lips. "What other conclusion would a Boston docter draw?"

"But Miss O'Keeffe described the woman as a friend, not someone of her mother's generation! How was I to know?"

"What if I told ye Miss O'Keeffe has but nineteen years, and her mother but thirty-four? She never had any rest from delivering babes, the first four in Ireland. Only a boy, the oldest, and little Ellen, survived the potato famine that year, before the family could flee County Cork. Mary O'Keeffe remarried, and once again, one, two, then three more babes. The poor woman never lived through the last of 'em, nor did her wee son, in spite of our prayers to Mother Mary and her blessed Son!"

Mother Bernadine crossed herself and passed her hand before her face, looking down so that James would not see her tears. Even at the height of the cholera epidemic, he had never seen the elderly nun cry. He felt awful. James knew that he could have prescribed some physic that would have induced a stillbirth in Ellen's mother; the risk to him and his practice would have been minimal if none other than the nun knew. Why had he responded so rudely without even fully comprehending Ellen's request?

James made a final attempt at redemption with Mother Bernadine by minimizing the personal nature of his interest in Miss O'Keeffe.

"Mother Superior, if indeed Miss O'Keeffe accepts the position I'm offering and acquits herself competently, which I have every confidence she'll do, I'll be in need of more copyists. These will be girls of your choosing. I understand you have instilled within them a great determination to labor on their own behalf, and you have given them the skills to do so. I would have Miss O'Keeffe train the brightest among them, too."

Mother Bernadine was surprised. This was not an outcome she had expected from Dr. Stone, whom she suspected of romantic rather than pragmatic motives. For a woman who had never had sex, the abbess had a surprising gift for identifying men with little else in mind.

Still, any opportunity for advancement was good for the young women in her charge; they had few prospects other than domestic labor, long days in the Lowell textile mills, or harlotry. She would see how matters progressed with Dr. Stone and Ellen before she made any further commitment.

James chose to interpret her silence as beatific, rather than reluctant, as she waved him toward her door. She hadn't pledged to recruit Ellen for his employ, but she hadn't denied his request, either. *That,* James thought, *was progress.*

~

The note was delivered by an Irish urchin whose nose was running almost as fast as his feet had. He shoved it into Sharon's hand when she answered the door at 6 Bowdoin Square and didn't wait for a gratuity. He knew he was in alien territory, and his impulse was to escape as quickly as possible.

Sharon delivered the folded paper to James, who thanked her. As always, she blushed, and then ran back to ironing the collars for James's shirts.

Examining the missive, he judged it to be written on a cheap variety of paper, judging by its heft and roughness. He opened it to discover a surprisingly well-composed message in the attractive hand of Ellen O'Keeffe. She explained that she was unable to attend him at his dispensary as suggested, and instead requested *his* presence at *her* habitation, 82 Endicott Street in the North End, that evening at seven. Miss O'Keeffe awaited the pleasure of his company, the note concluded.

James's confusion was now thorough. First the abbess had cautioned him for trifling with the reputation of a chaste young Irishwoman. And now Miss O'Keeffe was inviting him to her private chambers? Why would she wish to receive him there, surrounded, James imagined, by her drunken and indolent countrymen? Was her goal to shame him as he had shamed her at the hospital, in front of their judging eyes?

At the appointed hour, James stood freezing outside of O'Malley's, the grog shop on Endicott Street that was doing a steady business. He could

DALE M. POLLOCK

see light in the windows on the second story, above the saloon, where he presumed Ellen and her family resided.

The wind was fierce, and the first flurries of snow fell on James's wool overcoat. As if summoned by his curiosity, Ellen silently appeared at James's side. She wore a heavy red cape over a plain gray dress made from hard-finished wool. At her cuffs and throat were cheap lace frills. A dark bonnet covered most of her unruly red hair.

"I don't reside in a saloon, Doctor Stone," she said as he stared, open-mouthed, at her silent materialization. "I do live atop o' one, but that's no matter to ye, I'm sure.

James had difficulty meeting her gaze, as he had in each of their encounters. He wondered why he could not control his internal emotions in front of this girl. He tried smiling at her but wasn't sure what that smile could mean.

Ellen grew tired of waiting for a response and launched into her explanation for summoning him. "I could nae explain in the brief note I sent. The abbess said we must meet only by yer dispensary, and there must always be another soul present. She be on the lookout for my honor, the Lord help me that she does, for there be nae else to the task."

"I am pleased that she passed on my request," James said.

"I can't abide fretting Mother Bernadine," Ellen continued. "I must trust yer intentions be honorable, Doctor Stone, as I believe they've been since first we met. There were precious few like ye who came to our aid in that terrible time. I saw ye at the cholera hospital many a day, and none other in yer place when ye be absent."

Now it was Ellen's turn to color. The truth was that she had missed Dr. Stone when he was gone, and she had just come perilously close to declaring as much. She pressed on.

"I'm much pleased at the prospect of new and different work aiding ye in yer pursuit o' phonography, Doctor Stone. This be something about which I am most curious."

Then Ellen's tone shifted abruptly to one of resignation. "I suppose I must explain why I brought ye here. It's not me fault, but it is me stepfather's."

Ellen gestured to a man who stood at the corner of the saloon's bar, visible through the open door, his back to them. As if hearing his daughter's dismissive introduction, he turned and grinned mockingly at them before approaching.

James studied the Irishman William Haggerty as he drew near. He appeared to be in his early forties. His patched clothes sagged on his frame, which looked strangely hollowed out. A light-colored silk necktie, the only bright item in his grimy wardrobe, was clumsily formed into a bow below his collar. James's nose wrinkled in disgust; the man stank of new rum.

"Och, ain't ye none other than the good docter, the one wantin' to hire our Ellen, Lord help her, since nae other man wants her," said Haggerty, laughing at what he considered a witty remark. Ellen blanched at his words, making a hopeless gesture with her arm as if to brush them off.

Haggerty gave her a vengeful look as he proffered a hand to James. "William Haggerty at yer service, Yer Honor. Or rather, me daughter at yer service," he said, nodding toward Ellen. His attempt at ribald humor was accompanied by a leer and a wheeze.

James found himself greatly offended by the physical presence of Haggerty. But he knew that standing outside O'Malley's grog house when it was packed with customers was not the safest place to challenge a drunken Irishman.

"He would nae let me do the work, unless ye came here first and spoke to him," Ellen explained in a tired voice. She no longer tried to disguise her embarrassment. "I had nae choice. If ye nae longer desire me services, I'll understand. Little did I think there'd be any person willing to agree to his terms."

She gestured again toward Haggerty, this time with more bitterness than resignation. *Nothing was simple with this girl,* James thought. *He tried to imagine what she already had endured in her short life, if this brute of a stepfather was any example.*

"In the meantime, before ye go making all yer plans, allow me to remind ye of one small matter, if it please yer Lordship," Haggerty said in a thick Irish brogue. James believed the man was exaggerating for dramatic effect.

"Why, first, ye must give the money to me. I manage the money in this house, nae matter who's bringin' it in."

James was astonished by Haggerty's total dismissal of Ellen as an interested party in this conversation. "Miss O'Keeffe?" he exclaimed as he turned to her.

Ellen nodded her head in silent assent, then looked down. It was obvious to James that she wished to be anywhere else. He stewed for a moment, unsure what to do. *Should he pay this man nothing, ignore him, and remunerate*

DALE M. POLLOCK

Ellen directly? What trouble from her drunken stepfather would he visit upon her by following that tack? How would that rest upon James's conscience?

"With your approval, I shall assent to this man's request," James said, speaking only to Ellen, and ignoring Haggerty. "I'll bring him your salary every Saturday afternoon once our work has begun. I trust he will allow you to enjoy the fruits of your own labor."

"Fruit, oh, our Ellen loves her fruit, the banana, the apple, even the royal pineapple, nothing too good fer our Ellen, to be sure, Docter," Haggerty said. "Ye be sure to ask fer Will Haggerty when ye come to see me each and every week at O'Malley's, Docter, they all knows me, as I knows them."

"I'm sure I will have no difficulty locating you in a saloon, Haggerty," said James, concluding their conversation and turning his back on the man.

He faced Ellen and briefly pressed her hand, a moment of flesh-to-flesh contact whose memory he would retain for days. James then strode down Endicott Street toward the old North Church. *He could not bear to look back and see Ellen in service to that monster. He must find a way to free her from domestic bondage, if nothing else.*

~

10 February, 1850

Dear James,

I write you with best wishes for the New Year. I apologize for the tardiness of my response to your warm and confidential letter of 20 January. My affairs became quite hectic between Christmas and New Year's, and my cousin Raven Bradley Jenkins hosted a wonderful ball in Trenton on New Year's Eve that took up much of my time and attention.

I've also hesitated to communicate what I must now tell you, James. There is a man who has resurfaced in my life, someone I supposed had departed my existence forever, as thoroughly as if he had left for another planet. He has returned suddenly and unexpectedly from the Azores, where we were previously acquainted, and first became close friends.

When my guardian was transferred back to Trenton, this gentleman disclosed personal sentiments to me before I departed the Azores. These led me to believe we would become engaged, and marry after he joined me in the United States. All that remained was for this gentleman to meet my father and request my hand.

But this never occurred—my betrothed inexplicably vanished, with no trace of his whereabouts, or any indication whether he was dead or alive. I was forsaken and humiliated. My only consolation was that he never met my father, who was unaware of his and my feelings, and who was thus spared the constant pain I have suffered silently.

To my astonishment and initial dismay, this man has reappeared with a valid explanation that I cannot in good conscience disclose. If I tell you that I am satisfied by its veracity and compelling nature, that should be enough. In no way did I anticipate what would occur next—a renewal of his affections and a corresponding alteration of my formerly rigid attitude toward him.

I feel I can no longer in good conscience continue our intimate correspondence. I know this announcement seems abrupt, perhaps even hasty and ill conceived. I ask for both your forbearance and your forgiveness. The former for the impulsiveness of youth, and the latter for my unthinking and reckless behavior in my letters to you. Please destroy them immediately; they could cause me great shame once I am married.

I do not expect a response to this letter, which naturally you will regard as a perfidious betrayal. I do not disagree with this assessment, nor do I believe I deserve a response from you. My behavior does not merit one.

Please make no attempt to contact me. I ask that you remember that strength is born in the deep silence of long-suffering hearts, and not from joy. I pray that God will forgive me the wrong I have done you.

Always your respectful admirer,
Jennie Ray Gillmer

DALE M. POLLOCK

CHAPTER 11

February 1850
Beacon Hill and Hanover Street, Boston, Massachusetts

It was very cold. Snow fell at a moderate pace on this gray day in mid-February, and sleighs abounded on the snow-packed thoroughfares of Beacon Hill.

James Stone was recovering from a high level of caffeine as he finished his coffee in the warm confines of Cahill's coffee shop. Jennie's words—something like "I cannot in good conscience continue our intimacy"—would not leave his mind. He turned them over again and again, ruing Lucinda's matchmaking efforts and vowing never to follow her lead again.

James had to admit, in all honesty, he was not so much in love with Jennie Gillmer as with some idealized version of her that had motivated his ardent epistolary declarations. When James thought about Jennie's already close-set eyes further narrowing in disapproval at some future misdeed of his, he gave a small shudder of relief that he had avoided this match. A better one would surely present itself.

A scruffy boy burst into the coffee room, trumpeting sales of a just-published pamphlet. James called the boy over, gave him a coin, and began his examination of *The Boston Tragedy!! An Exposé of the Evidence in the Case of the Parkman Murder!*

This inflammatory thirty-two-page diatribe by W. E. Baxter convicted Webster before he was even formally charged.

James had attended the inquest at the invitation of Coroner Pratt, who had summoned him to confirm the initial identification of the remains. He had been surprised a week later to receive a $50 check drawn on the coroner's account for the postmortem examination he had conducted on that tumultuous day last December.

On December 13, 1849, Coroner Pratt had publicly announced in his report that the remains discovered in the Medical College, under and in the rooms occupied by Professor John Webster, were parts of the body of Dr. George Parkman. "Thanks to the work of Doctor James Winchell Stone, they have all been demonstrated to be parts of one and the same person," said Pratt's report. It made James feel proud, as if this one sentence justified his years of medical training.

The coroner's report also stated that Dr. Parkman had come to his death by violence, and it was the coroner's jury's opinion that Professor Webster had killed him with blows from an instrument "to the Jurors unknown."

There it was. A shy professor had been publicly and convincingly charged with murdering Boston's richest man and cutting him to pieces. A Harvard man stood accused of killing another Harvard man for the first time in the college's two-hundred-year history. James Stone, his alma mater, indeed the city of Boston, had never witnessed anything like it.

As James scanned the pages of the pamphlet, he was surprised by the specificity of Baxter's screed. The injuries reportedly inflicted upon Parkman were described in largely accurate detail. There was also much speculation about the murder weapon or weapons employed. One page bore an illustration of a brutish cudgel, along with a sharp and bloodstained knife. James tossed the pamphlet aside and regretted the waste of a dime on these senseless speculations.

He returned to the *Boston Herald*. Its editorial exclaimed: "We think that if Professor Webster be found guilty of killing Doctor Parkman, and we do not say he will, the gibbet must prove the legal end."

Yet Webster seemed in no particular hurry to engage an attorney. James, like the Boston legal community, knew the most qualified candidates to be Rufus Choate and Daniel Webster. The latter, although legendary as defense counsel, served in Washington as the senior senator from Massachusetts and had neither the time nor the inclination for the job. Webster had already politely declined a retainer of $2,000 offered him by the professor's supporters.

Choate was the popular choice, a man of whom James had heard it said: "He was never at a loss for *the* word." A tall Yankee with a long, angular face made more so by thick side-whiskers that crept below his jaw, Choate was considered one of the best lawyers in the United States. James had heard that Choate had offered Webster his services on one condition: that Webster plead guilty and allow his counsel to present an insanity defense that would save him from the hangman's noose.

Upon hearing this, the offended Webster was said to have abruptly ended Mr. Choate's jailhouse interview. He was innocent, Webster insisted, and would not plead otherwise. Choate had bowed and excused himself, the story went. Under the circumstances, he had said, he could not conduct the defense.

This rupture was well reported and discussed avidly wherever gentlemen gathered. James spent an animated supper with Lucinda and his brothers in which opinions and conclusions about the supposed event were much bantered about.

Jerome repeated a macabre joke he had heard Choate tell at Parker House, in which Parkman ventured into Webster's laboratory unannounced and was seized with a violent fit of ague, shaking himself all to pieces, one part of his body going here and another there, some down the privy and others into the furnace. James, who had seen the actual evidence, could not enjoy the humor. All else present laughed.

A little-known attorney named Edward Dexter Sohier became the sole lawyer willing to take up Webster's defense. He was joined on January 21, 1850, by Judge Pliny Merrick, a former member of the state senate and a judge of the Lower Court of Common Pleas. Merrick presented a benign appearance: a hatchet-shaped face, bushy side-whiskers, and thin spectacles. James had heard that Merrick's reluctance to decline an invitation was the best explanation for his unexpected participation in Webster's defense.

James saw little benefit for any attorney brave enough to defend John Webster. If the prisoner were acquitted, there would be charges of favoritism and privilege; a Harvard degree would be equivalent to a license to murder. If convicted, Webster and his defense would be faulted for an inadequate response to the mounds of circumstantial evidence, which was all the prosecution possessed.

James made sure to arrive at the massive, Greek Revival-style courthouse early on the morning of Friday, January 25, when the grand jury handed down its indictment, "charging John W. Webster with the murder of George Parkman, in the City of Boston on the twenty third day of November A.D. eighteen hundred and forty-nine."

Appearing at the courthouse for the first time together, Judge Merrick and Mr. Sohier were recognized as counsel representing Webster. They entered a plea of not guilty on his behalf. The trial would commence Tuesday, March 19, 1850. It would decide whether Professor John White Webster would live or die.

~

Frederick Ainsworth studied James Stone as they sipped liqueur at Hamilton House on Hanover Street. Rarely had he seen his friend this animated. James was no longer the shy, socially awkward classmate of years past. This was a man on fire.

"I tell you, I can change the entire manner in which courtroom trials are recorded. The public will have access to every word uttered by counsel, the witnesses, the defendant, even the judges!"

"Enough, James!" Ainsworth said in mock surrender. "I have no doubt your project will be an unadulterated success. May we now please discuss something else?"

"Is there any reason you can suggest for me not to proceed with my report?" James asked, holding up a hand to indicate this would be his last mention of the subject. "Do you believe the court will object and make my work impossible?"

"They'd have no right," said Ainsworth. "If you're a member of the public in the courtroom, and your new system allows you to translate the testimony you hear into these symbols you describe, who's to stop you? But remember, James: judges and counsel are in the habit of rewriting their arguments, they will be loath to give up that ability. Anyone can sound wiser and more judicious if given the opportunity to edit and revise their pronouncements."

"Aren't truth and accuracy more vital to our democracy than revised legal opinions, with all the life drained out of them? If a judge or jury wrongly condemns an innocent man, phonography will identify the victim and the crime committed against him. Isn't that of great benefit to society?"

"I caution you only that these court officials are proprietary when it comes to their traditions," Ainsworth said. "You won't change them or their practices easily."

James waved off Ainsworth's analysis; he couldn't be bothered, so great was this opportunity. "I agree there is risk, and I am willing to undertake it for the greater dissemination of phonography. I'm far along in my plans and ready to begin recording my report when the trial commences."

"How will you accomplish this task? It seems Herculean; you'll be working day and night if you hope to finish soon after the end of the trial."

James leaned forward to share his response with Ainsworth privately. "I've found the most talented young woman: an Irish girl, of all things. She has excellent handwriting and transcribes my notes effortlessly. She's called Miss Ellen O'Keeffe. It's as if she were designed for this work!"

Ainsworth again contemplated his manic companion and smiled suggestively. "Is it only her transcription skills that please you, James? Do I detect a special enthusiasm for Miss O'Keeffe?"

James flushed and shook his head. "No, no, it's just that our association grew out of a chance encounter during the Asian cholera epidemic last year. Her spirit impressed me, and now I find that she's perfectly suited for the task at hand."

Ainsworth's smile of complicit understanding did not waver. Instead, it made James hurry his words.

"Miss O'Keeffe also has found other girls who are literate, with good penmanship and work habits, so the transcription can take place in shifts, or as long as my voice holds out," he added.

Ainsworth was impressed by the effort James was putting into his enterprise.

"I'm moved by your passion for your undertaking, and I wish you only the best fortune," he said. "Really, James, I do. If I may be of assistance, don't hesitate to ask. I remain at your service."

CHAPTER 12

February 1850
Leverett Street, Endicott Street, Richmond Street, and Faneuil Hall Square,
Boston, Massachusetts

James Stone stood at the door of the Leverett Street Gaol, waiting for the pass that would gain him entry. Three to four inches of snow had fallen the night before; the streets were in poor condition on this late February day. Most Bostonians were keeping to their houses, but James had carefully contemplated his plan to interview John Webster in his jail cell. Webster was permitted visitors, but it was said that Mrs. Webster and her daughters had been allowed to see him on only two occasions since the night of his arrest.

James had journeyed to Cambridge shortly after the professor's arrest to pay his respects to the Webster household and to ascertain its status, which seemed perilous. No income was available to the family after Harvard halted its payments of Webster's yearly stipend. Friends of Webster's had initiated a relief fund. James had contributed the large sum of five dollars, which occasioned a note of appreciation from Mrs. Webster. His visit to the Webster family residence had a further result: he was contacted by Marshal Tukey, who told him that Webster had agreed to an audience with him.

James's throbbing stomach echoed his beating heart as he walked across the spacious yard that separated the two areas of the jail. A jailer met him, leading him into a gray granite building and then down a hallway reserved exclusively for prisoners on trial for their lives. James was deposited before a grated door that left Professor Webster exposed to the observation and inspection of any who passed by his cell, day or night.

Webster looked shorter and thicker than James remembered. He wore his spectacles and a dark suit, cravat, and starched collar, every bit the distinguished professor of chemistry.

The keeper came over and unlocked the professor's cell, which was filled with religious volumes, including a large and well-worn Bible. James saw copies of the *Boston Advertiser*, the *Boston Courier*, and the *Boston Herald* on the prisoner's bed. Foot mats offered some relief from the drafts that emanated from the cold stone floor. To one side was a small truckle bed, its straw mattress neatly made with sheets and a blanket. On a wobbly wooden table, surrounded by correspondence, sat the remnants of Webster's lunch, which James assumed came from nearby Pearl Street House. There were advantages Webster enjoyed due to his notorious celebrity; few other prisoners facing capital punishment were allowed such privileges.

Webster stood up to greet James warmly. He put his arm around the younger man and guided him to the cell's lone cane chair. The professor sat on the bed. He looked to be in good health, calm and self-possessed. James was surprised by how contented the defendant seemed in his confinement.

As if anticipating this reaction, Webster spoke first. "Yes, Doctor Stone, I do not perish in this horrid place. I have come to terms with my situation, although I shall leave here and never look back once my innocence is proven in court."

Webster gestured to the mass of papers next to the lightly sampled luncheon. "I finally possess the time to catch up on my epistolary correspondence with friends across the world. I have heard from so many of them."

These last words were uttered with a twinkle in his eye that surprised James. *Did this man have no idea what awaited him? Was he insensible to the mass hysteria his actions had provoked?*

"I'm pleased to see you so well, Professor Webster," James said, gaining control of his own thoughts. "I trust the treatment you receive here is fair and just. I speak for many when I say how concerned we've been for your well-being."

"The jailers have been most solicitous of my welfare," said Webster. "I'm free to meet with whomever I choose, and I can converse freely and without reserve in the privacy of this small chamber." Webster looked around the tiny enclosure, a half smile on his lips. "I am glad you came, James. I fondly recall you as a student."

"As I do you, Professor."

James was being untruthful, to avoid offending the man. Webster had been the most stultifying of his teachers at the Medical College. But the professor was not finished praising his young visitor.

"My wife and daughters informed me of your compassionate visit, and your contribution to the funds that help maintain my household. I am grateful for these kindnesses on my behalf."

For the first time since James arrived, the prisoner looked around furtively.

"I also must express my profound gratitude for your quick response on the night that I was taken into custody. You prevented an action that might have devastated my family."

James had never expected that Webster would express gratitude for preventing his suicide. In effect, Webster was thanking him for keeping him alive so that he might one day be executed. It seemed the professor was not quite done with his confession.

"I was a coward on that occasion. I feel only shame for my actions. I thank you especially for never sharing the details of that horrible night. It would be too much for Mrs. Webster and my daughters."

"You exaggerate my role, Professor," James said, unclear how to respond. "But I'm glad we sit here together. I hope to offer my assistance to you in a different matter. I'm sure you are familiar with phonography, the science of improved communication."

Webster shook his head in confusion. He had no idea what James was speaking about.

"Professor Webster," James began again, "I have a proposition for you. I have the experience and skill to render a full, unbiased account of your trial. I seek your permission to make a report of the entire proceedings employing phonography. I will take down each day's testimony as uttered, using phonographic notation that can equal the speed of human speech. A full and complete transcript of the trial will be published shortly after its conclusion. In this manner, there will be no question as to the veracity demonstrated by each and every witness, yourself included, of course."

Webster stared at James as if he were a lunatic. He either did not comprehend what was being asked of him or was so offended that he was liable to end the interview as abruptly as he had Rufus Choate's. James hurried on.

"A phonographic report of your trial will offer the public complete and uncensored access to your argument of innocence, Professor. There is no better way to spread the truth of your position."

Bringing the conversation back to Webster had been a wise tactic. He at last displayed some comprehension of James's proposition. He firmly nodded in agreement with what his visitor had just said.

"Oh yes, by all means, do what you deem necessary to demonstrate the mistakes inherent in these charges. I have assembled all the proofs needed to clear my name. If you think these may be successfully broadcast via your phono . . ." Webster stumbled on the unfamiliar word, and then abandoned it.

"James, there is one thing," Webster said, his voice trailing off. James remembered the same tone from the Professor's classroom, when Webster would beg his students to turn their assignments in on time.

"I know you will be called upon as a medical witness to identify the body parts that scoundrel Littlefield inserted into my privy by the most devious of means. Those do not and never have belonged to George Parkman, whose remains, no doubt, are rotting in some alley or ditch. This is all a plot by Ephraim Littlefield to cover up his illegal activities at the Medical College. You'll learn all this at the trial, of course, when I present my defense."

James was not surprised that Littlefield should be Webster's scapegoat. The accused couldn't ignore all the evidence pointing to his guilt, but he could attribute some of it to an attempt by the janitor to frame his employer. James wondered, *Was Webster about to ask him to lie at the trial, to pretend it was not George Parkman who had been hacked apart in Webster's chambers at the Medical College?*

"I appreciate your position, Professor. I'll do no more or less than my duty as a physician and a citizen in the coming days. Please always know that my best wishes and thoughts are with you and your family in the difficult times ahead."

Webster put a hand to his face and wiped away a tear.

"I know, my boy, I know. Don't concern yourself with me; the dear Lord and his divine son watch over all that transpires. Go and communicate how strong my faith remains. Nothing shall trample the soul of John Webster."

James rose to leave but was stayed at the door by a final comment from Webster.

"Remember, James," the professor said, his face suddenly gray and tired from the strain of maintaining such a determinedly upbeat countenance. "If this is allowed to happen to me, it can happen to anyone."

~

Ellen waited for the rest of the young women to walk through the door to the small brick building on Richmond Street that housed the Sisters of Mercy abbey. Mother Bernadine was generous in allowing her the use of the parlor for this meeting.

Ellen had gone throughout Fort Hill and the North End to find suitable young women between the ages of sixteen and eighteen. Potential recruits were domestics in private homes, boarding houses, or hotels, and those who labored at home caring for siblings, nieces, nephews, even grandchildren. Every Irish girl filing into the abbey had been educated under the watchful eye of the abbess and her nuns in scripture, reading, writing, and simple mathematics.

Moira Donoghue was the last to rush in, five full minutes after the time specified. Ellen glared at her. Tardiness would not do, her look made clear. Moira hastily took a seat on one of the straight-backed chairs. Ellen strode to the middle of the room and addressed the seven young women assembled before her.

"Thank ye for comin', and as for most of ye, arrivin' by the clock," she said, sending another glare Moira's way, making the poor girl squirm. "Comin' on time is a requirement for this position. Every day, when the business of the court be over, our labors are just beginnin'. First let me see that all who I asked here are indeed here."

As Ellen read her name, each girl briefly rose from her seat and looked around: Aileen Brennan, Maeve Byrne, Fiona Duinn, Oona Gallagher, Cathleen McCarthy, Mary O'Neill, and the tardy Moira Donoghue. All were present and accounted for.

"Doctor Stone and I will be choosin' ye for a most important duty," Ellen said. "Ye all know of the horrible murder of Doctor George Parkman and the arrest of Professor John Webster for committin' the crime."

"Docter Parkman was our landlord!" piped up Oona, a slight girl of seventeen who spoke in a rush of words with a heavy Kerry accent. "I once gave Docter P the rent! A tall, skinny man he was, I shall never forget how he bowed after takin' the rent from me!"

"Thank ye, Oona, that'll be enough now," Ellen said, guiding the conversation back to its intended purpose. "Now, the trial of Doctor Webster for murder, it'll begin in a fortnight. Each of ye has been vouchsafed by the blessed abbess herself for bein' quick of thought and of hand. Ye'll need that to serve as copyists for the report that will be made by Doctor Stone at the Webster trial."

Ellen looked around at seven rapt faces before continuing.

"Each evenin' we'll be gatherin' at 87 Court Street, on the second floor, where Doctor Stone has a room for all of us to work in. He'll be bringin' the day's testimony, and ye will be writin' it down as he reads it out loud. Ye all be working in shifts, one after t'other, so no one's writin' hand should cramp up too bad."

"Me, I've never had to write down anything a person might say," worried Mary O'Neill, seated in the corner of the parlor. "Will he speak slowly? What if we nae keep up?"

Ellen gave a confident smile to reassure the girls.

"I've already done this, taken down words spoke by Doctor Stone, and I can tell ye sure it's nothin' too difficult. Doctor Stone speaks slowly when he's reading his notes. And we'll be doin' this work for as long as the trial lasts, and maybe several weeks more until all the dictatin' be done."

Ellen looked around the room, trying to gaze into each young woman's eyes, trying to wake up people who had never been inspired in their lives.

"Workin' with Doctor Stone has been the grandest experience of me life," she said, radiating the pleasure she had felt during the time she and James were preparing the transcription room. "It's like goin' beyond myself. I wrote down what our great Senator Daniel Webster spoke, as if the words went straight from his own mouth to me pen and paper. This is something all ye can do, trust me."

"What will we be paid? And when?" asked husky-voiced Fiona, who had a great horse-like face and a mane of black hair flowing down her back.

"Very well now," said Ellen. "Ye'll be paid two dollars for each week of work. We'll be doin' this five days each week after court is done, and a half day on Saturdays. It'll be all day long when the trial is over until we finish."

Ellen did another survey of her charges, making clear her expectations for each of them. "I expect ye to be prompt in arrivin', and alert in yer work. Ye'll come in proper clothing, no dirty aprons or filthy coats, and ye'll keep mum about all ye hear and learn. Yer work'll be handed to me each evening, and that will be the last ye'll see of it. Nothing, and I mean absolutely nothing, is to leave our workroom. Am I being clear enough?"

James had insisted on confidentiality. He could not have the Irish girls reporting back to their beaux and their families everything that was said in court and inflaming the populace. The resulting scandal would terminate his experiment in short order.

Mary raised her hand with another question. "Who will be getting our pay, us or our fathers?"

There was an audible murmur from the other girls, while Ellen remained silent. This was a salient issue for these young women, including her. They could work more than sixty hours a week and watch their father, uncle, or brother drink up their wages in a single night of carousing. Ellen had experienced the same with her stepfather.

She had stood mutely by while Bill Haggerty demanded Dr. Stone pay her wages directly to him. If Ellen couldn't stand up for her right to the fruits of her labor, how could she expect these young women to act differently?

"I will be givin' the money to each of ye, following our half day on Saturday," Ellen said.

She would have to speak to Dr. Stone and ask him to ignore her stepfather and his instructions, and to pay her wages directly to her. Ellen knew that she was capable of managing her own affairs. Persuading William Haggerty of this would be something else altogether. He would not brook her true intentions if he came to know them.

Other questions now came forward.

"Do we work for ye, or fer Docter Stone?" one voice chirped.

"What about our supplies?" said a voice from another corner of the room.

Ellen pulled up a chair and joined the ladies in a semicircle. It would be a long evening.

~

James hurried through Boston Common to reach Faneuil Hall. He was late for the Sixteenth Annual Anti-Slavery Fair, where he was to be joined by Ellen O'Keeffe. This year the featured orator was Wendell Phillips, a Bostonian steeped in the reform spirit of the age. In addition to the immediate liberation of all slaves, Phillips advocated for full political rights for women, a radical position that James privately embraced. He was excited to share his views and political opinions, from women's suffrage to the slavery question, with Ellen, the first opportunity for them to have any sort of meaningful conversation.

At the entrance to Faneuil Hall, James's eyes alighted upon her, dressed in a plain brown frock, waiting patiently for him apart from the crowd. He stood still for a moment, savoring the opportunity to study her, unnoticed. *Despite her lowly status in Boston society, Ellen possessed an innate grace, manifest in the way she stood and moved,* he thought. He found this wounded him in an unexpected way. *He would never have this self-assurance, this place in nature that Ellen effortlessly occupied.*

She caught sight of him and waved a gloved hand, her face aglow with the pleasure of seeing him. James waved back, displaying the two tickets Henry had purchased for him. The price had been a thorough questioning concerning the identity of James's mysterious companion. James would not yield any information. He saw no need for anyone in his family to know about Ellen or her influence upon him.

"I feared ye were delayed by some medical matter," she said as James reached her. "Or somethin' to do with the Webster affair?" Ellen looked searchingly at him.

James was not yet prepared to share the bizarre conversation he had held with Professor Webster the previous day. "Henry could not find the tickets, and I was forced to wait while he went through every music case he could have put them in. They were, of course, in his pocket."

Ellen bestowed on James one of her easy, dazzling smiles. "I'm glad yer here, but I fear Mister Phillips will be startin' his speech. We ought to hurry to our seats!"

As they entered Faneuil Hall, they heard Phillips, already on stage, declaim in a bold, grand voice: "I am a teetotaler and a foe of capital punishment. I believe in animal magnetism and phrenology. I advocate letting women vote and hold office. But my main business, and our main business, must be the abolition of slavery. I hold that the world is wrong side up, and I maintain the propriety of turning it upside down!"

His words evoked waves of cheers from his partisan audience. James and Ellen took their seats and listened to Phillips explain how modern machinery was revolutionizing every industry, including the manufacture of cotton. Soon there would be machines to pick cotton, another development obviating the need for slaves. If America were to grow ever greater and stronger, Phillips asserted, it must shed the moral burden of slavery.

"We must further the cause of slave emancipation in every way available to us!" Phillips exhorted the crowd. "We must be ceaseless in our endeavor, for it is a right and just cause!"

James regarded Ellen, whose face was flushed with excitement as she applauded Phillips's inspiring words. James thought she had never looked more beautiful. Perhaps he should revisit his decision to take a public stance on the slavery issue. In his estimation, the abolitionists were overly self-righteous, and the Unionists too motivated by economic self-interest, better described as greed. As Phillips declaimed against slavery's brutal practice, James was aware of Ellen's growing fervor for the speaker's sentiments. Soon he found himself infected with the same passion as his companion's.

"I will not retreat one inch!" Phillips shouted from the stage. "I will be heard!"

The crowd of Black and white Bostonians stood and cheered, waving handkerchiefs and hats. James and Ellen both leapt to their feet spontaneously. He found the adrenaline animating the crowd to be irresistible.

Ellen squeezed his arm in response to the speaker's passion. Phillips's patrician features shone with sweat in the torchlight that surrounded the stage. James was unsure of exactly what was so stimulating: the excitement of the moment, or his physical proximity to this animated and attractive woman?

Ellen was not insensitive to the frequent glances that James bestowed upon her. They stimulated—and frightened—her. Always before her was the example of her dead mother, a woman whose sole purpose in life had been to produce babies, one after another, until the unending task killed her. Ellen had promised herself such a fate was not hers. Avoiding the company of men made her vow's accomplishment all the easier.

It was difficult to resist the gravitational pull that Dr. Stone exerted upon her. He was not conventionally handsome, not in possession of the rough good looks of Irish boys who had pursued her more times than she cared to remember. But there was something honest and forthright in James's visage. She could detect in his reveries an inner purpose she longed to share.

The idea of anything beyond the already unusual professional relationship they enjoyed had always been out of the question. Ellen innately understood this. Yet she could not stop thinking about James Stone, his slender fingers, and how they might feel interlaced with her own.

Surprising her, James took Ellen's gloved hand in his bare one. She stared straight ahead at the retreating back of Wendell Phillips as he left the stage to rapturous applause, feeling the warmth of James's grip through her cotton glove. She wasn't sure whether it manifested passion for the cause, or for her. They should be applauding, as everyone else was. But they weren't. They were just standing there, holding hands.

CHAPTER 13

March 1850
Washington Street and North Grove Street, Boston, Massachusetts

James Stone and Ellen O'Keeffe walked together down crowded Washington Street to the offices of Phillips, Sampson and Company, a publisher of historical works, including Gibbons's *Decline and Fall of the Roman and Empire*. James's brother-in-law Jacob Dresser was a cousin of Moses Dresser Phillips, a principal in the firm, and Jacob had helped effect this meeting.

The criminal proceedings in the Webster trial were scheduled to begin on March 19, in a week's time. James had taken to including Ellen in all matters concerning his report. Her presence helped him stay focused on the task at hand, which he considered the greatest undertaking of his life.

James had secured a room at 87 Court Street, above Copland's Confectioner's shop, where he, Ellen, and the female copyists could work. He had purchased reams of paper, boxes of steel nib pens and holders, ink, chairs, and tables. It was intended that the young women would bring their own supper to enjoy midway through the evening, when everyone would need a respite from the endless dictation.

By this time, James's family was cognizant of Ellen's existence, as far as his phonographic report was concerned. They had proven both accepting and resistant, as expected. Henry was drawn immediately to Ellen's intelligence and wit, and her love of music. The opposing reaction, unsurprisingly, was Lucinda's. She was appalled to see her brother openly consort with a single Irish woman. Who would believe the relationship was anything but improper, she demanded of James? This open liaison was detrimental, if not fatal, to James's matrimonial prospects, Lucinda scolded. The fact that his relationship with Ellen O'Keeffe was purely professional and completely chaste, as James insisted, was immaterial. If he had any hope of renewing Jennie Gillmer's affections, the gossip about James's "Irish whore" would put an end to it, Lucinda assured him. He ignored her.

Upon arriving at the publisher's offices, James and Ellen were greeted by an older male clerk who directed them into the study of Moses Phillips, a young, heavyset man in his midthirties with enormous black sidewhiskers. His dark, curly hair was combed straight back in a nimbus around his head, and with his black suit and neatly tied black cravat, he could have been an undertaker rather than a publisher.

"My cousin Jacob has spoken highly of you, Doctor Stone," Phillips said, standing next to his desk chair. He found himself unable to stop staring at the attractive Irishwoman accompanying James. "But he failed to make any mention of this lovely creature who accompanies you. He must have wanted to keep her existence a secret to himself."

"I apologize, Mister Phillips, allow me to introduce my business associate, Miss O'Keeffe," James said, with no embarrassment.

He understood that each man he encountered when accompanied by Ellen would immediately assume a sexual relationship between the two. Since he had done nothing improper beyond taking Ellen's hand at the abolitionist rally, James's guileless nature was an aid to him. He was believable in having nothing to hide.

James thought it best to launch immediately into his proposal. "As you know, Mister Phillips, public interest in the Webster-Parkman affair is at its height. This tragedy has captured the attention of the entire community, nay, the entire world, and will only increase when the trial begins."

"I wholeheartedly agree with you, Doctor Stone," Phillips responded, startling James with his quick assent. "How do you propose we best take advantage of this interest?"

"By publishing an accurate and timely version of this vital event," James said. "I can produce a thorough phonographic report of all testimony and evidence presented at the trial. There will be no account more accurate, nor any as speedily available to the public. My report can be prepared for delivery to you within two weeks of the trial's conclusion."

"What of the newspapermen from all over the country, and the rest of the world, who will cover the proceedings? They will file their reports immediately, leaving you with but a tired repetition of what has already been communicated."

"You do not understand the power of phonography, sir," James said, with the fervor of the religious convert. "This practice has evolved over centuries to meet a basic requirement: the practical yet profound demand to capture what people actually say, as they say it. Few have yet employed this system to record the legal proceedings of an entire trial, yet alone the most important trial of our lifetime. The press may communicate their *sense* of what is said and heard, but only my report will present the *reality* of what takes place in the courtroom."

"How is it possible for one man to do so much transcribing on a daily basis? Are you not also expected to be a witness, Doctor Stone? How will you take down your own testimony when you occupy the witness stand?"

"Through my work with phonography, I have become acquainted with Mister John French of the *Boston Herald*, who will also be present in court daily. He has graciously agreed to use his system of notation to record my testimony, which will be brief."

Phillips nodded. He knew John French, and if the veteran newspaper man took phonography seriously, he should also.

Feeling that he had succeeded in capturing Phillips's interest, James's voice rose as his sales pitch concluded. "As for the task of transcription, I've engaged several literate young women who will take down my dictation in shifts. I don't deny it will be a physical challenge, but it is one I believe to be worth the reward."

"Are you sure you possess the stamina to take on this prodigious task, Doctor Stone? I've heard that Thomas Lloyd, the founder of Lloyd's Register, attempted to use the phonographic method to record a session of Congress. The venture harmed his health; he was forced to abandon it. How will you manage this challenge?"

"I have put my medical practice in temporary abeyance for the duration of the trial and a period following," James said. He had anticipated these questions. "Thanks to the assistance of Miss O'Keeffe, we have assembled a group of well-trained copyists. When the day's proceedings in court are concluded, I will repair to a hired room where I will read my phonographic notes aloud to them, and they will take down every word I utter. Miss O'Keeffe will gather these as the record of the trial.

"If I tire, Miss O'Keeffe will proceed, as she can read my phonographic symbols as well as I. It is my goal to maintain good health and high spirits throughout the trial. Mister Phillips, imagine if we could have heard the parables and sermons of Jesus as he actually spoke them. Or Socrates's lectures, Cicero's orations, Homer's *Odyssey*, as they were orally delivered."

Phillips said, "Will all the witnesses, counselors, and justices have the opportunity to review their remarks, their testimony and their judgments, and make the necessary revisions? That is how these legal cases have been previously published."

"I fear not, Mister Phillips. Such a process would eliminate a most advantageous aspect of my proposal—your ability to publish a full account of the trial, in every detail, just two weeks after its conclusion."

Phillips's enthusiasm seemed to ebb. He looked unsure.

"I must admit, Doctor Stone, I'm troubled by the lack of opportunity your plan provides for review by the principals, particularly Chief Justice Shaw and his colleagues on the bench of the highest court in our state. Your report must be as precise as you promise, for it will function with the same power as the legal record. You must be sure above all that it is accurate."

"More accurate than what?" James said. "The official court record consists of whatever counsel and the judges wish they had said. An opinion expressed aloud in the courtroom vanishes as if it had never been uttered. Phonography as I employ it will end this practice of rewriting legal history."

Phillips thought for a long moment, his arms crossed over his substantial girth. He finally spoke.

"I am intrigued and interested, Doctor Stone. I can see the merits of Phillips, Sampson engaging with you on such a project. I need to discuss it with my partner, Mister Sampson. Could I impose upon you and Miss O'Keeffe to return in three days' time, at which point I hope we may discuss a publishing agreement?"

For the first time that morning, James smiled, the biggest of his smiles Ellen had seen. Phillips was correct. James's enthusiasm for his project was infectious. He stood up, and Ellen followed.

"I look forward to our next meeting, Mister Phillips. If there are further questions you or Mister Sampson has concerning my proposal, I am, of course, at your disposal. Miss O'Keeffe and I will see you on Friday this week."

Ellen looked gratefully at James for his inclusion of her as his equal. It was one of the many kindnesses he had shown her during their collaboration. They said their goodbyes to Phillips and were ushered out by the clerk. They walked out onto sunny Washington Street in a much better frame of mind than when they had walked in.

~

It had been weeks since James had first visited the Medical College at Dr. Lewis's request. He possessed vivid memories of that tumultuous evening last November. It now seemed like a malevolent dream. In that one night, he had identified pieces of flesh hanging in a privy, stopped a man from poisoning himself, and witnessed a possible murderer confronted with his alleged crime.

To satisfy his own curiosity, and in anticipation of what he might hear at the trial, James decided to visit Ephraim Littlefield. He knew from his time as a student that in return for his custodial work at the Medical College, Littlefield received a salary and a small apartment for himself and his wife, in the building adjacent to the storeroom and the dissecting laboratory. Littlefield had been employed there for over a decade, the first three years of which were at the Medical College's old location on Mason Street. He was a fixture at the college by the time James arrived in 1844.

As a student, James had heard rumors of Littlefield's connections to the shadowy world of grave robbing. While not a resurrectionist—a man who despoiled cemeteries of their most recent residents—Littlefield was well known for his ability to obtain corpses. A whole cadaver went for $25, while a severed head cost $5. These were useful specimens to practice on in preparation for the difficult physiology exams conducted by Dr. Holmes.

Littlefield also obtained requested body parts for the faculty to use in their lectures. On several occasions he had commandeered a supply of blood for Dr. Webster's chemistry demonstrations. Littlefield's facility in obtaining the dead and their various parts had become infamous. Finally, Professor Webster and other faculty had complained to Dr. Holmes that the janitor had fashioned an inappropriate and profitable business out of a sordid necessity.

Holmes threatened Littlefield with losing his job if his mortuary practices continued beyond what was required for the uses of the Medical College faculty. It was said that the usually placid Holmes actually lost his temper in his interview with the janitor and promised that Littlefield and his family would be put out in the street if he received another negative report.

James shuddered as he remembered the quality of the corpses and heads that Littlefield had sold to the students before exams—specimens rejected by the faculty as useless. There were tales of corpses shipped to Littlefield from the graveyards of New York City, men and women's bodies shoved into barrels of pickling juice and unpacked like side meat.

Littlefield was also tasked with sewing up the mutilated specimens after lectures by Dr. Holmes and other faculty members. He had seen hundreds of bodies cut up for postmortem examinations, James thought. He might even be considered an expert on the new practice of autopsy.

Arriving at the squat Medical College building, James went around to the side where Littlefield's apartment was located. Caroline Littlefield, a small, florid-faced woman mopping the worn stone floors of the couple's cottage, greeted him through the open door.

"Ephraim," she called out with a bigger voice than James expected to emerge from such a small frame, "Doctor James Stone has come to see you." Littlefield ascended from the cellar, where he had been sharpening dissection tools. He greeted James with a frown, not expecting the visitor and wary of his purpose.

"Is that you, Doctor Stone?" Littlefield asked, as he wiped dirt from his hands. "This is a surprise. I haven't seen you since that terrible night."

"I'm sorry if I disturb you, Mister Littlefield," said James, careful to address the janitor properly this time. "I come on no formal mission, bearing only a desire to speak with you about this cursed murder, and the trial that will soon decide who is at fault."

Littlefield was irritated by James's presence, his visitor could tell, but the janitor kept his voice calm and low.

"Any information I could provide I've willingly done so, at the askin' of Marshal Tukey and Doctors Holmes and Bigelow," he said, his tone injured. "I've nothin' to hide, Doctor Stone. Let me also remind ye that I've given up any claim to the reward offered by Mister Shaw and the Parkman family. I stated that to Mister Tukey himself, and he took that information to Mister Shaw himself. There can be no question of me profiting from this tragedy."

"Calm yourself, Mister Littlefield," James said with alacrity. "I'm not here to question your veracity. I am curious about certain matters that involve Professor Webster, whose actions before and after the disappearance of Doctor Parkman I find to be strange and mysterious."

Littlefield looked coldly at James. "What mysteries would those be, Doctor, and what have they to do with me? Have I not revealed all I know?"

"Is it true, Littlefield, that Professor Webster presented you with a turkey for your Thanksgiving dinner? Why would he do such a thing?"

"I've no more idea than you, Doctor Stone," Littlefield said. "On the Thursday before Thanksgiving, Professor Webster rang for me, and I went up the stairs to his rooms. He was reading a paper, and out of the blue, asked me if I had a turkey for Thanksgiving. I told him no. Then he gave me an order for one on Mister Foster."

"The shop next door to the Howard Athenaeum?" James asked, surprised. It was one of the most expensive food stores in Boston.

"The very one," Littlefield replied. "I was quite amazed because the professor never give me nothing before."

Mrs. Littlefield inserted herself into the conversation. "Give us something? We were fortunate if he gave us the time of day. He was the rudest man to my poor husband, never let him rest for a minute, always get this, bring me that, light my fire, put out my fire."

James ignored her and continued his cross-examination in as conversational a tone as he could muster. "What of Doctor Parkman? How often would you see him at the Medical College?"

Littlefield's face broke into a morbid smile. "Oh, Doctor Parkman, now there was a wonderful man. I don't care what people say, Doctor Parkman and me went back twenty years. He obtained for me my position, helped my family move down to Boston from New Hampshire. Doctor Parkman was a great man, no doubt of that."

"And you possess no doubts as to who killed him, in your estimation?"

"I am neither judge nor jury. As someone who lives and works in this college, I knows its goings-on as well as any. What Professor Webster was doing at the time Doctor Parkman disappeared were the actions of a guilty man. I believe this be the truth, and I'll so swear at his trial."

James gave Littlefield a long and measured look. He now understood how partial Littlefield had been to Parkman, and how unkindly he and his wife viewed Webster. James considered bringing up the scandal over Littlefield's wholesale selling of body parts, but he did not wish to further irritate the janitor, who was clearly losing his patience with their interview.

"One more thing, Mister Littlefield. Your rooms are but a few feet from where the remains were discovered, yet you heard nothing? No struggle, no raised voices, no open argument between Doctor Parkman and Professor Webster?"

"I heard what I heard and I saw what I saw, as I will testify. The person who needs to address your questions is Professor Webster. It's not me who must explain why doors were locked, why the sledgehammer was moved, why he was here all hours of the night, why the furnace was always hot, and the walls—ye could barely touch 'em. Why not bother the professor with these questions, rather than me?"

James supposed the publicity Littlefield had received in the press had gone to his head. He couldn't believe a common janitor would address a gentleman, let alone a doctor and an alumnus, in such a loud, aggrieved tone.

"I have been to see him, thank you for your suggestion, Mister Littlefield. And as you question his motives, he challenges yours. That is neither my concern nor my purpose in coming here; it was to ascertain that you truly believe Webster capable of such infamy. Clearly, you do."

"If that is all you've come to discover, Doctor Stone, I trust you're satisfied, and will allow me my peace."

"By all means, Mister Littlefield." James bowed briefly to Mrs. Littlefield, placed his hat on his head, and made ready to leave the cottage.

"One more thing, Doctor Stone," Littlefield called, and James turned back. "Will you be a witness at the trial? I look forward to your testimony. Without my discovery, you'd have naught to say."

James smiled at Littlefield. "I shall be a witness and more, Mister Littlefield. I am undertaking a phonographic report of the proceedings. Your words of testimony will be immortalized. Be careful in what you say, for this record will be accurate and timeless."

Littlefield gave a grim smile in return.

"I know what I'll say, Doctor Stone, the truth and nothing but. I hope you'll have the means to take it down truthfully."

Littlefield turned to the stairs to the cellar and shuffled back down them.

Dr. James Winchell Stone

Facepage of James Winchell Stone's phonographic report

REPORT

OF THE

TRIAL

OF

PROF. JOHN W. WEBSTER,

INDICTED FOR THE MURDER OF

DR. GEORGE PARKMAN

BEFORE THE SUPREME JUDICIAL COURT OF MASSACHUSETTS,

HOLDEN AT BOSTON,

ON TUESDAY, MARCH 19, 1850.

PHONOGRAPHIC REPORT, BY
DR. JAMES W. STONE.

BOSTON:
PHILLIPS, SAMPSON & COMPANY,
110 WASHINGTON STREET.
1850.

$3,000
REWARD!

DR. GEORGE PARKMAN,

A well known citizen of Boston, left his residence
No. 8 Walnut Street, on Friday last, he is 60 years of age ;—about 5 feet 9 inches high—grey hair—thin face— with a scar under his chin—light complexion—and usually walks very fast. He was dressed in a dark frock coat, dark pantaloons, purple silk vest, with dark figured black stock and black hat.

As he may have wandered from home in consequence of some sudden aberration of mind, being perfectly well when he left his house; or, as he had with him a large sum of money, he may have been foully dealt with. The above reward will be paid for information which will lead to his discovery if alive; or for the detection and conviction of the perpetrators if any injury may have been done to him.

A suitable reward will be paid for the discovery of his body.

Boston, Nov. 26th, 1849.   **ROBERT G. SHAW.**

Information may be given to the City Marshal.

From the Congress Printing House,(Farwell & Co.) 32 Congress St.

Handbill posted throughout New England

Lithograph of Webster murdering Parkman

A CORRECT LIKENESS OF DR. PARKMAN.
AS LAST SEEN PREVIOUS TO THE MURDER.

Parkman's remains found in Medical College (Courtesy of National Library of Medicine)

Dr. George Parkman on his rounds

THE NEW MASSACHUSETTS MEDICAL COLLEGE IN GROVE ST BOSTON.

Massachusetts (Harvard) Medical College, 1845.
Lithographer W. Sharp & Co. (Courtesy of Historic New England)

Restoration of Dr. Parkman's Skeleton.

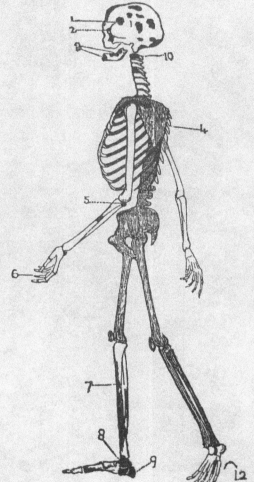

Designed by Rowse from a sketch by Dr. Jeffries Wyman, and engraved by Taylor & Adams Expecially for the Boston Herald.

The above is a correct copy of the diagram exhibited by Prof. Jeffries Wyman, in the course of his examination, on Thursday. It is the restoration of a skeleton, as made by Prof. Wyman, from the bones found in the vault, tea chest, and the furnace, in the part of the Medical College occupied by Dr. Webster.

The shaded parts of this figure represent what was found in the vault and tea chest; the black parts what was discovered in the furnace; and the white parts what was not found at all.

Restoration of Dr. Parkman's skeleton (Courtesy of National Library of Medicine)

For the Murder of
DR. GEORGE PARKMAN,
November 23, 1849.
Before the Supreme Judicial Court, in the City of Boston.
With Numerous Accurate Illustrations.

Professor John Webster (Courtesy of National Library of Medicine)

Illustration of trial of Dr. Webster, Supreme Judicial Court, Boston

Senator Daniel Webster

Chief Justice Lemuel Shaw

CHAPTER 14

March 1850
Court Street, Boston, Massachusetts

A murder trial is an exciting occurrence in a society. It engages people's best and worst impulses simultaneously: the elusiveness of evil, the difficulty of proof, the final question of guilt or innocence, the consequences of said determination.

These thoughts ran through James Stone's mind as he prepared for his first day in court. This Tuesday morning, March 19, 1850, would begin John Webster's trial for the murder of George Parkman. It would decide whether Webster would live or die, just as Webster might have made a similar decision in the fatal moment for Parkman.

Detailed exhibits and diagrams would be presented for the jury's study and reported in the daily press. The public would become secondhand spectators to the crime: the violence of the murder, then the devious, and failed, attempt to cover it up.

James knew the buildup to the trial would make his report an invaluable record. When all of the true words spoken in court were recorded, the populace could reason its way to its own decision of guilt or innocence, just as the jury would in this case. There would be no rumors or misinterpretations, only a factual collection of the utterances of counselors, witnesses, and the bench, leaving no one and nothing out. His skill would impress all.

James had fussed with his carefully chosen outfit for the first day in court. He would not testify until the next day, March 20, but his debut as an official phonographic reporter was auspicious, at least in his mind.

James was nervous as he walked the few blocks from 6 Bowdoin Square to the Suffolk County Courthouse in Court Square. Hundreds of people were gathered around the steps in the early morning sunlight of what promised to be a mild spring day. Many had waited all night in the hopes of gaining a coveted seat in the galleries, located one floor above the courtroom. Street traffic was obstructed for blocks: horses, carriages, carts, and pedestrians tied up in every which way.

James had to push through the crowd to the granite steps that led up to twin bronze doors, framed between four white Ionic pillars. He then passed through a full complement of Marshal Tukey's police force. Tukey's men had set up a heavy iron chain at waist height around the building; they unlocked it as needed to allow witnesses and dignitaries admittance. A side entrance was used to get the jurors in and out of the courthouse with as little fuss as possible and was heavily guarded at all times.

Middlesex County Sheriff Edward Eveleth had devised a scheme to allow the proceedings to continue unimpeded by the crowds hoping for admittance to the three-story granite courthouse. The inner area of the courtroom itself was reserved for important personages: judges, members of the legislature, clerics, physicians, citizens of a higher order. As many as 150 witnesses were accommodated in the neighboring grand jury room. The press was seated in a specially created area of the courtroom near the sheriff's desk, to the left side. By eight a.m., all available areas of observation were filled to capacity.

The gory details of the crime had amplified its morbid appeal. The populace, in and out of the courtroom, had devoured every grisly detail, every suggestion of murderous intent. More than one hundred constables armed with wooden batons ringed the outer walls of the courtroom and issued cards of admission to the waiting spectators at the head of a long line. In groups of twenty, the visitors were marched to the galleries, given a chance to view the proceedings below for ten minutes, and were then ushered out as a new group was led in.

James took a seat behind Attorney General John Clifford's table, where prosecutor George Bemis also sat, and nodded to several men of his acquaintance. There was Rufus Choate, the counselor who had declined Webster's defense. Seated next to him was Judge George Tyler, who would succeed Justice Wilde on the Supreme Court at the conclusion of this trial. He looked as if he wished he were already on the bench. The press had labeled Webster-Parkman the "trial of the century."

Attorney General Clifford seemed preoccupied with the task that lay before him. He possessed a handsome, unlined face and a dark beard sweeping down from one sideburn, passing under his chin, and climbing back up the other side into a matching sideburn. Clifford strode over to the press section, where he appeared to know many of its members by name and employer.

James was surprised by the prosecutor's vigor. Clifford was not known to be the most industrious of men. Some had called him downright lazy. He did possess a wealth of legal knowledge and experience as a prosecutor, although not enough for the Parkman family.

Robert Shaw had hired the family's own counsel to try the case alongside the attorney general. George Bemis, tall and clean-shaven, with the latest model of wire spectacles perched on his long New England nose, came from a prosperous Massachusetts manufacturing family. He was a graduate of Harvard College and its law school and was considered to be an expert in criminal law. At forty-four years old—experienced enough to be prosecuting such an important case—Bemis had attracted considerable attention as a legal scholar. In ten years, people speculated, he could be a Supreme Court justice if his health held up. Bemis was said to be possibly tubercular.

It was unusual for an attorney general to share his prosecutorial duties with an independent counselor, especially one chosen by the victim's family and paid the exorbitant fee of $1,150, or so James had heard, far more than Clifford's annual salary. The attorney general would give the opening and closing statements, his due as senior prosecuting attorney. Bemis would question the witnesses. The Parkman family gave Clifford and Bemis just one assignment: to ensure that Chief Justice Shaw pronounced a guilty verdict, and a sentence that would be enforced on John Webster at the end of a rope.

There was a stir in the courtroom when Daniel Webster arrived. Spontaneous applause (and a few hisses) greeted the senator as he seated himself in the second row of the dignitaries' section. Two weeks earlier, Webster had given a three-hour speech on the US Senate floor endorsing the Compromise of 1850, which, in effect, approved of slavery in the South to preserve the Union. He had been vilified by the abolitionist community throughout New England, but he remained a hometown hero in Boston.

Marshal Tukey, red in the face from rushing in and out of the courtroom trying to manage the crowds, tried to quiet the din with little success. A cacophony of conversation filled the large room, voices debating Webster's guilt or innocence right up to the moment of the trial's commencement.

James readied his materials. He had steel nib pens and holders from the British manufacturer Waterlow and Sons of London, several bottles of India ink, and more than a hundred sheets of foolscap writing paper. He was tempted to record his observations of the courtroom, its atmosphere and inhabitants, but remembered that his mission was to present solely the spoken word, an oral account of the trial's proceedings. He would restrict himself to recording what was said, with no editorial comment.

At ten minutes before nine o'clock, John White Webster was led into the courtroom, his hands bound by iron shackles. James noted that even in this extreme situation, Webster looked more the scholar than the murderer.

He carried a Bible in his right hand as he quickly crossed the left side of the courtroom, moving with a firm and elastic step despite his manacles. His countenance exhibited a calm and dignified composure. He walked by many friends, casually nodding to them as if passing them in the street. He climbed up and sat down on the wooden chair in the elevated prisoner's dock, surrounded by an iron railing, then reached out to shake the hand of a supporter who ran forward to greet him.

By no means did Webster communicate the air of a guilty man. Since James had last seen him in his cell, hope had regained control of the professor's faculties and had given him a sense of self-possession that seemed consistent with innocence. *This appearance would make a favorable impression on the jury,* James thought.

At precisely nine a.m., the bailiff's staff struck the floor with a resounding crack. All stood as the justices for the Supreme Judicial Court of the commonwealth of Massachusetts filed into the courtroom and took their seats at the bench, a long, elevated table facing the prisoner's dock. Chief Justice Lemuel Shaw sat in the center, Associate Justice Samuel Wilde to his right, Associate Justice Theron Metcalf next to him, and Associate Justice Charles A. Dewey on Shaw's left.

The presence of the associate justices was purely ceremonial. Court observers knew that only one individual would guide this trial and would do so in the manner he saw fit. Chief Justice Shaw was an enormous pile of a man with a huge head, shaggy hair, and mottled skin. To James, he surveyed the courtroom the way a hungry lion might eye an errant wildebeest.

The chief justice stared fixedly at a young man, a bit older than James, sitting not far from Senator Webster. James inquired of his courtroom neighbor John French who the stranger might be.

"Herman Melville," replied French, surprised James hadn't recognized the popular novelist. "Did you not know that Chief Justice Shaw is his father-in-law? He wishes Melville were anything but a writer and has secured for him a position at the Customs House."

James realized he wasn't the only one who saw the dramatic and literary potential of the Webster trial. Like many, he had enjoyed reading

Melville's Polynesian adventure, *Typee: A Peek at Polynesian Life*, a spirited account of the author's trip to the South Seas aboard a clipper ship. He wondered if he might someday read a Melville novel about a chubby Harvard professor accused of a heinous murder. James felt satisfied that his account of the trial would come out first.

The air was rent with a blast from the crier's box to the left of the bench: "Hear ye! Hear ye! Hear ye! All those having anything to do before the honorable justices of the Supreme Judicial Court gather round, give your attention, and you shall be heard! God save the commonwealth of Massachusetts! Be seated!"

James's pen took down every syllable of the crier's declaration with fingers that quickly spread phonographic symbols across the page. His pulse was beating rapidly. His great project had begun. The names remembered from this trial would be George Parkman, John Webster, and James Winchell Stone.

Seated at the table in front of him, Attorney General Clifford began loudly stating the obvious: John White Webster was present to be tried for the murder of Dr. George W. Parkman. He cited the grand jury indictment for said crime, to which Webster had pleaded not guilty. He then moved that the jury be empaneled to try the case. The trial was underway.

James turned his gaze on Professor Webster, whose nerves seemed to remain firm. When he removed his spectacles to wipe something from his eye, James could see how red Webster's eyes were, betraying many an anxious hour and wakeful night.

To everyone's surprise, the jury was quickly obtained. Fourteen men were excused immediately on account of their health or military duty. Webster's counsel, Pliny Merrick and Edwin Sohier, challenged another twenty on behalf of the defendant, and seven more were dismissed for believing Webster to be guilty before the trial had even begun. Chief Justice Shaw excused three more jurors for opposing capital punishment, which was required in Massachusetts for a conviction of willful murder.

By half past ten, the jury of twelve men and two male alternates was sworn in. The jury proper consisted of Robert J. Byram, a locksmith, who was elected foreman; Thomas Barrett, a printer; John Borrowscale, a slater; James Crosby, a clerk; John E. Davenport, a painter; Albert Day, a dry goods dealer; Joseph Eustis, a merchant; Daniel T. Fuller, an unemployed seaman; Benjamin H. Greene, a bookseller; Arnold Hayward, a carpenter; Frederick A. Henderson, a furnisher; and Stephen A. Stackpole, a clerk.

The jury occupied two rows to the right of the bench and professor

Webster's perch in the dock. Foreman Byram was in the first seat in the first row, where he could easily catch the eye of the justices seated above him on their elevated platform.

The clerk of the court read the indictment, stating that John W. Webster of Cambridge, on November 23, 1849, with malice aforethought, assaulted George Parkman with a knife which Webster held in his right hand, and rendered a mortal wound of one inch in length and three inches in depth. It was from this wound, the clerk intoned, "the said George Parkman then and there instantly died."

The courtroom fell silent. Webster looked away; he would not face the clerk as the reading continued. The indictment further accused Webster of hitting Parkman with a hammer upon his head, another mortal wound; of striking, beating, and kicking the head, breast, back, belly, and sides of Parkman's body; and of throwing Parkman to the floor and beating and kicking him further until he was absolutely, unequivocally dead. The grand jury, said the clerk, maintained that Webster "feloniously, willfully, and of his malice aforethought, did kill and murder, against the peace of the commonwealth."

There it was. A Harvard professor accused of murder. A Harvard man who might well hang. The clerk's enumeration of the murderer's foul deeds droned on.

Finally, the jury was informed that the prisoner at the bar had pleaded not guilty to the charges leveled against him. Chief Justice Shaw looked over and down at the jurors to address the men staring up at him. "Now you are here, upon your oaths, to try the case and true deliverance make," Shaw said.

That was it. The trial was begun.

The attorney general began his opening remarks with a preview of the testimony he and George Bemis would present to buttress their central argument: that John Webster's actions after his arrest demonstrated a consciousness of guilt. Clifford exhorted the jury to consider the matter, as he put it, "free of all excitement which might exist out of doors, but not here, gentlemen, in the clear, calm light of justice—in this temple of justice."

James's derisive smile was an inward one. As if there could be any abatement to the hysteria over this case that gripped Boston, much as a fever seizes a sick man. Clifford asked the court to sequester the jurors in a nearby military barracks and to order that they take all meals by themselves, with no outside visitors or newspapers allowed. Chief Justice Shaw so agreed.

Clifford emphasized to the jury that Parkman was "a well-known and highly respectable citizen of Boston, living in good health and cheerful spirits, on the morning of Friday, the twenty-third day of November last; that he was engaged in his usual occupations, on that day, up to fifteen minutes before two o'clock, at which time he was last seen alive, entering the Medical Building in Grove Street."

There was a low murmur in the courtroom. The rumors of Parkman's disappearance and reappearance in various parts of North America, as far south as Baltimore and as far north as Newfoundland, had never abated, and only grew as the trial neared. The attorney general was asserting that after Parkman's last known visit to the Medical College, he had not left the building alive, but only in pieces later hauled up from Webster's privy and storerooms and carried out on a pine board.

"It will appear that Doctor Parkman had at that time an invalid daughter to whom he was tenderly attached, in whom he was as much bound up as a father ever is in his child," Clifford explained. "And upon that day, on account of her condition, and to administer to her wants in the sick chamber, he had purchased a quantity of lettuce, which, at that season, was a rare plant, and which he intended to take home with him for their supper.

"Doctor Parkman left the lettuce in a shop near the Medical College, with the intention of returning to take it. He did not return. The lettuce remained. After he went to the Medical College, although he was expected to return in a few minutes to take it, he did not return, and he did not return to his home."

Very clever, that bit about the lettuce, James thought as his fingers moved across the page, the ink blotting slightly as his sleeve brushed it. He had a large blotter at the ready, but he could employ it only when the testimony paused. How many shirts of his would this trial ruin?

James became angry with himself for allowing his thoughts to stray. He must stay focused on the testimony. He comprehended Clifford's strategy: the invalid daughter humanized Parkman. Her caring father could not have been the hated, avaricious debt collector painted so crudely in the press.

Clifford then enumerated the body parts found in Webster's privy vault and the tea chest in his chambers, and he presented the medical conclusion that these were thought to constitute what remained of the body of Dr. George Parkman. James felt a swell of pride to have been one of the experts who came to this conclusion. Again, he tried to refocus his mind on Clifford's argument.

The prosecutor then listed the parts of Parkman that had never been recovered: his head (except for his teeth), his arms and hands, both feet, and his right leg from the knee down. What remained was still George Parkman; of that, there was no doubt, Clifford emphasized. "The evidence will show that the form was peculiar, as his was peculiar."

At this the galleries erupted, with shouts of "Murderer!" and "Hang him!" along with foot stamping and yelling. A scarlet-faced Tukey strode to the front of the courtroom and bellowed, "Quiet in the galleries! Silence!" He made a swift motion with his hand and the current spectators were hustled out, and a new, more subdued contingent brought in.

Clifford droned on for another two hours. James had to stretch his cramped fingers whenever he was granted a pause in the man's steady verbiage.

Periodically Chief Justice Shaw leaned over the bench and bellowed, "Stop one moment, Sir!" before posing a question. Poor Clifford was so intimidated by the chief justice's inquiries that he had difficulty resuming his remarks each time an interruption occurred. James treasured these short breaks for his aching hands. He also could see that Shaw enjoyed flummoxing Clifford.

As the attorney general finally drew to a close—he had spoken for almost three hours—he explained why the indictment had made sure that no possibility of mayhem was omitted. He was forced to acknowledge that the crime had no witness. No one had seen Webster strike Parkman, or cut up his body, or place its various pieces where they were found.

"Although you may not be able to put your hands upon a single particle of proof as to the mode by which the murder was accomplished, it will be no less your duty to return a verdict of guilty," Clifford said.

This was an interesting argument, thought James. *Not a particle of proof, but still guilty?* Clifford had ended his argument by putting the burden of proof on Webster to demonstrate that he had *not* killed Parkman. This, too, was a neat trick for the prosecution. It was their duty to prove their case beyond a reasonable doubt, not the defense's. James knew enough about the law to know that.

He also knew enough to know that it was rare for a man to be convicted of murder with no direct evidence. Not to mention no testimony from any eyewitness, no complete *corpus delecti*, and no confession of guilt by the accused. Clifford was asking the jury to make its own connections between the circumstantial evidence presented, the presumed motives of Professor

Webster, and what Clifford alleged was a web of lies, half truths and out-right deceptions concocted by Webster after Parkman's disappearance.

Testimony for the first day was concluded, but not before Mr. Sohier for the defense made a motion to have all the witnesses at the trial be seques-tered in a separate room until they were called. James panicked. Would he be forced to leave the courtroom, his report undone on its first day?

Clifford asked that the witnesses from the medical profession be al-lowed to remain in court to answer questions about the physical remains that were crucial to his argument. Shaw nodded his shaggy head in assent. James let his breath out. He had obtained a reprieve; his phonographic labors could continue.

CHAPTER 15

March 1850
Court Street, Boston, Massachusetts

Each day of the Webster trial evoked greater excitement and interest than the previous. All avenues leading to the main entrance of the courthouse were filled with those hoping to catch at least a glimpse of Professor Webster being led inside. The galleries were never empty; James marveled that the floor did not collapse under the weight of so many people streaming in and out.

In a ritual that he found puzzling, the names of the individual jurors were called at the commencement of each day's proceedings. All of Boston and beyond now knew their identities; they had become minor celebrities, although sequestered in a military barracks. They were stared at and even pursued by admirers as they took their morning stroll through Boston Common prior to being transported to the courthouse.

Charles M. Kingsley, a man James had heard much about but had never seen, was the first to testify for the prosecution. Kingsley was Parkman's "hatchet man," the individual responsible for drawing up his contracts, filing his lawsuits, and evicting his wayward tenants. Until his employer's demise, his life was organized around George Parkman and his daily schedule. Kingsley lived in one of Parkman's estates and had met with him daily to review real estate and business matters, and he was the first to remark upon Parkman's disappearance.

"He was very punctual in his habits," Kingsley testified in a nasal voice. "I never before was disappointed of meeting him at the dinner hour of two o'clock, when he dined with his family. Had called on him at least fifty times at that hour."

Kingsley said there still had been no word of Dr. Parkman or his whereabouts when he arrived at the residence the next morning, where a very worried and anxious family awaited him. Kingsley immediately organized a search that traced Parkman's path from his house, stop by stop, street by street, to North Grove Street and the Medical College.

The increasingly frantic hunt for a clue to the rich man's whereabouts went on until eleven at night. The next day, the police force began checking Parkman-owned properties throughout Boston, especially in Fort Hill and the North End, the two largest Irish neighborhoods. In every location where there was a rumored sighting of Parkman, Kingsley and the police hurried to it and searched, but in vain.

Their last stop was the Medical College, where Kingsley and one of Marshal Tukey's constables looked throughout the building, going into lecture rooms, offices, and the dissecting laboratory, accompanied by the janitor Littlefield.

At half past eleven that Sunday night, the men knocked on Webster's lecture-room door, which was locked. They were ready to depart, but Littlefield insisted Webster was there, and he shook the door violently several times. Littlefield was vindicated when Webster finally did appear, or at least a crack of him in the doorway. Kingsley explained the reason for their visit. Only then did Webster admit his visitors.

"Professor Webster very politely said we could look, but wished that nothing might be turned over," Kingsley added. He snorted and looked at the prisoner. Webster returned his gaze steadily, showing no sign of guilt or embarrassment. It was as if Kingsley were discussing the weather. The witness looked embarrassed to acknowledge that nothing incriminating had been found in Webster's rooms.

Parkman's man recounted his next encounter with Webster, which took place at the Leverett Street Gaol after he was taken from his home and failed in his abortive suicide attempt.

"When I went in, Professor Webster lay on the bed in the cell, with his face downwards. I asked if he was able to get up, and he said he was not. After a few minutes, they lifted him up. He had hardly strength to hold up his head and was so much distressed that I thought he would not live.

"He trembled and was so convulsed that I would not wish to see the like again. He cried out to have word sent to his family, as they did not know where he was. He mentioned his family a great many times, but when I said that there was another family, which also had been in great distress for a week, he would not look at me, nor respond."

Kingsley put his head down and roughly wiped away his tears. Clifford paused, letting the emotion settle for all to see.

Kingsley said he also had been present for the assemblage of the body parts by Dr. Stone and Dr. Lewis. Clifford asked him a direct question: "Were those the remains of George Parkman?"

Kingsley did not hesitate in his answer. "I should want to have it understood that I swear positively that the remains are the body of Doctor Parkman."

There was a commotion in the galleries at this statement, with cries such as "Are ye blind?" and "Get it over with, just hang him!" Chief Justice Shaw banged his gavel, and the police quickly pushed out the group occupying the galleries and waited a few minutes before bringing in their successors.

Robert Gould Shaw next came to the witness box to testify that he was the last relation of Parkman's to see him alive. They had met that morning, as they usually did.

"There was nothing unusual in his appearance; he looked to be in perfect health, and in very good spirits," Shaw said of the victim. "I parted with him about ten, and that was the last I saw of him."

Shaw also testified about his first sight of the remains. "I did see some marks which induced me to believe they were his remains; they were the hair on the breast and the leg, the color of which exactly corresponded with what I had seen. I did finally take charge of these remains, and I have had them interred as the remains of my brother-in-law."

Another audible murmur came, this time from those in the courtroom. *This was one of the issues upon which the outcome of the trial could hinge,* James thought—*were they or were they not the remains of George Parkman? What if the wrong man was buried in the Parkman family tomb? Why the rush to bury an incomplete corpse?*

Shaw also testified about his business dealings with Professor Webster, in particular the loan secured with the professor's minerals cabinet as collateral. The spectators seemed to hang on every word—the business dealings of the wealthy and powerful were rarely revealed in such sordid detail.

The day's testimony finished at seven o'clock. Shaw left the stand and strode out of the courtroom, glaring at Webster as he passed by the dock. The professor blinked.

Before court adjourned, Clifford asked that the jury be taken the next morning to the scene of the alleged crime, the Medical College. Accompanied by Mr. Bemis for the prosecution, Mr. Sohier for the defense, a contingent of Marshal Tukey's constables, and a small group of medical experts, the jurors would tour Professor Webster's lecture room, his laboratory, and his private rooms, and finally they would see the infamous privy them-selves. Chief Justice Shaw agreed to the request, but he required the jury to return to its duties by nine thirty in the morning, when court would resume. The gavel banged.

James stretched; his hands and arms ached deeply. *This was not even a full day's testimony! How would he survive this ordeal for another fortnight?* He consulted his pocket watch and realized he must quickly sup and meet Ellen and the copyists on Court Street. His work had only begun.

Eight women were busy in conversation when James, after climbing the wooden staircase in the back of the building, entered the rectangular room above 87 Court Street. Ellen O'Keeffe was seated at one of two tables in the front of the room, while the seven copyists occupied small desks that James had procured from a school that had closed down. There were wooden boxes of the steel-tipped pens, bottles of ink, and quires of writing paper.

Ellen leapt to her feet and clapped her hands, silencing the feminine chatter that had continued despite James's entrance into the room. "Let us welcome our good Doctor Stone, who must've had a long and excitin' first day in court."

James smiled, bowed to Ellen and the seated women. He enjoyed being the focus of attention for a large group of the opposite sex, something he had never experienced before.

He dutifully spread out his notes, carefully numbered in the order of their taking, drew back a chair from the larger table, sat down, and began to dictate what he had recorded.

Ellen and James had devised a method of transcribing that they hoped would prove productive. James read a page of notes aloud, and the first girl began transcribing. Once he finished a page, the next girl transcribed the succeeding page, and the first girl proofread her own work, making any necessary changes while the page-by-page process continued with the next young woman, and so on.

Ellen examined the transcribed pages, making sure the copyist had not omitted or missed an important word or sentence. Her duties required great concentration, since James was reading aloud the subsequent page as she perused the previous one. They thought it essential to have a backup system to ensure accuracy. James considered Ellen's recognition and un-derstanding of phonographic symbols to be equal to his own.

The work proceeded apace; everyone burst out laughing when James would make some desperate and unlikely guess at an unintelligible symbol he had scribbled. He was embarrassed at first but soon joined in the laughter. He was learning to relax among these young women.

As the hour of midnight drew near, James was finishing Mr. Shaw's testimony. He was barely awake; his bones ached with tiredness. He would sleep well that night, without his usual twitching and snoring.

Ellen was similarly exhausted. She had arrived early to organize the workspace, secure the necessary supplies, and make sure all the girls were fully prepared for their labors, which proved more time-consuming than she had predicted.

Ellen ushered the sleepy young women out, telling them to return home as a group. James had offered to engage a carriage to deliver them to the North End, but all had declined. They found greater safety in numbers and liked stretching their legs after the long hours of stationary confinement.

Finally, only Ellen and James remained. She extinguished the sooty oil lamps that provided the light required for their work, save one. It gave off an intermittent glow as he gathered his papers and made ready to depart.

"Miss O'Keeffe, I can't thank you enough for your efforts," James began, feeling less awkward now that they were alone. "The girls you chose did an excellent job this evening. I couldn't be more pleased."

"I'm happy that yer satisfied, Doctor Stone," Ellen said carefully. She was aware of their closeness in the solitude of the late hour, and she realized he was, too. It didn't concern as much as excite her. As James lifted his papers off the table, he brushed her arm. She trembled slightly.

He felt the tremor and looked directly at Ellen. He was as frozen as a deer on alert, not knowing what to do or say. This was always his problem. Inactivity was his byword. In matters of the heart, he felt confused and helpless.

And this was an Irish woman he was staring at. A desire for her contravened all the social norms of his world. James had always observed the unspoken boundaries between his world of Boston money and privilege, and Ellen's of Irish alienation, poverty, and drink.

As is to banish his thoughts, Ellen grasped his hand, hers dry and hot, still trembling.

"There be nae way for me to tell ye what all this means to me," she said. "All this," indicating the nearly darkened room and its tiny desks. "But also ye. I never met anyone like ye before in my life. Yer so different, so above me in every way! How can I . . ."

James placed a finger upon Ellen's lips. He was surprising himself this evening, not sure what he might do next. He found his other arm pulling Ellen to him, and he replaced his finger with his lips. The kiss was brief, but not light. It transfixed them both. They stood, helpless with unexpressed emotion, neither sure what might come next.

James came to some semblance of his senses first. He straightened and released Ellen, who quickly moved a few paces away. He was breathing heavily.

"My apologies, Miss O'Keeffe," he said haltingly. "I meant no offense by my actions. I hope you will not take any."

"Nae, Doctor Stone, I dinna. I think it best, though, if I left with the other girls tomorrow upon the end of our work," she said in a brisk tone. Ellen was trying to restore the normal decorum between a single man and a single woman in his employ.

"I promise not to place ye in this situation again," she said, failing to suppress a deep red blush that colored her features.

"That is a promise, Miss O'Keeffe, that I sincerely hope you will not be able to keep."

CHAPTER 16

March 1850
North Grove Street and Court Street, Boston, Massachusetts

James was permitted to join the attorneys, police, and jurors, along with Dr. Wynford Lewis and Dr. George Gay, on the early morning visit to the Medical College. The doctors were present as expert witnesses, available for any questions the jurors might pose.

The large party gathered at the foot of the twin staircases leading up to the college entrance. It was eight o'clock, and a biting wind blew, so different from the balmy weather of two days earlier. James shivered in his black wool overcoat.

As soon as they entered the dissecting laboratory, juror Albert Day came over to the physicians and asked, "Do you need special training to cut up a body?"

George Bemis, standing nearby, quickly interjected, "That topic will be covered at trial. Please wait until then before inquiring further."

"Can't one of the good doctors answer a simple question?" persisted Day, a dry goods dealer. Bemis could not afford to alienate a juror, however inappropriate his query. He nodded curtly to James that he was permitted to respond.

James had no idea what to say and hadn't realized Day's question was directed at him. The prosecutor looked impatiently at James. George Bemis, Esq., already had registered his disapproval of James's experiment with phonography, which he labeled error-ridden and of no benefit to anyone.

James's mouth went dry, and his palms moistened. But he knew the correct response, and to his surprise, it emerged as one coherent thought.

"My impression is that the individual who separated the remains had some anatomical skill," he said. "It's difficult for a person who has never done it to remove the sternum or the breastbone."

Now everyone was listening to Dr. Stone expound upon how George

Parkman had ended up as a collection of chopped-up body parts. An interested group of other jurors had gathered around Day.

"Dispensing of the arms and hands, and the feet, is a relatively simple task," James continued. "The appendages are always the easiest to chop off. To sever the head requires some expertise, along with an especially sharp knife. And the legs must be chopped off from the torso at the proper junction to be effectively severed."

James noticed a few jurors turning pale at his mention of chopping, but this is exactly what had been done with Parkman's corpse. When he'd first examined the remains, he had thought the butchering a clumsy job. He did not mention this to the jurors. That did little to mollify Bemis, who was flush with anger. He gave James an unhappy grimace when he had finished.

James silently vowed to keep his peace for the remainder of the tour and defer to his colleagues if there were future questions. He could not afford to antagonize Bemis and jeopardize the publication of his report. He worried that he already had made an enemy of the prosecutor.

Marshal Tukey led the jurors, trailed by the rest of the party, through all of Dr. Webster's rooms, then into Littlefield's apartment and down to the basement, where they viewed the hole he had burrowed into the privy vault. Littlefield stood by, clearly proud of his work. There was something about the man James didn't trust or believe. He had felt the same way after interviewing Littlefield a fortnight earlier.

The jurors jostled each other as they tried to peer into the hole, but nothing remained to be seen. James recalled his shock upon first discerning large pieces of a disemboweled body gruesomely dangling from fish-hooks. Nothing in his medical studies or practice had prepared him for the sight. It had both fascinated and disgusted him, and it remained etched in his memory.

The jurors were also shown Dr. Holmes's lecture room, immediately above Webster's. Before they departed, juror Benjamin Greene, a bookseller, remarked, "To think this was all taking place right under the very nose of Doctor Holmes!"

Two police carriages were waiting to ferry the jurors to the courthouse after they left the Medical College. The jurors traveled only with one another, except for one constable assigned to each carriage carrying six of them. James had to crowd into a third, smaller conveyance with Drs. Lewis and Gay.

"You should have kept quiet when that juror questioned you, Stone," said Lewis.

"I beg your pardon," James said, with a slight bow of his head. "I understood that we were asked to be present for exactly the reason Mister Day provided. I don't feel I spoke out of turn. I'm sorry if you do. My sincerest apologies."

"I question your true purpose in these proceedings, Stone," Lewis said, still lecturing his former pupil. "I've noticed you filling up quires of paper in the courtroom as if you were some chartered scrivener. I had supposed you were still a physician, bringing your knowledge of anatomy to the task presented to us. It seems you consider this business of phonography to be the more important skill for your career."

Dr. Gay looked uncomfortable and stared fixedly at the carriage's ceiling. Employing unusual self-restraint, James decided to add nothing further to the conversation. He would afford Lewis no further opportunity to speak down to him.

It had become clear that his devotion to his report was alienating some of his medical colleagues. He had crossed an invisible barrier by adopting a new profession, not the one he had been assigned to, trained for, and matriculated in.

So be it. James had identified a new course in his life. He would not be deterred from following it. Not by the machinations of George Bemis, nor the disdain and dismissal of Dr. Wynford Lewis. Ellen O'Keeffe had expressed no such doubts. She believed in phonography. And she believed in him.

~

It was past nine thirty a.m. by the time court resumed. Mr. Bemis began by wheeling in a large wooden model of the Medical College that could be disassembled in the courtroom to highlight specific locations where evidence had been discovered. The model showed the jury the building's interior in three dimensions. It had movable stairs, walls, and furnishings. The galleries marveled at its ingenious complexity.

James had not anticipated the prosecution's most effective exhibit, which was brought in next: a life-size drawing of a human skeleton that strongly suggested the outline of George Parkman's body, now familiar in shape and visage to the masses, variously shaded and keyed to the parts recovered from Webster's rooms.

At a glance, one could see which remains were found in the furnace (colored black), privy vault and tea chest (shaded), or never found at all (white). James was impressed by the clever manner in which the artist had positioned the skeleton in midstride, mimicking Parkman's distinctive gait. The two-dimensional skeleton also possessed a pronounced lower jaw that would fit the surviving false teeth, as well as documenting Parkman's appellation as "the Chin."

City Marshal Tukey sat down in the witness box after raising the wrong hand to swear on the bailiff's Bible. Tukey perspired greatly, his pleated white shirt visibly damp despite the cold weather outdoors. He wore a tall stovepipe hat that made his broad face look small and squat. He was always bestowing a scowl upon the world.

Tukey confirmed that Robert Shaw had notified him of Dr. Parkman's disappearance the morning after it was first remarked. Tukey had immediately ordered a police canvas of the West End, an area in which many people recalled seeing Parkman on the day in question, but not since.

The marshal also sent his men searching as far as sixty miles outside of Boston in all directions with no results, he reported. The railroads were supplied with a likeness of Dr. Parkman, as were constables in towns adjacent to Boston on the Atlantic seaboard, all the way down to Cape Cod.

"We searched over land and water, and under water," Tukey said, adding that twenty-eight thousand copies of four different handbills describing Parkman and offering a reward had been posted throughout New England in the days after his disappearance.

Tukey said he was notified of Littlefield's discovery on the afternoon of Friday, November 30, a week after Parkman's disappearance. He told how Littlefield led him, Lieutenant Derastus Clapp, and Constable George Fuller down a trap door to the basement of the college. They eventually came to a brick wall in which a hole had been made, about ten inches square.

"We got a light, and I took the lamp and reached into the hole with it and looked about. I saw what I supposed were body parts, pieces of flesh," Tukey testified.

There was an eerie silence in the usually boisterous galleries. This was the first eyewitness testimony about the final indignity suffered by George Parkman, parts of his person swaying from large fishhooks.

Suffolk County Coroner Jabez Pratt testified next and confirmed Tukey's account of the assemblage of the body parts. Pratt proved to be particularly observant of Professor Webster's behavior as the police searched his rooms at the college the night of his arrest.

"Someone had hold of Professor Webster by the arm all the time," testified Pratt. "He appeared different from any man I ever saw before. He called for water. When the water was offered him, he would seem to snap at it with his teeth, and push it from him."

Pratt had been the one to empty the furnace found in Webster's rooms. He testified to picking out bones and pieces of metal that looked like pewter or lead, along with fragments that resembled gold.

Pratt said he had discovered a section of jaw at the bottom of the furnace, which had been placed on the pine board for examination. A large block of false teeth had fallen through the grate of the furnace when Pratt removed the jaw, along with two or three individual teeth. These, too, had been placed on the board for the doctors' perusal.

Dr. Lewis took the stand next and listed the five pieces of the body that were discovered in the privy. After describing them in detail, he addressed how they might have ended up in that condition.

"There was nothing in the manner in which the parts were separated to indicate that it was a subject of dissection," Dr. Lewis testified. "There was no preservative fluid in the vessels, as there would have been if it was a subject. There could not be the least doubt that all the five pieces belonged to the same body."

The medical committee's report on the investigation of the remains, including the signatures of Drs. Stone and Lewis, was then entered into the record. It concluded with this statement: "The foregoing described portions appeared to belong to a person of between fifty and sixty years of age." Parkman, as everyone now knew, was sixty-one at the time of his disappearance.

Finally, it was James's turn in the witness box. John French, of the *Boston Herald*, had agreed to take down James's testimony using his own system of phonographic notation, which he told James was his "improvement" on Pittman's method.

The clerk of the court swore James in, and he sat down in the witness box feeling unsettled, his palms moist. James was especially nervous to face Bemis as his interlocutor, a man who had already formed a negative judgment of him. Despite a chilly formality in his questioning, Bemis showed little overt animus toward James, to the witness's relief.

His queries were rote. Bemis walked James through the various steps of the medical committee's investigation, which he affirmed were accurate. Bemis's next question was unexpected.

"Doctor Stone, was there any aspect to the body that was unusual, or extreme, in your viewpoint? Was there anything you discovered that surprised or startled you?"

"In fact, there were distinguishing signs," James replied. "The muscles of the lower body extremities found in the privy were unusual. They indicated that the individual had been accustomed to much exercise in walking."

This occasioned an audible reaction from the courtroom audience. If there was one quirk Parkman was known for, it was his mania for striding throughout Boston on foot.

Bemis moved on to more dangerous ground. James sensed that the prosecutor had been waiting for the opportunity to correct the impression he had given to the jurors in his explanation at the Medical College earlier that day.

"Can you tell us, Doctor Stone, whether it would take any special anatomical experience to have mutilated the remains you encountered on that fateful day? Did this butcher have medical training?"

The galleries were abuzz, and James had to raise his voice to be heard above the noisy courtroom. He paused while Chief Justice Shaw banged his gavel once, causing the babble to quickly die down. It gave James an extra moment to gather his thoughts.

"Whoever dismembered this particular body in all probability possessed some anatomical experience, particularly in the removal of the head and at least one of the legs," James said. "But it would take no special skill to remove the extremities, the hands, arms, and feet."

Webster, James knew, claimed no anatomical experience. As a chemistry professor, he had no need of such skills. Bemis's color was again rising; James had now thwarted him twice in his attempt to leave Webster the likeliest dismemberer.

The courtroom buzzed with possibilities. Tukey was obliged to stand up and demand silence. Bemis was not yet finished with his witness.

"Doctor Stone, was there anything else unusual that your examination revealed? Did you discern any evidence concerning the means of death?"

James said, "In my examination, as my notes indicate, I saw what looked like a cut into the specimen's ribs from a knife blade. The entire medical committee examined this cut. We could find no evidence that the wound, if even rendered by a knife, was the direct cause of death."

This conclusion seriously undercut the commonwealth's assertion that

Parkman had been stabbed while alive, one of several assaults that led to his death. Now James had disputed that argument, too. Bemis looked furious as his witness departed the box.

When James recovered his seat in the courtroom, French leaned over and shook his hand. "Very thorough, Doctor," he whispered. "But I fear you've given poor Mister Bemis apoplexy. Be ready for another medical emergency!"

James had to immediately resume his phonographic labors as Dr. George Gay was sworn in. Gay agreed with James that some anatomical knowledge had been exhibited in the dissection of the body that was recovered, although he used a different example.

"The separation of the head from the spinal column is not an easy act," said Gay. "They do not use a saw to do it, except when they wish to throw the parts away. A person without anatomical knowledge could not readily cut the head off."

Who had heard of doctors talking about cutting off human heads before? These were the gory details of a brutal murder the trial had promised and now was delivering. James could imagine the field day the newspapers would enjoy with the day's testimony, including his own observation about the knife wound.

Dr. Woodbridge Strong, a Boston physician who was an experienced practitioner of medical dissection, testified that he had often burned human specimens as part of his work. If all he desired were the bones, he must first destroy the flesh.

"I had a common fireplace. The body in question wasn't a large one, but muscular and had some fat. I made a fire of wood and flesh, and kept poking it, and keeping up a roaring fire. It burned all night, and up to three in the morning, and the mass still was not half burned up. Coal is bad to burn flesh with, but wood is good, though little flesh can be burned at a time. The smell is difficult to allay, and the operator would be apt to be found out through it."

Several of the jurors looked sickened. These matters were not discussed in polite society; no one wished to hear of burning human flesh. But their duty required them to listen, and so they did. *The advantage provided by Strong's testimony,* James supposed, *looking at it from the defense's perspective, was that no one had remarked on the odor of burning flesh, not even Littlefield, who lived adjacent to Webster's laboratory and furnace. Why had not someone detected such a distinctive odor?*

Bemis was happy to elicit testimony from Dr. Strong that he was certain that the knife slit in the ribs was indeed the result of an intentional attack, and most probably would have led to Parkman's death.

"I saw a perfectly clean cut made, so as to nearly graze the rib, which I supposed must have been given when the body was alive. I supposed it might have been the means of death."

Strong had contradicted both James and Gay on the fatal nature of the knife wound, but he was an older, well-respected Boston physician to whom the jury would pay attention. James felt embarrassment color his face. He remained convinced that his and the medical committee's observations were accurate. Strong was showboating.

Bemis led Dr. Strong to the conclusion he desired, as he inquired about any final observations concerning the remains.

"The body was unusual in its formation," Strong said, "from its narrowness across the shoulders, in proportion to the pelvis, and the tenuity in the upper part. It corresponded, in these respects, to the late Dr. Parkman's general appearance when alive." Strong also said he considered Parkman a personal friend.

"He had a peculiar appearance," Strong continued. "There was nothing dissimilar to what I would have expected to find in his remains. On the contrary, there were many points of resemblance."

Dr. Strong did impart an odd sense of humor to the otherwise grim proceedings. In response to one of Mr. Sohier's questions on cross-examination, Strong admitted, "I have never seen Doctor Parkman naked, yet I have a great interest in the living human body, the male and especially the female form." This admission led to gales of laughter in the courtroom, and Dr. Webster was laughing heartily with those in the galleries until Shaw intervened with a smash of his gavel.

When the chief justice adjourned court some minutes later, James felt spent. His day's work was but half over. Hours of transcribing lay ahead.

CHAPTER 17

March 1850
Park Street, Beacon Hill; Court Street and Bowdoin Square,
Boston, Massachusetts

The fireplace had been fed all evening, so the air was stuffy in the dark-paneled room in the Beacon Club on Park Street. George Bemis and John Clifford arrived directly from the courthouse, grateful for the compacted warmth awaiting them in the antechamber. Their arrival was anticipated. Robert Shaw, dressed in an expensive black wool suit, was standing in a corner of the drawing room, staring at the fire.

"Attorney General Clifford, Mister Bemis," said Shaw as the two men entered the room, leaving their overcoats with a Black servant at the door. "I have ordered supper for the three of us. I trust you don't object," he said in his usual terse fashion.

Clifford and Bemis were not sure why they had been summoned to the Beacon Club. What could concern Mr. Shaw so early in the trial to require their presence at the private retreat of the wealthiest, most powerful men of their city?

Another Black servant entered, announced that their table was prepared, and led them into the club's dining room. Only one other party, two older gentlemen at a table across the room, was present. Shaw glowered at them, and they bent to their meal.

Shaw, Bemis, and Clifford were ushered to a small, private alcove. After they were seated, the meal Shaw had ordered for them was served. As soon as the servers retired, Shaw wasted little time providing the reason for their gathering.

"Gentlemen, how do you estimate the case goes? How soon until Webster hangs from the gibbet?"

Clifford looked astonished. The trial had just begun. The prosecution was in the earliest stage of its presentation. Did Shaw expect the jury to retire the next morning, before any evidence had been presented?

Bemis was more phlegmatic, clearly accustomed to the whims of Boston's elite. He understood Shaw's anxiety and tried to allay it.

"We feel confident of our presentation today," he said. "The medical evidence overwhelmingly demonstrated that the body was that of your former brother-in-law, that he was killed by a knife wound before being dismembered, and that the individual who executed the dismemberment was not some rank amateur, but a trained medical professional who possessed full knowledge of the horrific act he perpetrated."

Shaw trained his keen gaze on Bemis.

"I share none of your confidence, Mister Bemis. You seem ignorant of what actually occurred in the courtroom today. Mister Sohier made fools of your witnesses, each and every one. He got them to state what *he* proposed. *You two*, to the contrary, did nothing to show guilt on the part of the murderer Webster. It is insufferable, I will not have it."

As Shaw's voice rose, the other two diners looked toward the alcove. An ugly scowl from Shaw returned them quickly to their supper.

"I beg pardon if today's proceedings caused you emotional distress, Mister Shaw," said Clifford in his most placating manner. "We understand and sympathize with the delicate feelings of the Parkman family. In a murder trial, the effort is to build gradually an unimpeachable mountain of evidence the defense will be unable to tear down. We have begun that work; we will continue it tomorrow and every day of this trial. Mister Sohier and Judge Merrick cannot possibly scale and disassemble such a mountain."

"Do you mean mountain, or tiny hill, Mister Clifford? I see no mass of evidence. I see only Harvard-trained doctors who don't seem to know the first thing about which they speak, yet they influence the jury greatly."

Bemis was quick to respond this time. "The knife wound is not essential to our case, Mister Shaw. It's not necessary we prove what implement caused Doctor Parkman to die. We only need prove who did the horrid deed, and we have sufficient motivation and evidence to demonstrate that it could be none other than Webster. The defense has no other person to suggest as an alternative."

"Let me be clear with both of you," said Shaw in a calmer voice that retained a wrathful aftertaste of his earlier anger. "I don't want witnesses called who do not point directly to the guilt of John Webster. I don't want useless testimony offered, like that of foundry workers and schoolboys.

"The case against Webster is clear," Shaw continued. "Webster owed my brother-in-law money, he would not pay, he was pressed, and the finest man I knew was brutally murdered as a result. That is what I want to hear in the courtroom, and little else."

"We're of one mind on this issue, Mister Shaw," said Bemis, his own anger rising. Who did this man think he was, powerful as he might be but certainly no attorney, to tell him and the attorney general how to prosecute a capital case?

"You must let us proceed in a manner that murder trials require, by accumulating enough evidence and sworn testimony that the jury will have no choice other than to convict," Bemis continued. "We're confident of achieving that end. We ask for your patience and forbearance in doing so."

"You have neither, Mister Bemis. This episode is more painful to my family than you can imagine. I don't relish my sister asking me each night when her nightmare will come to an end. I wish to tell her forthrightly. I wish to tell her the guilty will be punished."

"So they will, so they will," said the attorney general, in a reassuring tone no one involved in the conversation was reassured by. "We will prove without a doubt that Webster is the murderer. He will not be set free from these charges, for we possess little doubt that he will hang for the offense."

Bemis was startled by Clifford's promise of something the two of them could not necessarily deliver. A prosecutor cannot unfailingly predict anything, since juries are notoriously unpredictable.

Shaw looked from Clifford to Bemis, and back to Clifford. "I rely on your professionalism, and your word as gentlemen. Now, let us dine."

Bemis had lost his appetite. Shaw was pressuring them to obtain a conviction for willful murder, the only crime that mandated a capital sentence of death. Their host was offering his surrogates no alternative.

~

While Shaw, Bemis, and Clifford dined elegantly at the Beacon Club, James and his copyists enjoyed a more informal repast above 87 Court Street. When he entered the transcription room, he found the young women eating picnic-style at a trestle table covered with a cloth and a few dishes in tin pots.

Ellen rose to her feet when James arrived and rushed to him. "Oh, Doctor Stone, ye were most impressive in the witness box this mornin'. Yer by far the most informative and affectin' witness to testify."

James was surprised by Ellen's familiarity with the proceedings. He gave her a questioning look and was greeted with laughter from Ellen and the other young women.

"We were all there!" Ellen said. "We managed to get tickets from Colleen's pa, he's a janitor at the court building. We planned for our place in the galleries for just when ye were called forth, so we could all be judgin' ye together, and we all felt ye carried yerself very well indeed."

James looked embarrassed and the young ladies' laughter increased. Ellen turned to her throng. "Come, come, ladies. Time for us to clear away our supper and prepare for our work."

The copyists gathered their plates and cutlery, and moved toward the back door, where a slop can had been placed.

"Beg your pardon, Miss O'Keeffe," James interrupted. "Would you mind terribly if I ate something also? I've suffered a long and tiring day, and had no time to stop on my way here. A bit of supper would give me strength to continue our work this evening."

"I beg yer pardon, Doctor Stone," Ellen said, blushing; she could not believe she had forgotten to prepare a plate for their employer. She and James were both being careful to address each other by their surnames when in the company of the transcribers.

She brought James a plate with cold potatoes, a hunk of Irish soda bread, an apple, and a small block of cheese that smelled a bit dangerous. She brought the metal pitcher of water that James kept nearby when he dictated, and a tin cup. She busied herself with preparations for the hours of dictation to come, leaving James to eat alone.

James watched the women go about their business as he supped, impressed by their seriousness of purpose as they prepared pens and paper. The work seemed to go quickly that night, the copyists accustomed now to the rhythm of James's voice. The first three hours sped by. By the fourth, his eyelids drooped, his voice wavered, and he struggled to stay awake.

Ellen clapped her hands sharply, bringing everyone to attention, including the almost-dozing James.

"That'll be enough for tonight, ladies," she called out. "Thank ye again for a good evenin's work. I'll be correctin' yer papers from tonight, so, please pay close attention to my notes."

The young women fled before more criticism could be directed their way. As the last of them filed out, Ellen turned to James.

"Tell me again what it was like to be in the witness box, James," she said, switching to the informality of his Christian name now that they were alone. Her eyes were wide with curiosity. "It must give ye a whole new way of lookin' at the court, and all its many workin's."

James was happy to satisfy Ellen's interest; it gave him pleasure to share his thoughts with her.

"I must say that Chief Justice Shaw is more intimidating up close than at a distance," he said. "I supposed he might well lean over and bite my head off; it would be but a tidbit in those massive jaws of his."

They both laughed. James looked at Ellen, pleased that she shared his sense of humor, however sarcastic and mean-spirited it might be. He continued his recollections.

"Although I don't warm to the man personally, I admit that George Bemis is an effective counselor. He made that clear in his method of questioning. He is most difficult to evade."

Ellen teased James about the exasperated look Bemis gave him as he left the witness box. "It seemed he might prefer evadin' *ye*, James. Ye couldn't be off the stand quick enough to his likin'."

"He suspects all Harvard doctors of sympathizing with and shielding Professor Webster," James said. "I suppose these suspicions are natural, but I find it upsetting to be supposed to protect a murderer."

Ellen grew silent for a moment before asking guardedly, "Is that how ye see Professor Webster, James? As the murderer of Doctor Parkman?"

James did not expect such a bold question. He was at a loss for an immediate response; he had yet to allow himself to render a verdict on Webster's guilt or innocence.

"I'm unsure as to what I see, or how clearly I perceive it," he eventually responded. "My thoughts change by the day. I think if Professor Webster be the culprit, he didn't act alone."

Ellen was surprised. "Who else could that be? None has suggested an accomplice, have they?"

James regretted airing his private doubts. "Pay me little attention, Ellen; the hour is late, my brain is fatigued. These are the thoughts of minds that are overstimulated by a sensational trial such as this. Mine is no different. Let us both get a good night's rest. Perhaps matters will be clearer in the morning."

He smiled at her, hoping to restore the moment of intimacy they had shared about his testimony. He lingered by the door as Ellen gathered her things, but there would be no chaste kiss tonight. Ellen determinedly strode by him as he held the door open for her.

"I think I'm hearing the omnibus coming. I'll see ye on the morrow, James," Ellen said as she hurried down to the street. "Peace be with ye and yer thoughts tonight."

James decided to walk to Bowdoin Square rather than wait for the next conveyance. He had much on his mind: his testimony that morning, the trial itself, and, above all, Ellen. The more time he spent in her company, the more he desired her.

But Ellen had displayed scant awareness that she wielded any power over him. One of her most endearing aspects was her unselfconsciousness, her willful ignorance of the beauty of her face and form and of their impact on men in general—and on James Stone in particular.

He thought of potential outcomes for their relationship with a sense of dread. *It could lead only to scandal and ruin, the reaction that would greet any union between a Boston society doctor and an Irish immigrant. There was no room in the world James aspired to for Ellen O'Keeffe, just as James could never blend into in her Irish existence. They occupied two different planes of being, and no way to bridge them was in sight.*

The streets were largely deserted as James walked, the moon a luminous white orb in the sky, rendering the gas lamps redundant. Boston resembled a ghost city, the opposite of the pandemonium that clustered around the courthouse each day. *Why are people so transfixed by murder?* James wondered. *Do we all have a silent killer inside us, secretly scheming to do away with those who cause us pain and suffering? So quietly that we do not even realize it until the deed is done?*

It wasn't difficult to conjure up such a creature haunting the mind and actions of placid John Webster. James's knowledge of the chemistry professor and his overly calm demeanor in the courtroom suggested that Webster could be an effective actor when he needed to be.

The purpose of his charade still confused James. Webster stood little to gain by stubbornly proclaiming his innocence in the face of a weight of circumstance and detail against him. The more honorable path would be to acknowledge guilt and accept its punishment. James had learned from his medical practice how closely humankind clung to the life spirit, how unwilling anyone was to give up this existence in favor of an unknown afterlife.

He couldn't shed his suspicions that Webster did not act alone. The job was too taxing for such a piddling man. James estimated that Webster had neither the physical strength nor the moral fortitude to subdue Parkman, extinguish his life, and then hack him apart. Someone of greater strength and a stronger stomach must have assisted him.

No one at the trial had suggested an accomplice or helpmate for Webster. Perhaps James was foolish to think himself wiser in these matters than the police and the prosecutors. His foremost duty was to serve phonography with an accurate report, not to pretend to be a police investigator.

He ascended the steps to his chambers, long after Sharon had gone to sleep. No warm bath for him tonight. Still, he was happy to sink into his bed and allow Lethe to overtake him. He needed no more troubling thoughts. Just sleep, blissful sleep. Perhaps his bundle of misgivings would be broken up by morning.

~

James had little sense of respite when he awoke. His slumber had been fitful, his dreams vivid and disturbing. A man with a hacksaw had pursued him down a street that was dark except for a light at its end. No matter how fast he ran, the light remained just as distant, while his pursuer inexorably gained on him.

James reached for a nearby pitcher of water on his bedside table. The liquid was tepid but refreshing as it glided down his parched throat. He tried to recall his dream in detail, even as it faded from his memory. All he could remember was a sense of impending doom, and great panic.

The long days in court and the nights of dictation were taking their toll, James thought. There had been just two days of testimony, and already he was feeling the physical and mental effects of his grand undertaking.

Leaving Bowdoin Square after dressing in a conservative black suit, he strolled across the Common, taking a roundabout way to the courthouse. To his surprise, he came across the twelve jurors enjoying their morning walk accompanied by their keepers, two court officers. James observed passersby turn in astonishment as they recognized the men. What other group would be regarded so benignly, knowing they possessed the power of life and death? James smiled and nodded as he passed them. He could tell a few recognized him from his time on the witness stand and his eternal note-taking.

James arrived in court and made his way to his table, where his pens, ink and paper awaited him. The clerk nodded to him as he sat down; James rose and bowed back. He was now a regular presence in the courtroom. He had succeeded in making phonography a part of the judicial process.

The first witness called, Dr. Nathan Keep, had been a Boston dentist for thirty years, and the Parkman family dentist since 1825. If Keep identified the false teeth found in Professor Webster's furnace as Dr. Parkman's, the prosecution would finally gain what it so desperately sought:

conclusive proof that the butchered remains were those of the man buried in the sealed Parkman family tomb in Mt. Auburn Cemetery.

Keep testified that he was first shown the blackened block of mineral teeth by Dr. Lewis, the day after their discovery.

"I recognized them immediately as the teeth I made for Doctor Parkman in 1846," he said. "Doctor Parkman's mouth was a very peculiar mouth, in many respects. I remembered the peculiarity of the lower jaw with great exactness."

The galleries were abuzz with Dr. Keep's seemingly impregnable testimony. Who could now dispute that these were Parkman's remains?

Keep—who possessed no apparent neck, his large head seeming to rest directly on his high collar—recounted how he had searched among his inventory for the original mold for Parkman's false teeth. Upon finding it, he discovered that it matched exactly to the block of teeth that had survived the fiery furnace.

"There is sufficient left of these blocks to identify the place where they belonged in the jaw," Keep said with authority. "There is no mistake."

The blocks of teeth were passed among the jurors, then to the justices. Keep had difficulty maintaining his composure. As he spoke of examining Dr. Parkman on past occasions, he broke down in great wheezing sobs. James looked around to see several jurors and spectators also weeping. The justices, too, were moved by Keep's most personal recollections, save Chief Justice Shaw, whose intimidating visage remained undisturbed.

The next witness was Dr. Jeffries Wyman, who described in detail the condition of the bones he had catalogued and analyzed. He, too, believed that someone knowledgeable in the medical arts had dismembered the body. He also offered that he had been particularly struck by the quantity of hair on the back of the thorax found dangling in the privy.

"I never saw a person before with so much hair on their back," he marveled.

The human skeleton diagram, with the bones marked in various colors, was then brought forward for the jurors and justices to see. Wyman enumerated a list that could have been the leavings of a wild animal's savaging: several vertebrae, a joint of an elbow, some bones of the wrist, a few joints of the fingers, some of the bones of the right leg. He also revealed, for the first time, that he had tested the incriminating spots on the floor in Webster's rooms, and they proved to be tobacco juice, not blood.

There was a great uproar in the galleries, and Tukey leapt up in the courtroom, shouting admonishments. This time the crowd was slow to silence, and it was difficult to hear Wyman describe exactly what he examined. Shaw motioned for Tukey to sit down and allow the testimony to continue.

Wyman said he had found the right slipper and the left leg of the pantaloons seized from Webster's private room to be stained with blood, and he noted that a piece of paper found in the laboratory had two spots of blood.

James was confused. Had Webster spattered blood over his laboratory, or had he not? This was a crucial piece of circumstantial evidence the prosecution needed to convict Webster.

Wyman concluded his testimony by outlining his search for additional bloodstains. To be thorough, he had even taken up the brick floor, which was laid on sand, but no traces of blood had been discovered above or below it. Wyman had chips from the floor examined, and found no blood on them, either. *If Webster had slaughtered Parkman in his laboratory, he had been singularly meticulous about it,* James thought.

Finally, the moment had arrived for Dr. Oliver Wendell Holmes to testify. The packed courtroom was silent as the celebrity physician chose to identify himself as the Parkman Professor of Anatomy and Physiology at Harvard Medical College, where he was also the dean, thus linking himself immediately to the unseen victim and the location of the crime.

Holmes said he agreed with his colleagues that the remains indicated that the person who separated them knew where to cut.

"There is no botching about the business," he said peremptorily.

It was clear there was no need for further discussion on that point. He did address one fact much labored over in the press: the proximity of his lecture room to Webster's laboratory, which was located directly beneath his own lecture room.

"I have never heard noises from Professor Webster's room," Holmes said in response to Bemis's question, regarding the prosecutor stonily. "The students in my room sit on rising seats; I stand on the floor."

Bemis asked Dr. Holmes a few more meaningless questions, received brief, astringent replies, and then the famous witness was done. *The galleries seemed disappointed,* James thought. *Holmes had offered no defense of Harvard, no justification for the unseemly discoveries in the Medical College he supervised, and no words of praise for John Webster or George Parkman. Where was the erudition, the wit, the observant mind that all had come to expect from the "Autocrat of the Breakfast Table"? Gone home to his supper table, greatly relieved to be out of the public eye.*

CHAPTER 18

March 1850
Court Street, Boston, Massachusetts

Friday, March 22, dawned gray, windy, and dreary. The crowd in front of the courthouse huddled together for warmth. They awaited the first appearance of Ephraim Littlefield, the Medical College janitor who had solved the mystery of George Parkman's disappearance. There were rumors that Littlefield was preparing a traveling show that would present a facsimile of Professor Webster's laboratory, where the murder no one had witnessed would be staged in a dramatic fashion for all to view and wonder at.

Littlefield was the first and only witness of the day. He answered Bemis's questions in a flat, unvarying voice. He said he had been the janitor of the Medical College for seven years. He superintended the building, swept the rooms, made fires, and aided with the purchase and maintenance of the anatomical specimens.

Bemis wasted little time before directing Littlefield to recount the interview that took place on Monday evening, November 19 last, between Dr. Parkman and Professor Webster in the latter's private rooms in the college. In the scene Littlefield set, Webster had three candles burning and was reading a chemistry text, while Littlefield stood at the stove, stirring water for an experiment of Webster's.

"I heard no footsteps but saw Doctor Parkman enter the room from the lecture room. Professor Webster looked 'round, surprised to see him enter without being heard. Doctor Parkman said, 'Professor Webster, are you ready for me tonight?'—speakin' loud and quick. Professor Webster answered, 'No, I am not ready tonight, Doctor.'

"Doctor Parkman said somethin' else, I do not remember what. He either spoke of Professor Webster's selling somethin' mortgaged, or mortgagin' something sold. Doctor Parkman took out papers from his pocket, and Professor Webster said, 'I was not aware that it was so.' Doctor Parkman said, 'It is so, and you know it.' Professor Webster replied, 'I will see you to-morrow.' Doctor Parkman stood near the doorway, raised his hand, and said, 'Somethin' must be done tomorrow.' Then he went out, and it was the last time I ever seen him in the building."

Littlefield moved on to the day of Parkman's disappearance, Friday, November 23. He said that as usual, he made a fire in Webster's back room before sweeping it out. There he had noticed a sledgehammer behind the door, which had not been there previously. It was always kept in the laboratory itself, which is where Littlefield said he returned it.

The press had made much of the missing sledgehammer as a potential murder weapon. Its disappearance was considered particularly damning to Webster. Now Littlefield was suggesting that Webster had hidden the incriminating evidence.

Littlefield recalled looking out the window of Dr. Andrew Ware's lecture room, which he was cleaning on November 23, at about fifteen minutes before two o'clock. He saw Dr. Parkman approach the college, walking very quickly. Littlefield testified that he never saw Parkman actually enter the building, because he took out Dr. Ware's trash.

Littlefield then had to wait until Dr. Holmes finished his lecture before he could clean up his rooms. Holmes left the college at quarter past two in the afternoon, Littlefield estimated, leaving the janitor the last person remaining in the building. He said he did not hear anyone enter or leave Professor Webster's lecture room, nor any raised voices or sounds of violence.

Littlefield said he then encountered a puzzling situation he had not spoken about previously. He found every door leading into Professor Webster's private rooms bolted from the inside on that Friday. Twice that day, Littlefield said tonelessly, he witnessed Webster entering his rooms with a bundle under his arm.

"I heard him in there walkin'. I heard the water runnin'. I went up the stairs and tried the door to the lecture room from the front. I found it to be locked and bolted from the inside. I never knew Professor Webster's door to be locked before, on the night of a lecture day, since I been in the college."

The next day was Littlefield's sweeping day, as it was Saturday. In the course of his duties, he testified that he heard Webster at work in his laboratory, although he did not see him until Sunday evening, when he had another strange encounter with the professor.

Littlefield was standing outside the Medical College, discussing Dr.

Parkman's disappearance with a neighbor, when Professor Webster, walking from Fruit Street, approached Littlefield directly.

"The first words he said to me were, "Littlefield, did you see Doctor Parkman during the latter part of last week?'

"I told him I did. He asked me when I seen him. I said last Friday, 'bout half past one o'clock. Then he asked me, 'Where did you see him?' I said right about this spot. He asked me which way he was goin'. I said he was comin' right towards the college here."

Littlefield said that Webster, upon hearing this, startled him by striking his cane upon the ground. He said Webster claimed, "That is the very time when I paid him $483.60."

Webster told the janitor that he had counted out the money for Dr. Parkman in his lecture room, and that Dr. Parkman grabbed the money from the table without counting it himself and ran out of the college as fast as he could go.

Littlefield shook his head, as if he regretted what he was about to say.

"I remember he put the odd cents on. I told him I didn't see Doctor Parkman come in or go out of the college."

For the first time, Littlefield spoke with emotion.

"When Professor Webster spoke to me before, he'd look me in the face with his head up. He did not then, but looked down, and seemed confused and agitated. I'd never seen him look so before. His face was thoughtful. He was pale."

Littlefield made his observations as if he were an astute writer. James found his eye for detail remarkable, his recall impressive, if he were to be believed.

Webster's rooms remained locked on Monday, November 26, said Littlefield. Charles Kingsley arrived with Constable Starkweather that afternoon. They told Littlefield they could trace Dr. Parkman nowhere but to the Medical College. They had come determined to find him, possibly in the attic, they supposed.

Littlefield recalled that Dr. Holmes met the party as he came down the stairs, and Holmes instructed Littlefield to show them all around. The first stop was Webster's private rooms, which Littlefield wasn't surprised to discover were locked.

"We knocked two or three times, loud ones. Professor Webster didn't come at first. Finally, he unbolts the door and sticks his head out. I tell him what the officers were come for. We go in, look through the room, and go down into his laboratory. I don't recollect hearin' the professor say anythin'."

There was nothing to say, because no one saw anything untoward, reflected James. *If Webster committed such a gory crime, he had cleaned up well after himself, and quickly, too.*

The next day, Tuesday, November 27, Littlefield said he encountered Webster reading a newspaper in his private rooms, wearing a sort of smoking cap. Apropos of nothing, Webster inquired whether Littlefield had already bought his Thanksgiving turkey. Littlefield responded that he and his wife had planned to go to a hotel restaurant for Thanksgiving dinner.

Webster insisted that he pick out a nice turkey for his table and gave him the name of a provision dealer who would accommodate him. From memory, Littlefield quoted him: "I am in the habit of giving away two or three every year, and perhaps I shall want you to do some odd job for me.'"

Littlefield said he had been astonished by the unexpected generosity.

"It be the first time he give me anythin'. The idea of his givin' me a cent's worth is remarkable," he said.

This man is averse to any slight, James mused, *even when a free turkey accompanies it.* As his testimony continued, Littlefield displayed his less admirable traits, including sneakiness. He testified that the following morning, the twenty-eighth, found him crouched next to the door of Webster's laboratory, trying to listen to the movements he could detect within and discern their nature. But the catch over the keyhole was down, and he could neither hear nor see anything specific.

Littlefield told the court that he then lay on the floor, his face crushed against the wood planks, to peer under the door of the laboratory. He could not see above Webster's ankles, but he could make out the professor dragging a coal hod toward the furnace, the location where the burnt bones were eventually found.

Littlefield said he stayed prone on the floor for a full five minutes trying to determine what else Webster was up to. Later that afternoon, as he walked up the stairs to clean Dr. Ainsworth's dissection laboratory, Littlefield recalled feeling intense heat coming from the wall next to Webster's laboratory.

"I put my own hand upon it and it was so hot I couldn't even hold it there for a long moment. It was clear to me it proceeded from a furnace, where I had never known any fire, and never made any fire." Littlefield said he feared that the college might catch fire, the wall was so warm.

Littlefield's suspicions were now fully aroused, he said. He tried his keys to gain entry to Webster's rooms but found all still bolted from within. An hour later, he had managed to climb to the second floor with the aid of a ladder and clamber through a window into Webster's laboratory. He said he went directly to the furnace but was disappointed to find that it was barely warm. There was very little fire left in it. The stove had a soapstone lid, and the top was covered with pots of minerals. Littlefield said he was careful not to disturb anything.

He was also careful to note several anomalies. Two full hogsheads of water were depleted, after being filled by Littlefield just two days earlier. The pitch pine kindling Littlefield had prepared for a week's worth of lectures was also gone after only two days. On the stairs, Littlefield noticed stains he had never seen before, in a splatter pattern. He said he drew his finger across one of the spots and placed it in his mouth: it tasted like acid.

Littlefield sat upright in the witness box. The sweat shone on his pale, unmarked forehead. He was nervous, but his voice remained a steady monotone as he related the details of yet another police search of the Medical College, this time on Thursday morning, November 29, one as futile as its predecessors.

He recalled Lieutenant Clapp peering through a pane of glass in the door to Webster's privy and asking, "What place is this?" Webster was within three feet of Clapp, Littlefield said, when the janitor responded to the question.

"That be Professor Webster's privy. No one can get into it but himself."

Clapp looked as if he might inquire further, said Littlefield. "But Professor Webster seemed to me to draw every person's attention to another part of the room, and he unbolted another door leadin' to his storeroom," he said. "We all went into the storeroom."

Had Clapp pursued his instincts, James thought, *Littlefield would have had no glory in this matter and would still be an insignificant janitor whose opinions would interest no one.* Instead, the police asked to search the room where the remains of medical specimens were stored. Littlefield explained to them that only he had access to it, and that it was always locked, but Clapp had insisted. The janitor took them to a twelve by twelve-foot square room sunk below the dissection laboratory and lowered a lantern into it. The police could see that it was filled with bodies, a ghoulish gathering that reeked of preservation chemicals.

"All seemed satisfied that there was nothing there that didn't belong there," said Littlefield. But he remained under suspicion, he testified in an injured tone. The police searched all of his rooms thoroughly, as well as the entire basement under the building. While they crawled across the dirt floor, Littlefield said that he pointed out to one of the constables the brick wall that sealed off Webster's privy.

"I told him that this was the only place which had not been searched, and there was no access to it other than the locked door above, except by digging through the wall."

The police didn't share Littlefield's interest in the privy, but that didn't diminish the janitor's suspicions. On Friday, November 30, Littlefield began burrowing. He worked his way through two layers of brick in the thick wall before abandoning his labors by evening.

That night Littlefield and his wife went to a ball held by the Sons of Temperance in Cochituate. "There be twenty dances, and I danced in eighteen of 'em," he told the court proudly. There was laughter in the courtroom, but a grimace from Chief Justice Shaw quickly snuffed it out.

Littlefield said his wife hectored him to continue his work on the privy wall, but an unexpected visitor interrupted his plans the next morning: Professor Webster himself. Littlefield's narrative remained dispassionate, but James could imagine how shaken this unexpected encounter must have left the janitor.

"He asked me if I was hearin' anythin' about Doctor Parkman," said Littlefield, and before he could even respond, he said Webster related a report of a bloody bundle discovered in a hansom cab, then shook his head and went up the stairs to his rooms.

Littlefield said he next went looking for Dr. Wynfred Lewis in the anatomical lecture room.

"I asked him if he knew about reports and suspicions against Professor Webster. He said he knew there were. I told him what I had been doin', workin' on bustin' through the wall; he told me to go ahead."

Armed with the approval of his superiors, Littlefield set about his task in a serious manner. He obtained a crowbar, a cold chisel, and a bigger hammer from a neighbor, went home, and locked all the doors in his cottage.

"I told my wife not to be lettin' anyone in; but if Webster comes in, to be sure and let him in—but not before she gives me four raps on the floor."

Littlefield dreaded being caught by Webster, he admitted; how could he explain what he was doing? Littlefield said he worried that he might suffer the same fate as Parkman if Webster surprised him at his labors.

Littlefield recounted that he worked so assiduously that he blistered his hands. He made it through three and a half levels of brickwork, almost the entire thickness of the wall, when he heard four loud raps on the floor. In a panic, he dropped his tools and hurried upstairs, only to find that his wife had overreacted. The visitors were once again Kingsley and Constable Starkweather. Littlefield apprised them of his progress, saying he was about twenty minutes from penetrating the wall.

Kingsley and Starkweather departed, promising to return soon. Littlefield and his wife had just sat down to dinner when Webster appeared on his way out of the college. This time, the overly congenial professor told a tale of an Irishman offering a new $20 bill to pay a toll of one penny. This must have been the thief who robbed Dr. Parkman, Webster said. Littlefield had waited for Webster to continue, but he said the professor stood silent for a few minutes before abruptly leaving Littlefield's cottage.

Littlefield said the encounter with the man he suspected of murder left him shaken. He abandoned his dinner and resumed his efforts in the cellar, soon knocking out the remaining bricks. He chiseled a small opening about three feet off the ground that was eighteen inches wide and a foot high.

"I had difficulty getting a light through the hole, on account of the draft of air," said Littlefield. When he prevailed, what he saw took his breath away.

The rapt courtroom was riven by the thunder of the chief justice's gavel hammering down on the bench.

"That will be enough for today, gentlemen," he said, addressing the prosecutors, the defense, and the witness, Littlefield, who looked as if a rug had just been yanked from beneath him. "It has been a lengthy day, and I do not wish to tax either the witness or the jury too greatly. We will resume at nine o'clock tomorrow morning."

James thought Shaw could not have planned a better curtain drop, to retain maximum curiosity about just what Ephraim Littlefield saw dangling in that privy. James also enjoyed seeing Littlefield's discomfiture when the judge suddenly turned his spotlight off; Littlefield had been just warming up to the dramatic moment where his many suspicions became justified. Now, it would all have to wait until the next day.

Littlefield's testimony took hours to transcribe, and all departed Court Street exhausted, including Ellen and James. There was no romantic banter this evening, just a mutual desire to collapse into a mindless sleep in their respective beds.

The next morning, James was refreshed and eager to see Littlefield resume his time in the witness box. How would the great hero react to his grisly discovery? Unlike the courtroom audience, James understood exactly where this story was headed.

Littlefield still looked ruffled from yesterday's rude (in his mind) interruption by Chief Justice Shaw, and it affected his delivery of his discovery. He mumbled to the point where Shaw had to loudly interrupt him and demand that he speak up. Littlefield reddened, and had even more difficulty speaking clearly and distinctly. James had to lean toward the witness box to make sure he captured every word.

"On holdin' the light, I was thinkin' I could see the pelvis and the private parts of a man, and also parts of two legs. I came right up and told my wife what I had seen. I was violently agitated, so much so that I locked the trap door and went to see Doctor Jacob Bigelow."

The latter was not home, so Littlefield journeyed to Dr. Henry Ware's residence in Chauncey Place. Dr. Ware took him to Robert Shaw's home, where he was ushered into Shaw's study to relate his gruesome discovery. Marshal Tukey soon arrived. He instructed Littlefield to return to the Medical College, where Tukey's constables and the Harvard doctors would meet him.

When the reunited group gathered in the college basement, Littlefield testified, Tukey thought he heard Webster moving about, and he went up the stairs with his revolver out and cocked. But it was only neighborhood children running about outside; Webster was not present in the building. Littlefield said Tukey and his men left with Dr. James Stone to fetch Webster at his home in Cambridge.

Upon their return to the Medical College, after the lengthy stop at the Leverett Street Gaol, Littlefield said he was startled by Webster's appearance. "He was altogether supported by the officers. He did not seem to have the use of his legs at all."

Taking Littlefield and Webster with them, the police ascended to Webster's rooms and demanded keys for the small back room and the privy. Littlefield had already told them he had never possessed those keys; they belonged solely to Webster, who moaned that he'd had no chance to take any of his belongings when he was rushed from his home. The police found a hatchet under the sink and used it to break open the doors to Webster's back room and his privy.

Littlefield said he was most curious about the stove, remembering the heat of the wall from the prior week. He said he proceeded into the back room where the stove was located, saw that bones were in it, and took one out before being told sharply by Tukey to let all evidence remain as it was.

James was confused by Littlefield's testimony. It was as if he were taking credit for discovering the burnt remnants found in the stove, when previous testimony had clearly established that it was Constable Fuller who had found them. For all his demurrals, Littlefield was doing everything he could to keep himself front and center in the court's attention.

Bemis indicated that, after almost two full days of testimony, he was finished with his witness. Sohier rose to begin the cross-examination when Chief Justice Shaw banged his gavel and once again declared court adjourned for the day.

This time it was Edwin Sohier who looked stunned, like a man with an argument to make and nowhere to make it. Littlefield seemed grateful to exit the witness box. *It must have been an ordeal for the janitor, attempting to recall so many details from months past,* James thought.

In two days of testimony, Ephraim Littlefield had proved credible, an effective witness for the prosecution. James could see that the jurors were impressed by his down-to-earth manner and his seeming forthrightness. Sohier had his work cut out for him to impugn Littlefield's detailed recollections.

As he walked down Court Street to his nightly labors, James reflected upon Sohier's possible strategy. The janitor had stuck stubbornly to his version of events. No one in the courtroom could challenge him save the man in the prisoner's dock, and it was questionable whether Professor Webster would appear as a witness on his own behalf.

James had read the rumors printed in the newspapers: Webster was determined to testify; Webster was too terrified to testify. His lawyers would call him as their final witness; his counsel would never call him to the stand.

Littlefield's testimony would be difficult to sully, James imagined. Marshal Tukey had testified that on several occasions, Littlefield had verbally and publicly relinquished any reward money offered by the Parkman and Shaw families.

In court, Littlefield had displayed no personal animus toward Webster, although James remembered the look on Littlefield's face when recounting Webster's offer of a free turkey. It was the countenance of one who had been shamed and condescended to, and who remained indignant over slights both actual and perceived, although it had not prevented him from picking up the free turkey.

James arrived across the street from the workroom, where he now could see Ellen framed through the second-story window. It was a rare opportunity to study her unobserved. She went purposefully from desk to desk, straightening out the pens and foolscap, making sure every detail was just so. Her manner with the young copyists was that of an older sister: firm, yet capable of amusement and laughter, which James could almost hear.

James knew that his feelings for Ellen were complex, but he had given little time to sorting them out, with the press of the trial, the endless transcription of the testimony, and the continuing debate over Webster's innocence that raged within his mind

No matter how busy his life, he couldn't resist Ellen's magnetism, which drew him to her by the way she turned her head, the delight in her eyes when she beheld his approach.

There were moments when James thought his attraction to her would overwhelm him. *He had never experienced such a sharp sensation of desire evoked by a woman. Ellen touched something within him that he had not known existed.*

Jennie Ray Gillmer, at least in her letters to him, had never exerted such power over James. That laboriously written love affair had been calibrated to a higher level, unconcerned with sordid physicality. Yet all that had come to naught, and odds were so would this fancy for Ellen O'Keeffe.

James wished that he could occupy himself in relaxing more with women. Ellen left him doubly perplexed. He felt unable to either move forward or pull away. Thank God there was the business of the report to occupy them both, or these thoughts would drive him to distraction.

He walked across to number 87. Ellen looked down, saw James approaching, and moved to open the door at the top of the stairs, her face brightening at the sight of him as he climbed up. James smiled at her in a way that she cherished.

The dictation sessions were the highlight of Ellen's day. She looked forward to them all her waking hours. It was not just the startling sense of self-sufficiency and independence the job gave her. For the first time in her life, she was keeping her own money. To forestall Haggerty's complaints, she had paid for the next two buckets of coal the family would need to stay warm in this chilly spring.

James Stone had opened a window on a new world for her, where her intelligence and quick wit proved assets instead of liabilities. Ellen had never believed that a life outside the North End tenements was a possibility for someone of her lineage. James had broken that barrier in one short conversation with the Mother Superior. She could never repay his kindness, his belief in her potential.

Ellen knew James didn't expect her body in return for his beneficence. He was a gentleman. He had never treated her disrespectfully, nor made any forward advance.

There had been the brief kiss on the first night of the trial. It had transfixed and shaken her. She had been kissed before and pawed at by Irish men young and old over the years, from lecherous uncles to lusty beaux, but never had she experienced the depth of feeling James evoked within her. She didn't know what to call it, but he made her feel excited within her innermost core.

Ellen smiled as she greeted him. "Good evenin' to ye, Doctor Stone! Shall we begin?"

CHAPTER 19

March 1850
Court Street, Boston, Massachusetts

"What hour exactly on the evening of Monday, November 19, was it that Doctor Parkman came to the college?"

The cross examination of Ephraim Littlefield by Edwin Sohier began in a tone that made obvious the defense's lack of admiration for him and his memory.

This meeting, to which Littlefield had been the only witness, was critical in establishing Professor Webster's intent to settle his debts with his creditor. In Shaw's and Littlefield's testimony for the prosecution, Webster was presented as being under intense pressure to satisfy Parkman; murder might well have resulted.

Littlefield remained steadfast in his responses, never varying his reasonable tone nor his detailed recollections. Sohier kept probing. Yes, Littlefield admitted, he was in and out of Webster's rooms constantly because he did all the physical work for the professor: washing glass appliances, sweeping up, preparing the fires for his experiments. Sohier kept peppering him with more questions.

"Did you find the work dirty, Mister Littlefield? Beneath someone of your talents, your intelligence?"

"Sometimes it is dirty work," Littlefield acknowledged. James thought he was working hard to not show his resentment over the difference between his station and Professor Webster's. Littlefield testified that his suspicions about Webster's errant behavior began in earnest on Sunday, November 25. "I told my wife I was goin' to watch every step he took," he said.

Asked when he learned about the reward proffered by the Parkman family, Littlefield became agitated in the courtroom for the first time. "I never said I meant to get this reward, and *I defy you to prove it!*" he shouted at Sohier, who was startled, then satisfied. He had finally nettled Littlefield.

Chief Justice Shaw leaned over and rumbled, "Keep control of yourself, sir. There will be no shouting in this court!"

The janitor's face reddened, and after taking a moment, he more calmly claimed that he was not even aware of a reward until the Monday after Dr. Parkman's disappearance. "I stated my suspicions were all excited by Sunday night. I stated in my testimony all the circumstances that done excited them."

His encounter with Webster, on the night when the Professor insisted that he had paid Parkman in full, was the final provocation, Littlefield said.

"He didn't look at me when he struck his cane on the ground," he said. "I then start suspectin' him of havin' somethin' to do with the disappearance of Doctor Parkman. I suspected he dealt foully with Doctor Parkman."

Sohier focused on Littlefield's actions in checking up on Webster. He wanted to know why Littlefield examined the water barrels. The janitor looked embarrassed and lowered his voice for the first time.

"I didn't know but Doctor Parkman might be poked into the hogshead," he said.

The observation elicited great mirth in the courtroom. This led Chief Justice Shaw to rouse himself again. "Quiet in the court!"

All sound instantly ceased. Sohier looked to the chief justice before proceeding and continued his cross-examination only after Shaw's jowls quivered in silent assent.

Sohier had follow-up questions about Littlefield's suspicions concerning Webster's privy, which Littlefield said had been paramount in his imagination of places where foul deeds could have been hidden. Sohier wondered why Littlefield didn't try to gain access to the privy from above.

"I didn't try to get into the privy," Littlefield admitted. "Probably if I had a key that would fit it, I should've unlocked it. I shouldn't think it was a very common lock or key, but I didn't try to open it, and made no attempt to find any key that would fit it."

The suggestion by the defense, James realized, was that Littlefield had planted the evidence in the privy and needed a dramatic event to distract from his role. Had he been able to unlock the privy door so all could look inside, the impact of the discovery of the remains would have been greatly reduced, if no less gross. To James's surprise, Sohier didn't elaborate on this suggestion.

Instead, the counsel for the defense pressed Littlefield on how well rehearsed his testimony seemed. Had he studied on the matter for the trial? Littlefield stared contemptuously at Sohier.

"I may have made some minutes before the coroner's inquest. I kept them to look at, but I never made a new set. I never wrote them but once."

Next it was the turn of Pliny Merrick, Sohier's co-counsel, whose sallow features matched his thin frame, to shake Littlefield's smug bearing.

Under Merrick's cross-examination, Littlefield revealed for the first time that he had joined the general hunt for Dr. Parkman on the first night that his disappearance became known, crossing the bridge to East Cambridge to aid parties searching there.

For reasons he could not explain, he admitted that he had told no one of seeing Dr. Parkman visit Professor Webster prior to his disappearance, or that he had overheard their argument about money. He said he had no explanation for keeping this information secret.

James was surprised by Merrick's failure to pursue this confession and bear down on Littlefield for hiding important information. Instead, the defense counselor returned to the subject of the promised reward, again evoking vehement denials from Littlefield.

"I never have made claim to any reward. I have said that I never had made any claim, and never should. I say now that I never shall claim it."

Merrick's feeble cross-examination of Littlefield was soon done, but the janitor's story was not yet concluded. His wife, Caroline, was called to the witness box next. Her testimony proved more dramatic.

"On Sunday afternoon, after tea, Mister Littlefield, he went out. He came in, and beckoned me, Missus Littlefield, from the kitchen to the bedroom. He says now he believed that Doctor Parkman been murdered by Professor Webster.

"I says, 'For mercy's sake, what makes ye think so? Don't ye ever mention such a thing again! If the professor should hear it, it'll make real trouble for ye.'"

As she emptied the trash after her husband cleaned, Mrs. Littlefield, too, found normally accessible doors to Webster's rooms now mysteriously locked. She said she discussed this strange situation with her husband. This led to the first heated argument in court about admissible evidence.

Bemis led Mrs. Littlefield to testify that her husband had peered under the door and had seen Webster moving his coal hob to the furnace. Merrick strongly protested on behalf of the defense.

"We do not object to offering evidence that Mister Littlefield did try the door," he said, "but if you propose to show what Mister Littlefield saw when he was lying down, we do object."

The objection and assertions were registering so quickly that James could barely keep up. His fingers were speeding across his pages as he tried to capture every word. Chief Justice Shaw intervened at last and ruled that anything Mrs. Littlefield herself had observed might be stated, but not her conversations with other persons, including her husband. "What was done or seen can be testified to," Shaw gargled in his *basso profundo* voice. Bemis seemed delighted: he could now ask his question.

"Did you see Mister Littlefield lying on the floor, near Professor Webster's door?" The answer, however, was not what he expected.

"I didn't see him lying down," Mrs. Littlefield said in her clear voice, aware of the impact she was having. "I only saw him listening at the keyhole; and when he saw me, he came away."

Bemis looked disappointed, and there was an audible reaction in the courtroom. There was no one else to corroborate Littlefield's testimony. Ultimately it was his word against Webster's. Later, the newspapers reported that Professor Webster was said to be most eager to testify following Littlefield's appearance. It was also said that Messrs. Sohier and Merrick feared the damage Mr. Bemis and Attorney General Clifford would inflict on Webster, were he made available to them on the witness stand.

In the courtroom, Bemis concluded his questioning of Littlefield's wife with one final attempt at duplicating the horror of the janitor's discovery. "State then, what was your husband's manner when he came up from the discovery of the body?"

Mrs. Littlefield, her voice quavering, replied, "He was much affected. He burst into tears."

Mrs. Littlefield was dismissed, and Chief Justice Shaw adjourned early at one o'clock, given that it was Saturday and the court was mandated to provide "necessary relaxation" for the jurors. James began to suspect that the chief justice did not enjoy long days in court.

Shaw took pains to caution the jury that it had heard but one side of the question, and that it was too early for them to make up their minds as to the disposition of the case. James wondered what motivated the chief justice to issue such a warning. Did he think the evidence already proved Webster guilty beyond a reasonable doubt? Or the chief justice may have seen defects in the prosecution, in addition to Littlefield's weaknesses. There were no easy answers. There were only more questions.

CHAPTER 20

March 1850
Court Street, Boston, Massachusetts

The trial entered its second week, which meant a new week of courtroom transcription lay ahead. James felt unprepared for the grinding routine by which his life was now circumscribed.

No new witnesses were expected to equal the impact of Ephraim Littlefield. However, when Lieutenant Derastus Clapp approached the witness box, he brought the courtroom to life. Clapp was the founder of Boston's first detective bureau. Prior to the Webster trial, no one but criminals had recognized him on the street. Now he was mobbed wherever he went, a beneficiary of the wave of publicity washing over the policemen who had "solved" the crime.

Clapp produced a memorandum that he said he had taken from Webster's wallet on the night of his arrest. On it was written, along with various sums, this statement:

"Dr. Parkman came to the lecture-room and stayed till students went out. He came to me and asked for money. I told him to call Friday, Nov. 23. He was a good deal excited. Friday, Nov. 23 went to his house and told him to call at half past one, and I would pay him. He called, and I paid him $432.64, and he gave up two notes, and said he would go and get the mortgage cancelled."

The introduction of this evidence occasioned an explosive reaction in the courtroom. The galleries resounded with exclamations; the justices stared at each other before Chief Justice Shaw raised a heavily veined hand for silence. His injunction was obeyed, although given his glare at the galleries, not quickly enough to his taste.

Clapp testified that he was also with James, Marshal Tukey, and Officer Fuller when Professor Webster made his failed suicide attempt in the police carriage. The police lieutenant recalled that he had observed shock on Webster's face when he arrived at the Medical College and saw those present, from city and state officials to Harvard administrators.

"What does this all mean?" Webster asked, according to Clapp.

The Lieutenant said he responded, "We're done looking for the body of Doctor Parkman. We shall not look for his body any more, and you are now in custody on the charge of the murder of Doctor Parkman."

The galleries erupted again.

"The court will stand for no more of this clatter," Chief Justice Shaw said. Then he raised his voice, as if about to make a legal ruling: "I will clear the courtroom in the event of a single outburst more."

The resulting silence was total. As Clapp departed the witness box, many in the courtroom regarded Professor Webster, who sat calmly in the prisoner's dock, looking blandly ahead, as if regarding a great nothing. If he was reliving the events Clapp had described, he kept it to himself.

The next witness was Seth Pettee, a clerk at the New England Bank, who sold tickets to the Medical College lectures for the Harvard faculty. He said that the cost for a single chemistry lecture was $15, and Webster gave Pettee one hundred tickets to sell to students each semester.

Pettee testified that by the end of last November, he had paid Webster a net amount of almost $600 from the ticket sales. Sohier and Merrick seemed pleased by the clerk's testimony, which was honest and straightforward. James could see the jurors felt the same way about Pettee, a sensible and modest man, like many of them saw themselves.

Pettee also recounted his various conversations with George Parkman, who came to him that November to collect the money Webster owed him. Pettee reported that he'd said he had no funds in hand to pay Parkman: "I told him I had no control over the funds belonging to the professor. Doctor Parkman said that now he should be obliged to distress Professor Webster and his family. He seemed to blame me for not retaining the funds. He afterwards made some remarks, the import of which was that Professor Webster was not an honest or upright man. He called him a damned rascal, and a damned whelp, and he asked me to tell Professor Webster so. I never saw Doctor Parkman again."

Parkman has obtained a free pass in this case, James thought. *His character is beside the point in the question of Webster's guilt or innocence, but not in the larger issue of just how far a man can be driven before he breaks. Parkman was an expert breaker of men. John Webster was an unqualified and untrained combatant in the financial arena where he had met George Parkman.*

The next witness was Solomon Webb, the cashier of the Charles River Bank where Webster kept an account. He testified to the sad truth of Webster's overstretched and overmortgaged existence: on November 23, the balance in the bank account of Professor Webster stood at $139.15. Earlier in the month, his balance had been as low as $4.26, Webb said.

The picture of Webster emerging from the trial was that of an upscale pauper. This seemed to bother the defendant more than anything else he had heard. He kept his gaze upon his shoes throughout the testimony of the bank cashier. His sudden shyness was observed and commented upon by many.

The day's final witness was the Rev. Doctor Francis Parkman, brother of the late George Parkman. He confirmed his relationship with Professor Webster, who had attended the reverend's New North Church as a child, and whose grandson Rev. Parkman had baptized three months before his brother George vanished.

The clergyman was giving evidence against Webster for the murder of his brother, yet the accused had been under his pastoral care. No wonder Rev. Parkman was much affected. Weeping often disrupted his testimony. The jurors and justices, save Shaw, looked likewise moved. For the first time, the court heard of the anxious state of the Parkman family after the events of November 23.

"We were in great perplexity and distress," recalled Rev. Parkman.

The appearance of Professor Webster at Rev. Parkman's residence two days after Dr. Parkman's disappearance had brought some welcome news to the family, the clergyman testified. They were relieved to learn it was Professor Webster who had called that Friday morning. They had feared that Parkman had been visited by some stranger intending to do him harm later. Webster reiterated to Rev. Parkman his now-familiar tale of paying off his debt in full to his brother, but the reverend doctor was suspicious.

"There seemed to be in him great nervousness of manner," Rev. Parkman said. "He commenced upon his business immediately upon entering the room, and it was impossible for me not to remark that there was no expression of surprise at the mysterious disappearance, and none of sympathy."

This omission registered strongly on the clergyman. "What particularly struck me was the absence of that expression of sympathy naturally given to those in perplexity and distress."

James studied Professor Webster's reactions to this witness carefully. He saw more emotion in the little man's eyes than his usual studied

DALE M. POLLOCK

nonchalance and wondered what in Rev. Parkman's testimony had affected him so.

James was glad his job was only to take down the words uttered, and not to have to puzzle out the inner workings of the human mind.

～

It was almost midnight by the time the young women turned in their neatly printed papers to Ellen and readied to leave. Their hands were as weary as James' voice. He sounded dry and raspy after another long evening of reading aloud.

The work was progressing, despite the toll it took on his health, not to mention his pocketbook. He had gone surreptitiously to Jerome for an advance from his share of the family trust to pay for the mounting transcription costs. James knew that there would be the devil to pay if Lucinda discovered he was drawing down his capital.

It was not in James's nature to make unrequested disclosures, so he had said little to his family about his plans with his report. All were aware of his status as a key witness. He was the talk of Beacon Hill because of the valuable role he had played at the trial in identifying Dr. Parkman, or what was left of him.

James reminded himself that when he published the *Report of the Trial of Professor John W. Webster* mere weeks after the trial's conclusion, people would be discussing James Stone for his own accomplishments, not his proximity to a rich man's tragedy.

His back ached from the hunched position he always assumed when dictating. He grimaced as he stood that night to leave. Ellen noticed and came over, touching him lightly on the arm.

"James, I know this schedule must be wearing on ye," she said. "Is there any more I could do, to aid or assist ye?"

He hadn't realized how exhausted he must look. He was embarrassed to have revealed a weak constitution, but grateful for Ellen's solicitousness. No one other than his sister Lucinda had ever expressed concern for his physical well-being. He had been denied the warm affections of a loving mother from the age of three onward.

"I thank you, Ellen," he said. "I took up this task with full knowledge of the toll it would take on both mind and spirit, and now I must bear it. You help me greatly in this regard. I hardly know how to express my gratitude."

"Ye show it in the civil way ye treat me, and the other girls," Ellen said. "Nae been generous to us since we landed in these United States. These girls have been told all their lives the only purpose God intended for 'em was to birth babes, cook meals, and sleep beside a drunken husband. Ye've given them a higher purpose. As for me, ye've made all the difference."

Ellen looked away, her inevitable blush taking a few moments to subside. She'd surprised herself by revealing her inner thoughts to James for the first time. He had liberated her from a prison she hadn't realized she inhabited, it was so molded to her form and actions.

James was touched by Ellen's appreciation, and before fully understanding what he was doing, he took her hand in his. This time there were no interceding gloves.

He must have been listening to my thoughts, she said to herself.

"You've made a difference in my world, too," James said, looking directly into Ellen's eyes. "It hasn't been the same since you entered it. I've struggled to understand why. My feelings inform me more than my thoughts."

Startled by this declaration, Ellen did her best not to show it. She left her hand in James's palm. She could feel the heat of his hand around her fingers, reflecting the desire she saw in his eyes. He moved closer, bringing his other arm around Ellen's slim shoulder. What possessed him to do this? She wasn't sure; she didn't care.

Ellen stood still, leaning into James's arm. "Feelings can nae be trusted, Doctor Stone," she murmured. "I've learned that hard lesson in me life, as I'm sure ye have in yours."

"Do you share my sentiments, at least to some degree?" James asked. "I don't think I could bear it if you did not."

"Here we be, with nae distance between us, that should answer yer question, Doctor. But it leads to a hundred more. We have nae future, ye and me, nae here in this place, nae at this time. Maybe in some other world, but nae here."

"Are here and now to be overlooked because of an uncertain future? Can't we live for this moment, the two of us in a world of our own making, a world shaped and formed by our phonographic work?"

His fervor took Ellen aback. She had never seen him so excited. But these were not the words she was hoping to hear. James would never abandon the subject of his beloved phonography. She understood his enthusiasm, but this was disturbing. Could he not share with her what was in his heart? Ellen drew away, and James released her from his embrace.

"I beg your pardon," he said, ill at ease. He regretted his reference to their work, rather than to his feelings about her, which were so strong they defied easy expression. "I did not mean to place you in an uncomfortable situation. You know I have only the highest—"

Ellen put an index finger to James's lips. "Nae apologies, James, nae when ye've nothing to be sorry fer. I be a grown woman, and if I choose to welcome the touch of a man, that is me choice, and no one else's."

James had never before heard a woman declare herself in this direct manner, he found it both thrilling and unsettling. He hadn't considered that the licentious thoughts that had invaded his consciousness might also have probed Ellen's. Nothing in his limited experience with women had trained him for this moment.

Ellen made the decision for both of them. She turned and placed her arms around James's neck. She looked directly into his startled eyes.

"Kiss me, James. Do so quickly afore I lose my nerve and change my mind!"

As she leaned forward, James eagerly bent downward, and their lips met. It was a glorious kiss.

James felt himself stiffen below and was embarrassed. He had never been physically intimate with a woman other than a prostitute. In those circumstances, becoming hard was the entire point of the exercise. To be so grossly masculine with a woman he so admired, perhaps even loved, and unable to control his lewd desires, filled him with self-loathing.

Ellen was now in charge. She ran one of her hands delicately through James's hair, brushing her fingertips along the back of his neck. He moaned through lips that he pressed harder against hers. She could feel the involuntary jerk of his body as it came into contact with her own.

She removed her mouth from James's to pepper his face with short, quick kisses. She kissed his ear, leaving him gasping, helpless with desire. James grabbed Ellen by the shoulders and pulled her to him, grinding their bodies together as if trying to fuse them into one. He was unsure what to do next, only that he must complete this union he desperately desired.

James looked around the room for a suitable location. There was only the trestle table where he and Ellen worked—that, or the floor, too sordid even for James's inflamed senses. Grabbing Ellen by the forearm, he led her toward the table, sweeping it free of pens and paper with one hand, the other arm clutched around the waist of the woman who, at this moment, he wanted more than he had wanted anything in his life.

This is what I desire, Ellen thought as she let James guide her to a scene she had imagined in her mind but had never supposed would come to pass.

Ellen realized it was not too late to quit, to halt what was unfolding and stop it in its track, restoring some equilibrium to their relationship. This did not have to happen. Yet she wanted it to happen, and so did James. Of that she was sure. Ellen placed a calming hand on his shoulder.

"Let me go at my pace, James, and nae worry, we'll both arrive at the same place."

And they did.

DALE M. POLLOCK

CHAPTER 21

March 1850
Court Street and Union Street, Boston, Massachusetts

George Fuller was in the witness box, the constable who had been in the thick of things the night Littlefield sounded the news of his morbid discovery.

Fuller was an observant fellow, the kind of nosy person the city wanted for a constable, James thought. Fuller had interviewed Webster in his rooms at the Medical College about the debt that was allegedly paid to his creditor, and he possessed an excellent recollection of what had been said.

"I asked Professor Webster who was with him when he paid Doctor Parkman the money owed. He said, 'There was no one but the doctor and myself.' I asked the time of the occurrence. He said between half past one and two o'clock Friday past. I asked Doctor Webster where he and Doctor Parkman stood when he paid this money. He said, 'Behind the table, near the end'—that is, as he would stand facing the students, it would be to the left."

Fuller testified that he was also the constable who had discovered the remains in the tea chest. "I took the chest out into the middle of the room, and turned it over, and there were the remains of a human body—a thorax, and other parts. I also found a kidney. The neck end of the thorax was up, as it lay in the chest," he recalled.

The image of these random, gruesome body parts lingered in the courtroom. *No matter how often these grisly details were trotted out, they never failed to delight the galleries,* James thought.

Even the esteemed Oliver Wendell Holmes did not escape Fuller's scrutiny. Fuller revealed that he had experimented with sound, to see if someone in Professor Holmes's lecture room could have heard a violent struggle in Webster's rooms below. He said that with both doors shut, another constable shouted from Webster's lecture room, while Fuller stood in Holmes's lecture hall to hear if the sound carried.

"We couldn't hear each other," said Fuller, sounding disappointed that the experiment had failed.

His duty done, Constable Fuller retired to the back of the courtroom to help Marshal Tukey with crowd control, and George Parkman's nephew came to the witness box.

Samuel Parkman Blake had done more than just look for his uncle George. In the days after the disappearance, he had gone to the Medical College to confront Webster in the hope of obtaining more details of his meeting with Parkman on that fateful Friday. Blake was well acquainted with the chemistry professor, and had been "for a good many years," he testified.

"On my entrance, his manner was peculiar. It seemed to want that cordiality which was usual with him. He looked pale. He received me in a stiff manner. I think he didn't put out his hand to shake hands."

There was more, Blake said. His suspicions, hardly dormant on his arrival, were further inflamed by Webster's aberrant behavior.

"His manner, when he spoke of Doctor Parkman, surprised me," he said. "By his expression he was angry, at a time when my family was in deep distress. He expressed no sympathy. He let me approach him, instead of partly coming to meet me. He said very little about the search for Doctor Parkman. He made no inquiry about our family at all."

Blake was more than offended by Webster's behavior. He stayed with the man for no more than fifteen minutes, he testified, long enough that when Blake learned Webster had been charged, he was convinced of the professor's guilt. The look in Blake's eyes when he regarded Webster now, James could see, was one of plain hatred.

James discerned the plan of attack Clifford and Bemis were pursuing. They would alternate a policeman with a grieving family member, each presenting a different aspect of the case, detailing the impact of the murder upon both the family and the police investigation.

The jury was always moving back and forth between grim factual testimony and the emotional impact of the killing. James could see that this strategy was having an impact. There were fewer glances across the courtroom to see how Webster reacted to a statement or exhibit, and more attention paid to the Parkman family, the true victims of the tragedy.

The next witness called was Constable Charles Starkweather. He had been left to supervise Professor Webster in the Leverett Street Gaol after his arrest and failed suicide attempt. Starkweather said he told his prisoner of the grave charges he faced, and Webster, trying to clear his senses, re-quested details.

"I told him I wished he wouldn't ask me any questions, as it wasn't proper for me to answer them," Starkweather said. "He said, 'Where did they find him? Did they find the whole of the body? How came they to suspect me? Oh! My children! What will they do! How will they think of me! Where did you get your information?'"

While evading Webster's questions, Starkweather testified that he managed a few of his own.

"I asked the doctor if anyone had a way into his private rooms at the Medical College. He answered me, 'Nobody but the janitor who makes the fires.'" Starkweather was familiar with Littlefield; the policeman was part of the group the janitor had first led into the cellar.

Starkweather said that after relaying this information, Webster paused for some minutes. The constable had kept his peace, hoping for a confession to follow.

"And then the doctor exclaimed, 'Oh, that villain! I am a ruined man!'"

The constable testified that Webster said nothing more, "but wrung his hands and lay down."

Questioned by Sohier on cross-examination as to the veracity of his recollections, Starkweather was offended by the suggestion that his account was anything but truthful and accurate.

"I have given the exact words of conversation that were said in the jail," he maintained, in an irritated voice. "I wrote them down while the doctor was talking. I was writing atop a stove, which had no fire in it. I didn't write down my own language, I wrote down his."

It was almost two by the time the court adjourned for dinner. Snow was falling, a rare event this late in March. James's stomach was growling, and he was eager to be off to the Union Oyster House. There he was to join the dinner party of Senator Daniel Webster, who had journeyed from Washington to attend the trial, which was avidly followed in the nation's capital, as elsewhere in the country.

The Oyster House was crowded when James swung open the heavy door and entered the noisy establishment. His overcoat was wet with snow. He could see Daniel Webster's leonine head looming above a large table in the corner, surrounded by men eager for his thoughts and perspective, and James made his way toward the party, bowing and nodding to acquaintances.

"Doctor Stone, so good that you could join us," said Webster in way of greeting. James took one of the few empty chairs, sitting about four feet away from the senator. "We were discussing the Webster trial, of course," the senator said. "I noticed you taking detailed notes in the courtroom. What, pray tell, is your special interest?"

James hadn't thought about people observing his employment of phonography. He could imagine how strange his actions looked, scribbling mysterious marks and symbols. He needn't keep the plan for his report a secret. In fact, he hoped every man present would buy one upon its publication.

"I'm working on a personal project, Senator Webster," said James modestly. The men at the table halted their individual conversations, all eyes now focused on James. "I'm employing the science of phonography to record every word uttered during the trial, which I will collect and publish shortly after its conclusion."

There was a moment of confusion at the table, since most had no idea what James was talking about; phonography was a foreign word and concept to them. Senator Webster nodded knowingly.

"Well, Doctor Stone, if you do as fine work here as you did at the Sons of New Hampshire dinner last August, your efforts shall benefit us all. It was remarkable to read my remarks in the newspaper only days later, exactly as I had delivered them. You captured me down to the very syllable."

"Tell us, Senator Webster," said a man James didn't know. "What do you think of the mounting evidence against Professor Webster? Does he have any chance of acquittal?"

"The preponderance of evidence is most disturbing," agreed the senator, shaking his head. "I have known the man for years. When I first heard of this foul deed, I could in no way connect it to the John Webster of my acquaintance. He is an unlikely murderer, yet the evidence increasingly indicates otherwise."

"Does it not make sense for Professor Webster to take the stand in his own defense?" asked Thomas Russell, a Boston aristocrat whose fortune was made in the fur trade. James had danced with his sister Prudence at a ball. "After all, he was the only survivor of the final meeting between him and Parkman."

"I fear that Professor Webster wouldn't make the most credible witness on his own behalf," the senator replied. "He'd have to explain many instances of behavior that seem culpable in retrospect. He will have to answer for his actions, but his willingness to do so will only undermine him if he takes the stand."

"How do you mean, senator?" asked James.

He was puzzled by what Daniel Webster was saying. If Professor Webster could strongly refute the charges made against him, wouldn't that make testifying worthwhile? Or did the senator mean that there was no good solution left for Webster? If he did not testify, suspicions about him would be left unchallenged. If he took the stand, a thousand new questions would arise.

Instead of answering, Senator Webster turned the question on his interlocutor.

"Tell me, James, what is your opinion on the professor's guilt? You have been in court each day. Surely you have come to some conclusion."

Several lunch participants looked at Dr. Stone for the first time. He was the youngest man at the table.

"I admit to being troubled by the actions and motivations of the janitor, Littlefield," James said, choosing his words carefully. "He harbored a strong animus against Professor Webster and searched to uncover evidence that would implicate him."

"Littlefield is the least of Professor Webster's problems, gentlemen," Senator Webster said. "Are there no other observations to share with us, James? By taking your notes, you no doubt scrutinize the testimony more closely than anyone."

"My duty is to record, not judge, Senator. I've had time to reflect on what has been said because I must read it aloud to my copyists each evening. My report will give every man the same opportunity, to review all the evidence and come to his own conclusions."

"An admirable goal, James, admirable indeed," grunted the senator as he filled his mouth with a large piece of boiled turbot. "We shall await your report with anticipation. But of course, its publication will come too late to aid Professor Webster. His fate will be decided before your readers have the opportunity to judge the merits of his case."

Webster turned and beamed at the table of his admirers.

"This is the beauty of our democratic system and our Constitution, gentlemen. No matter how dastardly the crime you may be accused of, our system guarantees you a fair and open trial, like the one Professor Webster now enjoys. It won't be those around this table who decide the professor's fate, but a jury of twelve stouthearted men who must do their duty. I will say that I'm glad not to share their company. This is a sad occurrence."

The conversation continued around the table, but James was lost in his thoughts. *Was John Webster really receiving the fair trial that the senator promised? Was all the evidence being revealed, or just what pointed to Professor Webster's guilt?*

The longer the trial progressed, the more certain details nagged at James. He couldn't continue with half-formed doubts and suspicions. He must find out the truth, or the best approximation of it that he could discover.

~

The afternoon testimony commenced at half past three as the justices filed back into the courtroom, a group of old, frail men, thought James. Chief Justice Shaw limped at the head of the line. It was well known that he suffered from painful bouts with the gout.

Witness after witness was summoned to cast Professor Webster in a negative light. Mrs. Betsey Coleman was memorable: a heavyset woman with a strong New England accent and a no-nonsense attitude. She lived near the Medical College, on North Grove Street. She testified that Professor Webster unexpectedly called at her home at four o'clock in the afternoon on the day he would later be arrested, Friday, November 30.

"He inquired as to what time I seen Doctor Parkman last. I tells him I thought I seen him Thursday last, the day before his disappearance, as I was sitting by my window.

"'It was on Friday, you say,' says he. 'No,' I answered. 'I was busy on Friday cleanin' the lower part of the house.' 'How was he dressed?' he asks me. I told him in dark clothes."

Mrs. Coleman said she then asked Webster if he had heard of any new sightings of Dr. Parkman.

"He said that there had been a coat or cloak fished up, which was thought to be his, which had spots of blood on it. There was a hat found, likewise. I said then, 'O, dear, then I am afraid he's murdered!' He said, 'We are afraid he is.' He asked me two or three times if I was sure that it was Thursday that I saw Doctor Parkman, and I said I was. I saw Professor Webster to the door. He repeated, 'Wasn't it Friday you saw him?' I told him, 'No!' That was the last I saw of Professor Webster."

James saw all this as a measure of the defense's desperation. They needed an eyewitness to confirm that Parkman was still alive after he left the Medical College. As her testimony confirmed, Mrs. Coleman was not going to be that witness.

DALE M. POLLOCK

Gustavus Andrews, the keeper of the Leverett Street Gaol, testified next. He was at the Medical College guarding his prisoner when Dr. Webster was first presented with the evidence from the privy vault.

"When the remains were brought up, I was within nine feet of Doctor Webster. He appeared much agitated until all the remains appeared. He tried to stand upright but had to brace himself on a wall. I went out and called a police carriage. When we attempted to put him into the carriage, he appeared helpless, and had to be lifted in. He was like a man that had fainted."

Andrews continued with his account, the jurors, galleries, and justices hanging on every utterance.

"The first word Webster said, in the carriage, was, 'Why don't they ask Littlefield? He can explain all this. He has the care of the dissecting room. They wanted me to explain, but they didn't ask me anything. What will my family think of my absence?'"

Andrews recalled that when confronted with this man so fraught with anxiety and shame, he'd said to Webster, "My dear sir, I pity you. I'm sorry for you."

Andrews said Webster lashed out at him with a bitterness he had not previously displayed.

"He said, 'You pity me?! You are sorry for me?! What for?'

"I said, 'To see you so excited.' I don't recollect anything more being said, 'til we reached the jail."

Andrews testified that the following morning Dr. Webster offered another unsolicited comment: "'This is no more Doctor Parkman's body than it is my body; and how in the world it came there, I don't know.' He then said, 'I never liked the looks of that Littlefield, the janitor. I opposed his coming there all I could.'"

There it was, supposed James, *more evidence of bad blood.* James mused over this odd bond between the two men as his fingers flew across the page. He was finding it easier to take phonographic notes and still maintain some independence of thought. It made the work less tedious.

There was a final emotional moment in the courtroom that day. Andrews had legally seized a letter from Dr. Webster's cell because it contained incriminating statements. It was addressed to Webster's elder daughter, MaryAnne, and was dated Monday evening, December 3, 1849. At that point Webster had been in prison for three days. Andrews read it aloud in a gruff voice that became more emotional as he spoke.

My Dearest MaryAnne:

I wrote Mamma yesterday. I had a good sleep last night and dreamt of you all. I got my clothes off, for the first time, and awoke in the morning, quite hungry. It was a long time before my first breakfast, from Parker's, came; and it relished, I can assure you. At one o'clock, I was notified that I must appear at the Courthouse. All was arranged with great regard to my comfort, and the avoidance of publicity, and this first ceremony went off better than I had anticipated. On my return, I had a bit of turkey, and rice. Parker's sends much more than I can eat, and I have directed the steward to distribute the surplus to any poor ones here.

If you will send me a small canister of tea, I can make my own. Tell Mama not to open the little bundle I gave her the other day, but to keep it just as she received it.

Hope you will soon be cheered by my release, which is imminent. With many kisses to you all,

Good night, from
Your affectionate Father

P.S. My tongue troubles me yet, very much; and I must have bitten it, in my distress the other night. It is painful and swollen, affecting somewhat my speech.

James could see that the reading of this letter in court elicited much sympathy for Webster. The faces in the courtroom turned to him, and he looked downward, passing his hand briefly before his eyes. He straightened up, regained his composure, and stared directly ahead as if the letter had been of little import. *John Webster might buckle,* supposed James, *but he would not break.*

CHAPTER 22

March 1850
Court Street, Boston, Massachusetts

James allowed himself little time to reflect upon his sexual adventure with Ellen O'Keeffe, although he often wondered about her reaction to it. The pressure of the trial demanded almost all his attention and energy. When his thoughts did turn to Ellen, he hurried them elsewhere. He was both ashamed and proud of his behavior: embarrassed by giving in to his base desires, confident in his demonstrated manhood.

In their first encounter following their liaison, they both pretended nothing was out of the ordinary. James dictated his notes; Ellen corrected the girls' transcriptions. The erstwhile lovers kept their eyes steady on the goal of completing the report by their self-imposed deadline of two weeks following the end of the trial.

The reality of human touch and love had penetrated them and now their memories, and James and Ellen weren't the same. They could never be the same with each other. Their intimacy had altered their relationship. By necessity they would have to meet each evening until the trial reached its conclusion, and then, working together, they would complete the final manuscript. There was no way to avoid each other, and no means to deny what had occurred.

They simmered in an emotional stew of their own making. A prodigious effort was necessary for each to suppress their thoughts of desire, and the memory of the physical act that had consummated it.

Secure in his conviction that he suffered alone with the consequences of their actions, James could not imagine that the same was true for Ellen, but it was. She had to stop herself from caressing his soft skin or tracing her finger around his long face and smooth brow, ruffling his thick hair with her hands.

As the copyists departed, James realized he didn't desire a continuation of this palpable sexual tension. He was tired of wandering back to 6 Bowdoin Square, lost in the fantasies of a randy schoolboy.

"Ellen, I hardly know what to say," he began. "What happened the other evening was my doing. I bear full responsibility."

"If there's anythin' to be shared, it was what we did together," said Ellen. "It be just as much me decision as yer own. I imagine that I was takin' the same pleasure ye did. It certainly seemed so at the time."

James was disarmed by Ellen's sly smile at the memory of their lovemaking, which had been energetic. He, too, smiled, and they shared an easy laugh. His manner turned serious.

"We must find a way to complete our work without these moral lapses. This thing between us can be a distraction to our greater purpose. It cannot be allowed to continue."

"Don't be a silly man, James," said Ellen. "We can easily separate the two parts if we choose ta. The fact that ye employs me does nae change how I feel about ye. The one has nothin' to do with t'other unless I meself says so. I'm sure ye can do the same in how ye view me."

James was stunned by Ellen's matter-of-fact attitude. He had to admit to himself that it was exactly this brazen quality that excited him and made him desire her more. *She was the most modern creature he had ever encountered. She terrified and entranced him.*

～

The list of witnesses grew shorter as the trial proceeded, and one morning when the justices were delayed in arriving, James had a rare opportunity to study the jury, which already was seated.

These men held the power of life and death, he mused as he regarded the twelve now-famous citizens. He had watched bookseller Benjamin Greene throughout the trial because James could see that he paid careful attention to the testimony. Some jurors nodded off during the lengthy questioning (one snored so loudly that Chief Justice Shaw woke him one morning with a smash of his gavel), and others stared into space. Greene kept a notebook in his lap and made notes that James assumed would help his recollections in the jury room.

He wondered if Greene might share the skepticism he was feeling now that the testimony was almost all in. There seemed something shifty in what the attorney general and Mr. Bemis were doing, manufacturing a case that relied on nothing but circumstance. There was no direct proof, no eyewitness, nothing to implicate John Webster other than the location

DALE M. POLLOCK

where the remains were found, and the poisoned history between him and George Parkman.

The final witness for the prosecution was summoned at last; James supposed he had been saved for last in the interest of maximum emotional impact.

Dr. Fisher Boswell, a physician from Grafton, was the only eyewitness to see Parkman inside the Medical College on November 23. Boswell had had occasion to go to the Medical College on that date to meet a former student who was studying there.

"As I passed the foot of the stairs, I met Doctor Parkman right at the corner. He was going up the same stairs I was coming down. As I passed 'round the corner, I saw the doctor nearly at the top of the stairs."

The unspoken continuation of Dr. Boswell's story would take Dr. Parkman to the left at the top of the staircase, then just a few short steps into Professor Webster's laboratory, from which he would never emerge. Clifford and Bemis had strategized to save this chilling testimony until the very end of their presentation, when its power would be the greatest. Their hope was that it would linger in the minds of the jury while the defense mounted its case. *It was a smart idea,* James reasoned.

After James partook of a quick repast at Stackpole House on the corner of Milk and Devonshire Streets with John French, the two men hurried back to the courtroom to hear the opening statement on behalf of the defense, delivered by Edwin Sohier. He was an eloquent attorney, with a reputation for his skillful ability to play upon a jury's emotions. This had in the past often elicited him their sympathy, and occasionally, an acquittal for his clients.

Sohier began his presentation on an emotional note.

"I fear, gentlemen, that, should I permit my attention here to wander, I might be lost. I might, perchance, perceive nothing but the man who, for more than a quarter of a century, has been a respected professor in that university which is the pride of our state; a respected lecturer in that college which is one of the boasts of our city; the man under whose instruction many now present at this trial were educated, myself among the rest.

"I hate that I should see him struggling for his life; struggling for his reputation; struggling to avert infamy for himself and for his children, in that selfsame dock where we have been accustomed to seeing felon after felon, to abide the judgment of the law. I might think of these things, gentlemen, and I might wander from the case."

"The one great question, which, for months, has absorbed the attention and has agitated to their very lowest depths the feeling of a great community; to wit, is the life of Professor Webster, now the prisoner at the bar, forfeited because it has been proven here, beyond a most reasonable doubt, that he has been guilty of one of the most horrible offenses that can be found in the long, dark catalogue of crime?"

There was not a sound in the courtroom as Sohier presented the only two options he said were available to the jury.

"Yet, it does devolve upon you to say, whether the fire upon his hearthstone shall burn brightly, or whether your breath, Mister Foreman, when you pronounce the verdict, shall extinguish that fire, so as to cause all his honors to be scattered to the winds—to be forgotten by his friends, and be an aversion to his enemies."

The jurors seemed struck by the force of Sohier's address, as was James. Byram, the jury Foreman, looked particularly unsettled by Sohier's warning. He stretched his collar with two fingers, glanced around the courtroom to see everyone staring at him, and then looked down in embarrassment. The other jurors saw his error and did their best to appear unaffected.

"By no means are we to forget, gentlemen, or are we to suppose that you have forgotten, the great excitement which existed in this city when it was first bruited abroad that George Parkman was murdered.

"Do we now forget that men quit their avocations, that they were clustered together in the corners, in the doors, in the stores, the houses, and the churches—and that their conversation was upon this one point, and no other?

"Have we forgotten the great indignation that was excited in this community—so creditable to the community, but so dangerous to the defendant—when it was first announced that Doctor Parkman's body was found in the Medical College, in the chemistry laboratory? Have we forgotten the prejudice against Professor Webster? Have we forgotten these things? By no means! They are burned into our memories, and we shall not forget them!"

Unexpectedly, Sohier turned his attention to the distinction between murder and manslaughter. This alarmed James. *Webster's counsel seemed all too ready to concur with the commonwealth that he was guilty of one or the other. Did they plan to plead for a conviction of manslaughter, rather than murder?* Sohier's next statement answered James's question.

"Manslaughter is not deliberate. It is a sudden act. It is not a cruel act. But it is done in the heat of blood. Whenever death ensues from sudden transport of passion, or heat of blood, if upon a reasonable provocation, and without malice, or if upon sudden combat, it will be manslaughter.

"That, gentlemen, is the difference between murder and manslaughter. One is considerate, deliberate, cruel, and without provocation. The other is inconsiderate, sudden, in the heat of blood, and with provocation. It is one of the two."

James noticed that the justices seemed surprised by this legal strategy. Webster had pleaded not guilty, yet in his opening statement, Edwin Sohier seemed ready to concede his client's involvement in the inadvertent death of George Parkman.

Professor Webster remained as unperturbed as ever in the elevated prisoner's dock, nodding as Sohier made arguments that could support his conviction for manslaughter. James could not comprehend this strategy, nor why Webster would support it other than to save his neck from the hangman's noose. He guessed that was motivation enough.

Sohier finally did James and the rest of the puzzled courtroom the courtesy of explaining himself: this was indeed an effort to get the jury to spare the life of John Webster.

"For on one side is life, on the other, death; life, it may be encumbered with long and severe punishment; but still it is life—life which is clung to—life rendered radiant with hope."

Sohier went over the particulars of Parkman's death by actions with specific weapons, and how each of the counts in the murder indictment against Webster had specified a weapon used in killing of Parkman.

But the prosecution had offered no proof of these weapons, no evidence of their use, Sohier emphasized.

"The weapon is of no consequence; but that such a means were used is of consequence, and must be proved," he said.

A wise move, James thought. *The principal weakness of the commonwealth's case was the lack of an eyewitness to Parkman's slaying. They had enjoyed no better luck in proving a specific device to be the murder weapon. Only a knife had been recovered, and it appeared to have been wiped clean. The prosecution had not established with physical proof that the knife or any other specific weapon was the primary cause of Parkman's death.*

This was one basis for Webster's defense, James thought, *but surely not the only one.* Sohier continued down the path of introducing reasonable doubt into the equation.

"Has the government proved, beyond reasonable doubt, that Professor Webster destroyed George Parkman by striking him with a weapon?

That is the point. The government must prove the killing by the means stated. And if the killing is proved by the government to be in any other mode, then they fail. And if the jury, upon the evidence, are left in doubt, whether the killing was produced by the means stated, or by some other means, then they are bound to acquit, under their oaths; because it is the right of the defendant—it is his right and privilege, and it is every man's right and privilege—to have the government held strictly and distinctly to prove what they allege, in all its particulars."

Sohier made the issue very clear to the men occupying the jury seats.

"Here they allege, in these two counts, a striking by a weapon. If they fail in this, there is an end of the case. If you are left in doubt, there is an end of the case. If you believe that he killed him in this way, but you are left in doubt, then you are bound to acquit him."

Sohier kept turning to the reality that the prosecution had little to offer as physical proof of the crime.

"I am perfectly aware, gentlemen, that there is an idea abroad that this matter of reasonable doubt is something that the law accords to the prisoner as a gratuity; something that he is not entitled to; something by which guilty men sometimes escape punishment. But there never was a greater mistake in the world.

"What's our system? We take a man from his family. We arrest him upon the charge of a heavy, heinous offence. We lock him up in a jail. And while his mind is paralyzed by his position, he's told to procure a defense— to proceed and prepare for his defense. The matter is tried and adjudicated before a coroner's jury where he is not present. It is afterwards tried before a grand jury where he is not represented. An indictment is found; and then, with all this accumulation of public opinion necessarily formed upon these proceedings, he is brought into court, and put upon this trial."

If James followed Sohier's reasoning, Webster was the victim in this case, not Parkman. Sohier approached the jurors and addressed them directly.

"You may, any one of you, be charged with an offense done when you are alone. You can't prove that you didn't do it. But you can prove your previous character, and that there's a reasonable doubt."

Sohier came to his key point: the government's complete lack of physical evidence.

"Direct evidence needs no explanation. And, in point of fact, there is none of it in this case. There are opinions that circumstantial evidence is necessarily correct, that circumstances cannot lie, and various other sayings, that are totally false; sayings stupidly repeated, over and over again, that have received the dignity of proverbs. But, on the contrary, it should be remembered that it's always weak and uncertain."

Sohier approached the defense table and grasped a pitcher of water, pouring himself a full glass and draining it immediately. James did not envy the defense counsel this lengthy performance in front of an audience that was conscious of his every gesture and movement and seeming to be affected by his sometimes-stirring words.

Finally, Sohier arrived at his central argument.

"What is the government's evidence? Why, it consists of one great chain of circumstantial proof with which they have endeavored to surround the defendant, and by the weight of which they have endeavored to crush him.

"They say Doctor George Parkman was murdered. That's the very first point with which they start, that he came to his death by violence. How do they undertake to prove that? By various circumstances, all leading to one end: that Doctor Parkman, being in the Medical College, where it is admitted he was, never came out. And that's the circumstance upon which they build their chain.

"They say Professor Webster destroyed him by violence. Why? Because he was the last person with whom he was seen; and if he did not destroy him by violence, the government don't know who did."

Sohier then made an unexpected declaration.

"We say we do not intend to produce any direct evidence to explain by what means those human remains came into Professor Webster's laboratory, or beneath it. Professor Webster remains with the position that he originally took. He knows nothing about it.

"These are the remains of a human body. We can no more explain this than the government can. We can explain it only by hypotheses, as the government has explained it. The defendant stands as you would stand, if similar remains were found upon your premises, under the foundation of your house, in your workshop, anywhere. So he stands, and so he must stand."

James marveled at Sohier's nerve. *Who else had human remains discovered under his workplace or his home? Finding a butchered torso hanging in your privy was not an everyday occurrence.*

Sohier again turned to the question of Professor Webster's reputation.

"When a man stands charged, on circumstantial evidence and in a doubtful case, with the commission of a great crime, the very greatest weight is to be given to character. A man has a right to be judged by his fellow citizens on the character which he has earned and established by a long life."

Professor Webster nodded vigorously as Sohier spoke. He looked uplifted by the discussion of his character, which clearly was the principal strategy of his defense. His counsel had to convince the jurors that Webster was the least likely man to murder George Parkman. The weakness of the defense's argument remained in that they had no other suspect to put in his place.

"Professor Webster is charged with doing a violent, inhuman, and cruel act. And we will introduce evidence, with regard to his character, by which you will judge whether he would do this act. And I shall be very much mistaken if we don't establish strongly that he would not."

Webster's reputation for timidity and soft-spokenness was central to his defense, James reflected. As if reading his thoughts, Sohier began his concluding remarks.

"Professor Webster is a person who has all his life been devoted to the pursuit of chemistry. He is a person of nervous disposition, but a man exceedingly peaceable and harmless in his habits and his conduct. He may sometimes show petulance. But so far from being a violent man, familiar with deeds of blood, nothing could be further from this. He is naturally a timid man."

The reaction in the courtroom was considerable, and Chief Justice Shaw had to bang his gavel in a more animated manner than usual. It was the first time he had seen the man move all day. Shaw was like a giant, somnolent frog, whose tongue could lash out at any moment. James was nervous any time he felt Shaw's gaze upon his scribbling fingers. The chief justice could toss him from the courtroom on a whim, if so inclined.

Sohier then refuted Ephraim Littlefield's testimony, insisting that it was not unusual for Webster to lock himself up in his laboratory. It was no new thing for him to exclude the janitor when engaged in his chemistry experiments; that was the prudent course, practiced in all chemical laboratories, and Webster was acclaimed in his field, Sohier emphasized.

"We shall show you how Professor Webster passed the rest of the week; that he was at home every day at dinner, every night at tea." *In other words,* James thought, *the image of domestic tranquility.*

Edwin Sohier completed an opening argument that filled most of the afternoon, and by its end, he looked exhausted. Webster was visibly pleased by Sohier's performance.

James wasn't sure. He had heard Sohier all but acknowledge Webster's guilt in his discussion of manslaughter. Even when Sohier declared Webster's character to be unimpeachable, it was Webster's character that had led to his debts to Parkman and, eventually, to his financial ruin and his current situation.

The defense's first witness was Joseph T. Buckingham, a Massachusetts state senator from Middlesex County. He came to the witness box to deliver the first in an endless stream of character testimonials on behalf of Webster. He had known the professor for thirty years, Buckingham said. "I never heard that he was guilty of any act of violence or inhumanity."

Fifteen more men followed Buckingham to the witness box, all saying much the same: they had encountered only Webster's peaceable nature. The final witness was a pharmacist named Daniel Treadwell, from whom Webster obtained medicines for his sick wife.

Treadwell said, "He is generally considered a perfectly harmless man."

CHAPTER 23

April 1850
Bowdoin Square and Court Street, Boston, Massachusetts

James had barely settled into his armchair with the evening papers when he heard Sharon knock loudly at his door. It was past eleven o'clock on a Saturday night; he could not imagine what could have roused his servant at this hour.

"Docter Stone! Docter Stone! I'm sorry to disturb ye, sir, but there is someone here to see ye, demandin' to come in!" called Sharon.

James put on his robe and hurried to the door, opening it to find the flustered and frantic Irish serving girl in her bedclothes.

"I need you to calm yourself, Sharon," James said in a gentle voice, trying to settle her nerves. "Now, what's this about? Who is calling on me?"

"Oh, Docter Stone, there be a man down below, the likes of which has ne'er been here before. He's a rough sort, sir, I know his type, it's not the type ye should be havin' anything to do with!"

James could not imagine who his late caller could be, but he wasted no more time and headed down the wide staircase toward the old mansion's front entrance.

Waiting impatiently outside that entrance was Ellen's stepfather in his blue plug hat. James had last seen William Haggerty at the grog shop on Endicott Street when he went to pay to him Ellen's wages, the one and only time he had done so. Now James did as she requested and paid her directly. He suspected this visit had everything to do with those wages. How had the man found him, and why had he come so late?

"Mister Haggerty," James said, recovering from the surprise of the encounter. "To what do I owe this visit?"

"Good evenin' to ye, Docter, I hope I nae disturb ye," said Haggerty in a drunken, jocular tone, as if he and James were good friends, one paying the other a spontaneous social call. "I know it be a wee bit late, but I happened in the neighborhood, and thought I might stop by."

"State your business," James said, his tone clipped. "I have no time for foolishness at this hour."

"It hardly be the fool's business I be playin', Docter. If ye knew me at all, ye'd know that. Nae, it's nae foolishness I come about."

"Then, what is it?"

"It's my lovely daughter, Ellen, to arrive at the point, Docter. Ye been workin' her mighty hard, my Ellen, and ye be givin' me a bit of worry about the poor girl's health. Her ma had a weakness in the lungs, and methinks Ellen may be sufferin' the same affliction."

James knew there was nothing wrong with Ellen, who was the picture of health. No, Haggerty was there about something else.

"Ellen has never complained to me of illness," James said. "And I've detected no symptoms in her. Did she send you here to advise me of this?"

"Ellen nae wants me to worry, bless her heart, Docter. I care about me daughter, make nae mistake about it, Docter. And I notice things. I notice many, many things, I do."

James could feel the air being sucked out of him. Was Haggerty aware of the evening when he and Ellen had been intimate? That would be impossible, he thought. He couldn't conceive of Ellen disclosing their secret to her stepfather, of all people, or anyone else.

"Get to your point in coming here and rousing me from my bed, Haggerty. I wish to return there as soon as possible."

"I wants Yer Honor to be aware that I notice things. Like what time Ellen gets home, much later than the other girls, if I nae be mistaken. Maybe ye be devisin' extra tasks fer her, after the others have gone?"

Haggerty stood there obstinately, a half leer, half grin on his pale white face. James felt his own color drain as he stared at him. This man did know. If not in possession of confirmation, he had every suspicion lined up and trained on Dr. James Stone. What was next, he wondered; blackmail?

"I resent your insinuations, Haggerty, and I won't tolerate them any longer," James said. "Ellen is engaged by me for the purposes of transcribing my phonographic notes and supervising the copyists, and no other duties. I've been patient in trying to determine your true purpose in appearing uninvited on my doorstep. Now I see you have nothing but outlandish suspicions concerning your own stepdaughter to communicate to me. There is no purpose in continuing this conversation." He turned to go back inside.

"Ye may nae want to speak now, Docter Stone," said Haggerty, a poisonous tone to his voice. "But talk we will. I can promise ye, and me Ellen will be the subject. It nae be pleasant talk for a gentleman such as yerself.

For with me will be a friend that I employ in my service such times as I need him."

James turned back uneasily as Haggerty withdrew from his coat a shillelagh, a stout wooden cudgel made from blackthorn, and much favored by the Irish. He waggled it back and forth.

"Begone, sir!" said James, more frightened than he cared to show Haggerty. "I have no more use for you!"

Haggerty leaned in for the final word. "But ye do got a use fer me daughter, Docter Stone, my loveliest, sweetest, favorite daughter. Ye may call her me stepdaughter, but she be much more than that to me, ye'll see. We'll be discussin' her, sooner rather than later. Ye may rely on that."

With a wave of his weapon, Haggerty strode off the stoop at 6 Bowdoin Square and faded into the inky blackness of the night.

James had a sick, bilious feeling in his stomach. *He and Ellen had been found out. They should have supposed her comings and goings would be closely monitored. Haggerty possessed damaging information that could ruin James's professional career, his personal life, and Ellen's reputation. Information that could be leveraged for money: extortion, blackmail, hush money, whatever one wished to call James Stone's future.*

He thought first of Ellen. He could not imagine she could be aware of this visit. He was sickened by the cruel way her own stepfather was using her, without a thought to her feelings or her fate. He must think of a way to undo the damage he had inflicted on a bright young woman who wanted only to improve her position in life. Her brief liaison with him was a momentary lapse, one that he would not allow to occur again.

James squeezed his eyes shut. "My passions have undone me," he murmured aloud, but there was no one to hear him, no one to share his pain and regret. He had never felt so alone in the world, not even after his mother's funeral.

~

The crowds around the courthouse were larger than usual, as Webster's eldest daughter was scheduled to appear as a witness, and courtgoers anticipated dramatic testimony in her father's defense.

The intensity of public interest in the proceedings was a gathering storm. Bostonians milled about Court, Tremont, Washington, and School Streets, all bordering Court Square. Men and women were broken into clumps where ardent conversations about guilt and innocence were underway in the still-cold April weather.

It took James more than fifteen minutes to make his way through this human maelstrom. He was out of breath by the time he gained admittance through the chained entrance. James sidled into his seat just as the jurors took their seats. The justices followed, led by an unevenly balanced Chief Justice Shaw.

Pliny Merrick led the questioning for the defense this day, and under his guidance, a succession of witnesses continued the testimony from the previous afternoon: all stated that John Webster was unequivocally a peaceful, agreeable, nonviolent man.

James sat up straight as Harvard College President Jared Sparks approached the witness box. The courtroom was hushed as Harvard's official representative confirmed that he had known Professor Webster for seventeen years.

"I never knew of anything against him. I've heard many remarks about him since his arrest, but nothing to which I give credit. His conduct, as far as I knew before, was that of an amiable, kindhearted, and peaceable man."

Chief Justice Shaw banged for quiet as the galleries erupted noisily, following Sparks's endorsement of Webster. Here was Harvard pardoning Harvard!

The courtroom stirred mightily when MaryAnne Webster's turn in the witness box came. This was the first time a member of the Webster family had appeared in court. It was daring for Sohier and Merrick to have MaryAnne take up her father's defense. The two of them were known to be close. MaryAnne, not her mother, had been in charge of the household when James had visited just before the trial commenced.

"Since his arrest, I have endeavored to call to mind all the places where he was that week," said MaryAnne, in a voice that possessed a clear, bell-like tone.

She had a small nose and a well-formed mouth. Her flaxen hair was curled at the sides and pulled into a bun at the back. Her eyes were alert to everything in the courtroom. She was not the least bit intimidated by the crowds and the setting. James could see that Judge Merrick planned to use her to wring maximum sympathy for her plight, and indirectly, her father's.

MaryAnne said her father's behavior during Dr. Parkman's disappearance was nothing but benign. Professor Webster went to a small dinner party, he dined at home, he worked in his garden, he went to chapel, he prepared his lectures. MaryAnne offered neither titillation nor conspiracy: nothing suspicious, nothing unusual, nothing out of the ordinary. By her account and those of his friends, her father was the embodiment of ordinariness. Her assertions on his behalf appeared guileless.

Catherine Webster, the youngest sibling, testified next. She offered that she, MaryAnne, and her father had gone with a friend to Boston the night before Thanksgiving. "We left there about half past ten and came out in the eleven o'clock omnibus. While waiting at the tollhouse, I remember seeing a notice of a reward for Doctor Parkman. Sister pointed it out first; and Father read it aloud to us, as it was rather high up."

If Catherine were aware of the irony in this tale, she did not express it, but it left a strange image for those in the courtroom: Webster blithely reciting the particulars of an alarming broadside, concerning the mystery of a prominent citizen whom he allegedly had caused to vanish.

After the dinner break came a parade of defense witnesses intended to cast doubt upon the commonwealth's case. Philena Hatch, who said she'd known George Parkman by sight for fifteen years, swore that she saw him walking down Cambridge Street, on the same sidewalk she was on, heading toward Court Street on November 23, just before two o'clock—after Parkman would have finished his audience with Professor Webster.

Despite the efforts of George Bemis to shake her testimony, Mrs. Hatch remained adamant about what she witnessed. "I don't know but that Doctor Parkman turned 'round," she said in response to Mr. Bemis's query about whether Parkman had returned to the Medical College. "I was not his keeper."

As the afternoon drew to a close, James found it difficult to concentrate on his work. His head buzzed, his breathing was shallow, he worried he was coming down with some ailment. He must drink honey in his tea this evening. Possibly he could cut short his dictation tonight. Giving himself just one evening off should not alter the overall progress of his report. Ellen could read his notes aloud to the young women if need be. She was an expert decipherer of his crabbed writing.

The day's final witness was Mrs. Abby D. Rhodes, who said she had known Dr. Parkman for twenty-five years, well enough, she said, "to bow when I met him." She swore that she had seen him walking down Green Street, near Souther's apothecary store, at fifteen minutes before five o'clock on the afternoon of November 23.

"It was very near dark," Mrs. Rhodes recalled. "There was a man with him. I passed as near as I could, with my daughter between. He was walking quite fast. We bowed as we passed."

Mrs. Rhodes had called on the Rev. Dr. Parkman the week after his brother's disappearance and told him personally what she had witnessed. "I have never expressed any doubts or misgivings about what I saw," Mrs. Rhodes insisted.

Here was a witness who might have an impact, supposed James. *She was a down-to-earth, intelligent woman with a very specific memory.* Cross-examining her for the prosecution, Bemis could do nothing to shake her testimony. The more aggressively he questioned her, the more her jaw thrust forward in defiance.

Despite the defense witnesses accounts, James wondered if nothing short of Dr. Parkman striding into the courtroom could save John Webster now.

CHAPTER 24

April 1850
Bowdoin Square and Tontine Crescent, Boston, Massachusetts

James remained unsettled by his encounter with William Haggerty. Rattled to his core. Haggerty might not possess actual proof of a sexual liaison between James and Ellen, but that made his suspicions no less accurate.

James had no idea how to proceed. He could not discuss his dilemma with his brothers; they would question his sanity in embarking on an amorous relationship with an Irish girl. He would never recover in their estimation, and he might find himself emotionally and financially excluded from the bosom of his family, a possibility he found devastating.

He was due at Lucinda's house on Tontine Crescent for supper in an hour's time. He had canceled the evening's transcription work for a rare respite from hours of reading testimony aloud. It was also easier not to look into Ellen's hope-filled face at this moment. Everything in his mind was upset and in disarray.

Something had changed in his perception of their relationship when the senior Haggerty stepped forward with his threats, something irrevocable, James felt. It was no longer just his and Ellen's passionate secret, their private pleasure. It had been corrupted, fouled by that leering Irishman.

Haggerty's unexpected appearance had also, to James's surprise, deepened his affections for Ellen. She needed a defender, and James was to be the one to put a stop to this outrageous behavior. He would not allow Ellen to be used in this craven way by a man who purported to be her father but had no blood relation to her.

The young doctor finished straightening his cravat and looked in the mirror. On the surface, nothing was different in the visage he beheld—his usual sensitive face, his crown of black hair, his wry smile.

But for the first time, James could see a sense of purpose lurking around his features, instead of the recent aura of shame and fear he had been wearing. He and Ellen could not continue with Haggerty blackmailing him. Somehow, he would have to resolve this dilemma.

His reverie was interrupted by Sharon's knock on the door and her announcement that the Dresser carriage had arrived. James descended the steps two at a time to the front entrance and was just out the door when Sharon called after him and ran to deliver him his hat and gloves. He gave her a smile of appreciation, and as usual, Sharon blushed.

Varying thoughts occupied James's mind on his way to his sister's house, none staying long enough to focus on a resolution. The carriage clattered up to 18 Tontine Crescent. James descended the stairs pulled out by the footman. It was not a large supper party this evening: just the Dressers, the Marshalls, and the Stephenses, the couple who had hosted the ball last fall for Jennie Ray Gillmer.

Lucinda was at the door to greet her guest. "It's so good to see you, James, our very own minor celebrity," she said, patting his back. "Everyone I know has remarked upon your continual presence at the Webster trial."

"My work goes well," James reported, surprised by a rare compliment from his sister. "It's been exhausting, but I hope it will prove rewarding upon the trial's completion."

"When do you believe that will be?" asked Jacob Dresser, who had joined his wife. "I can't believe it's taken this long to establish that scoundrel Webster's guilt. His defense has amounted to nothing."

"I agree that his defense has lacked originality," said James, trying to remain neutral. He would certainly not share his suspicions about Webster's singular guilt with the Dresser family. "But the commonwealth also faces challenges in its prosecution. All their points rely upon circumstance, and it remains difficult to obtain a conviction for murder using only circumstantial evidence."

"You're one of the doctors who identified those pitiful remains as Parkman's, are you not, Doctor Stone?" said John Stephens, who had joined the conversation shortly after arriving with his wife, Anne.

"I was called upon by the coroner to aid in the identification of the remains, yes, sir."

"What mystery still exists? It should be clear to all that Webster owed Parkman money, couldn't pay when presented with the debt, and slew his creditor to stop his incessant appeals. Has anyone cast doubt on those events?"

"There was no witness to the slaying," James politely reminded Stephens.

"And the police have no murder weapon, nor much of a *corpus delecti*. I can personally vouchsafe that."

Lucinda interrupted the men with a lighthearted plea. "Cannot we have but one meal in peace without constant speculation on the matter of Professor Webster and poor Doctor Parkman?"

The arrival of Caleb Marshall and his wife, Martha, provided the transition that Lucinda sought. James thought he might avoid a new round of questioning by Marshall, another successful Boston businessman and a close associate of Robert Shaw's in the manufacture of textiles. His optimism was quickly dashed.

"Tell me, Doctor Stone," Marshall began, shortly after supper was served at Lucinda's long oak table. "When do you expect that cursed Webster trial to be behind us, so Boston can resume a semblance of normalcy?" He was seated across from James and seemed intent on taking full advantage of his access. "We lose business daily to New York and New Orleans," he said, "because of the ill repute this scandal brings to our shore."

"I hope to help restore our city's reputation with my phonographic report, which should be published within two weeks of the trial's conclusion. I'm confident it will gain a wide readership and dispel many of the rumors that have damaged Boston's reputation."

"I mean no offense, Doctor Stone, but what use will your record be when the trial is over?" asked Stephens.

"You are unfamiliar with the power of phonography, sir," said James, with enthusiasm. "My report will bring out the truth in the actual record of the court. Not a word will be missed, not a syllable absent. All the testimony will be offered for the reader's perusal, and ultimately, his judgment."

"James is a great adherent of phonography. It's British, you know," said Lucinda, trying to move the conversation of her supper party away from the Webster trial. "He recently recorded the remarks of Senator Webster before the Sons of New Hampshire. Or was it Vermont, James?"

"It was New Hampshire, thank you, Lucinda," James said. He hoped Lucinda would direct the evening to more cordial subjects.

As if she had read his thoughts, she stepped into the breach, but not as James might have preferred. "Mrs. Stephens, I understand you recently heard from your lovely niece, Miss Jennie Gillmer," she said, launching a new attempt to resuscitate James's doomed romance. "I hope she does well."

James flushed at the mention of Jennie Gillmer. He remembered the sting of humiliation when he'd read her final letter to him. Unlike his sister, he hoped Miss Gillmer did not do well at all.

"Very well, thank you for inquiring, Mrs. Dresser," said Mrs. Stephens. "She traveled back to the Azores, as I'm sure you've heard. She found nothing to keep her there, so she's now returned to New Jersey, where I believe she and her father plan to settle."

Lucinda continued with a conversation that unfolded so precisely that James thought it must have been preplanned. "But Mrs. Stephens, wasn't there talk of an engagement for Miss Gillmer? I thought I remembered hearing some such chatter."

Mrs. Stephens was so quick to dispel this rumor. "Oh, by no means was there any such thing, Mrs. Dresser. Miss Gillmer has had many suitors, and more than one marriage proposal, but she is determined to locate her ideal spouse, and will settle for nothing else."

Lucinda beamed at James. This was exactly the news she hoped he would hear; Mrs. Stephens could not have framed it better.

"If Miss Gillmer should journey to Boston, perhaps you could call on her, James," said Lucinda disingenuously. "If I recall, the two of you got on quite well during her previous visit."

"She has plans to visit us next week," said Mrs. Stephens. "She has shown great interest in the Webster trial and asked me to attend with her. May we see you there?"

James hated the idea that a trial for a man's life constituted a diversion on the New England social scene.

"I'm preoccupied with my duties in the courtroom," he demurred. "But if I shall happen to encounter you there, I'll be greatly pleased."

"So will Miss Gillmer, I should think," said Mrs. Stephens, with a private smile for Lucinda.

The two of them were up to something. Well, it wouldn't go very far. He had lost interest in Jennie Gillmer. She had made it quite clear that he held no special place in her estimation. Lucinda could scheme all she wanted, but James wasn't her marionette, a plaything to be trotted out upon a stage on command. He still possessed some degree of control over his own life, and he would make sure Miss Gillmer and her advocates understood that.

CHAPTER 25

April 1850
Court Street, Boston, Massachusetts

Edwin Sohier rose and approached the bench.

"Your Honors, the defense now rests its case," he declaimed, before bowing and returning to his table. *That was quick,* James thought.

The court's attention swung to Attorney General Clifford, who introduced his first rebuttal witnesses. These were five men who would help Clifford establish that there was a person who bore a strong resemblance to Parkman in form, gait, and manner, walking around Boston at the time of the man's disappearance. It was this individual, Clifford claimed, whom a variety of individuals had incorrectly taken for Parkman after his visit to the Medical College.

Merrick leapt to his feet to object. He begged the judge to not allow the witnesses to testify.

"I think this is entirely inadmissible, and contrary to the universal practice of the courts in questions of identity," said Merrick.

To the relief of Merrick and Sohier, Chief Justice Shaw saw the matter their way.

"The testimony in the present case is held to be inadmissible, as of a too remote and unsatisfactory nature," said the chief justice, his ruling interrupted by a hacking cough.

That was all that remained in the government's case, so Clifford rested. Now it was Pliny Merrick's turn for his closing argument, and James stretched his fingers, anticipating with dread his lengthy presentation. As he had demonstrated throughout the trial, Merrick was a longwinded speaker. But as James saw it, Webster's life hung in the balance. A strong, if lengthy, argument by Merrick might well save it. The defense counsel wasted no time in setting the stakes.

"A case, gentlemen, is presented to you, transcending in public interest any that has heretofore occupied the attention of our judicial tribunals," he reminded the jurors.

None of their number was unaware of this, but James supposed it was incumbent on Merrick to emphasize the gravity of the situation. He recounted the disappearance of George Parkman, the efforts of the entire community to locate him, the astonishing discovery of the mangled remains of a dead body. The suspicions about Dr. Webster, which accompanied this discovery, had only grown, said Merrick.

"Incident after incident was communicated to the public, and everything which could bear against this unhappy prisoner was spread abroad, as it were, on the wings of the wind. Every sheet that was published—every hour that passed—gave new tokens to the community, at once of the death of Doctor Parkman and, as it was supposed, the guilt of this prisoner."

Webster, said Merrick, was the true victim, at least in this regard.

"While every incident tending most unfavorably to affect him was the subject of daily communication and discussion abroad, he was alone, and without friends, without help, to repel these accumulating circumstances against him."

Merrick paused for dramatic effect.

"He waited, gentlemen, in silence, and in hope and confidence, because he had lived long in our midst, and knew who were finally to be his judges. He knew that a time was coming, when passion would subside, when prejudice would give way, when calm reason would intervene, and his country would try him fairly, in the midst of her tribunals of justice."

Merrick moved quickly to the essence of Webster's defense.

"By no direct evidence is it shown even that Doctor George Parkman is no longer in the land of the living; by no direct evidence that he was slain by the agency of another human being. By no direct evidence is it shown that the defendant had any direct agency in causing or procuring that death. But every one of these facts is sought to be proved by collateral circumstances."

The weakness of circumstantial evidence was the weakness underlying the commonwealth's case, Merrick emphasized. He cited the many witnesses who had identified Parkman on the streets of Boston after two o'clock on November 23, 1849. That meant, Merrick stressed, that Webster and Parkman had actually parted company after their meeting. And that meant that Webster was in no way connected to Parkman's subsequent disappearance.

"This, then, gentlemen of the jury, is the testimony upon which we rely to convince you that Doctor George Parkman did separate from Professor Webster; that Doctor Parkman went from that college, and was abroad, in various parts of the city," said Merrick.

"He did not return to his family, and that is strange. He was never seen afterwards, and that is strange. Something intervened that day that was very strange. Something occurred that day which we cannot understand, which we cannot reach or know. What that was, who can tell? Can you, upon the evidence that has been presented to you?"

Addressed so directly, a few jurors looked around nervously. Stackpole, the carpenter who seemed vain about his long blond hair, kept smoothing it as Merrick addressed the men.

Pointing at the display of Parkman's skeleton with the recovered body parts identified by shading, Merrick said, "If you are satisfied that this is the body of Doctor Parkman, that settles the point."

James saw Merrick's eyes boring into each juror individually.

"If you are not satisfied"—he paused for effect—"their case is gone."

Then, just as his co-counsel Edwin Sohier had done during the defense's opening statement, Merrick all but gave up the fight, conceding inevitable defeat. The courtroom sat in stunned silence as the defense commenced its capitulation.

"I am going to attempt to show you, taking all the government's case, and making the worst of it for the Prisoner, that the crime which was committed, if it was committed by Professor Webster, was not murder, but manslaughter, because the circumstances warrant the lesser crime," said Merrick.

He turned his back to Webster, as if he did not wish to witness the defendant's pained reaction to his statements. Yet Merrick could not ignore his client's presence in the courtroom. He had to acknowledge Webster's feelings and status.

"As the counsel of Professor Webster—called in here to protect him in this hour of peril, when his life is at stake—his counsel do not feel at liberty to stand exclusively on the ground upon which he stands. He denies that he took the life of Doctor Parkman. But gentlemen, his counsel cannot know what effect the evidence which the government has presented may produce upon your minds."

In other words, James saw, *Merrick was acknowledging that he and Sohier had lost their case. Why not challenge the government directly on the weaknesses in its presentation? Why not bear down on Littlefield for the true reason behind his animus toward Professor Webster? Why not fight to prove their client's innocence? Would no one do that for John Webster, not even the men professionally engaged for the task?*

Merrick continued to bury his client's hopes.

"We contend that the evidence in the case will warrant the jury in coming to the conclusion that, if there was a homicide here, that if Doctor Parkman came to his death by the hands of Professor Webster, it was under circumstances of such extenuation as reduces the offense from murder to manslaughter."

The reaction in the courtroom was muffled, and James, staring at Webster, saw him cast his eyes down with a grave expression. The professor continued to stare at the floor.

"You should find that Doctor Parkman's pursuit was constant, his purpose unchanged and inflexible, and his manner, I think, never calm in relation to this matter," said Merrick.

"So as early as Thursday evening November 22, there were irritating circumstances connected with this obligation. Doctor Parkman was aggravated. Rash language was used, and in the common parlance, vulgar language was used, which came in some way back to Professor Webster, certainly showing that there was not a kind relation between the two."

What was Merrick up to? James wondered. *Was he trying to demonstrate that the killing had occurred as a result of Parkman's harassment, not Webster's malice?*

"Is it strange that men, meeting under such circumstances, should get into a wrangle? Is it strange, or unnatural, that one party, who felt himself to be pursuing a dishonest man; that he had been personally injured; and therefore, that he would take, I will not say the law into his own hands, but take that which would do more for him than the law could do—he would pursue his debtor? Is it strange that the debtor, who has been thus pursued, should retaliate? That this should breed angry words, and that personal collision should be followed by death?"

James could not believe that Merrick was arguing for the guilt of his client under the circumstance of strong emotions. He was conceding that Webster's crime, if he did commit one, was one of passion, not premeditation.

"Professor Webster was a man of standing in society. He had a wife and children. He was poor. While his blood was hot, and passions high—his victim slain—he does one rash act. Before his blood cools, he does one act more. Surrounded as he was, the temptation came over him to conceal; and he did the first act of concealment. From that moment, all disclosure was too late."

As if for the record, Merrick repeated Webster's denials of responsibility for what was found in his rooms at the Medical College.

"His proposition, gentlemen, is, that by some way and means, and for some purpose or other, those remains were placed in that building, without his agency, and without his knowledge; and never has he professed to know how. He cannot now profess to be able to explain them. This he does say: 'I am guiltless of my brother's blood.'"

Then who was the guilty party? Merrick had, at last, an answer at the ready.

"The government's case does not exclude the idea that all these might have been placed there by another agent. If another man came there and did any of these things—that is enough. If another man came there and brought these remains, that man could dispose of them with a hammer, and, if he found a ball of twine there, could tie it round the leg of a human being. And, therefore, the twine and the hammer are explained, if at all, by the agency of the third person."

Get to who this third person is, James urged inwardly. *Say it was Ephraim Littlefield.* Merrick made no mention of the janitor by direct inference or name, and put aside the idea of an outside agent as quickly as he had raised it. *Why bring it up at all,* James wondered? *Was there madness or method in the defense's approach?*

Merrick suggested that the most important evidence was not the body parts, but the silver knife found in the tea chest. It was clean, with no trace of blood or chemical on it.

"Why hide this, a clean knife, in that tan? If Webster did so, why? If another man did so, he had a motive; that was, to bring in direct connection Professor Webster and these remains. And therefore, his knife may have been placed there."

Merrick had other questions about the condition of the remains.

"Where are the remnants or traces of the garments?" he queried, pointing out that the contents of the furnace revealed no evidence of cloth or leather having burned.

"And yet, gentlemen, it is certain that Doctor Parkman wore garments from head to foot; he had a coat, and a hat, a shirt, pants, and underclothes, and boots. And there undoubtedly was, as there is about all of us, something of an incombustible character—the buckles of our suspenders, sometimes the buttons on our coats, and the nails in our shoes. Somewhere have not remnants, or specimens of these, been found?"

Of course, they had not, Merrick continued, because they did not exist.

Dr. Parkman had exited the Medical College wearing his clothes because he was alive, as witness after witness had testified. *As many times as Merrick emphasized this,* observed James, *the jurors looked unconvinced. No heads nodded in agreement with Merrick's claim that Parkman might be alive to this day.*

Merrick at last turned to the questions concerning the testimony of Littlefield, whom he identified as the key participant in what Webster considered a conspiracy against him.

"Now, gentlemen of the jury, you must not misunderstand me. I will not take upon myself the fearful responsibility, in defending one man, to charge another with the same crime. Far be it from me to say that I will charge Ephraim Littlefield with this crime!"

There was much commotion in the galleries when it was pointed out that Littlefield sat in the courtroom, intently watching and listening to Merrick. He allowed himself no visible reaction that James could discern. Webster likewise stared ahead stolidly, paying no mind to his attorney or the janitor.

Merrick emphasized to the jurors their responsibility in weighing the veracity of Littlefield's testimony.

"I must say that we should be careful, extremely careful, where a man's life is in peril, not to place too much dependence upon a witness who, in giving part of his testimony, has fallen into error. A wide berth must not be given to witnesses upon whose testimony depends the fragile thread of human life."

Merrick now walked toward the diagram of the Medical College prepared by the prosecution. He traced Littlefield's search through the chemistry laboratory and Webster's other rooms.

"He was there four times; three times alone, and once with the police, and with an opportunity to search as much as he pleased!"

Merrick had succeeded in getting the attention of the jurors. They were digesting his every word.

"This is the first time that he enters that laboratory after the suspicion had come into his mind that Professor Webster had committed this awful crime. Would not his eye naturally have fallen on every object that could have attracted attention? Would his vision have been closed to anything, which would startle a man who was put upon his guard by the most grievous and horrible suspicions?

"And yet, he passed through that laboratory to the upper room, heard a part of the conversation, and turned and went back! Opportunity ample! Professor Webster he knew to be engaged. His own suspicions most strongly excited! Then he knew how those rooms had been watched and guarded, if he had been as vigilant as he says—and yet he makes no observations!"

James was pleased to see Merrick pursue Littlefield at last. He thought, *Merrick was absolutely correct in the direction in which he was leading the jury: to regard Littlefield's self-serving account with skepticism and suspicion.* The jurors' faces were tense and attentive.

Merrick referred to the numerous police searches of the Medical College in the days before Littlefield's grisly discovery. "Mister Littlefield says that he believed Professor Webster was a murderer; but he would not give a hint to Lieutenant Clapp that it was worthwhile to be a little more vigilant."

Instance after instance was cited of contradictory behavior on Littlefield's part: erratically sharing his suspicions; gladly accepting a Thanksgiving turkey from a man he thought a cold-blooded killer; never organizing a systematic search of Webster's rooms and effects. For inexplicable reasons, said Merrick, Littlefield settled on the theory that Dr. Parkman's body must be in the privy vault.

"Why should he go there? It was the privy that Professor Webster had excluded him from. Why not contrive some way or other to open the door and get in there? Perhaps all this painstaking of burrowing in would have been needless! Why not go from above? And, if the body was not visible from above, why not drop a light down the vault? It would have shown everything!"

Merrick paused to drink water and take a deep breath. His voice was beginning to give out; he spoke with a pronounced rasp. But he continued, his passion for his client's innocence for once sounding sincere. *James realized Webster was fortunate to have such a committed defender.*

"But no! This process was too simple. He goes below, to dig through the wall. But he works imperfectly; he does not accomplish it."

Merrick finally arrived at his true intention: to question Littlefield's trustworthiness, or lack of it.

"I believe the last reward for Doctor Parkman's body was published coincident with Mister Littlefield's exercise to break through that wall. Though he disclaims all intention of claiming it, yet I can see no earthly reason why he should not claim it. He went to work with this mighty conviction, and yet he left that work unfinished and incomplete!

"Was it the conviction that he was upon the very track of the murderer, and that he should find, decaying there, the body of Doctor Parkman, which could, the next day, be carried off to some other place—and yet he delayed for want of tools! He went to a party and danced eighteen out of twenty times, with the conviction that a dead man's bones were under his apartment at home, laid there by the hand of the wickedest criminal that has lived since Cain!"

James saw a few of the jurors blanch. None of them seemed to have considered the gaps and delays in Littlefield's efforts, from an incriminating perspective. Merrick was demonstrating his experience with jurors: who among them would turn down a large cash reward if their principled actions led to the arrest of the accused?

"Gentlemen, I bring you the facts in the case. If they are startling facts—if they demand explanations from Mister Littlefield, which cannot be given—I bring them to you only that you may say what ought, in justice and in truth, to be deduced from his testimony. If the want of credibility of this witness—if you, in short, do not believe, because of these internal difficulties, these intrinsic corruptions, in his testimony—then, gentlemen, this mass of network, these great theories and hypotheses of the government, crumble away, as the cloud and the mist are dispersed in the beams of the rising and refreshing sun."

Merrick went on to attack the physical evidence presented by the commonwealth.

"First, gentlemen, where are the traces of the crime? Where are the marks of blood in this laboratory? The physicians have told you the quantity of blood in the human body. Has any quantity of blood been found? A half a dozen spots on the left side of the pantaloons, and two or three upon the slippers, which have been in that room for years? Do you believe they came from Doctor George Parkman, and none else? Except for these traces, which might have been there before, there is not to be found the slightest mark of violence anywhere, either of blood, of stain, or of instrument. Nothing! The knife which is found is untarnished; the Turkish knife contains no blood! The floor is not marked with blood! There is no indication of violence!

"And yet it is said that at noonday, two men met—Doctor Parkman, a tall, vigorous man, and powerful; Professor Webster, such as he was, small, slight, with a paunch; that this mortal struggle occurred; that a mortal blow was given; yet no blood was found, though the pavement was taken up, though the walls were searched, though the garments were ransacked— and no blood found, save what might have been there years before! How is it possible that Professor Webster can have committed this crime?

"Nay more, gentlemen! Nay more! These improbabilities, that Professor Webster could have done this horrible thing, grow stronger and stronger; more evidence is presented for your examination."

Focusing on Webster's behavior after the alleged crime, Merrick again challenged the evidence presented by the prosecution.

"Follow Professor Webster from that place," he urged the jurors, pointing to the diagram of the Medical College.

"See him with his family that evening. The first part is spent, as usual, with his wife and children. Then we see him accompany these children to a neighbor's family hearth; then go by himself to Professor Treadwell's and spend two or three hours in social conversation—not absent-minded, not full of fits and starts, not frightened at the sound he has made, but self-possessed, calm, social as usual. Were ever human nerves made *that could do this?*"

Merrick let his last question hang in the air. The courtroom was absolutely still, focused on his every word. *James understood why Merrick had chosen to make the closing argument. He was good at this.* The defense counsel ended with a final plea for understanding and justice for his client.

"His character is here," he said, pointing to Webster in the prisoner's dock. The professor nodded graciously, as if he were being introduced for an award.

"He brings it and lays it before you. He implores you to weigh it well; and he asks only that your consciences, when your last day's work in this court shall be done, shall be pure and free; that you shall save him, in the hour of his affliction, to be returned to the world again, and yet arrive to that humble home of which no voice can adequately tell the sorrows that now sit there, or the joy that may yet be imparted to it!"

Merrick slumped in his chair. He had spoken from 11:30 in the morning to seven o'clock in the evening, with only the dinner recess in which to recover. James was equally exhausted. His fingers ached as they never had before; his head throbbed. The jurors also looked spent, and eager to have the proceedings come to a close. Webster stared straight ahead, ignoring whatever impact his counsel's impassioned plea to spare his life might have had. It was as if someone else were on trial in this courtroom, and John Webster just another casual observer.

DALE M. POLLOCK

CHAPTER 26

April 1850
Court Street, Boston, Massachusetts

James was so tired that he considered canceling the night's transcription session, but he couldn't afford the delay. There were only a few days at most left in the trial; the work must go on.

As he turned onto Court Street, he was accosted by a form that hurtled out of a dark corner and grabbed him about the shoulder and waist.

James's breath caught in his throat, thinking he was about to be robbed, or worse, murdered. He was powerless in the grip of the stranger, his arm grasped firmly as he was dragged underneath the canvas canopy of a trade goods store. He was ready to call for help when the man raised his cap and revealed himself. In the faint light from a nearby gas streetlamp stood William Haggerty.

"What's your purpose in this new outrage, Haggerty?" James said, throwing off the man's arm, and glaring at him. The best stratagem for dealing with Haggerty, he had decided, was to take the offensive and not let up. "I have paid every dollar and cent that I owe your stepdaughter, not that it's any business of yours. My agreement was with Miss O'Keeffe, and that's whom I have compensated for her excellent work. If you have complaints, they're of no concern to me. Your stepdaughter has acted in a most professional manner."

"Indeed, I do come about me stepdaughter—as ye calls her, Docter, I calls her me own flesh and blood—nae about the pittance ye pay her. And fer all her labor on yer behalf and to yer profit. Nae, Docter, I wish to discuss with ye the value of our Ellen in a diff'rent light."

James colored, furious at Haggerty's clear inference. As he had feared, the man was up to blackmail, pure and simple. Well, James wouldn't stand for it. Before he could respond, Haggerty made his mission explicit.

"Me Ellen's become a person yer familiar with, Docter Stone. So familiar it might be disturbin' to yer friends and yer patients in Beacon Hill,

Docter, where our kind ain't so kindly regarded, are we now? Not as kindly as ye regard our Ellen."

"How dare you!" said James, his voice louder than intended. He looked around to make sure there were no witnesses to this conversation. The street was deserted except for two men from different worlds. "Do you realize who you're speaking to? I could have you arrested for what you have just said."

"To be sure ye could, Docter, but we both be sure ye'll not. The court, that place ye spends yer days scrivenin', might want to hear my news. It concerns the good Docter Stone, who proves nae so good after all. What about me testimony, Docter Stone? Will ye write me words down, nice and neat, like ye do in the court?"

James wanted to erase the smirk from Haggerty's face with one well-placed blow. As if reading his mind, Haggerty cracked his knuckles, the sound reverberating in the air, achieving its purpose in discouraging any action on James's part. The resistance sagged out of him. He would have to pay.

"I take yer silence as agreein' with me," Haggerty said smoothly, as if he had offered an opinion about the weather. "And I trust there be nae more talk o' police or anyone bein' copped. What I'm proposin' is a simple bargain betwixt us, two gentlemens who agree to keep matters confidential-like. Nothin' wrong with that, aye, Docter?"

"You are no gentleman, Haggerty, and I will enter into no 'gentleman's agreement' with you. It's clear you propose to extort money from me. To spare your stepdaughter the embarrassment, I suppose I must succumb. Name your price. Let's do this quickly and be done with it."

Haggerty moved quickly to within inches of James's face, staring at him with his usual leer.

"Don't be speakin' to me in that tone, Docter, as if I'm some Irish dog. Remember who holds the upper hand here, and 'tis not ye. It was yer dirty thoughts that led ye to use my daughter, and now it's time for you to pay for all those evenin's ye spend with her."

"Do you present yourself as her procurer now? She is an adult. You have no right to intrude."

Ignoring James, Haggerty assumed a businesslike pose.

"It'll be twenty dollars in silver ye'll pay to me each month, 'til I say stop. If ye fail to do so, Docter Stone, ye'll be known for more than some fancy report. Scandal'll be yer boon companion."

"You would do this to your own stepdaughter?"

"I'm comin' to her aid, Docter. Our Ellen has been abused, oh yes, and by a rich and powerful man. Someone must stand up for her. That'd be me, her lovin' pa."

James felt walled in, unable to see a means of escape from his dilemma. His exhaustion descended upon him like a black cloud, fogging his thoughts and dampening his anger. He sighed.

"No more, Haggerty. I'll do as you demand. Present yourself to my apartments at number six Bowdoin Square Sunday next, I'll have your money ready. This will be the one and only time I'll pay. You don't have an endless rope around my neck; after Sunday you may pull all you want, I will not succumb."

"Ye hear so much talk o' ropes and hangin' in yer court, ye got 'em on yer mind. Ye nae needs be rude, Docter. This be a simple bargain, nothin' hidden about it. Ye go on seein' Ellen much as ye like, Docter, long as the money be comin' to me."

"There's no more to be said. I'll await you Sunday next. I warn you, if you so much as breathe one word of this to your stepdaughter, there will be no money. Instead, you'll find yourself in the custody of Marshal Tukey. I'll not have Ellen aware of our sordid business."

"Rest easy, good Docter. Mum's the word. Only ye'll come to me, and me own place of business. We met there before, if Yer Honor might remember."

James wondered if that would be the spot where Haggerty robbed and murdered him. But what would be the point? James had every intention of paying the blackmail, as much as it disgusted him. Haggerty wouldn't gain any more money if James were killed.

As if reading his thoughts, Haggerty's leer turned into a repellent smile.

"Nae trouble yerself, Docter. Yer worth far more to me alive than dead. Ye nae be tumblin' any time soon."

With that, Haggerty turned and proceeded down Washington Street, away from the canopy and the nearby gas lamp, leaving James alone under its muted glow. He was shaking with frustration. He had brought this on himself. There was no one else to blame.

By the time he reached the transcription room, his breath was no longer coming in shallow gasps. The copyists had not yet arrived. Ellen hurried over to him as he entered, concern on her face. He steadied himself; he had promised to himself to make no mention of the criminal enterprise perpetrated upon him by a member of her immediate family.

"Is everythin' all right, Docter Stone? I worried when the hour turned, and ye still hadn't come," Ellen said, as she helped James off with his over-coat and stovepipe hat.

"Nothing of concern, Miss O'Keeffe. I had to speak to the bailiff about the trial's conclusion. We must be prepared for matters in the court to end tomorrow, or the day after at the latest."

"And then what? When will they sentence Doctor Webster?"

James gave Ellen a sad smile. "So you, too, believe the only outcome to be a guilty verdict. I thought possibly the evidence I've dictated each night might make you think otherwise, as I now do. In fact, I no longer know what I believe."

The girls entered the room, chatting among themselves; when they overheard James, the room fell silent. Ellen looked at him.

"Do ye really think Professor Webster could be innocent? Does not all the evidence point to . . ."

James looked at Ellen with an intensity she had not seen since the anti-slavery rally. "It points, Miss O'Keeffe, but it does not show. A man should not lose his life for a crime with no witness, no murder weapon, and no victim. Is that proper?"

The copyists were surprised by James's display of emotion, which had built in him all day, now bursting out after his encounter with Haggerty. The young women had never before heard James express his personal views on the trial.

Ellen was more accustomed to this aspect of his personality, his abil-ity to draw conclusions from whatever evidence was presented to him, no matter its source. In fact, she was drawn to it.

"I'd nae meant to excite ye, Doctor," Ellen said, indicating to James that the female transcribers were staring at them. It was best to move on.

The work proceeded slowly, given that Merrick's closing argument had been endless. After four hours of dictation, James was having difficulty keeping his eyes open. There was no point in continuing; fully half of the defense argument remained to be dictated. The work would have to re-sume the following evening. This would set the report's completion fur-ther back, but it could not be helped. What James required now was a soft down pillow under his head.

Ellen blew out the whale oil lamps as he approached the door, coat and hat in hand. She surprised him, leaving the last lamp lit, and moving over to him quickly.

"What's it be, James?" Ellen asked in her Irish lilt, staring up at him. "What be disturbin' ye?"

James was no longer surprised by Ellen's acumen in discerning his moods, but he had vowed to himself that he wouldn't disclose her stepfather's blackmail.

"Simple exhaustion, Ellen. I can never remember feeling so tired. These proceedings have seemed endless. I'm sure to recover with a good night's rest once the trial reaches its conclusion."

"There's somethin' yer nae tellin' me, James. I know ye that well. Somethin's happened, and I wish ye'd share it with me. I might be of some help."

James took Ellen's left hand in his, gently, and stroked it, looking straight at her.

"Whatever matters preoccupy me concern only myself, Ellen. Don't bother yourself with them, they've nothing to do with you, and you may have no effect upon them."

This last comment was harsher than James intended, and he immediately regretted it. He wished he could confide in her, but, of course, he could not. She would despise him for paying her stepfather blackmail.

Ellen's voice tightened; she became more formal in her manner.

"Very well, Doctor Stone, if that's yer choice, I'm respectful of it. I nae wish to intrude upon ye."

James didn't have the energy to alter the wrong direction the conversation had taken. He really did desire sleep above all else, so he bid Ellen a quick goodnight. She looked after him with disappointment as he shambled toward 6 Bowdoin Square.

CHAPTER 27

April 1850
Bowdoin Square and Court Street, Boston, Massachusetts

It was the eleventh day of the trial, though it seemed like the hundredth. James arose at seven o'clock to prepare for perhaps his last day in court. He was relieved that it would bring the commonwealth's closing argument, to be delivered by Attorney General Clifford. An end was in sight.

The night hadn't yielded the blissful repose James sought. His thoughts had been plagued by reenactments of his encounter with Haggerty, imagining what he should have done differently. He should have walked away immediately, upon hearing Haggerty's demands. He should have told the scoundrel he'd have nothing to do with him. He should have called the police and had the Irishman arrested for extortion. He should have beaten the man to within an inch of his life.

He had done none of those things, James knew, because he was guilty of all that Haggerty had accused him. He was engaged in a carnal relationship with Haggerty's stepdaughter, although he might no longer be, given that he had just spurned her offer of comfort. He had to find a solution; he must find one.

James hurried through the rainy downtown streets. As he approached Court Street, throngs of bystanders surrounded the courthouse, their numbers larger than ever, despite the inclement weather. By now a familiar figure to Tukey's men, he was waved through the police chain and inside the coveted side entrance. Steam came off his clothes and those of the men around him; the wet wool gave the air a musty, pungent odor.

One constable, coming in from a shift outside, shook himself like a wet dog, spraying all around. Several spectators lined up to enter the galleries laughed. James noticed that one of those sprinkled was Robert Shaw, who, with imperious disdain, brushed the water off his expensive black velvet overcoat with a fur collar.

James hurried to his place as the jurors entered, followed by the justices.

The attorney general must be under great pressure, he supposed. *An unsuccessful summation could lead to an acquittal. Merrick had done an effective job for his client, sowing potential doubt about the government's singular use of circumstantial evidence; now it was Clifford's task to rebut him.*

John Clifford stroked his dark beard as he approached the jury. He began unexpectedly by praising the defense: "There has been nothing left unsaid or undone, which, consistent with the truth, could have been said, or could have been done, for this prisoner."

Clifford said he had hoped that Professor Webster would offer a credible explanation for the circumstances in which he found himself, a web that seemed to be irresistibly contracting to his doom. But that hadn't happened, Clifford concluded, shaking his head.

"And I grieve to say to you, that after all that has been done, and all that has been said, that hope has been utterly disappointed."

Clifford approached the jurors until he stood but a few feet from them and demanded that each place himself directly in Webster's position.

"I put it to the conscience of every one of you: if you were seized by an officer of justice and brought up upon the most heinous and revolting charge that could be made against a man, would you not turn 'round, after you had twenty-four, yea, forty-eight hours of reflection and time to recover from the first shock—would you not have demanded that the government show you the proofs upon which they charge you, an innocent man, with a crime like this?

"The complaint has been made that there is no direct evidence—strong as the counsel has admitted this mass of circumstantial proof to be—no direct evidence that the fact charged upon this prisoner is true; that the act committed by him was not witnessed by any human eye, and that that no witness has come upon the stand to say so."

Clifford mocked the defense's assertion that Parkman was not killed on November 23, 1849, but still alive when Webster was charged with his murder.

"Oh, would God it were so! Was there never a search, which not only disturbed the vigilant poise of this city, but made every man in it a policeman? And no tidings, no trace of him, living or dead, have been found, unless these mutilated remains, and these calcined bones, constitute parts of his mortal frame."

Clifford lowered his voice. "But their attempt has failed. I read it in your countenance. I read it in the proof which came from that witness box—that you have no more doubt that those were the remains of Doctor

George Parkman, than what I am now uttering to you is my living voice. Upon this part of the case there is not left a particle of doubt."

Going witness by witness, Clifford demolished the credibility of the alleged sightings of Parkman.

"Now, if Doctor Parkman were roaming about this city, as these witnesses describe, during the whole of that Friday afternoon, I ask you to say, upon your consciences, would they not have been able to produce here, to swear to the fact—not six, or sixty, or six hundred, even—six thousand, rather! Do you suppose that it would have been possible for him to have wandered about this city during a whole afternoon, and no human being, except these six persons, to have seen him?"

Finally, the attorney general came to the nettlesome issue of Ephraim Littlefield. Calling Littlefield "a humble and honest man," he made the janitor out to be the true victim of Merrick's argument.

Littlefield would have to bear the false accusations of a man he had served faithfully, Clifford said. He would be forced to live the rest of his life, at home or abroad, forever associated with this tragedy. *This was a neat trick,* thought James. *Make Littlefield the victim of an injustice. Make him the poor working man falsely accused by an elite of privilege and power.*

"I do not put Mister Littlefield upon this stand as a man of culture—of nice, delicate, moral sense; I put him here as an honest man, who fills reputably his position in life—a useful, though humble one."

The defense had produced nothing of significance to challenge Littlefield's veracity, Clifford insisted. The police did not contradict him, nor did the doctors who testified about the recovery of the remains. Even Littlefield's acceptance of the Thanksgiving turkey from Dr. Webster was justified.

"It don't appear that he ate it," Clifford said of Littlefield and the disputed bird. Laughter rippled through the courtroom, and even Chief Justice Shaw allowed himself a slight curving of the lips. "But it does appear that he did not dine at home on Thanksgiving Day; so that all the pathos and poetry of my learned friend, about his eating that consecrated meal, received from a murderer, is entirely lost.

"Then, if Mister Littlefield were not an honest man, and an honest witness—if he had a purpose to implicate Professor Webster, why did he not point out the tea chest? Why did he not point out the bones? He did neither."

All that occurred pointed to Webster's guilt, not Littlefield's, insisted Clifford.

"If a man has an object which he wishes to get rid of, the world's knowledge of the possession of which would be fatal to him, what is the most obvious thing that occurs to him, as the instrument and agency of destruction? Fire! Fire! For that reduces the organized structure to a mass of undistinguishable ashes.

"And so with this learned professor! When he has that body to dispose of, he had two things to do: one, to destroy the body, and all things pertaining to Doctor Parkman; and, at the same time, avoid suspicion. He was to keep up his natural and customary deportment. He was not to be caught anywhere, or at any moment, off his guard. If a person spoke to him in relation to Doctor Parkman, he was to meet the subject with calmness and self-possession."

Clifford used even Webster's impassive demeanor in the courtroom as another indication of his guilt.

"Gentlemen, you've seen him here, through these past two weeks; you've seen what his deportment has been during the solemnity and impressiveness that have marked the progress of this trial; you've seen him when others were moved to tears—when the Judge upon the bench, the counsel at the bar, the witness upon the stand, the entire audience throughout this hall, were unable to repress their emotions. You've seen him when his own daughters were upon the stand, and even the hardened heart of a public prosecutor was too much moved to subject them to cross-examination. Never has the defendant blanched but once—never but when detection, exposure, discovery, yawned before him. Then he drooped and fell prostrate, as innocence never did."

All eyes in the courtroom turned to Professor Webster, who as described, showed no emotion.

Clifford spoke for seven hours in total, as if trying to match Merrick, returning again and again to Webster's purported innocence, and all the reasons it could not be proven.

"We have waited for an explanation of this exculpating evidence, and we have waited in vain. Professor Webster is a man of high station, a professor at Harvard, an educated man, but that doesn't mean that he is innocent.

"Have you any doubt, from all this evidence, that Professor Webster had an agency in the death of Doctor Parkman? Can you doubt it for a moment? It is not a possible doubt that will shield you from your responsibilities—it must be a reasonable doubt."

Clifford turned toward Chief Justice Shaw. "And I invoke Your Honor's instruction to this jury, as to what a reasonable doubt is. It is a doubt for which a man can give a good reason, and not a mere possible doubt that somebody else may have done it.

"The juror who permits the guilty to escape convicts himself. If ever we have had a case which requires the jury to stand up firmly to the discharge of their great duty as citizens, it is here and now."

With that, an exhausted Clifford shuffled back to his seat. Chief Justice Shaw leaned his leonine head toward Professor Webster in the prisoner's dock and bowed slightly. His voice boomed from the bench. "Before committing this case to the jury: Professor Webster, you may address the jury with any statements you think fit and necessary for your defense. I ought to inform you, also, that this is a privilege granted to you, which you may use or not, at your own discretion."

Shaw was following common practice by allowing the defendant the opportunity to address the jury and not face cross-examination. His statement would be unsworn, so there was no obligation to state the truth, if it didn't help his case. He could say whatever he wished.

Webster didn't disappoint. He stood, turned, and surveyed the entire courtroom, his eyes lingering on three of his daughters (his wife had never once appeared in court), who sat together immediately behind the prisoner's dock. He was in no rush to speak. Finally, he put on his spectacles, pulled a sheaf of papers from inside his coat, and straightened them. He began to read.

"I feel indebted to Your Honor for this kind permission. I cannot go into an explanation of the network of circumstances which has been woven around me and would require many hours to unravel. On all the points, testimony had been placed in the hands of my counsel, and my innocence would have been firmly established if it had been produced. But, acting entirely under their guidance, I have sealed my lips, and from the first moment, I have trusted entirely to them.

"They have not seen fit to bring forward the evidence on a great variety of subjects, which, therefore, have been brought to bear, with consummate ingenuity, against me. I trust they will not be considered against me by the jury."

The prisoner flushed; his delicate hands trembled; his words began to make little sense. His speech halted. Webster looked wildly about the room. He looked at his notes, searched again for his daughters, yet avoided gazing at them. With a great sigh, he sat down, and waved his hand distractedly, as if dismissing these pesky charges of murder, vivisection, and conspiracy. Not for the first time during the trial, James felt an abject sympathy for John Webster.

Chief Justice Shaw was now the object of attention. He consulted sotto voce with the other justices, then turned to his notes. *His charge to the jury would define the matter,* supposed James. *He had to instruct the jury in a case where there was no key witness, no clearly identified murder weapon, and not even a complete corpse that may or may not be the victim.* Shaw lumbered to unsteady feet, forgoing the use of his birch cane, and faced the jurors.

"It is mainly a question of evidence, after all," Shaw said in a clear and precise voice, markedly different than the gravelly growl he had employed during the trial.

The evidence was not his to judge, Shaw told the jurors. He would make clear the rules and principles of law, and then the jurors would consider the evidence. At stake, he reminded the twelve men silently seated below him, was a man's right to life. James noted that Shaw spoke in a tone greatly affected by the circumstances; his countenance expressed his emotions.

The chief justice then unexpectedly took up the difference between murder and manslaughter, which he said hinged solely on the issue of malice. Was malice inherent in Webster's invitation to Parkman to meet at the Medical College, if he had the intention to dispose of him?

"It will be seen that the characteristic distinction between murder and manslaughter is malice, express or implied. This rule of malice is founded upon the plain and obvious principle that a person must presume to intend to do that which he in fact does; and that he must intend the probable consequences of his own acts. It is a settled rule that no provocation with words only will justify a mortal blow. If, upon provoking language, the party intentionally revenges himself with a mortal blow, it is unquestionably murder."

Murmurs rippled through the courtroom. Chief Justice Shaw paused, sternly surveying the spectators until they quieted. He offered numerous examples to illustrate his point.

"Where a pistol is discharged at another; where a heavy bludgeon or an axe is used upon another; where a knife is used—these are dangerous weapons and are indicative of an intention to kill. The law will reduce it to manslaughter if there be provocation sufficient for this. But words are not sufficient for this. It must be at least an assault."

Shaw, it seemed to James, *had just ruled in the commonwealth's favor.* There was no evidence of physical harm to Webster. He had apparently suffered no visible injuries from his presumed final encounter with Parkman. By defining the standard for manslaughter as a response to at least an assault, and murder as the result of malice "implied from any deliberate, cruel act against another, however sudden," Chief Justice Shaw had outlined an easy way for the jurors to convict Webster for murder.

Shaw acknowledged that the commonwealth was relying on circumstantial evidence to prove its case; "that is, nobody saw the act done." The prosecutors had provided a motive and various parts of a body, but little else. This absence of direct evidence didn't faze Chief Justice Shaw.

"Well, no witness saw it: but can it not be proved? Circumstantial evidence may be of such a nature as to warrant a conclusive belief that somebody did it; and it would be injurious to the best interests of society to have it so ordered that circumstantial proof cannot avail. If it were necessary always to have positive evidence, how many of the acts committed in this community which destroy its peace, which subvert its security, would go unpunished?"

Shaw leaned forward and studied the jurors, his jowls quivering.

"No, gentlemen, it is not so. There may be evidence quite as strong, indeed, sometimes considerably stronger, from circumstantial evidence, as from positive."

James regarded Webster, who looked noticeably paler. Sohier and Merrick listened morosely as the chief justice shredded their defense.

"The necessity, therefore, of resorting to circumstantial evidence, is absolute and is obvious. Crimes are secret. Most crimes seek the security of secrecy, and of darkness. It is, therefore, necessary to use another mode of evidence than that which is direct. Circumstantial evidence is founded on experience, and obvious facts and coincidences, establishing a connection between the known and proved facts, and the facts sought to be proved."

A final problem remained, the chief justice told the jurors. Lacking was a positively identified *corpus delecti*, the body of the crime. "Were those his remains? Was the body of Doctor Parkman found?" Shaw asked. It was a rhetorical question. "It sometimes happens that a body cannot be found, where the proof of death is clear. Because the body is not found, can anybody deny that the author of the crime is still a murderer?"

Webster reacted as if the chief justice had struck him physically. He recoiled and placed his head in his hands. His defense had crumbled; his advantages in a criminal proceeding (no body, no witness, no murder weapon) were being demolished by the most powerful man in the room.

"It is of importance to ascertain whether they were parts of one human body. If all the parts coincide with each other as one body—those parts found in the privy, and those found in tea chest, and those in the furnace, all corresponding—then the natural conclusion would be that the same person who concealed one did the whole, and that they do belong to the same body."

Who else but John Webster could be that concealing person? Only Ephraim Littlefield, James supposed. Chief Justice Shaw had been curiously silent about the state's key witness. Now he dismissed him as a potential suspect.

"I shall pass over all that has been said with regard to Mister Littlefield. I am not aware that the conclusion depends upon his testimony. You are to judge it and give that weight to it as you think it deserves, so far as it should command attention. His veracity is not impeached."

Shaw emphasized the debts Webster owed Parkman, and Webster's claim that he had invited Parkman to his rooms at the Medical College to settle their financial matters. Webster emerged from that encounter with receipts from Parkman that proved significant, Shaw maintained.

"If this engagement with Doctor Parkman was made by Professor Webster with the purpose of getting possession of those notes, and by means of this arrangement he did get possession of those notes, it would be a very strong case of murder by express malice."

That was, James supposed, *the final nail in John Webster's coffin. The life he had led was rendered meaningless in the chief justice's charge.* However exemplary the testimony offered by Webster's friends, coworkers and admirers, the jury was instructed to give it little credence.

Shaw finally concluded his lengthy charge.

"I commend this case to your consideration, gentlemen. Take sufficient time, weigh the evidence, and give such a verdict as will satisfy your own judgment and your own sound conscience, and I'm sure it will be a true one."

CHAPTER 28

April 1850
Court Street, Boston, Massachusetts

It was eight o'clock in the evening when Chief Justice Lemuel Shaw completed his charge to the jury and lowered his bulk back into his chair atop
the bench. He announced that the bailiff would lead the jurors to their de-
liberation room on the third floor of the courthouse. The court would be in
recess until 10:45 p.m. If the jurors had not reached a verdict by that time,
they would resume their duties the next morning when court resumed.

Sheriff Eveleth approached Professor Webster. Leaning into the prisoner's dock, Eveleth offered Webster the use of a private room in the courthouse until the verdict was rendered. The defendant looked grateful and
followed the sheriff out of the courtroom. Webster's handlers, for once,
refrained from manacling him as he left.

James still had to take down the reading of the verdict, and the sentencing, if Webster were found guilty. His fingers would soon be granted
their promised freedom from the incessant scratching of pen across paper.

The emotional events of this day had gone on longer than any previous
day of the trial, and hours more work awaited him if the jurors came to a
decision quickly. It could be early morning before James, Ellen, and her
troupe finished the transcriptions.

After the recess, people gathered in knots of ten or a dozen in the courtroom and around the courthouse. James estimated some two hundred persons remained inside, about fifty in the galleries and the rest on the floor
of the courtroom. They were lawyers, politicians, physicians, clergymen,
reporters, policemen. Any prominent male Bostonian able to wrangle a
pass was unwilling to depart and miss the historic moment.

No point in trying to eat this late in the evening, James thought as he
hurried to the necessary house behind the courthouse, where there was
already a long line. Trailing behind him was John French, the *Boston Herald*
owner and reporter. There had been some tension between the two since

French's paper had announced plans to publish, in daily installments, an accurate account of the trial that would commence immediately after Webster's anticipated sentencing.

James had already learned that French had devised his own style of transcription—not the phonographic alphabet developed by Sir Isaac Pitman, but instead a singular set of symbols and scratches. James had no idea to whom French dictated his accounts.

When he had received his own testimony as a medical expert from French, it had already been transcribed—and, he was sorry to say, inaccurately so. It made him nervous about the outcome of his own efforts, not to mention the competition from one of Boston's largest newspapers.

"How much longer do you believe we'll be in recess?" asked French, sounding as bored and tired as he usually did. "After the charge Chief Justice Shaw delivered, I thought a verdict would come posthaste."

"I hope they spend some time in their deliberations," said James. "Professor Webster deserves that much, at the least."

Three sharp blows to the wooden floor with the bailiff's staff, loud enough to be heard outside, interrupted the conversation. Everyone hurried back in, including James with a still-full bladder.

A deep quiet held the room as the bailiff strode in, announcing in a loud voice that the jury had agreed upon a verdict. *James marveled at the majesty of it all: the scales of justice about to be balanced.*

At twelve minutes after eleven o'clock, barely three hours after the jury had left the courtroom, Professor Webster, looking pale, was conducted to the armchair within the iron picket enclosure of the prisoner's dock, again without manacles. He moved to his seat with a quick, nervous step. James examined him closely and saw dejection apparent in the contraction of his mouth. His diminutive frame trembled.

A few moments later, twelve men, all dressed somberly in dark clothing, filed in slowly, taking their seats in the jury enclosure for the last time. The justices filed in and assembled at the bench, dignified in their gravity. A profound and painful silence followed their entry. Finally, George Wilde, the court clerk, broke it.

"Gentlemen of the jury, have you agreed on a verdict?"

James looked upon those who had the power of life or death in their votes, and he thanked God that he did not number among them. It was a terrible responsibility, one not easily dismissed after the trial was completed. This decision would haunt these men for the remainder of their lives.

Some of the jurors responded audibly to the clerk, while others remained silent. "We have," a sufficient number of male voices said. The clerk responded, "Who shall speak for you, gentlemen?"

"The foreman," the voices responded.

Locksmith Robert J. Byram stepped forward, flushing slightly, looking as if he wished he were anywhere else. The clerk spoke first, asking Webster to rise. James observed that the professor seemed to do so with difficulty.

"John W. Webster, hold up your right hand! Foreman, look upon the prisoner! Prisoner, look upon the jury! What say you, Mister Foreman? Is John W. Webster, the prisoner at the bar, guilty or not guilty of the willful murder of George Parkman?"

There was no hesitation in Byram's surprisingly strong voice. It rang out in the breathless courtroom.

"Guilty!" the foreman shouted. He brought his hand to his face, overcome by the painful duty he had just performed.

When Byram pronounced the word, Webster started, like a person who had been shot. His right hand flopped down upon the rail before him, his chin drooped to his breast. He sank into his chair and covered his eyes with his hands.

The clerk turned to the bench and repeated, "Guilty, Your Honor, guilty, he says."

James was surprised that pandemonium had not erupted. The courtroom remained clothed in a deathlike silence. All eyes were fixed in sadness on Webster, whose hopes had now fled. Several jurors were sobbing. Even the justices were moved. Justice Wilder had tears running down his face. Pliny Merrick, deeply affected, seemed so agitated that he could hardly stand.

James looked toward the Parkman family, seated in the first row of the courtroom. Robert Shaw had a grimace of satisfaction on his face, tempered only by disappointment that Webster would not be executed on the spot.

The clerk broke the unbearable silence.

"Gentlemen of the jury, hearken to your verdict, as the court have recorded it. You, upon your oaths, do say, that John W. Webster, the prisoner at the bar, is guilty of willful murder; so say you, Mister Foreman; so, gentlemen, you all say."

Webster remained in his stunned state, oblivious to all around him. Merrick went to the prisoner's dock to whisper words of consolation in his client's ear. The prisoner broke down in tears. He pushed up his spectacles and clutched his handkerchief to his eyes. It was the first time he had wept in the courtroom. Merrick reached out a hand, but Webster shrugged him off.

A deep, heartbreaking sigh came from deep within him that even James could hear, seated several feet away. Webster burst out, part cry, part scream: "Take me away. Why have me here to be gazed upon? Take me away!"

His jailers lifted him to a standing position, one on each side to keep his arms in their grasp, and then removed him to his cell, finally free from the eyes of the curious, the sympathetic, and the satiated.

No one else seemed willing to leave the courtroom, to break the spell that had kept all in silence except Webster, the foreman, and the clerk. Chief Justice Shaw, affected in a way evidenced by a huskier voice and a diminished demeanor, thanked the jurors and dismissed them. He gave the order to adjourn the court until the final sentence would be handed down. The spectators filed out, still hushed by the finality of the judgment rendered before them.

James felt moored to his seat, a welter of conflicting thoughts speeding through his brain. He could not shake his sense that an injustice had been perpetrated, but why this was so, he couldn't exactly say. This crime had bedeviled James from its outset. The guilty verdict now magnified his confusion. To put his own mind at ease, he had to answer the questions that were festering in it like inflamed splinters.

Who had aided John Webster in the murder of George Parkman? And why was Webster protecting his accomplice?

CHAPTER 29

April 1850
Bowdoin Square and Endicott Street, Boston, Massachusetts

James awoke late on the Sabbath morning. By the time the courtroom had emptied the night before, the hour had been too advanced to accomplish any work. Ellen and her copyists would gather with him again on Monday evening, following the scheduled sentencing of Professor Webster.

James did have one unpleasant task to fulfill. He had to visit the North End to pay the promised twenty dollars to William Haggerty. James had turned the matter of the Irishman's blackmail over in his mind countless times and had not come any closer to a successful response.

Despite his threat to Haggerty, James possessed no means by which to prevent the scoundrel from continuing his blackmail. He would remain at Haggerty's mercy, even if he stopped all contact with Ellen and never saw her again. Haggerty possessed information that, if properly distributed, would ruin James's reputation and career.

He found the strongbox that contained his ready cash money, which he kept hidden in his wardrobe, and removed twenty dollars in silver coins, putting them in a velvet sack. He must devise a way to rid himself of Haggerty, he thought, as he walked over to Revere House to catch the omnibus to Tremont Saloon. He was lucky enough to obtain a seat, and with detached interest, he watched passengers struggle to fold into themselves, bumping into one another as they reached for the leather straps dangling from the roof. The conductor made it through the horsecar to collect his fare just before the car arrived at James's destination.

He got out and walked to the North End. The wind had picked up. He felt that he could be blown easily into the bay. He made for Endicott Street, and soon the saloon where previously he had met Haggerty came into sight. Because it was Sunday, liquor sales were forbidden, and the saloon was not its usual boisterous hive of drunken activity.

There was still an infernal racket in the North End, as children swarmed the streets, street vendors shouted out the virtues of their wares, inebriated men staggered around with their diminishing beer pails, purchased at last call the night before and required to last through the one dry day of the week.

James hoped Haggerty had kept this meeting a secret from his stepdaughter. If he spotted Ellen, James decided, he would turn around and walk away. William Haggerty suddenly materialized, as if magically blown onto Endicott Street by the whipping wind.

"Docter Stone!" Haggerty hailed him as if he were a long-lost friend. "So good of ye to join me on this blowy day. I trust yer in good health."

Nothing irritated James more than Haggerty's false bonhomie, but he kept his temper in check and approached the Irishman, who clutched a thin jacket around his lanky frame in a vain attempt to ward off the wind's chill.

"There you are, Haggerty. I was afraid you'd wasted my time, having me here on a Sunday. Let's do our business, if I can call it that, and be done with one another."

"Docter Stone, I dinna understand yer sharp words. After all, me Ellen's done so much fer ye, in so many ways, that I think ye might show a bit o' gratitude to the Haggertys."

This statement was accompanied by his familiar phony smile. James wished he could strike Haggerty in the face just to see the stupid expression replaced by one of pain.

"Your stepdaughter is aware of my gratitude, but none is extended to you, Haggerty. You're a blackguard and a scoundrel, and the less I have to do with you, the better. Here's your money."

James thrust the velvet sack at Haggerty, who was so eager for its contents that he almost dropped it as he yanked it open. Silver coins tumbled into his hands. Haggerty counted them as quickly as they fell.

"You needn't worry, it's all there. I remind you of our agreement, that word of this shall never reach Ellen. If she is ever informed of this payment, I'll have you clapped in lockup faster than you can down a pail of porter. Marshal Tukey is a close acquaintance of mine, and he has a special appreciation for the Irish."

Haggerty's face clouded at the mention of Tukey, widely despised in the immigrant community for holding the Irish responsible for *all* the crime in Boston.

"I'd leave the marshal out o' this, Docter, for the benefit of all of us. He has nae ta say in the matter, this is between ye and me. Ellen has no knowin' of it, and she ne'er will."

Haggerty grabbed James's arm so quickly that he had no opportunity to pull from his grasp.

"This'll do fer now, Docter, but nae forever. I'll be back for more, ye can rest assured on that. Yer nae quit o' the Haggertys so easy."

James wrenched his arm away. "Watch your step, Haggerty. My patience is thin; it is almost worn away. I'm not without my own resources. Don't try me, I warn you. Our business is finished, for once and for all."

James turned and strode off, his heart thumping so loudly he was sure Haggerty must hear it. He did not turn around to see the man again. He kept walking, feeling the heat of the Irishman's hostile gaze upon his back.

CHAPTER 30

April 1850
Court Street, Boston, Massachusetts

There had been no time for a formal announcement that the chief justices of the Supreme Court of the commonwealth of Massachusetts would bring up John Webster for sentencing on a Monday morning in April.

There was no suspense about the result, either. Massachusetts's law required the death penalty for the crime of willful murder.

James arrived at the courthouse at half past seven in the morning to vouchsafe his admission; by eight o'clock, every space from whence a glimpse might be had of the unfortunate prisoner was occupied. Professor Webster was nowhere in sight, but it mattered not to the onlookers. A variety of opinions were argued, attacked, endorsed, and abandoned as discussions raged at every corner, in and out of the courtroom.

The gathered assemblage of dignitaries was impressive. James looked around and caught the eye of Senator Webster, who nodded slightly in James's direction. Next to him was Rufus Choate, looking mightily relieved that he had not accepted this lost cause. James also saw Governor Briggs, Mayor Beacham, President Jared Sparks of Harvard, and Dr. Oliver Wendell Holmes. The chief justice's son-in-law Herman Melville occupied a front row seat. Everyone looked properly grave, he observed, and he adjusted his own expression from one of curiosity to one of somber bearing, to better reflect the grim circumstances.

To the other side of the courtroom were the men of the press, representing all parts of the United States and several foreign capitals, as far away as Europe and South America. Many had their notebooks at the ready. Others were prepared to dash off to nearby telegraph offices the moment Webster's fate was announced.

James caught sight of Robert Shaw, sitting with George Parkman's widow, Eliza Parkman, and other members of the family. It was the first and only time she would venture into court. Shaw met James's eyes for a moment. They burned with a vengeance that was almost achieved. *If it were possible,* James thought, *Shaw himself would pull the lever that would snap Webster's neck.*

Precisely at ten minutes after nine o'clock, Professor Webster was brought into court. Constable William Jones had hold of one arm, and jail-keeper Andrews grasped the other. Webster looked downcast and nervous.

Attorney General Clifford spoke first, recapitulating the indictment and trial of the prisoner, emphasizing that Webster had counsel of his own choosing to help him prepare and conduct his defense. The evidence had been presented to the jury, and the jury had found him guilty of the charge of willful murder.

"It now becomes my painful duty to move that the sentence which the law of this commonwealth affixes to this offense should be passed upon the prisoner."

Clerk of the court Wilde, holding the indictment in his hand, addressed the prisoner, bawling: "John W. Webster, have you anything to say why sentence of death should not be pronounced upon you, according to law?"

At the mention of his name, Webster stood up and placed his hands upon the rail in front of the prisoner's dock. He looked calmly toward the bench, directly at Chief Justice Shaw, as if still pleading his case personally to the man about to order his execution.

For a moment, Webster seemed ready to speak; everyone in the courtroom caught his or her collective breath. But after a low bow, he resumed his seat without uttering a word. It was too late.

The deep bass voice of Lemuel Shaw boomed through the courtroom, breaking the silence.

"John W. Webster, in meeting you here for the last time, to pronounce that sentence which the law has affixed to the high and aggravated offense of which you stand convicted, it is impossible by language to give utterance to the deep consciousness of responsibility, to the keen sense of sadness and sympathy, with which we approach this solemn duty."

Shaw gave the barest acknowledgement of the justices arrayed on either side of him, a slight bow of his head in each direction.

"We are oppressed with grief and anguish, and nothing but a sense of imperative duty imposed on us by the law, whose officers and ministers we are, could sustain us in pronouncing such a judgment.

"Against the crime of willful murder, of which you stand convicted—a crime at which humanity shudders, a crime everywhere and under all forms of society regarded with the deepest abhorrence—the law has denounced its severest penalty, in these few and simple, but solemn and impressive words:"

The chief justice paused for dramatic emphasis.

"Every person who shall commit the crime of murder shall suffer the punishment of death for the same."

The prisoner was ordered to stand and face the bench. With difficulty, the chief justice hoisted himself upright and spoke in a loud, deliberate tone.

"That you, John W. Webster, be removed from this place, and detailed in close custody in the prison of this county, and thence taken, at such time as the executive government of this commonwealth may, by their warrant, appoint, to the place of execution, and thereby hanged by the neck until you are dead.

"And may God, of his infinite goodness, have mercy on your soul."

With a flourish of his papers, Chief Justice Shaw resumed his seat and looked around the courtroom.

Webster sank back in his chair and wept. He wiped his face with a handkerchief and placed his forehead upon the bar in the dock, an unsuccessful attempt to conceal his tears from the countless eyes turned upon him. He remained in this position undisturbed, for five full minutes, the entire court solemnly silent. Then the officers assigned to the convicted man took hold of him.

"Mister Sheriff, the prisoner is in your custody. Mister Crier, adjourn the court," the chief justice said.

At those words, John W. Webster was manacled and led away. As a precaution, his penknife and his razor had already been removed from his cell.

CHAPTER 31

April 1850
Harvard Square, Cambridge, Massachusetts; Prince Street, Worcester,
Massachusetts; Court Street and Richmond Street, Boston, Massachusetts

James remained dazed by what he had just witnessed. He proceeded down Court Street to the transcription office. The trial was over. His former college professor would soon dangle at the end of a rope. James had expected to feel relief at the conclusion of the proceedings, but he felt only more anxiety.

A great task lay before him: dictating the Charge to the jury, the reading of the verdict, and the sentencing. Moreover, he had to find a way in his Report to evoke the pathetic grief of the condemned man, and implacable Justice in the form of Lemuel Shaw's stern words.

Moses Phillips had communicated to James his growing excitement about the Report's commercial prospects. Boston and the entire nation were following the trial with tremendous interest. Once Phillips Sampson had announced plans to publish a full account of the trial with unparalleled accuracy so quickly after its completion, subscription orders had poured into the publisher's office.

"Good afternoon, ladies," James said as he entered the transcription office. Eight pairs of eyes brightened at his appearance. It was their first daytime session, but not their last. He estimated that the remaining testimony and concluding remarks would require them to work daytime hours at least through Wednesday. Thank God it was no longer all-night dictation.

James and Ellen would personally undertake the final proofreading of the manuscript. He had promised Moses Phillips he would deliver a completed report within two weeks of the trial's conclusion, and he was intent on meeting that deadline.

As James sat down in his familiar place at the trestle table, Ellen walked by and lightly brushed her hand against his. No one else saw the intimate gesture—she was careful—but James thrilled to it.

In his endless thoughts about Webster's guilt or innocence, the remarkable drama of the past two days in court, his impending publication deadline, and Haggerty's blackmail, Ellen's allure had become distant. Her beguiling scent, her trim figure and her warm hand reminded him of her impact on him. He wanted her in his presence, and not only in this room.

James sought her attention and found Ellen staring at him with a similar intensity. They both smiled, and he began his dictation. She walked among the girls, checking their work, keeping her eyes trained on him while the copyists labored, heads bowed, seeing nothing of the lovers' smoldering glances. If the other girls had noticed, at this point neither Ellen nor James particularly cared. The attraction between them had become too powerful to conceal.

∽

Six hours later the young women left the Court Street location where they had spent many an hour in productive labor. The dictation had slowed because of the verbiage of the closing arguments, with no pauses as in the testimony of witnesses. Every word of Clifford's and Merrick's addresses had to be exactly duplicated.

James' eyes were red and scratchy. He had underestimated the impact of the twelve-day trial on his constitution and felt depressed by the prospect of what still remained.

Ellen gave him a good once-over and said, "It be high time ye were home and put to bed, Doctor Stone. Would I could do it, but I don't think yer neighbors in Bowdoin Square would fancy yer Irish lover turnin' up at this time o' night."

James smiled at Ellen's description of him as her lover. *He never thought a "lover" would resemble the awkward, average-looking James Winchell Stone he beheld in the mirror opposite his tub. He never could have imagined the winding road of the relationship upon which he and Ellen had embarked when they first met at the cholera hospital nine months ago.*

He grasped her hands in his. "I'll rest, be assured. But I've too many theorems in my brain to leave off completely. I must act quickly, if I'm to impact the fate of Professor Webster."

"What could ye do now to save Professor Webster, James? He's to die at the end of a rope; ye were right there when sentence was passed. Do ye mean to break him out o' his cell? For I fear that will be the only way ye could stop his hangin'."

"No, I'm no jailbreaker or escape artist. I am of no service to Webster in that regard." James turned to Ellen, an anxious expression on his face. "Ellen, after hearing and seeing everything the commonwealth produced over the past three weeks, I'm convinced that Professor Webster did not act alone in the murder of Doctor Parkman. I do not think him capable of such a feat, neither physically nor mentally."

"Then who, James? Would nae such a person be known to the police? Have they nae asked the same question ye ask?"

"Not if the identity of the accomplice has been kept a secret. I believe Webster has his own reasons for presenting himself as the sole perpetrator of this crime. He's protecting someone, or something; of that I am sure. The police care only for a culprit and a conviction, and they had one at the ready."

"Are ye nae goin' a bit beyond yerself, James? Yer no policeman."

Ellen said this in a caring tone, but James flushed at her casual dismissal of the import of what he was saying.

"I'm all too well acquainted with who I am, Ellen. But I cannot remain silent while a man dies for a crime he did not commit alone. All my life I've quivered and quaked rather than standing my ground and following my beliefs. I can do it no longer. I've examined the evidence against Webster as thoroughly as anyone, and I refuse to believe that he acted by himself. He had aid, from someone whom he has chosen to keep secret for reasons known only to him. I feel compelled to discover who these conspirators are."

Ellen absorbed what James was telling her. She was as familiar as he with the testimony, although she had set foot in the courtroom only once. She had come to respect and admire the swift currents within Dr. Stone's thoughts. If this matter troubled him, it troubled her, also.

"Have ye thought of somethin' other than money that Professor Webster might've owed Doctor Parkman? Be there some other reason that led to bad feelin's with those two?"

"I've thought long and hard along those lines. I came up with nothing. They occupied different worlds. They didn't break bread, their families were not familiar, and their business was along greatly different lines. I can think of no other cord than debt that bound them."

"Then we must be lookin' in a new direction, James. What could make a man like Webster so upset that it took him to murder?"

"A dispute over property? Jealousy over an unfaithful spouse? Bad blood over debts?

"Nae, James, somethin' to make a man's blood boil. If they had nae in common, what about somethin' political?" Taken with a sudden thought, Ellen continued breathlessly. "What about slavery? 'Tis the great issue of the day, with strong feelin's held on both sides. Be that what might've divided these two?"

James had to admit that he hadn't considered the slavery question at all. It was indeed the great matter of their time, and in the Boston of 1850, one was either for it or against it. Few had not made up their minds.

"I heard nothing at the trial of Professor Webster's political views," James said. "These were kept private. His unpaid debt to Parkman was the only motivation presented or defended."

Ellen countered his caution with her usual enthusiasm. "We needs look to the activities of Professor Webster. I'll ask Mother Bernadine, who knows all the antislavers, for help. Her good word'll gain us well."

"I have an idea," said James. "I'll approach Edward Atkinson, a former classmate of mine. I saw him at the antislavery fair we attended at Faneuil Hall. He was an usher, so he must be well connected within the abolitionist movement."

"James, I'd very much like to aid ye in solvin' this mystery," said Ellen, grasping his hands and squeezing them.

James was relieved that Ellen seemed to share his doubts about Webster's unaided guilt. Buoyed by her support, he would finally act on his beliefs. He daren't hope to overturn Webster's conviction, but possibly he could help stay the man's execution, scheduled for August.

"You can best aid me in helping to finish our report," said James. He felt badly when he saw the disappointment on her face. "We must check and recheck for errata and omissions. The reputation of phonography depends on the quality of our work."

"I am here for ye, James. I've filled most of yer needs, have I nae?"

James colored. This time it was he who squeezed Ellen's hand, all the harder. She had satisfied his needs, all of them.

～

James headed for Cambridge Square as he walked out of University Hall at Harvard, where the records of college graduates were kept. His search had been fruitful. He had discovered that Edward Atkinson was a partner with his father in a successful cotton mill located near Worcester. Despite the business's dependency on cotton, Atkinson was a prominent abolitionist. James had known him for several years. He had been a friend, but not an intimate, at Harvard.

The plan was to visit Atkinson, conduct an interview, then meet Ellen back at the transcription office for a final review of the manuscript. That morning, James had received a note from Phillips inquiring as to its progress. The publisher had learned about the competing account the *Boston Herald* planned to publish and was concerned that Phillips Sampson would lose the race to be the first out with a verbatim account of the sensational trial. James's transcript must be turned in as soon as possible.

The omnibus arrived at Revere House, and James boarded, settling onto one of the two wooden benches for the ninety-minute ride to Worcester. He had much on his mind. *If Parkman had learned that Webster supported a cause he despised, it might have intensified their dispute and led to mayhem.* James felt his pulse quickening. He could see the markings of a trail toward understanding Webster's actions and motivations. It was about time.

~

James watched Edward Atkinson rotate back and forth in his new swivel desk chair. Atkinson was an intelligent but arrogant twenty-five-year-old who reacted with confusion to James's questions about their former chemistry professor, and the abolitionist movement.

"I don't understand the reason behind your request, James," Atkinson said. "I fail to see any correlation between you and Professor Webster's political beliefs."

"My apologies for not sharing my thoughts fully, Edward, but they are still in their infancy. Let me say only that I was present for every moment of the trial, and I remain unconvinced that Professor Webster acted alone in whatever action he undertook against Doctor Parkman."

Atkinson's eyebrows rose. "Are you suggesting Webster is innocent of murder?"

"In no way do I mean to vouchsafe his innocence, his lack of culpability. Please do not think so. But I do suspect the question of motive. In searching for what might have excited Webster to the point of violence, I came upon the issue of slavery."

James stopped talking and regarded Atkinson closely before he continued:

"Was Webster an abolitionist? Could this have fueled another dispute with Parkman?"

There. James had uttered it. He had opened himself for mockery and ridicule with an absurd theory that held no basis in reality. Atkinson looked down at his intertwined fingers, long, with perfectly trimmed nails. He stretched them so that one knuckle cracked loudly. Then he gazed up at his visitor.

"James, I compliment your intuition. John Webster was indeed an active member of a group of men with like-minded feelings. Yet I still fail to see how this information can serve your purposes, or the professor's."

"I'm not yet sure myself, Edward. My hope is that it might stay, and possibly overturn, his execution. Any detail you can provide will bring much-needed clarity to this situation."

Atkinson said, "I must talk to my colleagues to be sure that nothing that I could tell you would compromise our aims. We have a meeting of our group planned for July. I'll be in touch following that. I'll share what I can with you, James, I give you my word."

James's heart sank. Such a delay would prove fatal to Webster. A protest came immediately to his lips.

"Edward, there is no time for inaction. A man's life hangs in the balance. I beseech you, tell me now. Two months hence will undoubtedly be too late."

James knew he had placed his old classmate in an uncomfortable position, but his pleading look made Atkinson reconsider his reserve.

"Very well, James, you give no quarter, so I suppose I must relent. I cannot go into detail and will never yield the particulars, but Webster aided us on one of our most dangerous enterprises. This is the reason his affiliations have been kept secret. He proffered service that was valiant and dedicated."

"Can you share anything of a specific nature with me, Edward? I promise our conversation will go no further than this room, no matter the circumstance or the questioner. I give you my word as a physician, a gentleman, and a Harvard man."

Atkinson shook his head, a brisk no.

"I can tell you nothing more until our committee gathers, James. Otherwise, you might blunder and compromise our efforts without realizing so. You say Professor Webster's life is in the offing. Well, so are countless others, lives that God has placed in our hands to speed them from bondage to freedom. We play our small role in a grander scheme we will never fully comprehend."

James sat for a moment, wracking his brain for some way to entice Atkinson to divulge more details of Webster's activities. He could think of none. Politeness dictated that he should remove himself. Atkinson had said all he would say. James stood and bowed.

"Edward, I thank you from the bottom of my heart. If there's any matter on which I may render you assistance, medical or otherwise, don't hesitate to call. I'll be at your service. I thank you for your time."

Atkinson stood and bowed back.

"Remember, James, more is at stake than Professor Webster's life, as cold as that may sound. We live in significant times. I trust I've impressed you with that fact."

～

Ellen waited patiently for Mother Bernadine to finish her morning prayers at the Sisters of Mercy abbey. She had come to see the abbess, the best substitute for her poor dead mother that she could have hoped for, someone who had always listened to her complaints and hopes, who helped guide her on the right path, the one who had brought her to Dr. James Stone.

Ellen had also discovered that Mother Bernadine possessed a restricted view of what was possible for Irish women in Boston. Her advice for these women had always been to seek out a responsible and employed Irish immigrant whom a young woman could marry, and then to produce babies who would develop into loyal followers of Christ.

Ellen was sure she would marry some day, but at nineteen she did not feel ready to settle down into the life of grinding poverty and continuous childbirth that she saw wear her mother to death. Her relationship with James had shown Ellen that despite her pessimism about their unrelated worlds, an alternative did exist.

The abbess found Ellen sitting on a wooden bench, lost in her thoughts.

"Me child, it's good to see ye. How goes the work with Docter Stone? Are ye finished now that the trial's concluded? And may God have mercy on poor Professer Webster's soul."

"I've never worked harder in me life, Holy Mother. We're preparin' the finished version of the report for the publisher, Phillips and Sampson. It be a most excitin' time, I've had much to do."

There was an awkward pause. Then the abbess said, "Is this what you've come to tell me, child? If so, I'm happy to hear of it, but I have pressing matters before me."

Ellen rose quickly, motioning for the abbess to wait before rushing off.

"'Tis not, abbess. I've a great favor to ask. I was wonderin' if we could speak where none might overhear."

Mother Bernadine looked sharply at Ellen. "I trust ye do not bring me news of an unwanted pregnancy."

Ellen was offended by the suggestion. "'Tis on another matter completely!"

The elderly abbess looked ashamed for a moment, turned abruptly, and led Ellen to her office. She gestured to a trestle chair where Ellen promptly sat, while the abbess lowered herself into a leather chair behind a massive table.

"Proceed, child. What have ye to tell me?"

"I must ask fer yer help, abbess. Doctor Stone has done much lookin' at the evidence produced at Professor Webster's trial. He's come to the conclusion that all nae be right. He's convinced that further examination is needed as to whether Professor Webster be the only murderer."

Mother Bernadine raised her thick eyebrows in surprise, a gesture amplified by the stiff white coif surrounding her moon-shaped face.

"Ye and Docter Stone dinna believe Docter Webster be innocent, do ye? Did nae but the chief justice himself say that Docter Webster perpetrated this murder against man and God?"

"If he did, he was wrong to say so," Ellen said. "This is why I come to ye, abbess. Ye know the abolitionists in Boston; yer one among 'em. Ye've always seen the evil in slavery, as do Doctor Stone and me. But I needs ask ye, was Doctor Webster among 'em?"

The nun was puzzled. "What has this to do with the murder of Docter Parkman? What has one to do with t'other?"

"I know not yet the stitchin', but the good Doctor Stone and me believe it be all part of one garment. If we discover what we seek, it could stop Professor Webster's hangin'."

Mother Bernadine looked closely at Ellen, and then at her own thickly veined hands, folded before her on the desk.

"It is strange for ye to come here on such a matter, Ellen. This trial caused me soul great pain, imaginin' poor John Webster sufferin' so in the dock. He was a good man, a God-fearin' Christian who knows his Bible, even if he's not one of us. I can't believe that a man who saved lives could take one in such a fashion."

"What do ye mean, him savin' lives? He be a teacher of chemistry, nae a medical doctor like Doctor Stone."

Mother Bernadine was less than eager to explain her comment, which she now looked like she regretted uttering. "Nae, nae, he be a true doctor, trained in Paris. He has done other activities of which I know that make him a true hero, nae the terrible man the press shows. But Ellen, how can ye possibly gain his freedom?"

"I beg ye, Mother Bernadine. Share with me what ye know. I'll use it only to aid Professor Webster when he's at his lowest."

Mother Bernadine pursed her lips before speaking.

"This be all I can, and will, tell ye. Ye may've heard tell of an Underground Railroad, one that's helped many a slave flee the South. It is planned and aided by numerous persons in several states, all of whom hold slavery to be a mortal sin, God bless 'em. John Webster be among these, at least 'til his troubles. I come to know him as a good man, willin' to risk his high station to end this most evil institution. What was uttered at the trial described a man I did nae recognize."

Ellen said, "What did Professor Webster do exactly? Was his home a station on this railroad?"

"I have told ye more than I should, and even that is too much," the abbess said, rising to her feet. Their audience was concluded. She took Ellen by the hand.

"Be careful, my child. These waters be dangerous, and it be easy for 'em to suck you below. Docter Stone has nothin' to lose if his idea be wrong, but if ye go where it be none of yer business, ye'll be the worse for it. Things can happen in but a moment that can ruin a life, Ellen."

Ellen curtsied as she prepared to take her leave. "I'll heed yer words, abbess, I promise. No harm'll come to me, for I have Doctor Stone as my protector. He has been so good to me."

This comment alarmed Mother Bernadine more than anything else Ellen had said, but she had no time to address it; a full day of appointments awaited her. Ellen receded down the hallway toward the church doors, and the abbess sat down to her endless tasks.

CHAPTER 32

May 1850
Washington Street and Court Street, Boston, Massachusetts

Moses Phillips had a smile on his face as he accepted the pile of foolscap from James and his pretty companion, Miss O'Keeffe. Booksellers across the country had expressed strong interest in an accurate account of the murder trial that had gripped the entire United States and its new Western territories.

Phillips saw the possibility of significant profit, since he was paying James nothing for compiling and completing the report. James was so consumed with phonography that all his efforts were directed toward its promulgation. Phillips Sampson would pay him royalties, of course, but the publisher began from a position of sure profit, after accounting for printing and mailing costs.

"Mister Sampson and I look forward to publishing your manuscript with great anticipation," Phillips said, beaming at James. "I encounter everywhere debates over Professor Webster's guilt or innocence. Public interest has never been higher."

The smile had become greedier, thought James, as Phillips continued. "Our first printing is for a thousand copies, almost all of which are already subscribed. If demand grows, we will do a second printing, a third, even a fourth if the response warrants."

Ellen knew that James had no interest in business. She had realized it would have to be up to her to bring up the matter of payment for all their work over the past month.

"Pardon me, please, Mister Phillips, but when'll Doctor Stone be paid?"

James looked relieved that someone else had raised the onerous subject of money.

"Doctor Stone will receive a royalty of two cents for every copy of his report sold by a bookseller. If copies are purchased directly from our office, the royalty rises to three cents. We fully expect to sell out the initial subscription of one thousand and two hundred copies."

James was disappointed by how small the royalty payments would be, and a glance at Ellen told him she felt the same. Unless the report sold thousands upon thousands of copies, James would realize little money. He reminded himself, as well as Phillips and Ellen, that he had a purpose other than pecuniary gain.

"The royalty is not important," he said. "The report will demonstrate phonography's power to disseminate information quickly and accurately. It will also shed light on the workings of our justice system and our courts. That is its importance, not its financial success."

Ellen was disappointed by James's easy capitulation, but Phillips was pleased to move on from the distasteful subject of money.

"My partner and I hope there will be more opportunities for us to work together," he said. "We wish you to look upon Phillips, Sampson and Company as your literary home, Doctor Stone, always interested in your phonographic offerings."

James said, "I have other matters to attend to before undertaking future projects, so I must ask that you move forward with your publication of our report as soon as possible. Its dissemination may influence events that are of the gravest importance."

Ellen noticed the pronoun James chose to use to describe the report's authorship. It was the first time he had publicly acknowledged their collaboration.

Phillips said, "If you were concerned about competition from John French and his account for the *Boston Herald*, worry yourself no longer. Apparently Mister French's notes proved incomprehensible to all, including himself, and the project was abandoned. The *Herald* will publish a column of his reminiscences from the trial, but there will be no attempt to duplicate the testimony itself."

James could not deny a sense of relief that washed over him, but his hopes of delaying Webster's doomed walk to the gallows propelled him forward.

"I still insist that you publish as soon as humanly possible, Mister Phillips. Great matters are at stake."

"I fear I don't fully understand you, Doctor Stone. I can assure you that we'll move in a timely manner in your manuscript's publication. First, however, we must submit your report to Chief Justice Shaw for review and await any changes he may suggest."

James was startled. This was the first he had heard of this certain delay. "This defeats the purpose of my report, Mister Phillips. A virtue of phonography is its ability to record exactly what has been said. There is no need for revision or rewriting. What is in the report is what was uttered aloud in the courtroom. I should know; I recorded it myself."

Phillips was flustered. He looked to Ellen for support, but she stared directly back at him, offering nothing.

"Surely we cannot break precedent in this regard," he said. "Not only Chief Justice Shaw, but the attorney general, the prosecuting attorneys, and the defense counsel all must have the opportunity to review their parts in your manuscript and make appropriate corrections."

James's anger had been stoked each time Phillips mentioned another individual who would lay waste to his report. Ellen put a restraining hand on his arm, a gesture noticed by Phillips. James didn't care what Phillips thought.

"I must protest this practice in the strongest fashion," James said, "and I ask you to return my manuscript to me if these indeed are your intentions. They go against my sole purpose in this enterprise, which is to demonstrate phonography's speed and accuracy in recording human speech to the very last syllable. No corrections should be allowed to alter what was recorded as it was said."

Phillips had not expected James to react so strongly to normal business practice in the publishing world. Legal practitioners were experts in their field. How could a young medical doctor presume to know more about the law than Chief Justice Lemuel Shaw, who had spent fifty years on the bench?

"You're overreacting, Doctor. We must have accuracy in this account, above all else. Your reputation, and ours, depend upon it. We'll be accused of careless disregard if we act otherwise."

"There's nothing careless in my report, Mister Phillips. If you and Mister Sampson find yourselves too timid to publish the verbatim account I have provided, then I'll find someone with the gumption to do so. It shouldn't be difficult. As you say, interest in the subject has never been greater."

"Very well, very well, Doctor Stone, let's not be hasty. Allow us to deliberate, and we will continue this discussion. If all is as you say, perhaps you're correct. Phonography does bring a new skill to the enterprise of reporting upon criminal trials. The response to the first printing will tell us much."

"I await your decision, sir," said James, as he and Ellen rose together. "But if it's in the negative, then I trust you will permit me to enrich one of your competitors instead."

He bowed, Ellen curtsied, and Phillips nodded in reply, taken aback by James's rudeness. This was a strange man, and an even stranger couple, he thought as they exited his office. He wondered that Stone was willing to risk traveling in public with an Irishwoman with whom he was clearly in love. That mattered not if the manuscript was all that James had promised; Phillips, Sampson and Company would be significantly enriched by its success. However, the publisher still had to reckon with Lemuel Shaw and the legal establishment.

~

Ellen sensed how perturbed James had been by the meeting as they walked along Washington Street to the intersection of Court Street and their old transcription room. The space where she and James had worked, and made love several times over the past fortnight, was leased only through this evening. Ellen had sold the tables and chairs her team of copyists had employed, recovering most of James's investment, and the space was now empty.

She had been surprised by how emotional she became when parting with the trestle table. The office was the only place where she and James had enjoyed any privacy. She had brought a colorful quilt to spread over the table and make the space feel a bit homey. James's jacket became an improvised pillow. Their "love nest" was made complete.

If their idylls were to continue after the trial, Ellen supposed, they would have to find a new location, not an easy task in a crowded and nosy city. The larger question nagged at her: would a personal relationship continue now that the business one was coming to its conclusion?

Ellen had shut down any effort to dream about a future with James. He occupied a world where there was always hope for advancement; in hers, only the constant danger of failing. But he had used the word "our" when discussing the authorship of the report. That was something.

They reached their destination and began to climb the stairs. Ellen turned to James and spoke first.

"I be confident that Mister Phillips, when at last he reads our report, will doubt nae more. His greed'll make him print more copies. There is nae for ye to fear, James."

He smiled at Ellen, and after looking around, took her hand and led her up the stairs and into the now-deserted office. They surveyed the space in which they had labored as true collaborators, and then enjoyed each other as lovers. James wondered if, now that their trysting place was lost to them, their relationship would continue. He wasn't sure, but he had other matters to discuss with Ellen.

As if reading his thoughts, Ellen produced the familiar quilt from the voluminous bag she carried with her and spread it across the dusty floor so they could sit without dirtying themselves. James sat cross-legged. Ellen extended her long legs out in front of her, smoothing her skirt into place.

"We've much to discuss, Ellen. My mind has been like a river after a storm. I am flooded with thoughts."

"I trust ye be nae upset by Mister Phillips. He ain't worth the sweat of yer brow."

"No, no, Phillips is a fool who fails to understand that the future is upon us; we should give him no more thought, for if he chooses not to go with us, others will leap at the opportunity."

James grasped Ellen's hands, as he was wont to do every time he had something that excited him that he wanted to share with her. "I've more important news, Ellen. I had a productive conversation with Mister Atkinson, the mill owner, my Harvard acquaintance whom we met at the Faneuil Hall rally. He was most helpful."

"I, too, discovered much from Mother Bernadine," Ellen said.

James was pleased, which made Ellen so as well. "Then we both did well," he said. "Atkinson told me that Webster was a significant person in the abolitionist movement, holding a key position he would not divulge. Ellen, he said Webster did dangerous work. He rendered service that Atkinson called heroic."

"Methinks I know what that service be, James. Mother Bernadine told me Professor Webster helped slaves escape from the South. Somethin' called the Underground Railway, givin' these poor souls passage to Boston, where they could live like free men and women, or move even further north. Webster be a part o' this. Mother Bernadine said so!"

Once again, Ellen had arrived at the same conclusions James had. His mind raced. *Webster must have used the Medical College as a station on this secret railroad. He was protecting something far more important to him than the reputation of Harvard.*

"This is wonderful, Ellen! We're close to the heart of our mystery. Webster and Parkman must have quarreled over not just debt and money, but slavery itself. I know from my own conversations with Doctor Parkman's brother-in-law, Mister Shaw, that the two were proslavery to the greatest degree possible. It was good for their businesses."

"Be that enough for murder, James? Men may agree or nae about keepin' slaves, but Doctor Parkman wanted his money, nae a debate on slavery."

James agreed. Something still was missing, an occurrence that could trigger a battle to the death. Something happened in Webster's laboratory that had never been described in the courtroom.

He looked at Ellen closely. "Are you sure that Mother Bernadine is correct? Much depends on her veracity."

"The Sisters of Mercy be known for their help to the Blacks. If there be some railway passin' through Boston carryin' slaves, I be sure Mother Bernardine knows about it."

"We must puzzle this matter carefully," James said. "If Professor Webster were indeed a participant in the Underground Railroad, how could he be of assistance? He had no money to contribute, and it's unlikely he'd hide slaves at his home in Cambridge. He'd be too nervous about their discovery."

James stared upward as he continued with his line of reasoning. Ellen was impressed by his deductive skills.

He said, "It only makes sense that in some way the Medical College was employed in this activity. Webster had privacy in his chambers, rooms where a man or a group of men could easily be hidden."

"A slave could hardly be walkin' into the Medical College with no bother. Wouldn't Mister Littlefield notice?"

Ellen and James looked at each other. Littlefield! James knew the man was the key witness to Webster's guilt. Now could Littlefield be transformed into his savior?

"There be yer turkey fer Littlefield, James," said Ellen. "It musta been for Littlefield lookin' t'other way when Webster hid the slaves."

James shook his head. The solution could not be so simply explained. "Littlefield is not a man to settle for only a turkey. There are harsh penalties for abetting a slave's escape. We must discover what we can, in terms of facts rather than conjecture, and confront Littlefield ourselves. I shall enjoy seeing his face when he realizes how much we know."

Ellen had never seen James so excited. She put a steadying hand on his arm.

"Let us be goin' careful-like, James, at least fer now. From who could ye learn more of Mister Littlefield's business? It need be someone who would nae betray us to the janitor."

"Of course! Frederick Ainsworth is Littlefield's supervisor in the demonstration room. He's an old and trusted companion. I can speak to him with the greatest freedom and rest assured the conversation will go no further. I will go see him after his lecture tomorrow."

James pulled his watch from his vest pocket.

"I must be at my sister Lucinda's for supper in only ninety minutes, Ellen. Please excuse me, for I must bathe and dress."

"Do what ye must, James, but at least allow me to picture ye in yer bath afore ye hurry me out o' here."

Ellen laughed her warm, pleasant laugh as she and James walked to the door. They embraced silently, and then James broke away and went through the doorway. He had much on his mind. *No doubt, he was flattered by her desires. No one else had ever paid such attention to him. He must find a way to keep this woman in his life.*

CHAPTER 33

May 1850
North Grove Street and Bowdoin Square, Boston, Massachusetts

James had not entered the Medical College since those frenzied events surrounding Dr. Parkman's disappearance, Professor Webster's arrest, and the autopsy.

He returned to the site of spilled blood and spent passions, a place of learning transformed into a curiosity and a spectacle, still visited by hundreds each week. James had to walk through a crowd of gawkers who were stopping and pointing at various things, simply to gain access to the Medical College entrance.

He arrived at the first-floor rooms of Dr. Frederick Ainsworth at eleven o'clock in the morning and knocked sharply. Ainsworth greeted him, tall and smiling, before ushering James into the demonstration room, a large lecture space with a raised platform on which the dissection of cadavers could be displayed to medical students seated on risers.

"Pray tell me the purpose of this unexpected visit, James. I'd been thinking of you and that report you were scribbling throughout the trial. Will you really publish it? I have heard Chief Justice Shaw say that it will never see the light of day."

James was alarmed to hear that Shaw was discussing his report while knowing nothing about it. He could not let any doubt about its veracity be shown.

"Lemuel Shaw is not my publisher, Frederick. My report will be available, in the light of day and the dark of night, in a fortnight. I am introducing a different way to present a criminal trial to the general public, and I believe it will be revolutionary in its impact."

Ainsworth assessed James. His vanity was familiar from their college days, but there was now something different about James: a new gravity to his bearing that Ainsworth had not seen previously. He was intrigued to discover the purpose that had brought James to him.

"Of what help may I be, Doctor Stone? Can I assist you in a diagnosis or another medical endeavor? Although honestly, I can't imagine what I could do for you, given the state of my patients."

Ainsworth gestured around him at the specimen corpses, displayed in various stages of decay on three raised platforms.

James said, "I saw you in court many times, Frederick. I know you followed the proceedings of the Webster trial closely. Let me ask you a question you may find rude or blunt, for which I apologize in advance." Ainsworth nodded for him to continue. James said, "Did you have no doubts whatsoever concerning Webster's culpability? Did nothing seem amiss to you in the case presented against him?"

"I agree," Ainsworth said, "it was remarkable to see the jury convict so quickly on no more than a mass of circumstance and seeming coincidence. The defense presented only a litany of praise for Webster's character, nothing that counteracted the evidence found in his privy, his furnace, and his tea chest. How could any counselor explain all that away?"

"This is exactly why I come to you, good friend. All these elements are easily explained by the interference of the janitor Littlefield. I recall the unease we felt as students with his constant importuning to purchase a head, a limb, even genitalia. Now you work with him on a daily basis. If I may ask, what's your opinion of Ephraim Littlefield, Frederick?

Ainsworth lowered his voice before continuing, as if nervous that he might be overheard. "I've never trusted the man, and any suspicions of foul play immediately went to him when I heard of his sneaking into Webster's privy. But he acquitted himself well in the witness box. He didn't emerge as a liar or a fabulist, as I have known him to be. I was surprised by his equanimity under the pressure of Mister Sohier's cross-examination."

"I agree, he put on an effective performance. Tell me, Frederick, how does Littlefield procure his cadavers? Do they come from a single graveyard or other source, or are there many places he draws from?"

"The corpses are collected from all over New England. With the help of Doctor Holmes, Massachusetts has passed a law allowing dissection, so Littlefield has official sanction in his dealings. We're all aware he traffics in the dead far beyond the requirements of his work for this institution. Why, I have seen a dozen barrels delivered in a week when we needed only three or four cadavers."

"Barrels? The bodies come in barrels?"

"They're placed within by undertakers, along with saltpeter to reduce the odor. It proves the cheapest and most effective means of transport while offending the least number of people. Citizens would be sickened to know their train car or coach also carries the dead riding in barrels."

"No one here opens these barrels but Littlefield?" asked James, trying to keep his excitement under wraps.

"Who else would want to? I've been present for their unsealing, and believe me, the smell when they're opened is noxious. Littlefield unpacks the cadavers, preserves them with arsenic, mercury, and zinc, and brings them to my or Doctor Holmes's lecture room for display and demonstration. When they are spoiled beyond further use, Littlefield disposes of them."

"Are any of these barrels in your chambers, Frederick? I would very much like to see one."

"Littlefield brought up a new cadaver for me just this morning, and is at work on it," Ainsworth said. "I am sure there's an empty barrel in his janitorial closet." He pulled out his pocket watch and checked the time. "He may be at dinner now, but I wager that would be better for our purposes. Isn't that so, James?"

"Much better," replied James.

He followed Ainsworth out of the demonstration room and down the stairs to the basement storeroom, where Littlefield kept his closet of supplies and equipment. Sure enough, there were several barrels placed around the room, most with their tops off, all emitting the intermingled stench of death and saltpeter. James almost gagged, and he pinched his nostrils shut. Ainsworth was used to the odor and went around the room, peering into various barrels.

"I'll admit that you've raised my curiosity with your request, James. But I hardly see what any of this has to do with the death of Doctor Parkman. Do you think Webster tried to place Parkman in a barrel and cut him up when he wouldn't fit properly?"

James examined two of the barrels closely. They resembled any other hogsheads, large enough to encase a contorted human form. There was one strange aspect James immediately noticed: several holes were bored into the tops of the barrels, each about one inch in diameter.

Puzzled, James turned to Ainsworth. "The purpose of these holes?"

"Littlefield bores them so that the gases that accompany death will be released gradually and not overwhelm him when he first opens the casks. He's been doing this for as long as I've been the demonstrator. I never thought to question the practice."

"Nor should you have. I suppose that as easily as these holes let out the noxious fumes, they let in clean air. Do you think a living man could survive in one of these barrels?"

Ainsworth stared at James, whom suddenly he suspected of having ulterior motives for this visit. "I suppose he could, but why would a living man ever be in such a conveyance? For what purpose?"

"No reason, Frederick, just idle speculation on my part. I saw the strange irony of these holes allowing the dead to 'breathe' and wondered if the living might do so, also."

"Littlefield's duties lie with the dead rather than the living, James. I advance this to be the reason he so avidly searched for Parkman's body. No one in this college is more consumed with corpses than our janitor; it is little wonder Death occupied his imagination."

James had a final question for Ainsworth before he took his leave. "I know how you stand on the matter of slavery, my friend. I have seen you at abolitionist rallies and I know you signed the petition, with other Harvard faculty, to urge an end the evil practice."

Ainsworth bowed his head slightly. "I've been open in my feelings about the unholy institution and its deleterious effects on our students, our college, and our nation. I bear no shame for my stance, and I trust you won't affix any upon me, James."

"Have no fear, Frederick. My sympathies are fully with you. Did Professor Webster share your enthusiasm?"

"Most certainly he did. It was Professor Webster who first introduced me to Mister Garrison and Reverend Phillips, men who have exerted great influence on my thinking. But what have Webster's political views to do with his sorry plight? Do you believe slavery to be an element in the murder of Doctor Parkman?"

"I know not what to presume, Frederick. My mind's abuzz. When I've placed my thoughts in some order, I'll be sure to communicate them to you. I do have one final question. Was Littlefield also of this abolitionist sentiment? Did he agree with you and Webster in your sentiments against slavery?"

Ainsworth seemed surprised by the question. "I don't believe I've ever had a political discussion with the man, James. From what I've witnessed, I doubt the subject interests him. Littlefield is all about the business at hand. Beyond that, I know nothing of his views. I'm not even confident that he has any."

James nodded, took his hat and gloves from Ainsworth's desk, and bowed his thanks.

"I greatly appreciate your time and candor, Frederick," he said. "I'll be sure to send you a personally inscribed copy of my report upon its publication."

Ainsworth bowed slightly in return and put an arm on James's shoulder as he led the shorter man to the door. "Don't extend yourself too far on this matter, James. Webster's life is in God's hands now. Be content to see your labors justified by what I'm sure will be the success of your report. I've heard several colleagues speak of it with great interest."

James enjoyed being included in the latest Boston society gossip. If the doctors at the Medical College and Massachusetts General Hospital were eager to read his account, so would the rest of Boston's upper class be. His moment would soon arrive.

~

While rinsing his face in the tepid water Sharon had left for him in his bedroom, James experienced a familiar acidic unease in his stomach. He could not comprehend where his thoughts and suspicions were taking him, which bothered him. Logical thinking was usually his strength.

He grabbed a towel to wipe his face and sat down on his bed. He had no intention of proving Webster innocent. James was positive the timid college professor had at least been present at Dr. Parkman's killing and participated in its aftermath. But he could think of no individual mentioned at the trial or seen in the courtroom who possessed the strength to strike down a strong, aggressive, opinionated gentleman such as George Parkman, and who was important enough for John Webster to protect with his life.

It couldn't be Littlefield, James reasoned. If he and Webster were collaborators in the murder, would Littlefield have turned so viciously on his partner, without fear or consequence? If Littlefield were the actual killer, Webster would have declared so, clearing his own name and conscience. He would have faced prison, but not the hangman's noose.

James began working out a new hypothesis: Littlefield was smuggling live human beings, stuffed into barrels meant for the dead, into the Medical College, at Webster's and the Underground Railroad's behest. The barrels' breathing holes offered proof that men and women could have made their way into Littlefield's storeroom, and then onto the next stop toward freedom.

Edward Atkinson and Mother Bernadine had both suggested Webster was involved in the Underground Railroad. Wasn't that enough to implicate him in Littlefield's slave-smuggling scheme? Might have it actually been his scheme, with Littlefield simply carrying out Webster's orders?

James heard a loud knocking at his residence's front door. He was startled and a little frightened. Why had Sharon not answered? The knocking continued, now frantically; someone was very anxious to see him.

James put on a robe, donned his slippers, and walked down the broad staircase to the entranceway and asked loudly, "Who is it?"

"A friend," came a muffled voice.

"What friend would that be?"

"A friend of Ellen O'Keeffe's."

James panicked. Had something befallen Ellen? He feared she was injured, or worse. He opened the door, fumbling with the lock. Greeting him was Bill Haggerty, his thick shillelagh in one hand, his pipe in the other.

"I be pleased to see ye care so fer my Ellen, Docter Stone," said Haggerty in his thick brogue. "Ye opened that door considerable quick."

"Is Ellen all right? Has anything happened to her?" James asked, trying to hold back the fury he felt at seeing Haggerty again at his door.

"She be jest fine, Docter, jest fine. Methinks the only person could harm her be yerself, sir. We nae wish to see our Ellen get in the family way, now would we, Docter Stone? Maybe all ye sawbones has ways to make sure that don't happen."

Haggerty leaned forward threateningly. "Or maybe ye think ye can just dump her with some back-alley butcher in the North End and be done with her and the creature ye created inside o' her. It's them that killed her poor mother, me wife Mary, the sainted woman."

"Are you telling me that Ellen is with child? Is that the purpose of your visit?"

"Nothin' like that yet, nothin' at all. By rights we stay on the safe side, now, don't we, sir? We nae want scandal *and* a babe, do we? Nae, we want neither."

"What is it this time, Haggerty? Out with it."

"The first task ye give Ellen may be done with, Docter, but nae t'other. Ye still be payin' for Ellen's time, but this be more special, more expensive. It'll cost ye one hundred dollar, and if a wee babe should join us, the price, it'll rise. Another mouth to feed, ye know. If'n ye don't fancy me plan, Docter, then the folks at Phillips and Sampson, they might show some interest in me story. It be a corker, this one, about a fancy docter and his Irish whore."

Haggerty's face darkened, and he brandished his shillelagh. "Dinna take me lightly, Docter Stone. I got the means to ruin ye, and more. Ye bring me that money Monday evenin,' or ye'll be facin' a pack o' trouble."

Haggerty turned on his heel without giving James a chance to respond. But what could he have said? He was unable to stop himself from seeing Ellen. Yet he could hardly afford to have his reputation ruined by a singleminded blackmailer, just as he was on the precipice of celebrity and success.

Preoccupied by his thoughts, James never noticed someone else who had slipped into the darkness after his first visitor departed—someone with red hair ill concealed by the hood of a cape.

CHAPTER 34

May 1850
North Grove Street and Fruit Street, Boston, Massachusetts

The May sky was colored a brilliant blue as James set out for the Medical College. He was to meet Ellen there an hour before noon, when they would confront Ephraim Littlefield and try to settle for once and all his true role in the Parkman-Webster affair.

James worried that Littlefield might refuse to see them. He had become a celebrity. There were reports in the press that after frequently and publicly refusing the reward offered at the time of Parkman's disappearance, Littlefield had quietly accepted a $3,000 "donation" from Robert Shaw and the Parkman family. He was also planning a traveling exhibit of Webster's laboratory, where the reenactment of Parkman's murder could play several times a day.

James's previous visit with the janitor had not gone well, so he decided to bring Ellen along for this interview. Littlefield always had a pronounced eye for an attractive woman. It was no coincidence that he had gone dancing the night before he exposed Parkman's remains.

James knew that his hopes were unrealistic. He needed Littlefield to reveal how he moved slaves in and out of the Medical College, and the identity of the individual or individuals who had engaged him to do it. His acts were illegal, of course, and his willingness to admit to them was unlikely. It was a great deal to expect from this meeting.

What else did Littlefield know? Did Dr. Parkman come to the college on that fateful Friday November last to collect his money, but intending also to expose Professor Webster's use of the building for the illegal concealment of slaves? Or had "the Chin," appearing early in Webster's rooms, stumbled upon a delivery of a slave to the college that he had endowed, and, unable to check his outrage, attacked Webster? Did Littlefield witness any of these events, and pretend ignorance to shield his own involvement?

Ellen was waiting for him at the bottom of the Medical College steps. She looked nervous. "James, we must hurry to see Mister Littlefield, I fear he and his missus be ready to depart right away."

James quickly ushered Ellen to the side of the building where Littlefield's cottage was located. She pulled a cord affixed below a new small silver rectangle that read, "Ephraim Littlefield, Harvard Medical College." They could hear the bell ring inside.

The door was answered promptly, as if the Littlefields had been expecting their callers. Mrs. Littlefield dried her hands on her apron, while Littlefield seemed surprised to see Dr. Stone on his doorstep, accompanied a most comely Irishwoman. He extended an arm and motioned them into his tidy home, showing little enthusiasm for his visitors.

"Your appearance here is unexpected, Doctor Stone. My wife and I was about to leave to visit her ma and escape this hell. I been required to stay here for the whole of the trial, though I never understood why, once my testimony was done with."

Littlefield allowed himself a small smile. "After all, once I was done, so was the trial. Each suspicion I raised came true, every piece of evidence I uncovered led straight to Professor Webster and his terrible crime." Littlefield raised his eyes as if addressing a celestial audience. "I pray God rest that man's soul. His poor family'll pay a thousand times over for his sin, and for what? For trying to save a few hundred dollars?"

James was startled by Littlefield's enduring resentment against Webster. "Is that all you believe was behind this crime, Littlefield? A simple financial debt?"

Littlefield looked from James to Ellen and back again. He didn't look pleased.

"Given you're no longer a student here, Doctor Stone, I would thank ye for addressin' me as Mister Littlefield, as is proper. Please state the purpose of your visit, which I can't allow to delay us no longer."

Ellen spoke in her most soothing and sensual voice. "Mister Littlefield, my name be Miss Ellen O'Keeffe." Littlefield seemed surprised to be addressed by the Irishwoman.

"We've nae reason to delay ye and yer missus," she continued. "We but seek yer view of the trial, to aid us with the report Doctor Stone's been preparin'. Surely, more than anyone, ye knew Doctor Webster's state of mind, and we were hopin' ye might help us do the same."

Littlefield was mollified by Ellen's warm tone, so she continued, without looking at James. "Yer actions interest us greatly. I understand from some of me friends in the Free Soil Party that ye have been most helpful to them in a variety of ways."

At the mention of the antislavery Free Soil Party, Littlefield's eyes narrowed. "I have no truck with abolitionists and their prattle for the Black savages, who take all the honest jobs the Irish haven't already snatched," he said. Enjoying the moment, he studied Ellen and his thin lips formed a cold smile. "No offense, Miss, all that abolitionist talk came from Doctor Webster, never from my mouth. I had to plug my ears to stop hearin' him go on and on about his railroad, or whatever he called it, and what a fine thing we were doin'. As long as he paid me good hard cash, I didn't care what he said."

James interceded. "Paid you for what? What did you or he have to do with the Underground Railroad?"

In his haste to get answers, James had overplayed his hand with such direct questions. Littlefield took a step back and regarded Ellen and James coolly.

"I've no idea of what you're speakin', Doctor Stone. All I know of this matter was revealed at the trial. I held nothin' back."

Littlefield's reluctance to speak further made it clear he possessed information that he had no intention of revealing. James spoke carefully.

"You're aware of the new Fugitive Slave Act, Mister Littlefield, how it will prohibit all activities that aid slaves who flee their masters when it is signed into law? And you're aware of the punishment for such aid?"

"Are you threatenin' me, Doctor? I've faced down the attorney general of the commonwealth in court, I've stood up to Chief Justice Shaw, and it's me who's personally responsible for convictin' John Webster. I plan to be first among those at his hangin'. That's the punishment God and man has rendered, and it's just and proper for what John Webster done. Whatever he was up to, it's got nothin' to do with me."

James stared at Littlefield until the man met his gaze. He said, "We have evidence that indicates otherwise, and implicates you directly, Mister Littlefield."

Littlefield moved quickly. In a moment, he stood within inches of James's face, his complexion colored with anger.

"Stay out of affairs of which you know nothin', Doctor Stone. There are larger forces here than you or me, and you'll regret goin' against them. Look where Webster ended up."

Mrs. Littlefield advanced and Mr. Littlefield took her arm, his way of announcing that the audience was concluded. As if on cue, they bowed together to their visitors. Ellen and James had no choice but to bow in return and depart. As they passed through the door, Littlefield called after them.

"Have a pleasant afternoon, Doctor Stone, Miss O'Keeffe. Be sure to give my regards to Professor Webster when you visit him."

~

James was trembling as he and Ellen walked down Fruit Street. "Did that man just threaten me?" he asked her.

"Truth be, he included both of us," Ellen corrected him. "I give nae weight to his threats, James. Littlefield may be after money, where e're he can find it, but he got nae power, nor friends." Ellen smiled and added, "I trust there nae be a body he could hang in *yer* basement at 6 Bowdoin Square."

James laughed, but then grew serious. "Littlefield confirmed that he was paid to bring slaves to the Medical College. We know Webster supported the abolitionists, and through Littlefield, he possessed the means to help them. It follows that Webster paid Littlefield for his assistance, however begrudgingly."

Ellen listened closely to what James was saying but had questions of her own.

"'Tis' true that Littlefield was paid, but with what? From who did Webster draw his money? Of all people, yer professor had none at hand. He could nae even pay what he owed to Doctor Parkman."

"You're right, Ellen. Webster must have borrowed additional funds from Robert Shaw against his chemical collection to pay Littlefield, on top of his existing debts to Parkman. God knows how he managed to obtain the loans, given both men's low opinion of him."

Ellen said, "Remember, he'd pay just enough to keep Doctor Parkman at bay, until he owed too much. Not 'til Mister Shaw and Doctor Parkman realized they each had a mortgage on the same stuff do the Professor find himself undone."

"Webster would never have revealed the true reason for his indebtedness," said James, "for he knew the views held by men such as Parkman and Shaw. They would've destroyed him and his career had they learned of his involvement in the Underground Railroad, and in a Harvard building, no less. No trial would've been necessary."

"I think there be much here to study, James, in keepin' with yer aim. Now, we must decide what to do next. Should we nae go to Doctor Webster, press him, and tell him to part with the truth, and throw himself on the mercy of the court?"

James looked down at his hands as the couple walked. Faint ink stains remained on them from correcting proofs of the report. He had trusted that phonography would record the truth presented in court, untrammeled by prejudice. He now discovered that the testimony he had labored to take down so accurately was manufactured to hide something else, something Professor Webster valued more highly than the life of one of Boston's most distinguished citizens.

"You're correct, Ellen," James said, not breaking his stride, but turning left on Leverett Street. "We'll proceed to the Leverett Street Gaol posthaste. Either Professor Webster will allow us to save him from execution, or he'll send us on our way, and take his secret to his grave."

"'Tis his neck, his secret, his grave," said Ellen. "They all be his to do with as he please."

She took James's arm, and they walked toward the squat prison. It was a grim setting for the unpredictable encounter they were about to initiate.

CHAPTER 35

May 1850
Leverett Street, Boston, Massachusetts

The admission ticket for Dr. James Stone to enter the prison came soon enough. He had visited previously and was known, but one of the Leverett Street jailers hesitated before allowing Ellen entry into the noisy enclosure.

"She's with me," James said brusquely. "Professor Webster is expecting her as well, and we'll enter together or not at all." He knew that Webster had no knowledge of Ellen's existence, but James had no patience left to argue with the guard. Time was precious.

They were led to the office of Jailkeeper Andrews, who regarded James and Ellen coolly, in no hurry to grant access to his most celebrated prisoner.

"Your business, Doctor Stone? I seen you at the trial, but I don't understand your need to see Professor Webster now that legal matters have concluded."

"Has he not approved me, Mister Andrews? Isn't that the only requirement?"

"He most certainly hasn't approved your companion, sir. What might your name be, young lady?" he asked, turning his gaze on Ellen.

"She is Ellen O'Keeffe, an essential participant in the purpose of my visit with Professor Webster," James said.

"And that purpose might be?"

"As you no doubt observed in court, Mister Andrews, I was busy transcribing the entirety of the testimony given at Professor Webster's trial. The professor never testified, but I wish him to understand how his appearance and demeanor will be rendered in my phonographic report."

Andrews looked quizzically at James. He had never heard the word *phonographic*, and he had no interest in any report.

"That sounds all right," Andrews said, more pleasantly this time. "You both may go in but limit your time with the professor to no more than half an hour. If you're not out by then, we'll come get you."

"That won't be necessary," James said. "We hope to dispatch our business quickly."

He and Ellen were led on a path familiar to him, down a narrow corridor and up a flight of steps. As they approached the row of cells reserved for doomed prisoners, they saw Webster sitting on his narrow bed. Piles of mail, petitions, and newspapers covered the small table and part of the mattress. Two wooden chairs stood uneasily nearby.

"James, so good of you to come," said Webster, in a much friendlier voice than James had anticipated. "These visits mean the world to me. I'm a better man for each and every one of them. Please enter, be seated, I beg you."

James said, "Professor Webster, this is my associate, Miss Ellen O'Keeffe. She's been of great assistance in the preparation of my phonographic report, which will be published shortly, as you know."

"Miss O'Keeffe, it's a pleasure indeed to see one as lovely as yourself. Oh, yes, James, I saw you scribbling away with your pen, day after day. I wish my counselors had paid as close attention as you did."

"Would the outcome have been any different if they had?" James saw no reason now for niceties. He had to gauge where Webster stood on his own innocence, and whether he would be willing to entertain James's efforts on his behalf.

"It matters not," said Webster, clasping his hands and looking upward. "The good Lord decreed that I must suffer for the sins of others, and I do so with a happy heart. The Reverend Doctor Putnam and the Reverend Charles Spears believe this to be the best way forward. I need to approach my end on this earth as a new beginning in the next life."

Ellen stared at the man with admiration. "That be a beautiful sentiment, Professor Webster. To be sure, God'll grant ye peace in yer final hours. Me and Doctor Stone remain greatly curious about the events that led to yer trial. Since ye nae did testify, yer thoughts are a mystery to us, and the rest o' the world."

"And so they shall remain, my dear," Webster said, reaching out to take Ellen's hand in his small, chubby ones. It was a bold action to take just moments after meeting a woman, and Ellen flinched before allowing the liberty.

Webster continued, oblivious to the discomfort he had caused Ellen. "It can do no good to rail against my misfortune or take issue with Ephraim

Littlefield. You should know that I had an interview with Littlefield and his wife just yesterday. I begged his forgiveness, he asked for mine. There was many a tear shed. Well, all is in God's plan."

James and Ellen traded a glance. Littlefield had said nothing of this audience.

James said, "Professor Webster, was it at your instruction that Littlefield smuggled slaves into the Medical College?"

The question burst out of James as if shot from a cannon, but it provoked as intended. A look of complete devastation came over Webster's features, and then vanished, replaced by the same insincere humility he had manifested since James and Ellen's arrival.

"Let us not speak of these matters, which are now meaningless, I beg you, James," Webster said.

His wheedling voice reminded James of Webster's lecture classes and made him think of what Webster's entreaties to Parkman must have sounded like. James now could understand how they must have irritated and inflamed the wealthy man.

He said, "Has the slavery question become meaningless to you, Professor? Surely the actions you undertook derived from beliefs that put you and those you aided at risk. The evils of slavery still continue, do they not?"

Webster looked at James with a steady eye. "Go not where you're uninvited, Doctor Stone. The connection between Mister Littlefield and myself existed in the past, under particular circumstances. It was discontinued, and therefore no longer matters."

Now it was Ellen's turn to gently press the issue. "Did Doctor Parkman come upon yer business with Mister Littlefield? Is this what led to his death?"

Webster stared at Ellen with admiration, and a little fear. "Where did you find this perceptive young woman, James? She is smarter than Marshal Tukey and his men, and no doubt exceeds the mental capacities of Judge Merrick and Mister Sohier, too."

"Please, Professor," said James. "Our only hope is to aid you and see justice prevail. If you did not commit the murder of George Parkman by yourself, then please, tell us who aided you."

Webster replied, "It is a name you'll not know nor recognize, and I intend to keep it that way." He rose from his bed and paced back and forth in the narrow space available to him.

James and Ellen regarded each other. John Webster had just indirectly acknowledged that someone else had helped murder George Parkman. This accomplice presumably was still at large.

"Who do ye protect with yer very soul, Professor?" Ellen said soothingly. "Let us help ye bring the matter to light and spare yer life."

"It's not my life that concerns me, child." Webster sat back down on his bed, as if he had finally realized that further dissembling was useless. "It's the lives of those hundreds, nay, those tens of thousands held in cruel bondage, that concern me. Ever since I read the narrative of the former slave Frederick Douglass, I have pursued the abolitionist cause. When asked, I served. The answer you seek is that simple."

"Professor Webster, we know of your activities on behalf of the Underground Railroad," said James. "We've seen the barrels in which Littlefield brought runaway slaves to the Medical College, and we presume you helped those slaves along their path to freedom. Many other facts still elude us. Rather than engage in continual theorizing, we ask you plainly: share with us what happened. We'll do nothing with what you tell us that you do not authorize us to do."

Webster was silent for an uncomfortable length of time. He looked at Ellen first, then at James.

"I suppose it might do me well to unburden myself. I've told no one the true events of that horrible day, whose anniversary I won't live to see. But, Miss O'Keeffe, James, what good can come of this? Only the betrayal of a cause more important than any of us. I cannot sacrifice the safety and well-being of so many to expiate my own guilt."

James said, "The truth of these events will bring great attention to your cause, and more supporters to its fold than you may imagine."

"Nothing must be revealed about the workings of the Underground Railroad!" Webster spoke with a threatening tone that made James and Ellen nervous.

He continued, "If you must know, that is the reason for my silence. I bore assaults on my character from every quarter. The galleries peered at me as if I were a creature on display in a Barnum sideshow! I allowed falsehood and calumny to be leveled against me by all, and I said nothing! Now leave me be and leave this subject be!"

Webster was breathing heavily. James spoke calmly, trying to put him back at ease. "Miss O'Keeffe and I believe that your life could be spared if the true chain of events were to emerge. Surely, your wife and daughters deserve at least that opportunity."

Webster was again distant, as if James and Ellen occupied some other physical space, and not the tiny cell, where he was.

"Yes, I suppose they might," he mused, as if considering what his family might be planning for supper. "Harriet and my lovely girls, what will become of them? I've not provided adequately for their care. It weighs on me heavily."

"They would have more time with ye, if nae else, if ye let us help ye," said Ellen softly. "Surely that carries hope."

"Hope is something I abandoned long ago, Miss O'Keeffe," Webster replied, smiling sadly. "It has no place where I now reside."

His face was still sad when he turned to James and tried to assume a brisker tone. "I'll tell you what you want to know on the following conditions: that you disclose it to no one, least of all my family; that you do nothing to delay or halt my execution, which I've accepted as my ordained fate; and that you find some way, each of you, to support the cause for which I will donate my life. That would give me satisfaction, the only recompense I shall obtain from these circumstances."

James looked helplessly at Ellen. The price of total silence seemed a high one. What good was Webster's revelation if they could do nothing with it? Yet the man was ready at last to unburden himself, which they must allow him to do. James nodded his acceptance of Webster's ultimatum.

"We accede to your wishes, Professor. Miss O'Keeffe and I will tell no one of this conversation. But I beg you to reconsider the impact of a true account of your motives. Why embrace the noose, when I can publish a record of these events in my report, and your life may be spared? The entire world will know of your self-sacrifice."

"My secrets best go to the grave with me, James. Now I'll give you some solace for the endless worrying you've done on my behalf. If you're ready, I'll tell you the tale of a day I wish had been struck from the calendar!"

CHAPTER 36

November 1849
North Grove Street, Boston, Massachusetts

Professor John Webster was awash in paper. Yet these were not the examination books filled by his students at the end of each term at Harvard Medical College. They were the records of a man's descent into penury, Webster thought, as he sorted through promissory notes, loan papers, bank statements, and check drafts.

His shaky financial status was no secret. All his friends and relatives knew that even after many years of service to the college, he remained in debt, thanks to the pittance of a salary that Harvard paid him. That, along with the tickets sold to his students for the privilege (and requirement) of taking his chemistry lectures, barely gave him enough to adequately furnish his house and provision his family.

Webster had convinced himself that he always did his best to repay the sums he borrowed, but it was never as promptly as his creditors expected. Simply put, the man was ill-equipped to manage his own finances, especially when four other people depended on his earning power.

So the loans continued, and the promissory notes grew from a small pile to a heap that could not be contained in the drawer of his desk in his laboratory at the Medical College. But there was another cause for Webster's financial ills. He had become an advocate for a secret cause that further drained his resources.

John Webster had become a changed man in 1845 after reading Frederick Douglass's *Autobiography* and subscribing to his newspaper, *The North Star*. In short order he joined the Boston Vigilance Committee, led by Theodore Parker and Wendell Phillips. Members donated funds in secrecy to help fugitive slaves escape to Canada, in a complex process known as the Underground Railroad. In spite of the strain under which his household labored, Webster contributed substantial sums to the cause.

Finally, when he was no longer able to donate money, the professor decided instead to give shelter to slaves making their way north, using the Medical College as an Underground Railroad terminus. Most of the benighted souls who passed through Webster's rooms went on to Canada, the only true refuge from their owners, who continued to pursue them steadily so long as they remained in the United States.

William and Sally Craft, two escapees from Georgia, had first arrived at the Medical College in 1848 in barrels that were opened by Webster and Ephraim Littlefield. The Crafts soon had famed slave catcher John Capehart on their trail and were hidden in various locations owned by Vigilance Committee members in and around Boston until the couple could be spirited away in a boat to England.

Whatever Webster did for the cause, it had to remain a secret. Harvard College frowned on any display of abolitionist sentiment, and its president, Edward Everett, and his successor, Jared Sparks, had warned the faculty in no uncertain terms to keep their political beliefs to themselves. They were to take no action that could embarrass Harvard or hold it up to ridicule.

These strictures did not cause Webster's enthusiasm to wane, but his money woes intensified. These worsened when Littlefield—realizing the danger to which he was exposing himself by aiding Webster and the Vigilance Committee's smuggling of fugitive slaves—first requested, then demanded, additional payments for his cooperation and silence.

On several occasions, Littlefield threatened to expose Webster's work with the Railroad, although Webster's involvement was limited mostly to freeing the poor slaves from the barrels Littlefield had collected from Long Wharf. The barrels were usually smuggled on ships from Norfolk or Portsmouth in Virginia. After shooing Littlefield away, Webster would give the fugitives food and sustenance in his rooms at the Medical College, a place they were unlikely to be discovered. Often they would be picked up the same night and taken to the next stop on the Railroad, in Concord.

As time went on and the traffic increased, Littlefield's demands grew ever more outrageous, as did Webster's debts to his creditors, especially Dr. Parkman, who had been a great benefactor to Harvard but also to John Webster, helping to endow the professor's chair in chemistry.

The richest man in Boston had been generous with Webster personally, too. Parkman had accepted possessions of the Professor's as collateral, at various times and for various sums, including his mineral cabinet, filled with his specimens and chemical materials, and his collection of medical and chemical texts, the largest in New England.

Webster had learned from bitter experience that of all his creditors, Parkman must always be paid first. The man was unrelenting in collecting interest payments or the debt in full, regardless of the amount of money at stake. Parkman would have his money back, and anyone who stood in his way be damned. That was how business was done in Boston, the Parkman way.

Now Parkman's vengeance was being wreaked upon John Webster, and the professor knew he must accede if he were to survive. He had made one profound and stupid error: he had mortgaged his most valuable asset, his mineral collection, twice within weeks. George Parkman held one promissory note for $2,432 on the cabinet, and his brother-in-law, Robert Shaw, held a note for a subsequent loan he had made to Webster on the same cabinet, for $2,632.

The two brothers-in-law must have talked and compared loan papers, Webster thought. The duplication would be obvious, and the blame instantaneous. Webster knew, with devastating certainty, exactly what Dr. Parkman would say to him when they met here in his rooms at the college at the time he had scheduled, the rude way he would address him, the insults he would heap upon him.

The miserable Webster knew that he deserved it all. Even now, as he gathered the receipts and readied the documents for Parkman to sign that would acknowledge the most recent loan fully paid, his hands trembled. Parkman had the ability to ruin him. No self-respecting bank or business would extend him credit, and his home could be seized for unpaid rent, his family cast into the street, despoiled and homeless.

Who could have predicted that Ephraim Littlefield would knock sharply on the professor's outer door to announce a new delivery of a barrel to the college, just minutes before the punctual Dr. Parkman was expected?

Webster panicked. He opened the door and stared at the janitor, Littlefield, whose arm rested on a large oak barrel. Webster was in disbelief that the janitor and an escaping slave had chosen this moment to appear unbidden.

"What are you doing here, Littlefield? I wasn't told of any delivery for today. Remove that barrel immediately to the basement, where I will tend to it later. By what logic you bring it here, I do not pretend to understand."

But the aggrieved janitor had lost his patience with the slave-smuggling scheme, since the profit from his labors had not grown as Professor Webster had promised it would.

"Move it yerself, Professor, if ye be so inclined. My work is over, I done what ye warranted I should. This barrel got left on the wharf yesterday, and I took from my own time to fetch it back in my cart today; it cost you nothing, and me quite a bit."

Webster looked alarmed. "Do you mean to say that some poor refugee has been in that barrel well overnight and this morning, too? Have you no soul, Littlefield? Does human suffering not perturb you?"

There was no response from the other man, who looked down at his feet, unwilling to leave before he was compensated. "I picked him up on my own time, and you owe me for that time," said Littlefield. He was a stubborn man. "If not ye, then those fancy gents ye truck with. Either way, Professor, I need to get what you need to give."

Webster was flustered. The man was usually submissive to the point of genuflection, if resentfully so. Now Littlefield was making demands that gave Webster little choice but to demur.

He pulled out a large, worn leather wallet and thumbed through the bills. His plan had been to present Dr. Parkman with $432 to pay off one loan, although he would still owe him another $2,000 for the remaining mortgage on the chemical cabinet. He proffered two dollars in coins to Littlefield, who spat on the ground.

"That's typical of yer idea of fairness, Professor. But it won't do, as Missus Littlefield is fond of sayin', it won't do a'tall."

Webster scowled at the janitor but reached back into his wallet and this time offered a five-dollar bill drawn on the Bank of Boston. Littlefield nodded, snatched the bill from Webster's hand, and turned and stomped out of the laboratory.

"Wait, Littlefield, wait. You must remove this barrel immediately, I have visitors coming. Littlefield!"

Webster could hear Littlefield's boots going down the stone steps to the ground floor and realized that his shouts were in vain. He grabbed a long knife resting on a tea chest he used for storage of his materials and began prying the top off the barrel. Parkman would be there any moment.

He leaned onto the knife with all his strength, and the top came loose. He slipped the knife under and lifted, and almost immediately a dark head with tight wiry curls emerged from the barrel, frantically gulping for air.

"I am so sorry, you poor soul, are you all right?" Webster said, frantic with worry that at any moment he would hear Parkman knocking on the door to his rooms. He dropped the knife back on the small chest.

"Water, please, water," said the Black man, whose wide shoulders and powerful arms had also now emerged from the barrel. Webster hurried to a pitcher on his desk, poured water into a stoneware cup, and thrust it into the freed prisoner's hands.

"I cannot believe how unfortunate it is that this is the moment I had to rescue you from your prison," Webster said, trying to calm himself and act rationally under these extreme circumstances. "But you must hide yourself. Quickly, go into this room," he said, gesturing toward his storage closet. "Move behind the pile of grape stakes stored there for my fire. It is a space that I almost never utilize. I have a visitor coming, and you must not be seen or heard, not under any circumstances, do you understand? If he finds you, it will be our undoing."

The man nodded silently, still not having uttered a word other than his plea for water. He hoisted himself out of the barrel, reached down to touch his toes and stretch his back and shoulders, and then looked for where Webster had pointed. He was wearing a torn and stained white shirt and tattered dark wool pants, too small and riding high on his ankles. A dirty scarf served as his belt and held up his trousers.

"Quickly, quickly now, please," pleaded Webster. And no sooner had he freed the smuggled slave from his rancid conveyance and placed him in the closet than George Parkman came banging at his door. Webster hurriedly shoved the barrel into a corner of the room.

He had hoped for a moment to gather himself before greeting his visitor, but Parkman was already beating on the door with his cane, shouting fierce oaths. Webster could think of nothing else to do but to hurry and fling it open, just so the man would stop his confounded pounding. All was in jeopardy, Webster thought. If Parkman discovered the slave, the professor was sure he would have the two of them immediately arrested and imprisoned. On this one occasion his nerves would have to hold.

Even as he entered, Parkman berated Webster. "How dare you keep me waiting, sir! Have you no honor, or are you the leech, the parasite, the liar, and the charlatan all believe you to be? I, above all, know what a liar you are! What decent man sells the same bill of goods to two different men? Men who are only charitable, generous, compassionate in loaning him money in the first place?"

And charging him interest for the privilege, Webster thought, but dare not say. He knew, under these circumstances, the best policy was submissive silence. There was no point in arguing.

Parkman had let up in calling Webster a villain in every way, but he had moved on to new territory, where the Professor was even more vulnerable.

"Can a man like you be trusted in anything, Webster? Come now, what other falsehoods have you subscribed to? Need we check your medical credentials, and verify that you studied where you claim, and with whom? Can you stand that scrutiny, Webster?"

Webster was greatly alarmed. Would Parkman dare to deprive him of his livelihood? He had helped name Webster the Erving Professor of Chemistry, and he could just as easily have Harvard dismiss him, despite his years of service. In short, Parkman could ruin him and put his family out on the street, if he were so inclined.

Webster said, "Please, Doctor Parkman, let us not deal in oaths and threats, but instead as two businessmen, linked by many financial connections. I have a significant amount of money to give you toward my loan—"

"*Toward* your loan? Do you really believe I would accept any less than full payment on the capital amount of all of your loans, plus the accrued interest? Have you lost full possession of your faculties, Webster?"

Webster thrust out his wallet to demonstrate to Parkman that there were indeed funds he could pay. "Please, Doctor Parkman, accept this four hundred dollars as evidence of my good intent to replay each and every cent that I owe you."

But Parkman was no longer looking at Webster. He had smelled the fumes that still emanated from the opened slave-smuggling barrel behind him, and there was a filthy rag on the floor the escapee must have dropped when he exited the barrel. He walked over and poked at the rag with his cane.

"What might this be, Webster? Another place to hide your money, or some other nefarious scheme? I would hardly be surprised to see you engaged in any number of illegal pursuits."

Parkman approached the barrel, stuck his head into it, and gave the interior a great sniff. Webster was astonished by how much air the man could inhale through his nostrils. Parkman straightened and said, "Did you have a nigger in this barrel, Webster? I can smell one has been there! Why are you bringing niggers into the Medical College? What business could you have—"

"No, please, Doctor Parkman, you misunderstand. There is a man here, a janitor, who brings corpses of all races into the Medical College for our lectures and experiments, and this barrel had but one of those specimens."

Parkman was having none of it. "I see this for what it is, Webster. You are harboring and hiding fugitive slaves, no doubt a part of that cursed Underground Railroad. Well, this is the last straw. These actions will be the end of you. I will see you at trial for this shame you bring upon Harvard and its Medical College."

Something in Webster snapped. He could stand no more. "I demand you leave at once, Doctor Parkman. Here, take your money now and be gone, you may supply my receipt at a later day. I will not stand for your accusations a moment longer."

Infuriated, Parkman swung his long wooden cane directly at Webster's head. Thanks to his short stature, the professor was able to duck the blow, but Parkman continued to strike him, hitting him in the back and ribs with the cane and knocking Webster to the ground. He averted his face, but Parkman struck at him wildly, hitting his body again and again. He tried to rise, but Parkman knocked him to the floor and struck him again.

Webster shouted as he struggled to his feet. "Do you intend to me leave me dead, Doctor Parkman? I shall be left dead from your assault!"

At that moment the tall, powerfully built escapee burst out of the closet with one of the grapevine stakes in his hand. Webster ran to the man and wrested the wooden stake from him. Parkman looked confused, then apoplectic. He moved immediately toward the pair, lashing out with his cane and striking the Black man across his broad features.

"How dare you, Webster! You are a liar and a traitor!" Parkman bellowed.

Webster's fury, once finally unleashed, could not be contained. The short, rotund man rushed his adversary and smote Parkman directly on the head with the grapevine stake, knocking him to his knees.

Parkman put his hand to his brow and looked up at Webster, who was hovering above him.

"Webster, what have you done?"

Parkman toppled over onto the floor. Webster remained motionless; he could see that the blow had probably proven fatal.

The Black man also stood there, still as a rock, blood dripping down his lacerated face. Webster bent over Parkman, trying to help the doctor regain consciousness, but it was too late. Dark blood welled out of the wound on his scalp, just above his forehead. Webster wasn't sure if his time had already passed, and he bent over Parkman's body to try to hear his breath.

Suddenly the former slave jumped onto Parkman's prone form and drove the knife he'd found on the small trunk straight into Parkman's chest.

"Enough!" Webster shouted, and the man dropped the knife, which was covered in blood. His effort had been unnecessary; Webster was convinced that Parkman had already expired from the blow the professor had rendered to his skull.

As the two survivors both rose from the corpse, for the first time Webster saw the escapee's bare back, which had been scarred by the lash many times. Not a single spot was exempted. It was the most grievous punishment he had ever seen administered. Now Webster understood the man's animus toward the white man he had slain.

Webster felt panicked. He had no idea what to do next. George Parkman lay dead upon his floor, his life finished at Webster's hand. He had only two choices: go to the police and admit his crime, and hang for it; or hide the body and hope that Parkman's disappearance would remain a mystery. The next thing he knew, he was aiding the slave in dragging Parkman toward his back room. They brought him to the sink built against the wall and stood the body partially erect in the corner.

"What is your name? I am John," Webster said to the escapee, trying to gather his senses. He had made the choice for concealment, and now this man was Webster's accomplice in a murder.

"Meshach," the man said, "my name is Meshach. Give me the saw, give me the knife."

It turned out that Meshach had been trained in butchering. He used Webster's pruning saw and the bloodstained knife to hack off the limbs as if he were slaughtering a hog. Meshach had the limbs removed quickly, the blood running down the drain in the sink. Webster was careful to make sure that none was spilled on the floor or the walls.

Removing the head was the most difficult task. Webster had closed Parkman's blue eyes just as they dulled with death, but the rich man's physiognomy was so distinctive that it was impossible for him not to resemble himself, even in death.

Meshach instructed Webster to hold the head and turn the face to the left while he sawed through the neck and spine. It was a much more gruesome process, Webster thought, when you knew the identity of the victim.

Webster's plan was to burn everything: Parkman's papers, pocketbook, limbs, even the head. His clothes, including the boots, he gave to Meshach, and they fit him remarkably well, the slave also being tall and lean.

They used the slave's ragged clothes to wipe up the blood that had spattered the floor when Webster first dealt Parkman the fatal blow, along with every spot and stain they could espy. When they were finished cleaning the laboratory and the sink, Webster would not allow the slave to discard the bloody rags.

"Keep these with you, hidden from any to see, and burn them when you reach Concord," he told Meshach, who seemed dazed by the reality that he had just participated in his first slaying of a white man. Meshach nodded his acquiescence to Webster's plan. Then the chemistry professor started a fire in his stove for a purpose never required in his lectures: to dispose of the human flesh of his benefactor.

Before the fire was heated to the proper temperature for the task, there was another loud rapping on the outer door to Webster's lecture room. Again, he knew who his visitor would be: another member of the Vigilance Committee, who was there to transport Meshach on the next step of his journey.

Webster closed the door to his inner rooms; bade Meshach wash his hands, face, and body of any blood; and then opened the door only so far as to vouchsafe that the visitor was indeed there to pick up Meshach and convey him to Concord.

Webster's concerns were not all addressed, however, by the departure of Meshach on his journey to freedom. There remained the matter of Ephraim Littlefield.

CHAPTER 37

James and Ellen sat in stunned silence as Webster concluded his narrative. Finally, James asked a question with which he had long wrestled.

"Was Littlefield aware of Parkman's murder? Has he used this to blackmail you further in some way?"

Webster looked rueful. "He didn't need to blackmail me on this account. He had many other opportunities. His turning on me was motivated more out of fear that he would be blamed for Doctor Parkman's death. And he wanted the reward money. A disclosure of my activities for the Railroad would have ruined me, but it would have also exposed him, since it was he who actually brought the runaway slaves into the college. I was protected therefore on that count. Littlefield realized his income from smuggling slaves was at an end, as were my payments for his silence. The most I could offer him was a Thanksgiving turkey, and he took the gesture as an insult, although I will point out that he also took the turkey."

Jame said, "So Littlefield had nothing to do with hiding the evidence of the crime, or placing the body parts I helped identify into your privy?"

"He knew nothing of what actually transpired in my final meeting with Doctor Parkman. His desire for revenge drove him, but also greatly hindered my own efforts to dispose of every trace of the slaying. Each time Littlefield spied on me—I knew when he was lying outside my door—he frustrated me. With the help of potash, I managed to burn all of Parkman's papers, his cane, and some parts of him, his hands and feet, and so on.

"I had a roaring fire built up one night and could have finished the job had Littlefield not come weaseling around. I feared he would enter my rooms at any moment, and I would be undone. It was necessary for me to force what was left of Parkman into an old tea chest I possessed. The torso, the genitals, one thigh, all these were too big to fit, and I had no other hiding place available. That is when I purchased the large fishhooks and fishing line, to put those parts out of view.

"The rest you know, as does the world. I didn't intentionally murder George Parkman, but I may as well have, for that's what all believe, and it's that crime's punishment I shall suffer. Why should I not?"

He stared penetratingly first at Ellen, then lingered longer on James. "Remember, James, I ask not only for your silence, but also a pledge to action. I don't expect you to work on the Railroad, fear not. I do demand your support in other ways, perhaps through phonography, to distribute the abolitionist message. When I ascend the gallows twenty days hence, it will be a comfort to know my work continues in the person of you and Miss O'Keeffe."

"Ye may rely upon it, Professor Webster," Ellen said, with great emotion in her voice. "We don't wish to disappoint ye."

"I'm glad to hear it, child," Webster said, looking tired and ashen-faced. "Now, it's time for you to go. I'm weary, and my telling of these events has made me relive them in my mind, where they remain as horrible as when they occurred."

Webster stood. The audience was over. Ellen touched Webster's arm in a final gesture of empathy as they made their way out of the small cell. James put an arm around Webster's shoulder until they reached the iron doorway.

Webster spoke once more before his visitors were led down the long hallway.

"Remember your vow. I'll be thinking on it when they place the hood over my face. My prayers will be with my family, but my thoughts will be with you, and the good you will do in my stead."

~

James and Ellen were eager to go over their interview with Professor Webster, but they had nowhere respectable in which to do it. Their former refuge at the transcription office was given up, and James couldn't be seen escorting Ellen to his own chambers in Bowdoin Square.

He hit upon the idea of William Lee's ice cream parlor, on Washington Street. It was respectable, if not advisable, for an unmarried woman to enter such an establishment on the arm of a gentleman. James strode in confidently with Ellen, pointed out the ice creams made on the premises, and ordered one served in a jelly glass for each of them.

They stood in a corner of the establishment where conversation was encouraged, and speaking softly, they reviewed the astonishing tale Dr. Webster had told them. They marveled at every unanticipated detail, wondering aloud whether Meshach the escaped slave was an invention or a flesh-and-blood human being who had jeopardized, then saved, the life of the man providing him a route to safety.

If James revealed what he and Ellen had learned, an injustice could be righted, and a man guilty of only manslaughter might be spared the gallows. If they remained silent, as they had promised Webster, James would feel forever responsible for not stopping the man's execution, even if that was the wish of the condemned.

They left Lee's shop and made their way toward the North End and Ellen's home. As they walked, the cool breezes of the late afternoon came off the harbor, but they were unable to calm James's fevered mind.

"What next, Ellen?" he asked miserably. "We're caught in a web not of our making, but which has us stuck firmly within it. Whichever way we turn, someone is undone."

"We must keep our word to the professor, above all, James. We owe him that much. As to his fate, I see the man is at peace with it. I saw nae weakness in his soul. If he can keep his secret, so can we."

"Should I amend my report to include what Webster told us, even indirectly? The uproar it would cause would do wonders for phonography."

"Or for the linin' of yer own pocket," Ellen said, disturbed by a mercenary side of James she was seeing for the first time. "That's nae what we be about, James. I'm surprised to hear ye say it. Professor Webster had a high purpose; we needs have one, too. We gave him our word."

James was embarrassed that Ellen had caught him thinking about profit, for that was indeed the motivation for amending his report, with a story that could have been devised by the great Edgar Allan Poe. She was correct; they owed Webster the right to his privacy. Once again, James appreciated Ellen's role in improving his moral character.

"You know that profit has never driven this enterprise, Ellen," he said, trying to redeem himself. "I gave in to temptation when I heard this fantastic tale from Doctor Webster. We must be devoted to phonography, just as Professor Webster saw his duty to the abolitionists. Each of us acts with a purpose. We must stay true to ours."

"I meant nae offense, James, I beg ye. Our chat with Doctor Webster affected me greatly. He was like a priest in church, summonin' us to a higher callin'."

James looked at Ellen. *She was his better in every way. In moments such as these, she inspired him to fulfill a better version of himself. How could he not keep this spirited, beautiful woman in his life? He had always yearned for a woman who could be a true partner, not just in a conjugal way, or the spirituality that Jennie Gillmer was always going on about. That wasn't it.*

Ellen was what he wanted. He now realized that no matter what obstacles his family or Boston society put in their way, he was destined to be with Ellen. Her beauty, her charm, her tenacity—all was there for the taking, and she wished him to take it. Of that he was sure.

They arrived at Sullivan Square just as the sun began its downward descent. A golden hue embraced the squalid North End. It was the most romantic setting James might have desired. He took Ellen's hand in his own and turned to face her. Some words were going to come out of his mouth, although he wasn't sure exactly what they would be.

Instead, a hand grabbed James's left shoulder and whirled him around. He ended up face to face with William Haggerty, who stank of stout beer and barely stood upright. It was just past seven o'clock in the evening, and the Irishman was completely soused.

"Docter Stone," mumbled Haggerty incoherently—it came out sounding more like "Okerone." "It be a pleasure and a surprise to see ye here in our neighborhood this very evenin'."

"Get away from us, Haggerty," James said. "You reek of liquor." James pulled Ellen behind him. He looked around. They were alone on the dirt street.

"O, now it's ye that'll be protectin' me from me own daughter? The one ye've ruined?" Haggerty had great difficulty pronouncing the final word; it emerged as "rined."

"Shut yer mouth, William. Yer not my pa, and ye never will be!" said Ellen. "You nae know nothin' of us. But I know ye! I know ye been stealin' money from Docter Stone here, money ye told me nothin' about. Ye take money for my honor? I be the only one in possession of me own honor! Yer only in possession of the drink!"

Haggerty tried to straighten himself, swaying all the while. He lashed out with the back of his hand, striking Ellen viciously above her left ear, and sending her tumbling to the dirt street.

"I'll teach ye how to speak to yer father!" he bellowed. "I'm the man of this house, and nae woman'll give me orders!

James hurried to Ellen's prone form in shock, not sure what had just happened. In one moment, his entire world had shifted.

Ellen lay utterly still. James lifted her head gently and discovered below it a flinty, sharp rock. Thick, dark blood matted her red hair, the two colors shocking in their contrast. The rock was a mess of hair, blood, and brains.

James brought Ellen's head to his ear and strained to hear a breath, but none came. Her blood stained his hands, which cradled her skull. There was nothing to do. Ellen O'Keeffe was gone. The essence of the woman he had loved with all his heart had departed in an instant. What remained was a shell with two shades of red in its hair.

James had a feeling of leaving himself, of being no longer tied to his body but looking at this scene as if from a great distance, far, far away. This is what tragedy feels like, he thought dimly. It's as though you are taken from your own life. He wondered if he would ever return, and if he did, how diminished would his life be?

CHAPTER 38

June 1850
Mt. Auburn Cemetery, Watertown, Massachusetts; Bowdoin Square;
Tremont Street, Beacon Hill; and Washington Street, Boston,
Massachusetts

The hackney pulled up to the main gate of Mt. Auburn Cemetery. James got out and paid the driver. He could have taken the omnibus, but he preferred the privacy of a hired carriage. He had no desire to share his misery. His grief, like the love that had preceded it, would remain secret.

Now he was the principal actor in a drama as horrible as Webster's, James thought grimly, as he made his way through the Egyptian gates and chose at random one of the paths that led into the cemetery. He, too, had caused the death of another, and he had no convenient runaway slave on whom to blame it. Yes, Haggerty had delivered the fatal blow to Ellen, but only because James had sustained him, paid him the dirty money he demanded, and by doing so, kept Ellen in continued jeopardy. It had cost James the only person in his life he had truly cared for.

The path wandered past stone monuments and brass burial vaults. James wished he could bury Ellen in this pristine place, but those intended for Mt. Auburn had to shine in Boston society. He now knew he would never join what he had once aspired to. He had lost his hunger for that measure of success.

James still believed in phonography as an improvement in human communication, but it was no longer the Holy Grail he had once pursued. *What use was communicating half truths, made-up stories, evidence that concealed what it purported to reveal?* James now doubted there was any such thing as truth. *Each participant in an event saw only his or her own perspective and gave meaning only to that viewpoint.* James marveled that there could be so many different versions of one event, whose "truth" can never be "known." The killing of George Parkman demonstrated that.

James had completed a task alone that he and Ellen had undertaken together. His report was a secret tribute to her, dedicated to the memories that he would carry with him for the remainder of his life. William Haggerty couldn't deprive him of that, not in the same way he had taken the physical manifestation of Ellen from him.

Haggerty posed a remaining problem for James to solve. He had given much thought to the matter of revenge. He feared his reluctance to fight might prevent him from acting, but now he was more cognizant of his strengths, his logic, and his imagination. After witnessing Webster's complicated schemes and stratagems, he came up with one of his own.

He couldn't go to the police and accuse Haggerty of homicide. He would have to explain his presence at the scene. It would doubtless emerge that he was the lover of the slain girl and enabler of her blackmailer stepfather. He had come to terms with the truth of his situation. There would be no peace for James Winchell Stone so long as William Haggerty breathed.

James shook his head. *He couldn't believe he was contemplating the murder of another human being. Yet what other means to avenge Ellen were available to him? He had spent weeks watching a man held accountable for just a few moments of rage, which resulted in his victim's death. Could he claim a similar exemption, commit a crime of passion, not of planning? Or was his determination to make Haggerty pay for his fatal assault on Ellen a vengeance he would have to carefully plot and execute?*

The sun was settling over the hills as James made his way out of Mt. Auburn. The visit had served its purpose. It had quieted his roiling emotions and stiffened his resolve. He would not be like John Webster and dissemble. He would act.

~

On June 6, the public declaration of guilt that James had anticipated from John Webster finally came. As promised, Webster employed the Rev. Dr. Francis Parkman, brother of the late victim, as the vehicle for his "final" confession. Parkman had published a letter he received from the condemned man. Webster wrote:

> *I cannot leave this world in the peace of mind for which I pray, without addressing you as the head of that family which I have so deeply injured or affected, to make known to you and them the bitter anguish of soul, the sincere contrition or penitence I have felt at having been the cause of the affliction under which you and they have been called to mourn.*

For the first time since his arrest, Webster expressed remorse for his actions.

I offer no excuse for any wicked and fatal ebullition of passion, but what you already know, nor would I attempt to palliate it. I had never, until the two or three last interviews with your brother, felt towards him anything but gratitude for his many acts of kindness and friendship. The feelings excited in me on that one occasion so entirely overpowered me as to take the life of your brother, and my own temporal and external welfare, I can, even now hardly realize.

There it was. John Webster had finally acknowledged that he had been the sole murderer of George Parkman. Yet James knew this to be a lie. Had not Meshach stepped between Webster and Parkman, a different man might have sat in the prisoner's dock accused of willful murder. But Webster, now joined by James Stone, would reveal none of this.

The convicted professor also made a final attempt to protect his wife and daughters from any association with his guilt.

I beg to assure you, I entreat you to believe me, no one of my family had the slightest doubt of my entire innocence up to the moment when the contrary was communicated to them by me. That they have your sincere pity or sympathy, I feel assured.

What actually passed within the walls of Professor Webster's laboratory on that November Friday afternoon would never be revealed. One of the participants was dead, the other was about to be, and the third, a free man in Canada, would never speak of it. If James had learned one thing over the course of the previous nine months, it was that life holds little certainty for those who seek it. The truth is a slippery eel.

⁓

James's medical practice had practically expired during the Webster trial. Following its conclusion, he attempted to resuscitate it by contacting the few patients whom he had regularly treated. But they had moved on to new practitioners, and none looked back. It seemed that his role in the trial and his association with the Medical College had tarnished him; his patients exhibited a kind of fear of him. James had never felt more like an outsider, no longer privy to the gossip and gatherings of the Beacon Hill elite. He was very much alone.

Therefore, he was surprised when Sharon brought up an expensive note card that had just been delivered by a servant of Robert Shaw's, requesting Dr. James Stone's presence at the Beacon Club for supper that evening. James was pleased to be invited, and not summoned for a lecture, as he had been that night at Dr. Bigelow's, less than a year past, during the cholera epidemic. It seemed like a decade ago.

His original intent upon taking up his project was to have his report provide the social entrée he had long sought. Now, with it due out at the beginning of the following week, he was stricken with guilty thoughts. How could he behave so badly, seeking acclaim so soon after the tragedy of Ellen's death? *He hadn't deserved her love or her respect, all that she had willingly bestowed upon him. He was unworthy of her in every way.*

Contemplating the memory of Ellen O'Keeffe oppressed him, made him feel futile and useless. *He needed to reassert himself in society, and find a new identity to mold and shape into his own. He must prove he had no further need of comfort or support. He would go it alone, since that was the position in which he had always found himself.*

Before the Webster trial, James would have purchased a new tailored suit and hired an expensive carriage for the short ride to Beacon Street. The Beacon Club's members were the most powerful and wealthy men of Boston, and the earlier version of James Stone would have been thrilled to receive this invitation.

But this James Stone was not the same parvenu doctor he once was. His reckoning with John Webster, the senseless loss of Ellen O'Keeffe, and the report's impending publication had altered him. Of all things, he now exhibited a quiet confidence in his own skills and perseverance. The approval of rich and powerful men meant less to him than it once had.

Nevertheless, after dressing carefully and wearing his best hat, he turned up at the luxurious Beacon Club promptly at seven o'clock. A Black butler showed James into a slightly smaller version of a British castle's great hall, still baronial in expanse and decoration. A group of men stood talking in one corner of the room; Robert Shaw separated from them and motioned James over.

His heart sank as he drew near and saw with whom Shaw was conversing. He instantly recognized the shaggy, huge head of Lemuel Shaw; the nervous energy of Edwin Sohier; and the imperial disdain of George Bemis. James now knew that he was the fox, tricked into entering the lair of the hounds.

"Doctor Stone," said Robert Shaw, his countenance on more of a simmer than a fast burn. "We're pleased you could join us this evening. I trust these other gentlemen need no introduction, nor you to them." He smiled thinly, like a snake contemplating its dinner without allowing itself to relish the prospect too much.

Justice Shaw nodded his impressive cranium magisterially, Bemis gave James a clipped nod, and Sohier tried unsuccessfully to smile at him. James smiled back, uneasily, bowing to each man in turn, praying that he was not there for the reason he now suspected. Robert Shaw quickly disabused him of any hope on this count.

"As you have no doubt surmised, Doctor Stone, we gather here for a single purpose. Like us, you are a Harvard man. We pass no judgment on your merits as a physician, or as an expert on anatomy. Your testimony at the recent trial was most helpful in identifying my brother-in-law. Nor do we question your background as a gentleman of benevolence and attention to our needy. I recall your service during last year's cholera outbreak; along with Doctor Bigelow, you helped Boston avert a great tragedy. The community owes you its respect and thanks."

As if on cue, all three of Shaw's guests nodded gravely, as if they, too, personally extended their thanks to this medical hero.

Shaw was getting to his point, and James felt faint, for he knew where this was headed.

"But the community must not become too excited," Shaw said. "The community must not become overwrought. This trial, although achieving the proper result, has been a bane on the commerce of this city and of all New England. Trade has ceased as people debate this nonsense. As if anyone could seriously believe that monster Webster to be innocent." James thought he had never actually heard someone scoff, and now he had.

Sohier bristled slightly at this characterization of his former client, but an indignant look from Lemuel Shaw led the defense counsel to gaze downward and remain silent. The chief justice looked carefully among his companions. No one was about to disagree with him.

The justice turned to James and said, " Doctor Stone, you must abandon this project of yours, this phonographic record, or whatever you call it. It will only inflame the populace, lead to further distraction, perhaps even riots. Doctor Webster is to be executed, that is the end of this matter. The guilty must be punished, and extirpated from our midst, as he will be. We need waste no further time on it."

George Bemis spoke up for the first time, regarding James as if he were very far away instead of just a few feet from him. "Don't be concerned, Stone. The trial will be well documented. I'm preparing a thorough and complete account that will stand as the official record; all parties are co-operating with me, each will edit or rewrite his part, as it should be put down. Your experiment with rapid note-taking is no longer required."

"Surely you understand, Doctor Stone," Sohier chimed in, adopting a tone of greater respect than the scorn Bemis had just exhibited. "This is the most important case any of us will work on. Its accuracy is vital to our reputations. Any account of the trial must be assembled in the proper manner. I have discussed with Judge Merrick the publication of a notice stating that no reliance can be placed upon the accuracy of your report."

James remained outwardly calm, though he could feel his pulse hasten for the fight. "Excuse me, gentlemen, I greatly respect your experience and wisdom in these matters. But I am aware of no law or prohibition that would prevent publication of my phonographic report. You should all welcome this new age of phonography, in which your literal words in court will be shared with the world, earning its respect and admiration."

"You have no understanding of the law, Doctor Stone," Lemuel Shaw said, "and it's folly for you to proceed." He turned the full force of his piggy eyes upon James. "What was uttered in the courtroom is not the official record of the Webster trial. We," and he included the entire group in the sweep of his arm, save James, "are the trial of record. We conducted it, we will review it, we will document it, and then we will be done with it. That is how these matters are handled. I do not give a fig for your damned phonography, nor for you, sir!"

Shaw raised his voice for emphasis on this final dismissal, as if he still sat on the high bench in the court and had just dispensed with a pesky motion. Sohier nodded in agreement with Shaw; Bemis just glared. He looked as if he might just as soon strangle James.

There was nowhere for James to look for support, certainly not in the direction of Robert Shaw, who had remained silent after his effusive praise for James, and now, arms crossed, awaited James's response. James knew he must present a defense. He was surprised by his willingness to challenge the chief justice of the Supreme Court of the commonwealth of Massachusetts.

"I have the greatest respect for your traditions, Your Honor," he said, bowing his head to Shaw. "I am, more than anyone, aware of the tremendous burden borne by all of you in the recent proceedings. As I stated earlier, we are in a new age of communication. You were no doubt cognizant of many newspaper reporters crowding the courtroom, able to dictate passages from the testimony and have these instantly transmitted via telegraph to points far and wide."

Of those present, only Sohier seemed interested in what James was saying.

"News of Webster's trial and conviction has spread around the world," James said. "There is no holding back. People have already read testimony reported to them, and they are eager to read more. Why not provide them with a neutral, accurate, and timely report via phonography?"

Robert Shaw, losing what patience he had maintained up to that point, finally broke his silence.

"Please, Doctor Stone. The chief justice and counsel have made their positions clear. They wish nothing to do with your report, they will make their own, and that will be the official record. I request your word as a gentleman that you will abandon this project of yours posthaste and inform Phillips and Sampson that you are withdrawing your report."

James looked around at the group arrayed against him. He knew he was ignoring legal traditions that had been in place since the founding of the United States. He was aware of the power, politically and socially, that this group of men had amassed over decades. If he went forward with his report, he would jeopardize everything he had worked for in his adult life, professionally and personally, and potentially damage his siblings and their families, too.

James knew he had no other choice. He had abandoned Ellen O'Keeffe cold and lifeless on a dirty sidewalk. He had left John Webster in a grubby cell, intent on ascending the gallows for a murder that was a crime of passion. The Boston political and legal establishment was now ordering James Winchell Stone to renounce both, and the work that had revealed the truth to his eyes.

He would not comply. Turning to Lemuel Shaw, he said, "I regret that I cannot accommodate you, sir." His voice did not seem to know how to behave in this rare act of defiance. "I have the greatest respect for you gentlemen, but I cannot accede to your wishes. I've labored too long and too hard to produce an accurate phonographic report that will bring your wise words to the great masses. I had hoped for your encouragement, even your endorsement, but your refusal doesn't dissuade me. I must continue with my plan, and Phillips and Sampson will publish my report one week hence."

Bemis broke in at this point. "You should consult your friend John

French, Stone. We had a similar discussion with him and his staff at the *Boston Herald*. He promptly agreed to our request. If you persist in this foolhardy scheme, you will be alone in inviting public ridicule. No one of import will take your account seriously."

James replied in as measured a voice he could muster. "John French abandoned his project because his notes were worthless, not simply to please you. Why not let those interested in the recent events that have gripped our city make the decision themselves? No one will be compelled to read my report. But Phillips and Sampson anticipates great interest in an accurate and unbiased account of the trial."

Lemuel Shaw's face was almost purple with indignation over this medical upstart, who hadn't a clue about the law or the courts. He sputtered hoarsely: "Have you lost your senses, man? You're in possession of no accurate information! We are, the court who labored in the pursuit of justice in that courtroom, while you sat there and played with your pens! You have no more knowledge of legal matters than a cockroach in that courtroom would!"

Robert Shaw, in a move that must have offended the Chief Justice, interrupted him, and crystallized the consequences James would face if he followed his course.

"You think you may do as you will, Stone," said Shaw in his quietest, and therefore most threatening, voice. "A free country, free speech, free action for free men. You will learn otherwise. You will pay a price for your 'freedom' to publish your report, much higher than you can now imagine. You will be cut, sir. No one will patronize your medical practice. No one will marry his daughter to you. You will not be invited to their supper parties, their balls, their weddings, or their funerals.

"You will be an outcast, Stone, no matter how many people you think admire you in Boston. They will be rid of you, done with you. They will forget you existed. Your report may gain you some momentary attention, but the cost is your future. In this city, you will no longer have one."

A servant approached Shaw and whispered in his ear. He turned to his guests, his back to James, and gestured toward the dining room. "Gentlemen, our supper awaits us."

Shaw led the men away, leaving James behind as if he were a piece of refuse left rotting on the ground. No one had bothered to look at him as they walked away or bid him good evening. His banishment had begun.

~

DALE M. POLLOCK

James made his way down Washington Street to the offices of Phillips, Sampson and Company early the next morning. His sense of trepidation was high. His report already may have been canceled, if the group from last night had also visited his publisher.

To his surprise, Moses Phillips did not seem cowed in the least when James was ushered into his office, which, as always, was overflowing with manuscripts, published works, and correspondence.

"Doctor Stone, so very good to see you! Our project moves ahead ever so smoothly. We should have proofs to share with you by tomorrow eve. I'll need your greatest cooperation in returning a corrected version within two days, at the latest. We must have our editions at the booksellers by the beginning of next week."

"I'm heartened by this news, Mister Phillips," said James, with enormous relief. "Recently I've been the object of scorn and calumny for my efforts, and I feared greatly that outside pressure was put upon you and your partner."

"Oh, pshaw, Mister Sampson and I face such complaints each week, it seems. Someone or another is outraged by an upcoming publication and does all in their power to compel us to abandon it. Well, we do not succumb. Phillips and Sampson has never yielded to outside influences in our decisions as to what we publish. We live in a country with a Constitution and a First Amendment that guarantees us the right to publish what we see fit, as long as it does not alarm the public or incite ill feeling or violence. Your report does the opposite. It will calm agitation within the public by giving them the facts of the Webster trial, not only the speculation of the press. Our advance orders for your report are the largest in our history. We anticipate printing as many as five thousand copies, to sell at 38 cents apiece. That would bring your royalty to 5 cents per copy. Your work has great significance. Don't let anyone tell you otherwise."

The tragedy had eliminated James's stirrings of pride. His goal from the start had been to disseminate phonography, and by doing so, demonstrate its accuracy and scope. Due to his and Ellen's efforts, the first manifestation was about to materialize. If there had ever been a moment in James Stone's young life for pride, this was it.

Yet he felt none. Ellen's death had numbed him, left him walking through his life as if a shadow. The clothes of a dandy now seemed like irrelevant frippery to him. There were no more parades on the Common; the peacock had lost its plumage and its spirit.

CHAPTER 39

June 1850
Garland Street, Boston, Massachusetts

It wasn't until he walked into the antechamber of Anson Stone's mansion that James Stone realized that something was terribly wrong. Anson and his brother Jerome stood awaiting him with troubled faces; he knew the reason why.

"Don't tell me, let me surmise why you've summoned me," said James, sarcastically. "I'm sure this has nothing to do with my phonographic report."

Anson motioned for James and Jerome to follow him into his study. James walked behind his brothers into a room darkly decorated with wood and leather; Anson slammed the door shut.

"James, I see that you're aware of why we're conducting this conversation," Anson said, wasting no time. "You have the potential to ruin this family if you continue with your publication. We've been told," at which point Anson regarded Jerome, who nodded his assent, "that if your report on the Webster trial sees the light of day, no one will be inclined to do business with us. Can't you comprehend what this would do to your own family?"

James looked at his brothers with a wry smile. At this point the daily advice he received on what he should and shouldn't do regarding his report provided him with bitter amusement. Better to laugh sarcastically than to spend his hours lamenting his decisions and their outcomes; little good would come of that. He struck a triumphant tone in his response to his brothers' complaint.

"Phillips and Sampson will publish my report; the citizens of Boston, nay, the entire United States, will flock to read it; and a great good will be accomplished in the name of phonography! One that may resound to the Stone family name."

"Curses on your damned phonography!" said Anson. "For the sake of the family, I must insist that you abandon your report immediately. I'm willing to pay Phillips and Sampson whatever they believe necessary to recover their costs. You can also leave your medical practice, such as it is, and join us in our real estate ventures."

"I don't wish to be difficult or disrespectful, Anson," James said. "But I cannot follow your directive, and I beg you to excuse me from it. My report will be published in two days' time, and I believe it will prove popular and beneficial to the public good, as well as our family and its reputation."

Lucinda opened the door and motioned for the three brothers to come to supper.

James thought he'd had quite enough of surprises as he followed Lucinda into Anson's dining room, but what awaited him there startled him. Seated at the table between her aunt and uncle was Jennie Ray Gillmer, his former and never-again love, whom he had succeeded in putting out of his thoughts completely. As his love for Ellen had grown in the weeks before her death, his affections for Jennie had diminished to the point of no return.

James shot Lucinda a look of pure hatred. "How dare you trick me like this?" he muttered behind a hand he put to his mouth.

Lucinda ignored James's aside and reintroduced him to the Stephenses and their niece, who was again visiting her Boston relations.

"As you're no doubt aware," Lucinda said to her guests, "James has just concluded his duties at the horrid trial of Professor Webster. My brother is quite the object of attention in Boston these days!"

James declined to meet Miss Gillmer's gaze; he stared fixedly at his place setting. He was seated directly across from Jennie, thanks to Lucinda's plotting, but James wouldn't look in the young woman's direction.

Jennie made the first overture of peace. "We followed the trial every day in the New Jersey newspapers, but of course, no one enjoyed the special access you did, Doctor Stone. What struck you as the most peculiar occurrence in the proceedings? Was it the reaction of Professor Webster himself?"

James permitted himself to look at Miss Gillmer full in the face, for the first time in almost six months. She hadn't even come to his mind since his loss of Ellen, and the sentiments he had expressed to her in the past were so distant as to seem unreal.

"This tragedy was so filled with peculiarities, I hardly know where to begin," James said, managing now to keep self-importance out of his voice. He was aware of the entire table hanging on his every word. "There's the irony of Doctor Parkman meeting his end in a location he donated to

Harvard College. There's the confusion in assembling a body that was cut into pieces, which are found here and there in Professor Webster's rooms. There are the many sightings of Doctor Parkman all over Boston after the time he was supposedly murdered. And finally, you have Littlefield the janitor, acting on his own suspicions that he doesn't bother to share with anyone at the Medical College, save his wife."

"It's a wonder you were able to keep up with all the details," said Jennie, who looked genuinely impressed. "Will these facts and themes be in your report? When may we read it?"

"In just two days' time," James said, and looked at Anson. "It's the most complete version of the testimony and judgments at a criminal proceeding ever attempted. My publisher, Phillips, Sampson and Company, has great expectations for its reception."

"Will your report be available at all booksellers?" inquired Mr. Stephens. "I am very familiar with Mister Little and Mister Brown, and their store downtown, but I have heard nothing from them about your publication."

James supposed that Robert Shaw had already visited Little, Brown and Company, and made sure their bookstalls would not feature his title. But Phillips, Sampson controlled the loyalty of several local booksellers.

"Those who wish to find it will have little trouble doing so," James said, which he hoped would be true.

Lucinda tried to divert the conversation back to her larger goal, which had nothing to do with James's report. "How long do you plan to visit, Miss Gillmer? I hope you'll be able to stay in Boston for our lovely fall, which will unveil itself in the coming months."

Mrs. Stephens answered in the young woman's stead. "We're so pleased our niece has agreed to make this visit open-ended. There's nothing in Trenton or the Azores that require her presence, so we hope she will remain the rest of the year with us."

James understood what Mrs. Stephens intended him to grasp. The adventurer who had proposed, disappeared, then reappeared to make good his promise apparently had vanished again. Why otherwise emphasize the lack of ties binding Miss Gillmer to her distant home?

Jennie laughed at her aunt's presumption and put her hand on Mrs. Stephens's arm. "Please, Aunt Ann, don't sentence me to a lifetime in Boston yet! I'm still not sure what I think of this place. Each time I've visited, the city has been in a whirl! Now that the trial has concluded, I hope to share in what you most love about Boston, Doctor Stone. I'm particularly eager to visit Mount Auburn, which I have heard described as a new Eden."

The irony amused James. There was a time when he had envisioned a future paradise in which he was Adam, and Jennie Ray Gillmer his Eve; but a snake had entered the garden in the form of the reappearing suitor, and Adam was banished. Now the snake was gone, and Adam was invited back in. Was the invitation sincere? Was it worth taking? Would it dishonor the memory of Ellen?

James and Jennie were oblivious to the mundane conversation going around the table. Instead, they gazed at each other thoughtfully, but politely. James would not have thought it possible, but he sensed that perhaps Jennie Gillmer had reappeared in his life for a reason.

CHAPTER 40

July 1850
School Street, Washington Street, and Union Street, Boston, Massachusetts

On Wednesday in the first week in July, James set out on a more than or-dinary stroll. His destination was the Old Corner Bookstore at the corner of School and Washington Streets, where his phonographic report on the Webster trial was to go on sale that morning.

As he continued on his way to what he thought was his destiny, his mind was still awhirl with images of Ellen O'Keeffe, not Jennie Gillmer. Ellen leaning over his shoulder as he perused his trial notes. Ellen lectur-ing the Irish girls on the importance of accuracy. Ellen settling back on the trestle table, her red hair in an aura around her pale, freckled face.

Now was the moment of triumph, and Ellen was absent. Horribly, wrongfully absent. Encountering Jennie again had, surprisingly, renewed his affections for his lost lover. Staring into Jennie's eyes brought James a keen sense of betrayal. Ellen maintained a hold on him from the grave. His memories of their time together were inescapable and would not recede from the physical presence of Jennie.

As James approached the bookstore, he first went to one of the two large bay windows on either side of the entrance and peered through the glass. Just as Moses Phillips had promised, a large, round table was heaped with copies of the report bound in dark green cloth. The cover bore an or-nate, leafy stencil in gold filigree with no words, and the spine carried the title—"Trial of J. W. Webster"—in gilt letters on a black square. The sight so excited James that he had to breathe deeply to calm himself.

He entered the Old Corner Bookstore and made his way to the display. An older woman and two men in dark suits were standing at the round table, each looking over one of the volumes. James hovered, hoping to over-hear a stray comment. He was disappointed when no one said a word and put their books back on the table and departed.

He was dejected. Was this the fate that awaited the hundreds of hours he and Ellen had spent recording and dictating every word of the trial? Was there a surfeit among the populace? Were they no longer curious about the scandal? Was it even a scandal any more? Time moves on, and while Webster's hanging was still to come, Boston might have moved on, too.

James was concerned enough to walk back up Washington Street to his publisher's offices, less than a block away. There, for the first time, James encountered Charles Sampson, the more retiring elderly partner, who spent much of his time reading manuscripts and choosing titles for publication. He and Phillips were in fine fettle, greeting James with pleasure and affection.

"Doctor Stone, so good to see you on this auspicious day!" said Phillips, grasping him warmly by the arm and leading him to a comfortable armchair in his office. "We have nothing but positive news for you. Your report has warranted one of the largest printings in our firm's history: five thousand copies!"

James reported the depressing scene he had witnessed at the Old Corner Bookstore, and Sampson smiled at Phillips. "Don't be concerned with those who don't buy your book, only the many who will," said Phillips. "We've supplied bookshops throughout the Northeast with four thousand copies. I have already received telegrams from booksellers in Providence and New York ordering more! It's still too soon to predict success, but I believe the interest warrants it."

Finally, old Sampson spoke up, his voice hoarse and scratchy.

"We have the first complete record of the Webster trial, an unparalleled event in the minds of citizens everywhere," he croaked. "The only means of discovering exactly what was said and done at the trial is through your report. As the people learn of it, the book will sell. I've been at this business longer than you have been alive, Doctor Stone."

James felt restored. All wasn't lost; his report might still be a success. Again, he felt a pang of loneliness for Ellen, who would have been giddy with delight at this news.

He decided to treat himself to a celebratory dinner at the Union Oyster House. As he walked along Milk Street to the restaurant, Rufus Choate appeared, walking toward him. James hadn't seen the attorney since the conclusion of the trial, which Choate, too, had attended every day. James removed his hat and bowed, but the man seemed to not even see him. Choate's hat stayed on, his eyes remained focused on the distance, and he strode directly by.

James felt the fool, hat in hand, treated as if he were a hitching post by the side of the road. He had known Choate for years, had shared a table with him many a time at the Oyster House, and had enjoyed conversations with him at the courthouse during the Webster trial.

James recalled Robert Shaw's prediction: *You will be cut.* Could Shaw be so powerful as to alter relationships James had cultivated for years?

This trip to the Union Oyster House had gained new significance. His dinner would provide a test, he supposed, his anxiety growing by the minute. There would likely be many friends there whom he had known since his medical student days, from the august Senator Daniel Webster to the waiter George, who always minded his every need. Would they, too, turn against him?

James entered the noisy and bustling Oyster House and headed for his familiar seat at the soapstone bar. It was occupied, so he looked around, searching for acquaintances. He spotted Senator Webster at his usual table, seated at its head and engaged in conversation with multiple partners.

The senator caught James's eye and looked down for a moment, as if pondering whether to respond. His long, fine, white fingers motioned James over but did not indicate for him to sit. He had to stand by Webster's side and lean down to converse with him.

James said, "Senator Webster, we're so pleased to have you still in Boston. My phonographic report is now published. I would be honored to present you a copy at your convenience."

"James, I shan't even speak to you, in all honesty," the senator said in a loud whisper that his seatmates could easily overhear. "You transgressed an important boundary, one that keeps our system of justice efficient. The bench and counsel summarize their arguments and rulings. Your assistance in these matters was not required. In fact, it was not desired, and now has proved a catastrophe."

"Senator, I'm sure you will understand when I explain—"

Webster cut James off, something that had never happened before. "I've no need of explanations. You were asked to withdraw your publication, and for reasons I cannot comprehend, since the request was a reasonable one, you refused. Now you must suffer the bitter harvest of what you have sowed. I can no longer associate or dine with you, now or in the future. I shouldn't be conversing with you at all, so we are done."

Webster turned from James and resumed his conversation with the men at the table, all of whom had witnessed this encounter. James was left standing next to a man he had greatly admired, a man who now pretended that Dr. James Winchell Stone did not exist.

James left the Oyster House and leaned against the structure's outer wall, his mind reeling. His hopes of surviving in Boston were dashed, as Shaw had promised they would be. The cause of his banishment was his greatest accomplishment, his phonographic report.

As he wandered away from the Oyster House, everyone who passed him on the street or rode by seemed to look right through him. He had been rendered invisible, a man rejected by society. Good things inevitably led to bad things, it seemed to James. Perhaps they were forever mixed up, the positive and the negative, success and failure. Only death offered a true separation. Ellen was proof of that.

CHAPTER 41

August 1850
North Allen Street, Commercial Street, and Long Wharf, Boston,
Massachusetts; Main Street, Waltham, Massachusetts

James walked out of the Bulfinch entrance of Massachusetts General Hospital onto North Grove Street. The hour was turning late; it was almost nine o'clock on this humid late August evening. James was sweating as he made his way from Fruit Street down Commercial Street toward Bowdoin Square. He paused briefly to mop his wet forehead with his handkerchief when a pair of arms came at him, grabbed hold of him, and silently dragged him toward a dark alley.

James no longer panicked. This wasn't an assault or robbery. By now he was familiar with the tactics of William Haggerty; they had been practiced on him before. Well, this time, matters would be different. James had anticipated this visit, figuring that news of his report's success would eventually reach the North End and the ears of Ellen's killer, her drunken and greedy stepfather.

"Evenin' to ye, Docter Stone, it be my good fortune to see ye by chance," Haggerty said, his wheedling tone unchanged: half-importuning, half-threatening. "I were just partakin' of the fine air in yer parts, and thinkin' how fortunate be the rich folks that live here, such as yerself."

"You do poorly in your mathematics if you count me among the wealthy," James said. "I no longer belong here, and soon will not reside here, either. I have forsaken my medical practice and will leave Boston. Your trip tonight is wasted, Haggerty. I have no business left with you."

"No, I suppose ye left that business bleedin' in the street when last we seen each other, Docter," Haggerty said, in a sorrowful voice.

"Our poor Ellen, done in by a blow from her lover, who turns and walks away, leavin' her wee body cold in the dirt!"

James's voice shook with a violence that surprised both of them. "What say you, man? I am Ellen's murderer? No, we both know who killed your stepdaughter, Haggerty, there were but the three of us there! If you try to implicate me for your crime, you will follow Professor Webster to the gallows, I promise you!"

"Who be speakin' of crimes, who be speakin' of gallows?" Haggerty retreated a few steps and put his hand to his chest in mock protest. "Nae meself, nae meself. Me and ye, we can settle our business like the gentlemens we be, nae bring any gallows into it."

"You are the devil's idea of a gentleman, Haggerty! If you don't leave here immediately, I'll have Marshal Tukey round you up and toss you into a pit where your drunken Irish friends will never find you."

"Do Marshal Tukey know Miss Jennie Ray Gillmer? For she's the one methinks most curious about relations that shame my family from the grave. If there be shame to me family, then there be shame to yer family, too, I promise ye that!"

James stopped short. "How did you learn that name, Haggerty? I demand you tell me. That person has nothing to do with our affairs."

"O, now it's 'our affairs,' is it, Docter Stone? Ain't I headed for that pit ye jest invited me into? My news might not go as far as that fancy pamphlet of yours everyone's been crowin' about, but it'll reach the people it needs reach."

"This is the last time we speak of these matters," James said in a flat voice that brooked no argument. "You'll meet me at the foot of Long Wharf tomorrow night at eleven o'clock, and you'll bring no one with you. Before I pay you one cent, you'll sign a document stating that you extorted money from me. If you ever approach me again, that statement will be mailed to Attorney General Clifford. It's an admission of guilt on your part, and you won't escape its punishment." James paused. "I presume you can sign your name?"

"I can make my mark," Haggerty said, not at all embarrassed by his illiteracy. "Be sure to bring five hundred dollars with you tomorrow, an' somethin' to carry 'em in."

"Are you mad, Haggerty? What makes you think I have that kind of money?"

"If ye nae have it, Doctor, ye know where to get it. Yer kind always do. If ye don't have the money, perhaps Miss Gillmer do."

"Don't mention her name again in my presence, Haggerty. I'll deal with you and you alone at eleven o'clock tomorrow night at Long Wharf."

"Bring the money, Docter Stone, and ye'll be rid of me forever and a day. But it need be the full five hundred."

With that, Haggerty strode away. James smiled grimly. His trap had sprung. He had a stop to make.

~

James spent the next day preparing for his encounter with Haggerty. This was the man who had taken Ellen from him, deprived him of the best thing in his life. Haggerty's violence to his daughter had cut short her existence; his greed was noxious; he was a drunkard, a bully, and a blackmailer. James despised him and looked forward to delivering a comeuppance that was sorely deserved.

His plan was to frighten Haggerty as never before, beat him if necessary, and force him to sign a confession admitting himself to be an extortionist. He hoped the drunkard would be surprised by a show of force and rattled enough to give up his scheme and leave James in peace.

His final preparations led to a hackney cab trip to Waltham. There he found Mr. Savin, who sold the thick grape stakes that were presented in court as damning evidence against Professor Webster. The one that had been used to slay George Parkman with one blow, when wielded by an enraged debtor. James had thought it the ideal weapon: solid, hard, and capable of being swung with great momentum.

After he returned home, James cut one stake free from the bundle. He slid it halfway down his left pants leg so he could grasp it with his left hand. But it made him stiff-legged, which would draw Haggerty's attention. The stake was too big to keep on his person. He would have to hide it nearby.

James ventured out again late in the afternoon to determine the right location for his encounter with Haggerty. James had grown up around the docks, spindly wooden piers that had become wide and solid structures since the years of his childhood. He and his brothers had played tag, hide-and-seek, and find the devil behind barrels and bales, ships' stores, and exotic cargo.

He walked over to Long Wharf, which had become a commercial center and was no longer the smelly dumping ground for fish guts that it had been in James's early years. He soon found an appropriate hiding place for the grape stake, his response to Haggerty's shillelagh: a dark space between two barrels of molasses, situated near the end of the pier. He could

DALE M. POLLOCK

smell their sweet tang. The stake fit neatly between them. James thought the isolated location ideal. He wanted no curious passersby to witness this encounter.

The night mists gathered over Boston Harbor, but the wet, clammy feeling was familiar to James as he left 6 Bowdoin Square and walked east. The sea air's sounds and smells were like balm to him. As in his childhood, they calmed his inflamed nerves.

James usually walked abroad with only a thin wallet in his pants, but tonight he was weighted down. In one hand he held a lantern, whose flame danced in the wind. Inside his linen jacket, a pocket held a pen and a folded piece of parchment, upon which he had written the confession to extortion that he would demand William Haggerty sign or at least make his mark. In another pocket rested a handkerchief and a small vial of ether. He hoped he would not need it this evening—the grape stake should be more than adequate—but if circumstances warranted, it was at the ready.

James checked his pocket watch. It was ten minutes shy of the hour of eleven o'clock. His plan was well thought out: the men would meet at the end of Long Wharf, almost two thousand feet from the shore, with nothing around them and nowhere for Haggerty to hide an accomplice.

The possibility of a hidden accomplice worried James. If Haggerty were accompanied, he would abandon the enterprise. If forced to fight, he first would employ the grape stake. If that failed, he would douse the kerchief with ether and try to smother his assailant. He had no intention of killing Haggerty, but he did want his message to be taken seriously: stay away from James Stone, now and forevermore.

His conscience continued to torture him for doing exactly what Haggerty accused him of: leaving Ellen's bloodied form in the dirt. The scene had never left James's mind since he walked away from her inert form, a reaction he now regarded with deep shame. He never should have left her. He should have gathered her body in some conveyance, taken her to an undertaker and given her a proper burial.

He had done none of those things. He had slunk away like some guilty witness to a crime he wished he had not seen. He would not be that abject coward again. There was only one way to avenge her death. He would rid himself of this leech and achieve a small measure of retribution for Ellen.

James was to begin a new life. Robert Shaw's promise had come true, and James had lost all of his social standing. But so had Jennie Gillmer, it turned out. Tales of her misadventures with her mysterious suitor had reached Boston, and Lucinda had informed James gravely that the young woman was now considered "damaged goods," unsuitable for marriage. James was in the identical situation, for different reasons. He took pride in thumbing his nose at the Beacon Hill elites he formerly admired when he proposed, and gained the acceptance of Miss Gillmer to be his wife.

James and Jennie were to announce their engagement in September. He had found a house in Dorchester, an agricultural town on the outskirts of Boston, that he could afford to buy. He had a new occupation as a tax collector for the commonwealth of Massachusetts, and he still saw a few patients, mostly local families around Dorchester.

But none of his plans could move ahead without the disposition of William Haggerty, whose blackmail would continue until James put a stop to it.

James finally heard muffled footsteps coming down Long Wharf. He listened carefully: only one set. James was relieved. Haggerty was arrayed alone against him, and the man would likely be in the liquored condition that was his norm.

James changed his mind again, removed the grape stake from its hiding place, and bundled it in his coat. He hoped it would do the job and teach Haggerty a lesson in the language of brute force, the only one he understood.

Haggerty stopped twenty feet from the end of the pier where James waited. The Irishman peered into the mist.

"Who be there? Docter Stone?" he called, his Irish accent thick with drink. *Yes,* James thought with satisfaction, *he's tight, his words are slurred.* Haggerty's addiction to alcohol would allow James's plan to proceed that much more easily.

"Over here, Haggerty," James called, beckoning the wobbly Irishman forward.

"I can't see a bloody thing, Docter, ye must come to me. I be goin' nowhere near the end of this pier, mind ye, I dinna care for the water. Can't swim worth a lick, so I'll be stayin' right here, if ye don't mind."

"My light is here, I have it shielded; if I walk to you, we'll lose the light and waste our time. If you want your money, you'll come to me."

Haggerty, heeding the mention of money, grumbled his assent. He moved forward, weaving a bit, stopping frequently to steady himself.

"Why in blasted hell did ye choose a place like this, Docter Stone? What ye got goin'?"

Haggerty looked around suspiciously, expecting James to have a hidden associate. James's heart shuddered. Did the man smell his plan? Was he prepared for what James was about to do?

"Our agreement, Haggerty," James said. "That's our only purpose in meeting, and I vow this will be the last time we do so."

"To be sure, to be sure, Docter," said Haggerty, grinning as he contemplated how many more times he'd be able to put the squeeze on a fool like Stone. No need to go to California to chase gold when there was a ready supply before him.

Finally, the Irishman drew up close to his mark. James withdrew the paper and pen from his jacket, and motioned Haggerty closer. He laid the document on one of the nearby molasses barrels, and proffered his pen, shifting the lantern to his right hand.

"Sign here," he gestured. With his left hand, he slid the grape stake out from the folds of his jacket and kept it at the ready. He placed the lantern next to the document.

As Haggerty bent toward the light, James looked over the man's shoulder and pointed where he was to sign. As he had expected, Haggerty was illiterate, and made an X on the line James indicated.

Without warning, Haggerty whirled around and brandished a knife in James's face. "What do ye got goin', Stone? Tryin' to murder me, are ye?" He lunged at James, who backed up, then gained his purchase.

He grasped the hidden grape stake, raised it high, and brought it down hard on Haggerty's shoulder. The knife went flying.

Haggerty fell in a heap, shouting, "I be undone! Jesus, Mary, and Joseph, Jesus, help me! I be undone!"

James continued to strike the Irishman, not uttering a word, but methodically laying the grape stake on Haggerty's prostrate form. Hurriedly, he set the lantern down on the pier.

Striking out with his feet, Haggerty hit the lantern and sent it flying over the side of the pier. Both men were plunged into total darkness, broken only by white wisps of fog.

James tried to keep his head, although his heart was beating so loudly, he supposed the entire city must hear it. He had lost the grape stake when reaching vainly for the lantern, and he could barely see Haggerty in the dark.

Somewhere nearby, Haggerty rolled back and forth on the rutted pier, moaning in pain. James thought he must have broken the man's collarbone. He was still a physician making a diagnosis. He struggled to make out Haggerty's form in the pitch-black night.

James got on his hands and knees to crawl through the darkness, desperately searching for the grape stake. He needed to have one final conversation with Haggerty before he beat him into submission. It would have to take place in the dark.

James's hand caught an edge of the grape stake. Grasping it firmly in his left hand, he hauled himself to his feet and approached the writhing figure of Haggerty, who yelled curses at James and threatened him with the wrath of the devil.

James nudged the Irishman with his foot, and Haggerty kicked back at him. James brought the stake down hard on one of Haggerty's knees, and the Irishman screamed in pain and anger.

"Each time I touch you with this stake, Haggerty, think of the woman you killed. Every blow you receive, and they will never number enough, is for a blow you visited upon poor Ellen."

"Go fuck yerself, ye pox-ridden piece of shite," Haggerty spat out, in between cries of distress.

James realized that if he wished, he could re-create the murder of George Parkman, who in all probability had been killed by a grape stake identical to the one James clutched.

"You'll remember this conversation, Haggerty, because it's our last one. You'll never see me again, I promise you. I'll beat you to an inch of your life to make sure you remember. Our business is done. There is no more money, just more of this!"

He lashed out with his boot at Haggerty, catching him in the chest and driving the man backward. James had not realized how close they were to the edge of the pier, and he felt Haggerty grab at his foot, afraid he was about to topple off the pier and into the cold, dark water.

James yanked his leg back, fearing that Haggerty would pull him over the edge, too, and reached forward to grasp the Irishman and haul him back onto the pier. Haggerty, fearing another attack, scrambled backwards, all the momentum he needed to begin a quick descent into the water, screaming all the way.

Out of breath, James looked over the edge of the pier. There was no sign of Haggerty in the water. He had sunk as if weighted down with the cares of his miserable life.

James could not believe what had just occurred. *He had come with no intention of killing Haggerty, yet the man was now gone. If his death wasn't directly at James's hand, it was uncomfortably close. He had tried to save Haggerty at the end. He knew what his intentions were, and they were not to murder him. Of this he was sure.*

What would the law say? James wondered. *Guilty or innocent? Or was that not so black and white anymore?* If James had learned one lesson from the Webster trial, it was that nothing was as it seemed on the surface. There were always subtle gradations of gray, with some good and some evil in our actions. James wondered which quality was more present in himself.

He thought back to the drowning of his own father. *Both William Haggerty and Joseph Stone were drunk at the time they met death. Like James's alcoholic father, Haggerty had met his end in his least favorite substance: water.*

CHAPTER 42

August 1850
Leverett Street, Boston, Massachusetts

The morning of Friday, August 30, was a sweltering one. James Stone had dressed lightly, but by the time he neared the Leverett Street Gaol, his white cravat hung soggily from his neck. He passed several placards posted on walls and fences that equated public justice with murder.

A steady stream of people headed toward the prison yard, where the gallows had been erected. The vehicles carrying spectators ranged from the humblest milk cart to the smartest landau. The grass was brown and dead in the yard, the result of the recent heat wave.

Although it was seven o'clock in the morning, and the execution was not scheduled until nine, James saw crowds of men, women, and children as he approached the jail. Hundreds more had commandeered the rooftops of adjacent houses on Lowell and Leverett Streets. The scaffold was erected so close to Webster's cell that every blow of the carpenter's hammer that morning fell on his ears.

Two weeks earlier, James had received in the post a card that said, "Admit James Winchell Stone To Witness the Execution of Dr. J. W. Webster, Signed, John H. Clifford, Attorney for the Hangman." *What an odd way for Clifford to identify himself,* James thought. *Imagine, an invitation to watch a man die in public, as if it were some kind of celebration.* It had been sent, James knew, by John Webster himself.

A total of 150 passes had been issued; James felt fortunate to be in possession of one of the cardboard squares. He saw about twenty members of the press, another hundred or so sheriff's deputies, Boston constables, and various city officials filling the yard.

James's eyes searched the crowd, and in no time he came upon the hawklike visage of Robert Shaw, who was also scanning the entrance to the jail yard. His eyes met James's for a scalding moment and moved on.

James wished to be done with this man for good, never having to think again if one of his actions would displease Mr. Shaw.

James didn't see any other Parkman family members present, other than Shaw, nor did his careful survey of the crowd reveal Webster's wife or daughters. James had heard that the Webster family was kept in ignorance of the date of the execution, and that in their last visit together, Webster had been careful to not betray that it would be the last time he should see them on earth.

Everyone in the jail yard was moving toward the enlarged archway of the Leverett Street entrance. The crowd grew silent, and James heard the thin, high voice of the Rev. Dr. Francis Putnam, offering a prayer that he said was delivered at Webster's request. Putnam prayed that the hearts of the people of Boston be softened toward Dr. Webster and his innocent family, and the bereaved family of Dr. Parkman.

As the press of spectators grew, James realized that the sheriff and the Boston police were losing control of the crowd. An unruly mob pushed toward the dwellings and commercial buildings on each side of the jail. At the first sight of Professor Webster, led in a small procession from the jail entrance toward the high scaffold at the center of the yard, there was a subdued roar from the crowd; no jeering or yelling, but a deep collective moan of fascination. Webster wore shoes of a common sort and a shabby black coat.

Sheriff Eveleth and six of his deputies led twelve legal witnesses to watch the execution. They would attest to its effectiveness after the hanging was concluded. Jailkeeper Andrews followed, holding firmly onto one of Webster's arms. At his other side was the Rev. Dr. Putnam, who clasped Webster's slumped right shoulder. Both the prisoner's arms were tightly pinioned to his body with rope.

Webster, head bare, looked deathly pale and subdued, almost drugged. James recalled the conflicting emotions in Webster's eyes after he drank poison and thought his expression to be similar. *It was the look of a man who welcomed death, even as he feared it.*

Everyone in the crowd removed their hats as Webster passed by. James was shocked to see how many women and children were present. He did not think highly of a parent who would bring small children to such an event.

All present stared at Webster as he ascended the scaffold steps unassisted. He didn't exhibit the tremors and trembling that had characterized his previous behavior in extreme circumstances. It must not have been easy climbing with his arms and hands bound, but Webster finally gained the top of the wooden structure. The crowd was sad, silent, somber, maybe even sympathetic. James observed that no one jeered, no boys threw stones.

Deputy Sheriff John Coban called the attention of the witnesses to the executive death warrant, which Sheriff Eveleth proceeded to read. *This mob doesn't understand a word he's saying*, James thought; *not that it mattered. Words hadn't saved Webster's life. It was his actions, however motivated and understandable, that had led to this moment. Words were just words.*

After the sheriff concluded, Webster moved to the side and awkwardly tried to shake hands with Rev. Putnam. The minister clasped the condemned man to his chest, and then stepped back. Webster was seated on a chair to have his legs pinioned, too, and then was aided in standing up again.

When the rope was placed around his neck, Webster's face colored rapidly from its former chalk whiteness. He attempted a clumsy handshake with Sheriff Eveleth and spoke a few words in a low voice. These were later reported to be: "Father, if it be thy will, let this cup pass from me; if not, then thine, not my, will be done!"

Eveleth placed a black hood over Webster's head, adjusted it to fit snugly, turned to the crowd.

"In the name of and by the command of the commonwealth of Massachusetts, I will now do execution on the body of John White Webster. God save the commonwealth!"

It was thirty-five minutes after the hour of nine o'clock. Webster stood still, awaiting the final plunge. Eveleth turned and pressed the spring. With a metallic clang, the platform fell open and Webster's body plummeted seven feet downward, jerking violently at first, then growing still. His legs spasmodically twitched a few feet off the ground. Webster's pants darkened, the natural response of the body when the windpipe was crushed and the muscles loosened. James felt nauseated.

Silence reigned for several more minutes, and then, as if by some mysterious signal, a riotous, celebratory noise erupted from the crowd. James felt those waiting outside the jail surge closer, hoping for a glimpse of the slowly swinging corpse. They would have plenty of time, since the body had to hang in place for thirty minutes until the official time of death could be announced.

At 10:05, Eveleth cut the rope, Webster fell in a heap to the ground, and his body was placed in a rude pine coffin.

Those spectators still inside the jail yard now filed over for a final viewing of the condemned man's body. Andrews propped the open coffin up at an angle of forty-five degrees so the blood would drain and would not discolor the dead man's face. As James approached, he was surprised that Webster's features still resembled those he had in life, with little distortion. Only a ring of purple flesh around his neck testified to his violent demise.

Dr. Henry G. Clark, the newly appointed city physician, and Dr. Charles H. Stedman, a friend of Sheriff Eveleth's, officially confirmed that Webster was deceased.

Webster's widow, Harriet, had signed a document giving up the body to Edwin Sohier, Webster's counsel. Owing to the crowds that still roamed inside and outside the jail yard, the coffin remained under the sheriff's protection for now and would be removed later. Webster had procured a plot in Mt. Auburn for himself and his family, but the Parkman family had blocked any plan to inter Webster in the same cemetery as his victim. Now the family's intention was to bury Webster in an unmarked grave in Boston where they hoped it would remain unmolested.

Webster had achieved what he'd hoped to, James supposed. *He had gone to his death a martyr, his life sacrificed to a greater cause, albeit anonymously.* James wondered if he would be able to approach his own death with Webster's calm and equanimity.

Greatly affected by the execution, James hurriedly left the crowds massed around the jail. He had a final funerary rite to perform, but not for John Webster. He was not present when Ellen O'Keeffe had been laid in the ground, in a plot he had paid for, but he would now visit her resting place and pay tribute to her memory. He owed her that much, and more.

CHAPTER 43

September 1850
St. Mary's Way, Dorchester, Massachusetts

The hackney cab brought him to the wrought-iron arch that framed the words "St. Mary's Cemetery." James tried to avoid thinking of the sad irony that Ellen's resting place was less than a mile from the new home he and Jennie would occupy in Dorchester.

James had no idea how to locate Ellen's grave at St. Mary's. He looked toward the nearby church, a shabby, peeling structure, and saw a small man in a leather apron come out of one of the building's side doors. James strode over to him, the question already on his lips.

"Can you tell me if a certain individual was buried here in the last month? I purchased her plot sometime back, but I was unable to attend her funeral," he asked. "She was a young Irishwoman," he added, as if that would clarify matters.

"Have you checked the register? Every decedent is entered on the register," said the man in a bored, rote voice. James stood, still confused, until the little man nodded toward a small shack with a prominent cross above its doorway. James pointed, and the man nodded again before heading around the back of the church, pulling tools from his leather apron.

An elderly man, apparently the church deacon, was inside, copying names from a large register book as James entered.

James said, "Can you tell me please where I might find the final resting place of a young Irishwoman who was buried here in the past month?"

"Do you have a name?" croaked the deacon.

"James Winchell Stone."

"No, no, not you! The poor unfortunate!" he rasped, irritably. "Do you possess her given name?"

"Ellen O'Keeffe. The date of death was"—James thought back to that horrible night in the North End, Ellen lying pale and unmoving in the twilight—"July 7. She was to be buried here, in a plot I paid for, and I wish to ascertain that she was."

"Let me see, let me see," mumbled the old deacon as he pulled the register toward him and began flipping through the massive pages. "You say July 7, do you not? And the name was O'Keeffe? Eileen O'Keeffe?"

"No, *Ellen* O'Keeffe," said James. He realized how few times he had actually pronounced her full Christian name. "I fear that whoever brought her to this place for burial couldn't read or write, so I can't vouch for how her name might appear in your ledger."

"Do you think we let the Irish write down the names of their dead?" the deacon asked. "We'd never be able to read a one of them, since few of these potato eaters can even make a mark, let alone write down a Christian name. No, *we* take down the names, so if she's here, I'll find her."

The deacon spent some minutes flipping the heavy parchment pages back and forth until he stabbed his finger near the bottom of one.

"Here it is, just as I thought. July the ninth, at three o'clock in the afternoon. Ellen O'Keeffe, deceased, brought here by three members of the immediate family. Let me see, row 3, halfway down."

He turned and looked up at James. "That's where she is, that's where you'll find her. Row 3, halfway down, that's what the book says, the book says row 3." The old man continued to stare expectantly at James.

"Very well," said James. "I thank you for your assistance." Then he realized why the deacon was still staring at him.

"Is there a fund I may contribute to?" James asked, not knowing how else to refer to the obvious solicitation.

"No fund, no fund, just me," cackled the deacon. "You may contribute to me, since I does all the work. That's the thing, I does all the work here, you see. All the names, I know where they are, all the bodies that go with them names."

James was anxious to find row 3 and be rid of this old man who had spent too much time in proximity to a cemetery. He placed two coins upon the table next to the register and backed out of the shed. "I'm much obliged for your assistance, sir," he said. "Much obliged."

There was a tall, crooked fir tree on the left as he approached the rows of graves. Scrub brush, not yet dug up for graves, grew on the right of the path he walked on. He counted the first three rows and walked down the middle of the third one. A cheap wooden board was shoved into the dirt; already the name on it was fading. It read:

Ellen O'Keeffe
1831–1850
Beloved Daughter

The words Helpmate *and* Lover *could also have been appended,* James thought, gazing at the rough wood. By next spring, this pitiful marker would be gone, rotted by the snow and rain.

This pathetic grave can't be all that remains of her, he thought. He would order a small marker of Millstone Point granite from Connecticut, maybe three feet high. He had seen such a grave marker for a niece who had died. It had an angel flying with a cross, with the girl's name beneath it in a flowery script.

He knelt at the foot of Ellen's grave. *She lies just a few feet away from me,* he thought, *in the cold, cold earth. I look down upon her and she looks up to me, just as we did on the trestle table.* Tears sprang to his eyes, and he rubbed them on his sleeve.

Still kneeling, James reached into the wide side pocket of his jacket and pulled out a copy of the *Report.* The leafy design in gold filigree glittered on the green cloth cover; the book still smelled new.

"I've brought you this, sweet Ellen, the fruit of our collaboration, so you may rejoice in it as I have been unable to, without you to share it with. Without you, I would've failed. Together, we are triumphant. Would that you were here to celebrate with me!"

He placed the book near the bottom of the crude wooden tablet. He wiped his eyes again, pressed the book deeper into the soil, and turned back to the shack. He had to see about purchasing a marker.

George Parkman was dead. John Webster was dead. William Haggerty and Ellen O'Keeffe were dead. Enough, James thought.

Jennie Ray Gillmer would be the companion for the life he would have to settle for, now that his first love story had been ended senselessly. He had the funds generated by the success of his report, which had sold fifty thousand copies. He would marry a woman who would regard him as her best—her only—prospect, as he did her, and he would no longer carry the torch of phonography.

For all its usefulness in science and industry, phonography had failed James Stone. He had completely believed in its ability to reveal the truth of the word as spoken, as if that truth stood above all others. It did not.

Phonography had not revealed the true killer of George Parkman; it had not exposed the perfidy of Ephraim Littlefield, who profited from corpses and slaves. It had not punished William Haggerty for his crimes and evil disposition. It had not saved the life of Ellen O'Keeffe. It had not spared James Stone actions that he would regret for the rest of his life.

Exact words, faithfully recorded, never tell the whole story. Truth is contained in the spaces between words, in the silences, in the knowledge not revealed.

AFTERWORD

The origins of *Chopped: A Novel* began with my wife's great-great grand-father, Dr. James Winchell Stone, and the surviving family copy of his original publication of *The Trial of John W. Webster,* published in 1850. Pamela O'Keeffe, my wife's mother, had assembled research and notes for a potential book, but lost them. Fifteen years ago, my wife and I decided to pick up the pieces she had left behind.

In *Chopped: A Novel,* all testimony from the Webster trial comes directly from James Stone's phonographic transcription, taken daily by Stone personally in the courtroom, and printed in what he called his "phonographic report."

All of the characters in *Chopped* are also based on real individuals who lived in Boston at the time of the murder of George Parkman and the murder trial of John Webster, 1849-1850. The only invented characters are Ellen O'Keeffe, her family, and her stepfather William Haggerty; Mother Bernardine of the Sisters of Mercy abbey; and Sharon, James Stone's maid. A gallery of historic images appears after page 126.

I would like to thank Myles Thompson, Joyce and Ron Della Chiesa, David Lubin, Joe Mills, Diana Greene, Karen Dorr, and my daughter and son-in-law, Zoe and Will Di Novi, for their advice on and assistance with the manuscript; Gary Brown and Michelle Harden for their efforts toward publication; the Rare Book Room staff at the Boston Public Library for their research assistance; and Julie Allred and Brent Winter for their in-valuable contributions to helping to realize this book.

Above all, I have to express my love and appreciation for my wife of almost fifty years, Susie O'Keeffe Pollock, not only for her forebears, but for her undying passion, commitment, and drive to seeing this story pub-lished. It would not have happened without her.

Dale M. Pollock
Autumn 2022

CAST OF CHARACTERS

MAJOR CHARACTERS

Dr. James Winchell Stone—medical doctor and phonographer
Professor John White Webster—professor at Harvard Medical College
Dr. George Parkman—John Webster's creditor, the richest man in Boston
Ellen O'Keeffe—young Irishwoman and James' love interest
William Haggerty—Ellen O'Keeffe's stepfather
Robert Gould Shaw—George Parkman's brother-in-law
Ephraim Littlefield—janitor at Harvard Medical College
Jennie Gillmer—eligible young woman whose family tries to match her
    with James Stone
Jacob Bigelow—prominent Boston doctor, mentor to James Stone

FAMILY

Anson Stone—James Stone's brother
Henry Stone—James Stone's brother
Jerome Stone—James Stone's brother
Lucinda Dresser—James Stone's sister
Jacob Dresser—Lucinda Dresser's husband

TRIAL FOR MURDER OF GEORGE PARKMAN

Chief Justice Lemuel Shaw—presiding justice
Judge Pliny Merrick—defense counsel for Webster
Edwin Sohier—defense counsel for Webster
John Clifford—attorney general, prosecuting attorney
George Bemis—privately retained prosecuting attorney
Daniel Webster—US senator from Massachusetts
Dr. Wynford Lewis Jr.—James Stone's anatomy professor; Harvard
    Medical College lecturer

Dr. George Gay—witness

Dr. Nathan Keep—Boston dentist; witness

Dr. Jeffries Wyman—witness

Rev. Doctor Francis Parkman—George Parkman's brother; witness

Francis Tukey—marshal, Boston police force; witness

Derastus Clapp—lieutenant, head of detectives, Boston police force; witness

Constable Charles Starkweather—Boston police officer; witness

Gustavus Andrews—keeper of the Leverett Street Gaol; witness

The twelve jurors—Robert J. Byram, a locksmith, who was elected foreman; Thomas Barrett, a printer; John Borrowscale, a slater; James Crosby, a clerk; John E. Davenport, a painter; Albert Day, a dry goods dealer; Joseph Eustis, a merchant; Daniel T. Fuller, an unemployed seaman; Benjamin H. Greene, a bookseller; Arnold Hayward, a carpenter; Frederick A. Henderson, a furnisher; and Stephen A. Stackpole, a clerk

John French—owner of and reporter for the *Boston Herald*

Edward Eveleth—sheriff of Middlesex County

ADDITIONAL CHARACTERS

Dr. Frederick Ainsworth—demonstrator of anatomy at Harvard Medical College

Edward Atkinson—partner in a Worcester cotton mill; prominent abolitionist

Mother Bernadine—abbess and Mother Superior of the Sisters of Charity

Albert Doyle—unemployed fishcutter; patient of Dr. Stone's

Dr. Oliver Wendell Holmes—Dean of Harvard Medical College

Jared Sparks—President of Harvard College

Charles M. Kingsley—George Parkman's "hatchet man" and first to notice his disappearance

Moses Phillips—partner in the publishing company that agrees to publish James Stone's phonographic record of the Webster trial

Wendell Phillips—Boston abolitionist

Rev. Dr. Francis Putnam—clergyman who prays at Webster's execution

Charles Sampson—partner in the publishing company that agrees to publish James Stone's phonographic record of the Webster trial

Sharon—James Stone's Irish maid